Editor: Jovana Shirley, Unforeseen Editing, www.unforeseenediting.com

Developmental Editor: Becca Mysoor, Fairy Plot-Mother, www.fairyplotmother.me

Cover Design and Formatting: Jillian Liota, Blue Moon Creative Studio, www.bluemooncreativestudio.com

Out with the Tide

Julie Olivia

- *Author's Note* -

Out with the Tide is the second book in *Never Harbor*, a series of contemporary romance novels inspired by *Peter Pan*. They are not a retelling of the original story.

This book is a standalone and does not need to be read with the series. However, there will be spoilers for previous books.

Please be advised that this book is a **slow burn, open-door romance**, meaning there is **on-page** sexual content. Mature readers only.

Finally, while this rom-com is 95% heart-warming small town moments, there is also about 5% angst, including discussion of absent parents and workplace harassment. Be kind to your heart when you read, friends.

Now, go! Fly off to Never Harbor!

xo Julie O.

- Dedication -

*To everyone who feels like they're
slowly drifting away.*

*I hope this book can be your 'otter'
for a little while..*

- Playlist -

Gold Dust Woman - Fleetwood Mac ♥

Apple Pie - Lizzy McAlpine ♥

The Joker and the Queen - Ed Sheeran (feat. Taylor Swift) ♥

Lavender Girl - Caamp ♥

I Want to Hold Your Hand - Kate McGill ♥

La Vie En Rose - Emily Watts ♥

First Light - Hozier ♥

To Build a Home - The Cinematic Orchestra, Patrick Watson ♥

Here with Me - d4vid ♥

My Love Mine All Mine - Mitski ♥

Chapter One

THE HIGHLY INAPPROPRIATE LITTLE BOOTS

Marina

I didn't listen to my gut.
I should have.
But I didn't.
Instead, I freeze when *it* happens, as if I were surprised. Like there weren't a million signs warning of *it* before.

It.

A hand reaching closer. A smile. I don't have time to understand what's happening before his fumbling fingers curl around my ear, clumsily tucking a strand of hair behind it.

It's funny what goes through your mind in a moment like this. For some reason, my immediate thought was, *You didn't need to do that.* The braid in my hair secures most of the stray waves from my face. *Seems unnecessary actually.* But once I'm finally aware of the touch, I jerk back.

"Whoa," is all I can think to say.

"Whoa," my boss repeats with a smile.

My boss.

Dustin Barrie's polished shoes scoot forward on the carpet, dragging his butt across the coffee table's glass and closer to the sofa I sit on. His knees cage me in.

"The way you've been looking at me lately … your smile is like sunshine on a rainy day."

"Wish it weren't," I blurt out.

That's when his face falls.

I never say the right thing at the right time. I wish I could say this is the first time I've given mixed signals, but it isn't. My dad says I've got the type of face people can trust, just like my mom. Turns out my boss, Dustin Barrie, might trust me more than he should.

I believe in signs. When I interviewed and realized this company was owned by Dustin Barrie—the son of my hometown mayor—it felt like kismet. A fellow Massachusetts local, all the way out in California? What are the odds? It felt great—not at all like the gut feeling I get now. But I should have guessed that a man who grew up sitting in the royal high chair always gets what he wants, even three time zones away from Never Harbor.

Overall, I like working the reception desk at Barrie Wine & Spirits. I'm good at it—the spreadsheets, the meetings, and the fast-paced environment. Everyone walks with a mission here, like they have the whole *life purpose* thing figured out. Every single person—all the way to our mail guy, Ben—seems content. He says he's trying to support his daughter, but I'd believe it if he said this was his dream job.

I might not have a dream job, but I like it here. Unfortunately, the most "life purpose" I have is tending to the small nursery of plants behind the receptionist desk. But I'm finding my way. Slowly. Surely. At least my botany degree hasn't fully gone to waste.

Barrie Wine & Spirits didn't give me any red flags—not like the flags that had waved high when I filled out applications to pharmacy school. Even after I scored in the top two percent of my PCAT, the idea of spending hours filling pill bottles for the rest of my life made my skin crawl. Like a plant, I need sunshine, water, and soil. I've been searching for the right job since dropping my post-grad pharmacy plans, but my gut always told me I'd find it. Eventually. Hopefully.

I thought this was the one.

My gut let me down.

No, I simply didn't listen to it.

I was seconds away from leaving for the day, having stayed late to finish emails, when I heard my boss call, "Mind stepping in here?"

Slinging my beige tote over my shoulder and cradling the terra-cotta pot of my ficus, Fido, I walked to his office door and smiled. "The golf course shut down or something, boss?"

He chuckled, waving an open palm to the sofa across from his desk. "Take a seat, kiddo."

Dustin Barrie told me on day one that he didn't like formalities, which is why he's *boss* and I'm *kiddo*. I like—or *liked*—the casual nature of our relationship. It served as a little wink and a nod to our shared past.

We're both pesky Never Harbor kids.
Look at us! We escaped the small-town life.

I lowered onto the sofa. "I'm not getting fired, am I?"

He laughed, sauntering around his desk topped with only a closed laptop and cell phone. It's the desk of someone who is either a neat freak or doesn't have much to do. Judging by the haphazard bookshelves, filled with golf magazines and trophies, I assume it's the latter.

Resting on the edge of the desk, Dustin took that pseudo-sitting position with one ankle crossed over the other and palms folded over his thick thighs. He's all about casual.

"How was your weekend?" he asked. Very casual.

"Good," I answered brightly. "Got through another season of my show, so can't complain."

Dustin tilted his chin up, as if assessing me under his horn-rimmed glasses. He's objectively good-looking—a product of wealth that can afford braces, prescribed skin care, and proper nutrition. But he also has the haughty appearance of a man whose never been told no.

"*Survivor*, wasn't it?"

"That's right. *I'm not here to make friends*," I mocked, then added conspiratorially, "But they always make friends."

"You said the same thing on your first day," he teased.

"Hey, I absolutely did not say that!"

Dustin pushed off from the desk and rounded the coffee table. He took a seat on the edge with his thighs spread apart. Something felt *off*, like an incessant tapping on my shoulder. I clutched Fido closer, a sort of security blanket stitched through greenery and soil.

"You've been a surprise since day one, kiddo," he murmured. "We've got this new label coming out soon, and you've been rocking the release. Truly. Just spearheading it with ease."

"Yeah, well," I said, giving a smiling exhale, "I do what I can."

"You do. You brighten this office so much. Hell, even accounting likes you."

"They're easy. I keep a bowl of candy out just for them."

"That's right," Dustin mused. "Your bowl of candy."

"Well, who can resist a sweet tooth?"

"Not me," he said. "I can't resist anything as sweet as you."

The hand reached out. He tucked hair behind my ear.

And here we are.

He pulls his hand away with little finesse—almost as much as when he assaulted my hair. He smiles, probably thinking my *whoa* was a *whoa, how magical.*

"Mr. Barrie?" I finally get out.

"Mr. Barrie?" He laughs. "No. Please. Call me boss."

The little inside joke crawls down my skin like a roach in the night, skittering down my spine.

"No, no, I don't think so." I blink, finally processing *what the hell is happening.* Then, I laugh because *what else do I do?* "I think, uh, you're Mr. Barrie, and I'm Marina Starkey, and …" I'm blabbing. I hold up my watchless wrist. "Look at the time. I should go."

He blinks. "Go?"

"Yes, because this is …" I let out another choked laugh, waving my palms between us, as if gesturing to the whole situation. I'm trying to lighten the mood, but, *God*, how do you lighten *this*? "*Highly* inappropriate."

His face falls. "Inappropriate," he echoes, sitting up and pulling in a hiss of air.

Dustin clicks his tongue and sneers out the one word I've heard too often in my life: "You *tease*."

Slimy and malicious and not dissimilar to when my high school guy friend said it. Or my college guy friend. Or that one friendly guy I met on a cruise. I've learned to stop being friends with guys altogether.

"God, you're such a little tease," he mutters more to himself than me.

It never gets any less jarring.

I feel my eyebrows furrow in. "Pardon, what?"

He rolls his eyes with a groan. "Working extra hours at the soup kitchen with me? Coffee on my desk every morning? Wearing those"—he laughs—"*highly inappropriate* little boots of yours?"

I open my mouth, close, then open again. "I was already volunteering that day. I didn't know you'd be there," I explain. "And I like making coffee for people. I do it for Jess too. And"—I glance down at my ankle boots, only a sliver of skin showing between the top stitch and my long dress hem—"I'm teasing you by wearing *shoes*?"

His face contorts into harsh lines. "You knew what you were doing, Marina. And now, you're making me look and feel stupid."

My lips part in disbelief. "I'm not—"

"You flirt with me since day one, and you're telling me it meant nothing?"

"Yes," I say quickly. "I mean, no. I ... I didn't flirt."

"Really?"

"Yes." But I hesitate more than I should.

I didn't, right?

This is the same issue I've had with previous guy friends. I've been told that I'm too friendly—smiling too long and laughing too easily. It feels unfair that I'm forced to enjoy friendships *less* because other people see what they want to see.

"Sorry if I sent mixed signals," I say. "That was *not* my intention."

"Then, what was?"

I'm at a loss for words.

I like this job. I *liked* feeling like I belonged.

My eyes sting. *No, no, no.*

Dustin gives a haughty sniff. "Just leave. And don't take your laptop or your badge."

I blink. "Leave? Am I getting fired?"

He says nothing in response. Nothing for an agonizing ten seconds. I slowly stand, the leather sofa cushions whining beneath me as they inflate. My legs bump against his bent knees as I shimmy away from the tight space.

Shakily, I exhale.

"Are you about to cry?" Dustin asks.

I swallow. "No."

I am.

My dad always taught me to be strong, but I'm a crier at my core. One level above or below happy, and my nose stings with tears. As an independent woman, it's embarrassing, like I'm proving the world right by having emotions. But I'm not proving anything to Dustin Barrie.

I'm only about to cry because I'm angry, but he wouldn't know the difference.

I hug my plant—my beautiful Fido, who would never make me cry—and leave.

I somehow hold back tears all the way to my dingy apartment building with the brown carpet, creaking stairwell, and cracked paint. I ascend the five flights of stairs, ready for a night of bingeing more *Survivor*, only to find a pink slip taped to our door.

EVICTION NOTICE. FAILURE TO PAY RENT.

I shift Fido to my other arm and dial my roommate. She doesn't pick up. Not on the first or second or third try. Then, her texts go from blue to green.

She freaking blocked *me?*

Finally, the tears fall.

Shakily exhaling, I close my eyes and lean my head back to stop the embarrassing sobs. But just like with Dustin, I know this is my fault. This is what happens when you find a roommate through an online ad. I knew she had a spending habit for designer clothes, talking about my thrifted dresses like they were an assault to her moral code. Something in my gut told me she was pocketing my monthly rent check.

But I didn't listen.

Again.

I text my landlord, begging for another week while I figure my life out. Thankfully, because he likes me—and I have enough savings to bribe him—I'm granted an extension.

I look at my bank account. There's just enough remaining to book the cheapest flight I can find one week out—a red-eye straight to Boston, Massachusetts.

Just one plane and two trains back to my hometown of Never Harbor.

- *Chapter Two* -

THE QUIET HOUSE

Cassidy

"You've got one more in you—I know it."

"I do *not*, you masochist."

I bark out a laugh. "Yes, you do. Go full beast mode. Absolutely wail on it."

"Hmph."

"No hmphs," I correct. "Just go for it. Do it for you."

With my palms steadied under the barbell, Bobbi lowers the loaded weight to her chest. Her thin arms shake. Gloves whine against the metal. She huffs out a breath, sending wiry gray hairs wisping around her scrunched face. A bead of sweat rolls down her temple.

"C'mon. Halfway there. You got this," I murmur.

Grunting, Bobbi pushes the weight back up. Up, up, up and …

The weight is raised once more! I assist in replacing it on the rack behind her. Bobbi stares at the drop ceiling with wide, unblinking eyes.

"Hell yeah! That's my girl!" I pump my fist in the air. "Bobbi freaking Mullins!"

"Well, how about that?" she breathes out.

Cupping my palms over my mouth, I yell through the empty gym, "Superstar weight lifter, everyone!"

"Oh, hush, mister." She waves her hand out. "You're gonna give an old woman a complex."

"Impossible. You're amazing, and you know it." I bend at the knees by the bench, resting my forearms on my thighs so I can look up at her. "Hey." I hold up my palm for a high five. "You *did it.*"

Bobbi's face slowly pulls into a genuine grin, the one that makes little checks in the brown skin beside her eyes.

"I sure as shit did," she says in a conspiratorial whisper.

She slaps her hand to mine so hard that it stings my palm.

That—*that right there*—is my favorite expression in the world. It's the moment people realize that hard challenges can be overcome. I love the intensity of these moments. The energy in the gym is palpable.

I shake my head with a smile. "Nah, I need that louder. You *did it!*" I yell again, looking around the echoing weight room once more, as if signaling her victory to the invisible guests.

"Cass!"

"Come on."

She groans. "You're insufferable."

"Bobbi …" I drag out the request, lightly nudging her knobby knee.

She hums, twisting her pursed lips to the side in thought, before blurting out, "I DID IT!"

I hold my finger up to my lips. "Shh. Jeez, Bobbi."

Shoving my arm, she leans in again and squints. "Did I beat Mags?"

I laugh. Bobbi is always trying to beat my mom's personal record on bench press. The fact that two women nearing the age of sixty are competing to out-bench each other makes me feel like I'm doing something right.

I tsk, rising up again and crossing my arms. "Not yet."

"What's her personal best?" Bobbi asks.

"You know I can't tell you that."

"What's *your* personal best?"

I shrug. "Can't even remember."

"Liar."

I bite my lower lip to withhold another laugh. I hold out a palm and assist her off the bench. Bobbi's in impeccable shape for someone of her age—I don't know her exact number and will never dare to ask—but owning the local coffee shop isn't easy. That is where I come in. I help her become strong enough to carry bags of flour and coffee beans day-to-day. I make sure she's building the energy to do what she loves.

I snap my fingers. "Oh! I have something for you. A celebration gift."

I dig in my gym duffel and pull out a package.

"Cass …"

"Humor me." I hand it to her.

It's not wrapped prettily because all I had was Never Harbor's newspaper, but she still unwraps it gently, like it was gifted to her by an eager little kid. Admittedly, I can't stop smiling. I love gifts.

She barks out a laugh. "Cass, you didn't! The licorice jelly beans? They're my favorite. How did you know?"

"Because nobody else likes licorice," I say with a laugh. "They have tons at Live, Laugh, Taffy. It was either that or mint chocolate, right?"

"Mint chocolate?"

"Isn't that your second-favorite flavor?" I ask.

"Peppermint is," she corrects with a finger point. "That's why I'm adding it to the drink menu this summer."

"Peppermint coffee in summer?"

"Would you rather me make licorice-flavored coffee? Wait, actually …"

She tucks the candy in her bag. When she turns away, I whip out my small notebook and pen from my duffel, quickly flipping to the page titled *Bobbi*. Under *licorice*, I scratch out *mint chocolate* and replace it with *peppermint*. I close it and zip both back in my own bag.

I hand her a towel. "I'll see you in"—I check my watch—"twelve hours."

Digging through rattling keys and crinkling receipts, Bobbi emerges with a checkbook. "And what do I owe you?"

I laugh. "For what?"

"For the extra hour."

"Oh, stop." I wave my hand. "I stayed late because you needed it."

She growls a little. "I should be paying you for your time."

"This is a full-time job. If I stay late, it's not a big deal."

"Then, I should tip at least."

"Are you gonna throw ones at me, Bob?" I ask with a wink. "Should I get a fancy pole?"

"If you call me Bob again, I'll take it all back."

"Good to know, Bob."

She shoves a wad of money at me irritatingly. "You deserve more money for all you do for me."

"The community center pays me just fine," I insist, resting my forearms on the racked barbell.

11

Bobbi leans in like we're conspiring together. "You don't need 'em."

I bark out a laugh. "Actually, I do."

"No. Start your own business. If Steve is trying it, you can."

"Whoa, is he opening his own paper business?"

"Trying," she repeats. "But he's gonna have to get over Laura first. He spends too much time and money pursuing her."

I gasp. "He's into Laura? Does she know?" I gasp again. "He's, like, what, seven years younger than her?"

"You gossip," she says with a sly grin.

"Pot calling the kettle black."

"You're forcing us off topic," Bobbi says. "Start a business."

"Is me staying late not good enough?" I tease.

She sniffs. "No. Because I want you to get paid what you deserve. You don't get overtime, do you?"

I tongue my cheek with a grin. "Of course I do."

I don't, but it doesn't bother me.

Bobbi hmphs, then shrugs. "Well, I'm aiming for Maggie's personal best tomorrow," she insists, tossing her tote over her shoulder.

"Still won't tell you what it is. Want me to carry that to your car?"

She waves me off. "Please. Go home. You've stayed too late already."

"Never too late for you, Bob."

She points a single finger at me. "You'll pay for that."

"Hope so."

Bobbi leans back to laugh, then pats my cheek. "Good kid."

"I do what I can."

I wave as she crosses through the fogged glass doors. She gives a final *Breakfast Club*-esque frozen fist bump in the air. I mirror the motion with her.

By the time I leave, it's late in the evening. I push through the community center's double doors and am greeted by watercolor wisps of pink and purple across the sky. Bobbi was right; I did stay too late. And that's when I check my phone and see a couple of missed texts from Jake at the hardware store.

Crap.

I book it down Main. It's the start of May, and the seasons have just changed from blustery to radiant. The breeze off the ocean thankfully doesn't chill to the bone anymore. If I'm hurriedly breathing in outside air, it could be worse. Never Harbor's a delightful perfume of salty sea and vanilla—a lingering scent from our four ice cream shops.

I burst into the hardware store, the bell signaling my arrival with a light *ding*.

"Sorry, Jake!"

He's in the back, already chuckling. "You're doing this for free. I'm not concerned."

I help Jake carry in his deliveries—something I promised to help him with last week.

After that, I drop by the candle shop to help Moira rearrange the top-shelf candles she can't reach—another agreement I made when I ran into her at the grocery store two days ago. I peer into the flower shop, too, since Lulu normally needs help, but the lights are off. Flowers wilt in the window. The counter is messy with paperwork. I laugh. Lulu's parents are gonna kill her.

I keep busting through doors like the Kool-Aid Man, tardy to one place, then the other, like a landslide of lateness. Thankfully, nobody seems to mind. I think people just expect it by now. I'm an overcommitter by nature.

But I love Never Harbor. I love not saying no.

By the time I've made my rounds through Main, I finally journey home. It feels like the only person I don't talk to is Rafe, standing outside his screen print shop and surprisingly granting me the slightest chin nod. I was compelled to stop for awkward conversation, but his narrowed eyes signaled, *Keep moving, Cass*, so I left with my small victory of acknowledgment instead.

A five-minute stroll later, exactly one block from the sea, is my own townhome. I moved in a few days ago, so it's still squeaky clean. A healthy flower bed is perched under the open kitchen window. The stoop steps have been power-washed. The door looks freshly painted. I grab a package off the porch—probably not mine—and walk in. No need for a key. Locking doors in Never Harbor is basically unheard of. But when the door snicks shut behind me, suddenly, the house feels *too* clean.

It's quiet.

Uncomfortably quiet.

After finally moving out from my parents' house at twenty-seven, I'm not accustomed to a bare house without six loud siblings. The walls aren't crowded with family photos. The hardwood isn't dinged up from years of running children and snapping shoelaces. The curtains aren't worn in with messy patches and fabric snags. All I have from home is our lumpy antique sofa. It's a stark contrast against the townhome's neat interior.

I should be proud of my accomplishment on moving out, but instead, it feels like I've been relegated to time-out in a corner. Do people seriously like this type of quiet? It's an eerie silence. It's too much like the days before Mom and Dad found me. Pre-seven-year-old Cassidy doesn't like this feeling.

I place the package on the counter, noting the name. *Marina Starkey.* My landlord's daughter keeps getting her packages sent here, and I keep forgetting to tell him. I add it to her growing stack and sigh. The pile of brown parcels is the only decoration I have.

Flicking on the living room lights, I start my silent, evening routine.

A shower followed by dinner with baked chicken and mixed veggie leftovers. That meal is one of three dishes I've learned—the other two being scrambled eggs and making a mean peanut butter and jelly sandwich. Never underestimate the power of PB&J.

Finally, I end with one uninterrupted hour of television, watching some reality show my little sister recommended. I text her to talk about it, but she doesn't respond. They're probably all eating dinner.

I click off the television and crawl into bed earlier than I should. The only sounds whispering through the house are my air conditioner and the faint ocean waves seeping through the open bedroom window. It's like sleeping in a house that isn't mine again.

None of my younger brothers are yelling downstairs. My dad's music isn't flowing up from the kitchen. My sister isn't bursting in randomly with high school gossip, and my three older brothers aren't dropping by to steal food from Ma's fridge.

I know I should have moved out earlier. My older brothers didn't hesitate. But they also had dreams. College, business ambitions, life curiosities. They've always been more motivated than me. I only moved out because it was time. But now, it's just me, lying in this one-bedroom bungalow, staring at the ceiling until I fall asleep in silence.

For the first time in days, I have a good dream. A really good dream actually. The mattress sinks as a woman crawls into my bed. At least, I think it's a woman.

"Hey, Dad," she whispers.

Huh. I'm not generally into being called *Daddy* in bed. But this woman smells soft, like lavender, and I bet if she asked really nicely, I could get used to *Daddy*. If she wanted me to.

"Hey, honey," I murmur back.

In my dream, I roll over, running a hand over the woman's smooth skin. She feels like silk, like she could truly be right here.

Then, I hear a bloodcurdling, nails-on-chalkboard scream.

The beautiful woman scrambles out of bed, mouth gaping open, screeches bellowing through the room.

My stomach plummets down like a ten-ton weight, and then it hits me.

This isn't a dream at all.

I'm here. In bed. Awake. And the strange woman snatching the side table lamp, ready to smack me over the head, is very, very real.

- Chapter Three -

A DAVIES

Marina

"Who the *hell* are you?!" I screech.

I jerk the bedside lamp from its post. With a small *pop* and skittering of a cord trailing over the floor, I hold the weapon over my head.

"Who are you?!" I repeat.

The stranger is groggy. "What?"

I turn around and flick on the light. He immediately covers his face, shading his eyes from the light.

"Tell me who you are!" I shriek.

If he's not blinded, then he'll be deaf soon. I'm fine with either because a *stranger* is squatting in our family townhome rental.

"I'm the man who lives here!"

"No, you don't!" I insist.

"I don't?!"

"No, because *I'm* the owner of this house."

I know for a fact that our family rental house should be vacant. Dad told me our last tenant, Wendy, moved out months ago. So, when I walked in to see it furnished with a sofa and kitchen table, I figured maybe Dad was staying here again. His apartment near Never Harbor's docks always smelled like fish anyway.

This rental was meant to be an investment property, but Dad always said either of us could use it if we needed to. So, I did. I waltzed through the unlocked door and plopped Fido's terra-cotta pot right on the kitchen counter. And when I heard my dad's snoring in the back room, I kicked off my sneakers and hurried down the squeaking hallway.

The bedroom door was cracked open. Warm light from the streetlamps outside illuminated the bedsheets, kicked around the bulky frame of a man. It was Dad—or who I thought was Dad.

I crawled on the bed beside him. I needed his comfort, like I had when I was a kid. I remember thinking he must have changed his cologne because Dad didn't smell like his usual cinnamon spice. It was more like a fresh shower. Different. Clean. Nice.

"Hey, Dad," I whispered.

Dad.

Oh God, I called this strange man *Dad.* The memory alone squeaks down my spine like nails on a chalkboard.

"Hey, honey," he answered.

Dad had never called me *honey.* The tone was a little less gruff than his usual morning voice, too, not with the rasp of a man who had spent half a lifetime as a smoker. My gut feeling was twinging, and for once, I was ready to listen. But by the time he shifted beside me, turning on his back and then side, I was too shocked to do anything. Because this man didn't have my dad's craggy beard. Not his tattooed neck or his cracked smile.

No, it was a man with gorgeous, curly brown hair. A sharp jawline. A smattering of a five-o'clock shadow. A small dimple, like he was smiling, even in his sleep.

And it was definitely not my dad.

So, I screamed in the face of a man I didn't know, and I haven't stopped screaming since.

My stranger squints at the lamp held over my head then, realization setting in, his eyes widen.

"Whoa! Hang on! Hang on!" He raises his palms in defense. Then, after a moment of both our chests rising and falling in unison, he squints. "Wait, Marina?" His lips kick into a chuckling smile. "Marina," he repeats softly, lowering his palms, exhaling relief. "It's me."

I can't figure out who Me is, but I just noticed Me's shirtless body and … holy *God.*

I only took one art history class in college, but it was enough for me to equate this man's body with an artist's rendering. He's a chiaroscuro, dark and light contrasts, a study in form. His hard chest rises like a rolling hill, only to dip back into his stomach, sketched with lines boxing out paths of abs. Each movement shifts like rippling brushstrokes.

I start to lower the lamp, and he breathes out a sigh.

"See? It's fine," he says. "It's—"

I raise the lamp again, and his palms shoot up.

"Wait! Wait! It's me! I'm Cassidy!"

"Cassidy?" I ask.

"Cassidy. Cassidy Davies."

I pause. "A Davies?"

The air gets pulled out of him in a small chuckle. "Yes. *A Davies.*"

Oh.

I know the Davies family. Who doesn't? His parents are staples in the community. Mr. Davies chaperoned most school trips, and Mrs. Davies was my physician, growing up. Then, there are the children—Peter and Milo and Bonnie and honestly a multitude of other siblings, but they start to jumble together after a while.

"We went to high school together," he clarifies. "Your dad works with my brother at the docks."

And then it hits me exactly *who* he is. Cassidy. Football quarterback. Voted Class Clown as his senior superlative. The guy whose boisterous laugh could be heard from the stage at graduation.

Cassidy Davies looks … different now. Built. Bulky. His jawline displays his growth into an older man—no longer the grin of a teenage boy, but instead a confident, charming smile.

I know this man. At least there's that.

"Okay," I finally say, slowly lowering the lamp.

But in a split second, I raise it again. His hands swiftly follow the motion, ready to catch the lamp, exhaling in exhaustion from our game.

"But what are you doing here?"

A laugh leaves him in nervous starts. I'm glad he finds this so funny. I'm the one with the lamp, and he's the victim in only boxer briefs. Very well-fitted boxer briefs, I might add.

"I was sleeping," he answers.

"Dad didn't tell me someone moved in."

He shrugs sheepishly. "Doesn't change the fact that I live here, honey."

I try to ignore the rush of adrenaline with him calling me *honey* for the second time. Instead, I notice his unsteady hands.

I narrow my eyes. "Nervous, Cass?"

His deep brown eyes flick to the lamp, then back to me. "Sure, I might be a *little* on edge," he answers. "There's a woman in my bedroom, threatening me with a lamp."

"Hmm. Fair."

"Can you lower it, please?"

"Can you prove you live here?" I ask.

"Call your dad."

Cautiously, I place the lamp back to its rightful place on the side table, my eyes not leaving Cassidy for one moment. The lamp rattles on its base when I let go. I finally lower my palms by my sides and swallow.

"Sorry."

"Don't be," he answers. "Well, I mean, yes, *do* be a little," he jokes with a grin.

"Where's my dad?"

"Out late. He told me not to wait up for him."

"What? You're roommates?"

He grins, that dimple popping once more. "I'm kidding. Starkey's still at his apartment by the docks."

"Oh. Funny." A smile twitches at the edge of my mouth. "Got it."

His expression matches mine, and a zip rolls through me.

"When'd you move in?" I ask.

"Only a few days ago. He didn't tell you?"

"He doesn't know I'm here. I was going to surprise him."

"Are you gonna threaten him with a lamp too?"

"He could only be so lucky."

Cassidy laughs, and, God, it's so low and gentle. But it doesn't color the reality that sets in.

Somebody officially lives in our family rental. I now have no place to stay.

This is what I get for being impulsive.

Again.

I'm off to a terrible start.

I sigh. "I should head to my dad's."

"Let me drive you."

I shake my head with a laugh. "No. I can walk."

"Please."

Cassidy's already getting out of bed. The sheets fall to the ground in a lump by his bare feet as he walks to the closet in just his boxer briefs. My eyes shamelessly trail over his thick thighs and toned calves. They disappear when he tugs on sweatpants, and his abs do, too, when he pulls a hoodie over his head.

Shame.

Cassidy clears his throat, jolting me from my admiration. I let out a weak laugh. He grins, kind dimples dented into his cheeks.

"You coming with me or what?" he asks.

The car ride is silent, but short. Most places in Never Harbor can be walked to within fifteen minutes, driven in five at most. But Cassidy was insistent … or maybe his dimple was.

I sit in the passenger seat with my duffel in the back seat and Fido clutched to my chest. We ride through past Main and toward the docks with the windows rolled down and the lapping sea at our side.

He rolls the car tires onto the sidewalk next to my dad's apartment complex. I sit for a quiet moment, then smile.

"Well, thanks for the ride."

"No problem. Stop by anytime," he jokes.

I laugh and tease back, "Don't make me take you up on that. That bed is comfy." But the moment I say it, I regret it. It wasn't supposed to be a flirty comment, but this is why I get in trouble—why I get fired from jobs. I clear my throat and quickly murmur, "See you around, Davies."

"Hope so, Starkey."

I exit the car, but not before Cassidy does first, snatching my bag from the back seat for me and gently settling it on my shoulder.

"Thanks," I murmur.

Cassidy shrugs. "Like I said, anytime."

I wave when he leaves, his cologne or body wash—whatever it is— still sticking to me.

Clean. Fresh. New.

I twist open the front door, excited to finally see my dad, but what I find is almost as upsetting as crawling into bed with Cassidy.

No, it's ten times worse.

Because my dad isn't alone in bed.

- Chapter Four -

A GIRL AND HER SHADOW

Marina

Everything creaks in my dad's dockside office. The wooden chair squeaks when I sit. The metal desk whines. Even Dad's back crinkles like a disposed water bottle when he straightens up from the coffee machine tucked beside his filing cabinet.

"You should get that checked out," I observe.

When he looks at me sideways, I curl my lips in. Some might be intimidated by my dad's stares—the plethora of tattoos, combined with a stern brow and craggy beard, isn't for the weakhearted—but Charles Starkey has always just been Dad to me.

"So, we're gonna talk about this morning, aren't we?" I mutter.

He slides me a chipped mug of steaming coffee with my exact three sugar packets. "You know it, Guppy."

I puff my cheeks and blow out air. "Thought we could breeze over it."

"Not when you show up, unannounced, at five in the morning."

"That early, huh?" I joke.

"That fuckin' early."

"Whoops."

I look around at anywhere but him. My dad's office consists mostly of yard-sale finds I've gifted him over the years: a framed painting of a boat; a pencil holder, shaped like an open whale mouth; and even the faded wood table I sit at beside the stained glass—literally *stained* from fingerprints and sea salt—overlooking the Never Harbor docks. Dad sits in his desk chair, the old leather moaning beneath him, as if begging to be put out of its misery.

I squint out the window, absentmindedly tearing open one sugar packet after another.

"Huh. I didn't know Noodler could drive a boat."

"You're changing the subject," he says.

"And it looks like he's doing it backward."

"Marina."

"Are you sure he's qualified?" I ask.

"Guppy."

"Hmm?"

My dad tilts his head to the side. "Why didn't you tell me you were moving back?"

"Why didn't you tell me you were dating Auntie Bobbi?" I counter.

He slowly nods. "Maybe let's not call her that anymore."

I cringe. "Fair."

Bobbi Mullins has been one of my dad's best friends for nearly thirty years. I spent many evenings after school doing homework in the back of her coffee shop, Peg Leg Press, while I waited for Dad to get off work. She let me drink however much hot chocolate I wanted and promised to never tell him. But now, I can't shake the unease in my stomach, knowing that Auntie Bobbi—no, just *Bobbi*—was in bed with my dad last night.

"I should have told you," he admits.

"No, it's fine," I say quickly.

A slithery, guilty impulse whispers that I should have known. He hasn't dated anyone since Mom left when I was thirteen years old. I never think to ask if he's dating because he simply *doesn't*. Is this a secret, or have I really been absent that long?

"Is it serious?"

"Yes," he admits. "Things've definitely been going on—"

"Oh, I saw."

The tips of my dad's ears redden in sheepish embarrassment. I found my dad and Bobbi curled together in the sheets with—thankfully—their shirts on. It could have been worse, I guess.

"How long has it been going on?" I ask.

He clears his throat, giving me a stern look. "A good bit."

I twist my lips to the side. "What, like a few days?"

He grunts.

"A few weeks?" I ask.

"A few months," he finally replies.

"Oh."

Suddenly, I feel like all those bellyfuls of hot chocolate at Peg Leg Press are gonna empty onto this floor.

He didn't tell me for months?

Where have I been? What have I been doing? How did I miss my dad dating one of his best friends? How did I miss my dad being *happy*?

"Anyway, your turn," he says gruffly. "Why the sudden move?"

I shift in my seat and try to think of a response that doesn't mention Dustin Barrie, my terrible roommate, or the fact that my savings are almost depleted. I'm an embarrassment on all fronts.

All I conjure up is, "I wanted it to be a surprise."

The problem with Charles Starkey is that nothing surprises him. Even this morning, when he emerged from his bedroom, rubbing the sleep out of his eye, he didn't flinch after spotting me on the sofa. He lazily cupped my temples between his meaty hands and kissed my forehead.

But now, as he tips the coffee cup to his bearded mouth, I sense my dad knows I'm bending the truth. This type of parental attentiveness only comes from him.

"What?" I ask innocuously.

"Why didn't you tell me beforehand?"

"Told you, it was a surprise. It really wasn't a big deal."

He snorts. "I don't believe you. My daughter doesn't just randomly move back to town without telling anyone."

"Fine. You caught me," I tease, hands held in the air. "I robbed a bank. I stole a horse. I'm an outlaw."

"Marina."

"I got fired."

He sputters into his coffee, the overflow landing on his work shirt. He rubs a meaty palm over the stain and glares at me. "You what?"

"Yeah," I say, drawing out the word, running my fingernail over the chip in my mug. "It wasn't working out."

"And why not? That was Barrie's company, yeah? Why would they fire you?"

Dustin Barrie. Just the name sets me on edge. It's bad enough he's the reason I left, but in a small town, everyone knows everyone.

"It just wasn't working out," I repeat. "Too boring. Too many fluorescent lights." I straighten my spine and force a smile. "I think I just need to find some … I don't know … some stability?"

"Impossible," he grunts, laughing. "You're too much like your ma."

That comment wasn't meant to be cruel, but my stomach drops all the same.

My mom left Never Harbor and us when I was thirteen. She'd felt stifled by the small town. She'd claimed her spirit couldn't soar and, in fewer words, said she was overwhelmed by motherhood. Though that conclusion I finally drew in my early twenties through therapy.

Dad had let her leave. He didn't even question it. Her free spirit was why he loved her. But when we received a call one night, saying she'd died in a motorcycle crash, I think Dad compartmentalized all the good and bad memories of Mom from then on. When I'm happy and wistful, I'm the good version of her. When I'm reckless, I'm the bad version. A real girl and her shadow. Either way, I'm *her* through and through. It's funny how the carefree nature I'd inherited seemed less exciting and more like shackles around a destiny already laid out for me. I've been fighting it since.

"No, I'm ready to settle somewhere for a bit," I say. "Maybe it'll only be for the summer, but I need a change of pace. West Coast life was getting boring."

"How is *that* life boring? Too many adventures to choose from? Surfing? Rollerblading? What else do they do out there?"

I stick my chin up. "I'm actually already having more adventures here than I did there."

"Are you? Like what?"

"Well, I snuck into bed with Cassidy Davies last night."

My dad firmly places his coffee cup on the counter. "Explain yourself now, Marina Starkey."

"In the townhome. I didn't know he lived there."

"Oh." Then, his eyes widen in realization. "*Oh*. Oh no. You didn't."

"I sure did."

Dad covers his mouth with his palm and erupts into laughter. I can't help but join in. I like how similar my laugh is to my dad's. But beneath our laughter, I'm remembering everything from last night, and it's a little *less* funny. Cassidy's smile. His arms. His boxer briefs—

"Well"—Dad wipes the tears from his eyes, chuckling—"I'll need to apologize to him soon. For now, you can stay with me. Don't worry."

"No, I can't. That's your place."

"Too smelly?"

"Maybe," I joke.

He chuckles. "Bobbi tells me all the time we need to get away from the docks."

I freeze. "Does she live there too?"

"She just moved in."

I shake my head. "Well, that's settles it for sure. I *definitely* can't stay there."

"What? It's fine."

"No! I'm not disrupting your cute little love nest."

He sighs. "I really do wish I'd known you were coming into town."

"So I could have the family rental?" I tease. "Well, me too. But *somebody* rented it out."

He holds up his palms. "Take it up with Cass. He practically begged me for it."

There are quite a few things I've considered doing with my dad's tenant the last few hours—very impulsive, inappropriate things that might involve some sort of begging too—but kicking him out of his new home isn't at the top of my list.

"Maybe he needs a roommate," I joke.

"He's a good kid," Dad says. "Ten bucks he'd offer it himself."

Dad pulls out his phone, holding it away from his face and tapping with a single index finger over the screen.

I snort. "What are you doing?"

"Sending texts for tonight."

"What's going on tonight?"

"The Hideaway." He swivels his eyes to me. "If you're gonna live with me, you'll have to keep up."

I grin. "I'm not living with you. I'll find someplace. It's only for the summer anyway."

His face falls. "You're really not staying in Never Harbor?"

"Oh. No. I mean, I'm just getting back on my feet, y'know?"

I don't plan to stay here. It's Never Harbor. The smallest of small towns. The place where people never leave if they're not careful. But I won't tell my dad—the man who's lived here forever—that judgy truth. Even I know that's unfair.

Dad nods slowly, and I think he's forcing a smile when he says, "Well, I'll help any way I can."

I give a weak smile in return, but it can't conceal the plunk of a pebble sinking in my stomach.

- *Chapter Five* -

NO SURPRISES

Cassidy

"You've got registration covered, right? Cass? Cassidy Davies?"

"Hmm? Oh." I was zoning out, and the look on my supervisor's face says she knows. "Yes. Sorry, Laura. Of course. Got it."

"Out late again?"

"Nah," I answer with a laugh, rubbing my palm over my face and across my stubble. "Just had trouble sleeping, is all. But I'm fine. And one hundred percent ready to go." I clap my hands together. "In fact, I am ready to wrangle a music festival. Aren't you?"

It's the start of summer, which means we're planning every Never Harbor festival known to man, and our small town sure loves events. They kicked me off Taste of Never Harbor after I kept sneaking food samples last year. This year, I'm on the Never Harbor Music Festival committee. Probably a better decision.

I slap the conference room table. "I vote to add a petting zoo."

Peter barks out a laugh. "To the music festival? Why? So the loud saxophones can tip the goats over?"

I look down the table at my older brother, running a palm through his wild mess of sunny-blond hair. Peter is sitting in his usual spot at the head of the table because Peter Davies knows everyone and everything in Never Harbor. Laura tried to convince him to join the community center full-time last year. If he wasn't already running his own restaurant and bar, he might have.

"We won't get fainting goats," I clarify. "Well, maybe. I don't know. That's not a bad idea, Pete." I lean back in my chair, balancing on the back legs, whipping out my phone from my hoodie's front pocket and mouthing my search out loud, *"Do goats faint at the sound of saxophones?"*

"You're gonna fall," Milo observes.

My other brother smiles at me, adjusting his horn-rimmed glasses as he watches me sway on the chair. I force the seat to wobble under me, raising my eyebrows and opening my mouth into a mock, surprised *whoa*. He shakes his head at my blatant carelessness.

Laura sighs. "I wouldn't trust you to wrangle goats, Cass."

"Hey, I'm good with animals," I counter with a scoffing laugh.

"The chair," Milo warns again.

"I'm fine," I say, waving him off. "Anyway, I can absolutely lead registration. You know I love talking to people. It's my greatest strength. Even Pete thinks so."

"He's better with people than me—that's for sure," Peter compliments, which has the corner of my mouth kicking up into a smile.

"See?" I say, throwing a thumb his way.

Peter's confidence in me is nice, but I know, out of the three Davies children sitting in this room, I'm the one brother people expect the least from. I can't blame them. I didn't start a restaurant, like Peter, and I don't read a ton, like Milo. Even our eldest brother, Jasper, renovates houses with his bare hands. Then, there's me, a man Laura has to second-guess giving goats to. In her defense, I am a little distracted today, but I know exactly why.

Marina Starkey.

Just the thought of her name has me grinning.

Marina and I were never close friends, only as familiar as two people growing up in a small town together can be—the type of passing acquaintance you play with on the monkey bars throughout elementary school until puberty introduces cliques. Like two ships passing in the night.

I was voted Class Clown, and Marina Starkey was voted Best Smile. I threw footballs every Friday night, and she was the head cheerleader and talent show winner. Nearly ten years later, I'm still just all muscles and not much else, but she's still an absolute knockout.

The most beautiful woman I've laid eyes on.

Dramatic? Sure.

But she's gorgeous. Stunning. I'm not sure many words could accurately describe Marina Starkey, but if I knew them, I'd use them.

I haven't stopped imagining how her honey-blonde hair fell in a beautiful mess of tangled waves. And if I close my eyes, I can see those green eyes like the warm, foggy shade of the small plant she clutched against her chest.

Don't think about her chest though.

Don't think about the way it rose and fell to rustle the plant leaves.

Damn, but it was hard to miss that she wasn't wearing a bra in the car. The pebbled peaks of her nipples were outlined under the loose fabric.

No. Bad idea to think about your landlord's daughter.

It's not that I'm scared of Charles Starkey; it's that I'm technically under his roof as I pay toward owning the townhome. That was the deal we made a few weeks ago, and I respect the guy.

Though I also respect that his daughter does *have nice breasts.*

Milo's hand shoots out. "Whoa, Cass—"

My stomach plummets right as the chair falls off-balance. My palms whip out to grab the corner of the table. I catch myself in time, but the chair is lost to the ground, clattering and echoing through the conference room.

I cringe and send a weak smile to Laura. "My bad."

"Our chairs were not meant to handle you and your ... bulk." With the final word, her eyes trail over my arms, still flexed as I hold on to the table.

"Okay, so I can't handle chairs," I joke, "but I can handle registration, all right?"

She bites her lower lip and nods slowly. I can't blame her apprehension. I am the same guy who just knocked over a chair.

"Okay, so ..." Laura says absentmindedly, scribbling on her clipboard. She likes to think out loud. "I still need to meet with Mayor Barrie about reserving the big stage." She tsks. "God, I can never get in touch with that man. Milo, are you still friends with his son? Maybe we can sneak in the back door?"

Milo shifts in his chair. "No. He's out in California, last I checked."

I don't know why he looks so uncomfortable. Milo and Dustin Barrie were stuck together like glue their senior year. As for me, I wouldn't say I'm upset they don't talk anymore.

I always got the sense Dustin didn't like me. I couldn't keep up with their conversations of books, I didn't care to understand the college application process, and I swear Dustin rolled his eyes every time I beat them at Mario Kart, calling it *luck*.

Whenever he drawled, "Nice one, Cassie," after every joke of mine, I could taste the sarcasm.

"I need to talk to Mayor Barrie about our new sponsor too," Laura says. "I'm apparently meeting them tonight. He says it's a surprise."

"You hate surprises," I note.

She groans. "I almost punched my sister at my last surprise party." She waves her hand in the air frantically. "Maybe don't jump out at people randomly, y'know? Anyway, Pete, if you've got catering covered …"

"On it," Peter answers. She doesn't need to finish her thought because Peter's reliability is just implied. He's chaotic day-to-day, but professionally, he flips a switch, and he's suddenly Superman.

"Milo?" Laura prompts, but my other brother isn't an issue either, and we all know it.

"I have Charles Starkey practically busting down my door with his trombone," Milo says through a smile. "Easy."

Charles Starkey.

Don't think about his daughter's breasts.

"Y'know what? How about Cass books the bands instead?" Laura suggests, smiling at me. "Like you said, you're great with people. And you won't be on a strict timeline, like you would be with registration."

I catch eyes with Milo. He gives a half smile, but I can't decipher it. It seems to say, *If you want*, but maybe he agrees with Laura too.

"Sure," I concede with a smiling shrug. "Wherever you need me."

"Less on your plate that way," Laura says with a kind smile.

But the sentence settles in my gut as I nod and return it. "Absolutely."

Peter clears his throat. I look over, and he's giving me a silent thumbs-up. Then, within seconds, my phone buzzes in my pocket. I tug it out to see a new text in our family group chat.

Peter
Music festival kickoff party?

Peter is intuitive in that way. He always knows how to make me feel better.

Cassidy
Let's goooo!

Milo digs into his pocket, giving Peter a smirk as well before whipping his fingers across his phone screen.

Milo
You plan a party for everything.

Peter
You're telling me this doesn't need a celebration?

Bonnie
There's a party?! But I'm studying tonight!

                                          Cassidy
                                             Boring!

Bonnie
I'm so close to finally being out, I can taste it! *crossed fingers emoji*

Our younger sister graduates high school in a few weeks. Sometimes, I'm happy she can't come out. We can get a little wild—something she probably doesn't need to see.

Milo
You can't drink. You're underage.

Bonnie
I'm eighteen! I can still go!

Peter
Doesn't sound like twenty-one to me.

Bonnie
You're no fun when you play the Responsible Bar Owner card.

                                         Cassidy
Ooh, does a Bar Owner Simulator exist? Bet that's fun.

Peter:
You're missing out too, Bon. I have it under good authority Marina's in town.

My chest tightens, and I shoot Peter a look that he dismisses with a snort. I told my brothers about last night. I should have expected some level of ribbing.

Bonnie
WHAT?! Okay, I'm skipping studying.

Milo
Why?

Bonnie
She's ridiculously cool. You wouldn't understand, nerd.

Cassidy
I didn't know you were friends with her.

Bonnie
She used to babysit Lu. She let us eat whatever
we wanted when I came over. It was the BEST.

Cassidy
I always forget you and Lulu are wee babies.

Bonnie
We're not babies!

Milo
The word "teen" is still in your age.

Bonnie
It's not in Lulu's!

Milo
Okay, so Lulu's not a baby. But you are.

Cassidy
LOL, you played yourself, Bon.

Peter
So, Hideaway? Party time?

Cassidy
Excellent!!!

Peter
You're my favorite brother.

Peter
Speaking of, where's Jasper?

> **Cassidy**
> Rude.

> **Jasper**
> Not going

All three of us let out varying laughs, causing Laura to glance up from her clipboard. It's unsurprising that our oldest brother, Jasper, would prefer a night at his cottage with his girlfriend and seven-year-old son instead.

> **Cassidy**
> Booooo!

> **Peter**
> Booooo!

> **Milo**
> Boo.

> **Wendy**
> BooOooOooO.

> **Bonnie**
> Wendy! Aren't you supposed to take his side?

But it's also a good thing his girlfriend is more outgoing than he is. This past year, she's slipped into the family group chat easily, like she's always belonged.

> **Wendy**
> What? I like booing Jasper as much as the next person.

> **Wendy**
> And I wanna go!

> **Jasper**
> Fine we'll go

> **Peter**
> I'm sorry, was that the sound of a whip in the background?

After the fiasco of last summer, I cringe. The Peter-Wendy-Jasper triangle is one shape I want no part in. But if Peter can joke about his ex-fiancée dating his older brother, then more power to him. I know Wendy is perfect for Jasper—we all do—but she's also not my ex to tiptoe around. Leave it to Pete to stomp instead.

Bonnie
Marina AND Wendy are going?! I wanna go!!!!!

Jasper
You're studying

                                        Cassidy
                                           Booo!

Peter
Boooo!

Wendy
As a teacher, I can't condone booing of education.

Milo
I work at a library. I stand with Wendy.

Bonnie
Booooo.

Peter
Party time!!!

                                        Cassidy
                                     EXCELLENTTTT.

Peter
See you never, Bonnie! *peace sign emoji*

Bonnie
You guys suck.

I almost tuck my phone back in my hoodie pocket, but it vibrates before I can. This time, I freeze. It's Charles Starkey.

Starkey
sorry about marina. heard she woke you up

                                        Cassidy
                                     No worries!

Starkey
we're going to hideaway tonight if you wanna grab a drink

Starkey
apology beer

Cassidy
It really wasn't a big deal!

Cassidy
But you are speaking my language.

Plus, I don't miss the *we* involved. Is he referring to his usual crew of best friends, Bobbi Mullins and William Jukes? Or does that include Marina as well?

Don't think about her chest.

Laura stacks her phone on top of her clipboard. "Okay, since all of you are clearly checked out, I think that's a wrap for today."

I laugh. "Hey, you were texting too."

"It was Mayor Barrie," Laura says pointedly. "Speaking of which …" Her smile fades into a grimace. "Can I ask a teensy little favor of one of you?"

My brothers and I chime a collection of, "Anything," "Absolutely," and, "All ears."

"Mayor Barrie says I have to meet the new sponsor at The Hideaway tonight," she explains. "Can someone possibly, maybe, definitely join me? I hate that kind of stuff."

We all exchange a grinning look before chorusing, "Yes."

Music festival kickoff party, drinks with my landlord, meeting the new festival sponsor, *and* seeing the woman with the beautiful blonde waves again?

Looks like it'll be one of those nights where The Hideaway is packed.

My favorite type of night—a night for shenanigans.

- *Chapter Six* -

A NIGHT FOR SHENANIGANS

Cassidy

The Hideaway is located down a winding road of drooping willow trees, holding up to its namesake as a truly hidden bar. The three-tiered structure, split between a first-floor restaurant and tiki bar upper levels, is a place most locals call home. This means the lot is always overflowing after five o'clock.

I walk through the double doors to greet the heart of Never Harbor. Warm string lights wrap around exposed wooden bars overhead, and tree trunks shoot through the center like support beams to this adult tree house.

Walking into The Hideaway is like walking into your own birthday party. There are calls of my name from every direction, fist bumps exchanged, and distant chin nods. I clap a hand on Steve's shoulder, our local paperboy—or paper *man*—leaning on his bicycle near the bar. I tap elbows with Donna, Never Harbor's elementary school principal. I only make it five more feet before a shot is pushed toward me across the bar.

Finally, in the back, at their usual booth, I spot Bobbi Mullins, William Jukes, and my landlord, Charles Starkey—a tattooed crew flush with drink.

And across from all three of them is Marina, sitting under the glow of the hanging string lights, illuminating her head like a sunny crown—just as stunning as I remember. She's got a cheeky look to her, lips tinged pink and tipped up into a smile. She's wearing another one of those loose dresses, the kind with thin straps that slide down her shoulders. I can still imagine her soft skin beneath my palms last night.

I walk over, place my hands in my pockets, then remove them before pocketing once more.

"We've *got* to stop bumping into each other," I tease, grinning.

Marina spots me and laughs, her finger rotating over the lip of her glass. "Darn, and I forgot my defense weapon this time."

"I was hoping for a rematch too."

"Next time," she says.

I can't stop lingering on her beautiful smile.

"Sorry about all that, kid," Starkey interjects.

"Nah, it's no big deal," I say, holding out my palm to shake his hand. "Things happen. Didn't realize fighting for my property was in our contract."

He chuckles. "Should have warned you."

"Cass wouldn't hurt a fly anyway," Bobbi says from beside me.

"Whoa, there's my superwoman!" I lean down to hug her, cradling her wiry limbs.

"Sit, ya goof," Bobbi insists. "We were just talking about what Marina's gonna do here."

I take the chair next to Marina, watching her shift in her seat uncomfortably. Though whether that's due to me or the conversation, I'm not sure.

"And I was politely ignoring that," Marina responds, playfully sticking her tongue out at Bobbi.

"Cop-out answer," Jukes rasps out.

"But we'll let it slide this time," Bobbi says.

"No, you won't." I laugh. "You three never let up."

"Hey!" they collectively say, hands flying in the air in protest.

"You told everyone about that time I skipped out on the town hall meeting to skinny-dip." I point a finger at them. Bobbi swats it away. "And I explicitly wanted *nobody* to know."

"We told nobody!" Bobbi protests.

"Yeah, nobody!" Jukes's Boston accent gets thicker, making me laugh again.

I lean back in my chair, smiling at Marina, who looks between the four of us in wonder.

"So, what are you gonna do?" I ask.

She bites her bottom lip and shakes her head. "I don't know actually."

"You'll stay with us," her dad says, hanging his arm over the back of the booth, resting a palm on Bobbi's opposite shoulder.

Marina smiles sweetly, eyes lingering on her dad's hand. "I can't."

"Where else can you go?" Jukes jests.

Maybe it's the uncomfortable conversation, or maybe it's just me being me, but I blurt out, "I could always use a roommate."

I say it without thinking. What is there to think about anyway? She needs a place to stay.

Around the table, there are varying degrees of processing, but it's her dad who passes a wink to Marina.

"You owe me ten bucks, Guppy."

Marina shakes her head. "No, that's your house, Cass."

"Technically, it's not," I clarify. "Not yet. I could use the extra rent."

"I have no job," she counters.

"Ah. Well, I could use the company then." I tend to speak before I think, which is why that comment has my nerves halting in place. I didn't realize it was true until it came out. "The townhome is really quiet," I admit. "And ... well, I can't *not* help someone without a place to stay."

"I mean ..." Marina starts, stops, then laughs. "No. That's ... I don't even ... no." She parts her lips to say more, but whatever was intended is interrupted by a separate arm looping through hers.

"Marina! Ahhh!"

I'd recognize that voice anywhere.

"Oh my God, hi, Lulu!" Marina says.

My sister's best friend, Lulu Kitt, grabs Marina's shoulder and pulls her into a hug, swaying them both back and forth. "Girl! You're back! Okay, okay, I'm *demanding* we get drinks! And I guess you can join too, Cass."

"Wow, thanks," I deadpan with a smile.

Lulu grins, and I know she's joking.

Marina points over her shoulder. "Well, I came here to hang out with—"

"No, no. You guys go have fun," Starkey says, waving his palms out. "You're sure?"

"Yeah. You need friends for the summer that aren't me."

She's only here for the summer?

Marina gives a weak smile and nods. "Oh. Okay, sure, yeah."

Lulu drags Marina toward the open-air stairwell. Her long black hair matches the length of Marina's, swishing like spilled ink behind her and serving as a guide through the crowd of more familiar faces. I follow behind.

"Cass, Laura's by the bar upstairs, looking for you," Lulu calls back to me.

"Good thing you came downstairs then."

"Duh, that's *why* I came downstairs."

Lulu's exaggerated eye roll says it all, but she turns around to smile at me, as if I were in on the joke as well. I don't know what joke, and I can never tell with Lulu anyway.

We ascend the stairs to the second floor—she drags Marina, more like it—then trail up the last flight to the third floor. The Hideaway's top level is an open balcony, cooled by the breezy summer air with the scent of the sea rolling in from Crocodile Cove below. It's our usual go-to spot, and most of my family is already crowded around the bar.

Lulu rushes over on clacking heels to sit on the stool beside my brother Milo. A finger rests on his temple as he peers down at a torn bright-yellow paperback, spine damaged and cracked from the years he's likely read and reread it. Lulu leans over his shoulder as if she's reading it too.

When Milo catches sight of me, he tips his chin up with a smile in acknowledgment. He stands from his stool, tucking his book into his back pocket. Milo's considerate like that, knowing when he can disappear into pages versus when it's time to be social.

My oldest brother, Jasper, doesn't have the same social cues installed. He's on the opposite side of Milo, sipping his whiskey and staring into it like its ripples could pass the time faster.

"Cass, I got us pink drinks!" Wendy calls, one hand on Jasper's shoulder.

I throw my fists in the air. "Hell yeah, pink drink!"

I sidestep past Milo and Jasper to pull Wendy into a big hug. Even though she's dating my brother, it's far from weird. She was my friend first anyway. This beautiful, kind girl was my English partner in middle school, and I've kept her around since then. It was good luck that she fell in love with my brother.

"Last one for me tonight," she says with a shrug. "Pete's still got me on a drink limit."

"Such a stickler, that guy," I tease.

Peter is a stickler for nothing but his own bar rules. I guess that's why he's so good at what he does.

But just over her shoulder, Marina gives a teasing smile. While I'm sure Jasper would disagree … although Wendy is pretty, it's Marina who takes the breath out of me.

"Good call leaving when you did," I tease Marina, pulling out of the hug from Wendy. "Those three get wild."

"My dad and his friends?" she asks.

"Yeah."

She shrugs. "I think I can handle wild."

And God if that doesn't do something to me.

I laugh. "I'm just saying, they're on a different level from everyone else."

"As his daughter, I've got the same gumption, I think." She puffs out her chest.

"I could see that last night."

"Wait, am I missing something here?" Wendy asks, glancing between us. Her eyebrows are raised, head tilted to the side. I don't trust her innocent elementary school teacher facade one bit.

The rest of my family is just as nosy. Milo suppresses a knowing smile. Jasper blinks between us, finally drawn out from his drink, more interested than he'll ever let on.

"Okay, okay, don't get any ideas," I say, holding up my palms and waving them around. "She thought the rental was empty."

Marina shrugs, innocently adding, "I got into bed with him."

"Ow-owww!" Lulu crows, jutting her red cowboy boot out to nudge Marina's sneakers. The two shots in each palm almost slosh over.

I shake my head at Marina. "Why're you stoking the fires, huh?"

She smiles satisfactorily. "Told you I can be just as plucky as my dad."

"Plucky?" I ask. "Who says plucky?"

"I do." Her confidence has my heart racing. "Anyway, Cass is right. It wasn't like that at all."

Wendy bumps her shoulder to mine. "Okay, so a woman you barely know crawled into bed with you," she says. "What *is* it like then?"

"It's *like* being woken up at four a.m. to screams," I respond.

"Not fun ones," Marina adds.

I tilt my head to the side. "You're a menace."

Marina scrunches her nose. "Maybe."

God, she's cute.

"So, no fun things?" Lulu pouts.

I don't look away from Marina this time as we both answer, "No."

"Boring," Lulu drawls, handing me one of the shots.

I faintly hear Wendy jokingly whisper, "You flirt, you."

I laugh. "Wait, what?"

"Shot, Cass!" Lulu demands, directing me away from Wendy's accusatory eyebrow lift. I swear she got that expression from Jasper.

I tap my glass to Lulu's, slam it on the bar, then knock it back. Lulu shakes her head with a hiss, high-fives me, then waltzes back over to the other three, leaving me at the end of the bar.

Alone.

With only Marina.

"So, you're here," I say dumbly.

"I am," she answers with a grin. "For a bit at least."

"Thought I caught that. Any reason why?"

She laughs. "You mean, why would I stay?"

I open my mouth to talk, then close it, and nod. But when my words fail me, she supplies some instead.

"Where's Peter?" she asks. "This feels like his territory of partying."

"Didn't know you were so familiar with my family."

"Who isn't familiar with Pete?"

I grin. "He's got a reputation, I guess."

"All of you do to some degree. Milo's the smart one. Jasper's the hermit. Bonnie's the only girl."

"Oh, she'd hate knowing that's how you classified her."

Marina smiles. "Your mom was my physician, growing up," she continues. "And your dad was PTA president for most of elementary school."

"That's true," I agree with a laugh. "So, who am I?"

"I don't know. Who *are* you, Cassidy?" she asks, leaning in like it's some secret, and I like the way her voice grows husky with the hushed whisper. "What's your reputation?"

"Clearly, a Davies," I answer. "Maybe a house thief. Or ... a roommate." I tip my drink to her, and she laughs. "I can be whatever you'd like."

It's a blink-and-you-miss-it moment, but Marina's green eyes shadow over. As soon as the expression came, it's gone, and she's smiling again.

I clear my throat. "Hey, I'm sorry for freaking you out last night, by the way."

"No, no." She waves me off. "I should be apologizing. I could have hurt you."

"Oh, sure. That was a *very* intimidating lamp."

"It was! Trust me, I'm lethal with household items. You should see me with cords. I use 'em like whips."

"I'll keep that in mind next time you're at my house at four in the morning."

Her cheeks flush, and the freckles dotting her nose nearly disappear. The tips of my ears burn when I realize what I said.

"I didn't mean—"

"So, you're telling me you unintentionally leave innuendos hanging out there?" she says. "That's two for two."

"Two?"

"Is that Laura?"

Out of the corner of my eye, I see my boss, Laura, sitting at the bar, cradling a drink with an umbrella swirling along the side. She's waving me over. I wonder if I'm late.

When I walk over to Laura, Marina follows. Admittedly, I kinda like the companionship.

I lean my forearms on the countertop. "What are you doing all the way up here?"

Laura sighs. "I'm preparing."

Marina twists her lips to the side. "Preparing for what?"

"Our music festival sponsor."

"Whoa, you've met him?" I ask. "Who is it? Is it a celebrity?"

Marina gasps. "A celebrity host?"

It's cute how easily she gets excited.

"I like where your head is at, Starkey," I say. "Maybe it's Bob Saget!"

Marina's face falls.

"Wait, Bob Saget isn't alive anymore, is he? Bob Ross?"

Marina winces, rubbing a hand down my arm with a pitying, "Oh …"

I don't have time to consider what celebrities are alive with her hand on me like that.

But before I can comment again, Marina looks over my shoulder, and her eyes grow the size of two full moons. I twist around and follow her line of sight to a man ascending the stairs, swinging car keys over his fingers. He's in a tailored gray suit. His hair is slicked back with too much mousse, maybe a couple of strands hanging here and there. And his glasses, so similar to Milo's yet somehow more pretentious, are perched at the end of his nose.

45

My stomach drops.

Laura sighs. "Our sponsor is Mayor Barrie's son."

"Dustin," Marina breathes.

- *Chapter Seven* -

A GOOD BIT OF FOUL

Marina

I hate the phrase, "What a small world." When you grow up in a small town, everyone knows everyone. But the proof of a truly, infinitesimally small world is Dustin Barrie standing in The Hideaway, eerily out of place, like a butcher knife on a cabin's entry table.

My sneakers are cemented to the ground—not my old boots because I threw those *tempting* things away. Nerves that were once zipping like a hummingbird's wings around Cassidy are instead gnawing, grating, chewing.

"Cassie?" Dustin calls over. His grin is wide, akin to how he'd greet a golfing buddy.

I hate it.

Cassidy's eyebrows pull toward the center of his forehead, clear confusion on his face. I wonder if I look as shocked as I feel too.

"Dustin," he says, though more to himself than anyone else.

"Dustin!" Laura waves her hand, gesturing him over. Her teeth grit together as she mutters to us, "The mayor's son. What the hell, right?" She's grinning again. "Dustin, hi! You know Cassidy?"

Dustin smiles, and it's slimy and *off*. "I know little Cassie," he says, and I don't like it. It's one lip curl away from a sneer. "Youngest Davies kid."

"Middle child," Cassidy says with a good-natured laugh. "Bonnie and The Twins are the babies."

"Right. Forgot about the whole brood."

"We're a handful."

I know Cassidy is trying to be nice, but I'm hanging on by a thread. My nose stings, and tears start to bubble behind my eyes, but it's not out of sadness or fear.

It's anger.

Why is he sponsoring the festival? Why is he here?

I freeze when his eyes lock on me like shots of ice.

"Nice to see you, kiddo."

All I can do is nod, and I hate myself for it. From the corner of my eye, I see Cassidy's mouth tilting down.

"Yeah," is all I say. "Nice to see you too."

"You two friends?" Cassidy asks, pointing between us.

"She was my employee up until recently," he corrects.

"Didn't work out," I finish for him.

Yep, angry tears are definitely coming, along with the shame of it all, which only makes me tear up more.

Lulu appears by my side, looping an arm through the crook of mine, and tugs me away, chanting, "Shots, shots, shots."

She flashes a grin at Dustin, and he returns it, waggling his fingers in greeting. Her face flushes pink.

I want to circle back—maybe I'll spit in his face or something—but Lulu tugs my arm more, leaving Cassidy watching with a stunned expression as I'm dragged away.

"Girl, you okay?" Lulu asks once we're out of earshot. "You look like you're gonna cry."

I force out a laugh. "I'm definitely not."

One hundred percent was.

"Then, who's that?"

"The mayor's son."

"Get out," she breathes. "Dustin?" She looks over her shoulder. "Damn, it's been a while since I've seen him." She twitches her lips into a smile. "He got hot."

"Okay, *no*," I say quickly. "He's a walking red flag."

She lifts an eyebrow, and the subsequent smirk tells me that red might be her favorite color.

I shake my head with a scoff. "Lu, you're better than him."

She tips her chin up in pride. "I don't think I'm better than anyone, thank you very much."

"Cute."

"I am who I am."

And Dustin Barrie is who he is because when I turn back, Dustin's eyes have landed on us—focused in a way that has me feeling like my hand has been caught in the cookie jar.

I'm mortified when Cassidy turns on the spot to follow his gaze. The embarrassment sluices over my spine like cool aloe dribbling in thick gobs after a summer's day. But there's no relief, just a hissing inhale of pain.

What if they're exchanging some type of unspoken guy code, saying, *Oh, hey, she hits on her bosses?*

I don't know why I care what Cassidy thinks—I barely know the guy—but he's nice, and I've always been one to imprint on people easily. Call it my mommy issues, if you'd like. My old therapist did, in nicer terms.

"Okay, forget the mayor's kid," Lulu says. "Whatever. Anyway, how long are you staying in town? What's your plan?"

"I don't know. A couple of months maybe?" The words catch while I'm stuck between here and the conversation I left.

Distantly, I hear Cassidy say, "So, sponsoring the music festival, yeah?"

"Yeah," Dustin answers. "About that ..."

"We should totally hang out," Lulu interjects. "I'm bored out of my mind every day. Bonnie's still in school, and the flower shop is a mess. I swear, one more missed event, and my parents will disown me ..."

But her words fade into the background as I watch Dustin's crooked smile stretch across his face like it's plastered on the wrong man. It should be charming, and maybe I considered it to be once—as a friend or his employee—but never in the way it looks now with white teeth that feel too big for his face.

In fact, it's interesting how different he and Cassidy look, standing side by side.

I got a good look at Cassidy last night, but how does he look even better with more clothes *on?*

His curls are tamed back, sprouting from behind a headband's hold like coral in the sea. A white pocket T-shirt pulls taut over his chest and arms. Jeans barely contain his thighs. Cassidy's sneakers look comfortable, but not outdated. You can tell a lot about a person by their shoes. The tops are creased, like they've got some miles in them, but they're still crisp white. I wonder if he scrubs them clean. He must prefer looking presentable. Practical yet frugal.

Dustin's shoes look untouched and freshly polished, like maybe he bought them this week. I wonder if he ever wears the same pair twice.

They're definitely not the same person.

"I actually want to adjust a few things," Dustin says as I continue to shamelessly eavesdrop.

"Oh, okay," Laura says. "Well, we just started planning, so that's not a big deal at all. Let me pull up my Notes app ..."

"I was thinking, instead of a music festival, it's a wine mixer."

"A wine mixer?" Cassidy laughs, but it still manages to sound friendly. "In Never Harbor?"

"We've got this new product that we're launching," Dustin explains, and I want to groan.

Of course Barrie Wine & Spirits is involved. He's sponsoring this for him and him alone.

"Yeah, but the music festival is about ... music?" Cassidy responds, chuckling again.

"Right, right," Dustin interjects hurriedly. "And we can still have some booths. But think about it: you're not just capturing average tourists, looking for some weekend at the beach with some saxophones, but *wealthy* tourists."

"I mean, it's not really about the money," Laura kindly explains, but I can hear the irritation lying underneath. "The town looks forward to this every year. We barely break even, and we're okay with that."

Cassidy chuckles. "I think Jukes might throw his saxophone in the sea if we cancel."

Laura must agree because she laughs too. Dustin's late laughter doesn't carry the same jovial nature.

"Right," he responds, dragging out the word with a fake smile. "Right."

"Marina?"

I jump on the spot, brought back to my own side of the bar and face-to-face with Lulu's crossed arms.

"Were you even listening?"

"I ... no." I wince. "I'm sorry."

She turns around. "Mayor's son again?" Then, she pumps her eyebrows with a smile. "Or Cass?"

I choke out a laugh and shake my head. "What were you saying again? I'm listening."

"Oh. Well, ugh"—Lulu leans back on the heels of her cowboy boots dramatically—"the flower shop has been a disaster. I royally messed up arrangements for prom."

"I didn't know you owned a flower shop."

"Aw, you've been gone so long. Poor thing." She places a hand on my shoulder. "Wait, oh my God, you should drop by!" Then, like an idea hits her suddenly, she goes, "Ahh! Yes, please stop by. You majored in plant stuff, right?"

I have to catch my smile from falling. It feels like yet another life I left behind. I tend to have a lot of those.

"I did," I answer. "But it's been so long."

"It's better than what I can do. I'm killing these things left and right. The place smells like a funeral home." She cups her hands together in prayer. "Please-please-please?"

"Maybe," I answer through her continued pleas. "But, hey, I think I'm gonna turn in for the night."

She furrows her brow. "Wait, why? Because of Dustin?"

"No," I protest too quickly. "No. I'm just a little tired, y'know? I'm used to another time zone. Text me. We'll hang out."

"Sure you don't need me to go slap the guy?"

I laugh. "Please don't."

"Maybe he's into that."

"*Lu.*"

She giggles as we pull each other into a hug, her side lingering with a final squeeze, and before she has enough time to make sense of my excuse—how my old time zone was actually three hours *behind* ours—I slip away to exactly where Dustin is blocking part of the stairwell and the only exit.

He, Cassidy, and Laura pause at the steps.

Dang it.

I inhale, my heart pounding with every step, trying to look at the ground or the railing, anywhere but at him.

I walk behind them. Maybe if I just sneak by …

If I could only find one more inch …

But when I do, I accidentally budge Laura.

Like a terrified rabbit, Laura screeches.

She jumps. I jump. We all jump.

Her feet trip over one another. I grab her arm, but she slips from my grasp.

Then, it's slow motion.

Slow as molasses.

Slower than time will allow as Laura bumps down The Hideaway's staircase.

"I am so, so sorry, Laura."

It's the fiftieth time I've apologized, and Laura's been flashing me a kind, absolutely-not-genuine smile for about ten minutes now. But the guilt of seeing her with one arm in a sling and the other resting over a crutch is enough to make me want to crawl into a hole and die.

It's only my second day in Never Harbor, and I'm nearly killing people.

We're standing in Never Harbor's clinic, pacing the waiting room's tiled floor and white walls, colored only by bright magazine racks and framed art portraying local landmarks.

"I said it's fine," Laura says. "I just don't like getting surprised."

"Marina didn't mean to scare you," Cassidy says.

"I know. I know," Laura repeats. I swear her eye twitches. "It's fine. How much do I owe you, Mags?"

Cassidy's mom, Maggie Davies, stands behind the receptionist desk, sipping from a Peg Leg Press to-go cup. "Don't worry about it for now, Laura. Go home and rest."

Cassidy tosses his hands in the air with a satisfied grin. "See? No harm, no foul, boss."

"Lots of harm," Laura corrects grumpily.

"A good bit of foul," I add with a wince.

Cassidy laughs. At least he finds all this funny.

After Laura's topple down the stairs—to put it lightly—Cassidy and I carried her straight to his car. Dustin asked once if he could come with us, but after Laura's polite protest, he didn't insist a second time.

Cassidy drove us to his mom's clinic, calling her on the way. Maggie Davies met us outside on her electric-blue moped within minutes. Not only was she prompt, but she also arrived in style—leather jacket, boots, and a grin. Her black hair, interspersed with gray, flew in every direction like a mad scientist as she ripped off her helmet. I wish I could be even half as cool as her.

"Thanks. You're a saint, Ma," Cassidy says. He pulls her into a hug, burying her in his arms, like not even a passing hug should be half-assed. He sniffs. "Wait, why do you smell like licorice?"

She tips her to-go cup. "Bobbi's new drink."

Cassidy's nose scrunches up. "She already started making those?"

"There's a licorice drink?" I ask.

"She's clever, that Bobbi," Maggie says.

I nod to myself. She is. I've always loved that about her. She's a business guru. And now, she's dating my dad. No, living with him. It's so wild to me how things change, yet somehow are still the same. Maybe it's a small-town thing.

"Bobbi's been at The Hideaway for hours," Cassidy observes. "How old is that cup?"

"Long day. I've been reheating it."

He scrunches his nose. "Reheated licorice?"

"Okay, well, be careful, Marina," Maggie says, ignoring her son's remarks with a grin. "Maybe don't scare anyone else soon."

"Why," Cassidy chimes in, "when it's such a talent of hers?"

He winks. All thought of anything else leaves my head. I nearly stumble back. My body feels hot. I didn't know people still casually winked like that. Somebody needs to tell him to holster that gun.

"I'm lethal, apparently," I reply with a choked laugh.

"I'll keep an eye out for future victims coming in here," Maggie says. "Now, Laura, go home. Stay in bed. Don't do anything at all, okay? I'll have your prescription ready tomorrow."

"Thanks," she grumbles, adjusting her crutch.

"I guess we should get going, huh?" Cassidy walks over to place a hand on Laura's back, likely sensing, just as I do, that Laura is annoyed and wanted a bed two hours ago.

We say our goodbyes to Maggie and escort Laura out the front door, down the porch, and to Cassidy's car.

He tucks her into the passenger seat, then rounds to the front as she buckles.

"Hop on in, Starkey."

I wave my palm. "No, it's all right. I'll walk."

He pauses, placing a palm on the hood. "What? Don't be ridiculous. Let me drive you home."

I shake my head. "No, really. I prefer walking."

"It's a forty-five-minute walk at best," he counters with a laugh.

I look up at the sky. "And the moon is nice tonight."

He thinks for a moment, running his large palm over the door.

"But you'll be alone."

I shrug. "What's new?"

I didn't mean for it to come out sounding so pathetic, which is why I follow it with a cringe.

Cassidy laughs, considers me more—enough to make me feel like I'm standing in front of him, naked—and then knocks on the roof. "All right then. I'll see you soon."

"See you later." I wave as he pulls out of the lot with Laura. She does not look back at me.

The road ahead is illuminated by only occasional lampposts and porch lights from neighboring houses. Some railings have fresh paint. Some are just as dilapidated as they were when I was in high school. Another part of Never Harbor that's changed, yet it's still the same. Familiar.

I smile to myself and start my trek.

I wasn't lying when I claimed to love walking. Sidewalks are one of the things I missed most about Never Harbor. Nothing beats the rushing waves beating against rocks just beyond the railing. The city has a lot of good things, but it doesn't have this type of calm. The only other sound is a low hum from outside radiators or buzzing porch lights. It's hard to not love it.

I wonder how much calmer tonight would have been without Dustin Barrie though.

I can't believe he's back in town too. And for how long? A weekend? The summer?

That possibility feels like a death sentence.

And how long has he been planning this? Wouldn't I have known about it? Why is his sponsorship so sudden?

I cross the road, trailing down the wooden plank ramp to the pebbled beach shore and take a seat on the rocks. I close my eyes and only listen to the rushing in of the tide lapping against the rocks. Then the withdrawal, drifting out once more.

And I breathe.

I don't know how much time passes, but the cooling breeze tells me it must be late. I don't want to look at my phone though. I don't want any part of the world to seep into this peacefulness. But Dad might be worried if I'm not home soon.

I'm in my late twenties. I have a degree I don't use. I have no job. No money. And I'm living with my dad again—not just my dad, but his girlfriend too. I feel like I'm careening fifty steps back from my already-stunted progress.

I stand and dust off my skirt, but suddenly, the ocean is illuminated by car headlights. Someone drives by, slowing to a rumble by the beach, before pulling into the post office's empty lot.

Never Harbor is the safest town I've ever lived in, but my old roommate watched enough true crime documentaries for me to know that existing as a woman anywhere means I shouldn't ignore the goose bumps skittering over my arms.

I need to listen to my gut.

I swallow, striding back up the ramp and onto the sidewalk again, bypassing the stalling car.

The engine cuts off. From behind me, the driver's door opens, then shuts.

Shit.

I walk faster.

"Hey, wait!"

I pick up speed.

And the person laughs.

Laughs.

Is this a game to them?

Screw. That.

I spin on my heel and point a single finger like I'm wielding a weapon.

"Back the hell off," I snap. "I have a knife!"

"Jesus!"

There is no creeper. It's Cassidy jogging up behind me, hoodie strings snapping against his chest. He was smiling, but that expression got obliterated after my outburst.

"Do you seriously have a knife?"

"No," I admit sheepishly.

He blows out a breath. "You're a scary woman sometimes."

"Why are you here?"

"To walk with you," he explains, like it's the easiest thing on the planet.

"What?" I ask, laughing.

"Told you I'd see you soon."

"You drove back here just to walk with me?"

"Yeah."

I blink at him. "But you have a car. And I've still got maybe thirty minutes left."

"Then, we should probably get going."

"And abandon your car?"

He pockets his hands in his hoodie and shrugs. "I'll pick up my car in the morning."

"No," I say, closing my eyes. "It's not ..."

"Hey, if you don't want me to walk with you, that's fine. Just figured you'd want the company." Cassidy gives a crooked smile, the kind that indents his dimple. "But I know what it's like to be alone too much. Not good for the soul, y'know?"

He is too kind for his own good. Something about him and the casual way he falls into step beside me gets me smiling. I wonder if this type of thing is normal for him.

"Wait." I pause and laugh. "The soul?"

"Yeah," he says. "Oh, don't tell me you don't believe in a soul."

"Oh, I believe in souls."

"Perfect. Can't wait to hear all about your thoughts for the next"—he looks at his phone to jokingly check the time—"thirty minutes." He brings his arms behind his head and looks up at the stars. "God, what a night, huh?"

I can't stop the grin spreading up to my flushed cheeks.

"Yeah," I say. "What a night."

- *Chapter Eight* -

LAWN MOWER SUMMER CAMP

Cassidy

The fact that Dustin didn't come to the clinic initially pissed me off, but I'm having a hard time being too mad about it now. Laura is safe—I tucked her in like a baby, setting Tylenol and water by her bed—and now, I'm walking side by side with a stunning woman on a beautiful summer evening.

Life could be worse.

Marina and I trail down the winding sidewalks of Never Harbor. She kicks pebbles, knocking one to me like a soccer ball that I pass back.

"Does your mom accept gifts?"

I laugh. "Yeah. Why?"

"I'll need to tell her thanks somehow. She's my hero for the night."

"Mine too," I agree, but that's an understatement. Ma's been my hero since I was seven years old. "And she likes lilies, by the way."

Marina smiles. "Good to know."

"So," I say, kicking another pebble, "Dustin, huh?"

She nods slowly, more to herself than me. "That guy."

"He was why you left the West Coast?"

She lets out a small groan. "No. Yes. I don't know. Not *him* exactly. We just didn't end on good terms. I was fired. Sorta."

"Sorta?"

"Yeah."

"Such a bad employee," I tease.

She runs a tongue over her teeth and into her cheek, giving me one of those grins with only her eyes.

"Apparently, I *wasn't there to make friends.*"

"*Survivor*-style."

She giggles, and I wonder if I touched on something. "Yeah. I didn't turn in stuff on time. Bought too many plants for the office, I guess."

"You monster."

"Monstera," she says. When I furrow my brow, she adds, "It's a plant."

"I knew that," I reply, my aloof tone making it clear *I definitely didn't*. "Can't imagine he was the best boss though," I continue.

"What makes you say that?"

"Eh"—I shrug—"you seem smart." Then, I blurt out, "And he's a tool."

She gasps. "Cassidy Davies. Such words."

"He was my brother's best pal at one point, but can't say he was my favorite guy."

"I think I might like you more and more."

"So, is that why you're in town?" I ask. "You left your job?"

"Well," she answers with a sigh, "yeah. Couple reasons. I lost my job. My roommate stopped paying our rent—"

"That's a terrible friend."

"Not exactly a friend. She's a stranger I found online."

I bark out a laugh. "So, let me get this straight. You quit your job—"

"Got fired."

"And you lived with someone you didn't know? What's next, breaking into someone's house at four in the morning and crawling into bed with them?"

She slowly smiles, but it's delayed, like maybe she took a minute to process. It only makes the delivery that much sweeter. "You'll never let me live that down, will you?"

"Not anytime soon."

"Fair enough."

"If it makes you feel better," I say, "sponsors from corporations like Dustin's normally leave after the first brainstorming meeting. They like feeling important for a day, and then they just call or email after that. Maybe they'll come to the final event. Maybe. If we're incredibly unlucky."

"That does make me feel better," she admits.

I trail down to her sneakers. There's a hitch in her step.

"You all right?" I ask.

She winces, sucking in her lip.

"Yeah. Turns out these shoes ain't made for walking," she says with a forced twang. "They're new."

I take a step in front of her, halting her walking as I lower down to a squat.

"Come here then."

"Wait, what?" Her words stumble out through a laugh.

"Hop up."

"You can't be serious."

"I am."

"Cass, no." She's still laughing at least.

"We've got tons of time left. Those shoes will kill your pretty ankles. I can hold you. Promise."

Marina's quiet, maybe considering for a moment then. With a shake of her head and a smile, she smooths her palms over my back and over my shoulders.

"Easy does it," I say, trying to mask the shiver that runs down my spine by reaching back and hooking a palm under her knee. When I grab her other side, she jumps, and I hoist the rest of her up to straddle my back.

"You're really gonna carry me the rest of the way?" she asks.

"Please. You weigh half of what I dead lift, honey." I bounce her in my arms. "See? Light as air."

"And they say chivalry is dead."

"Who is *they*?" I ask.

"You know," she says, "people."

"Oh. How could I forget *people*?"

She giggles again, and I find I like the sound a lot.

We stride down the sidewalk, her long hair lying like a blanket over my shoulders. The heat of her breath, slightly tinged with vodka from hours ago, occasionally huffs along my neck. I clutch beneath her hamstrings. They're smooth under my roughened palms.

"So, you're in charge of the music festival?" she asks.

I grunt, "It's a wine mixer now, apparently."

"Gross."

"Right?" I say, the words chuckling out of me. "And, nah, not in charge. Just helping get performers scheduled. They give me the easy jobs."

"Why's that?"

"I …" I laugh again because I don't know what else to say. "Just makes sense, I guess."

"Oh, Mr. Busy Man over here."

"No. I'm not *busy*. I'm just … well, okay, I'm busy."

"Aha!"

"But it's not like that. I just tend to be late to things."

"Poor time management, huh?"

I clear my throat uncomfortably. It's not something I'm proud of. "Yeah, and Laura knows what she's doing. She knows everyone's strengths."

"And yours is …" Marina coaxes.

"Carrying women across town."

She laughs. "Seriously, what's your strength?"

"I can bench press—"

"Cassidy," she pleads as a protest. "What are you good at?"

"I don't know. I'm just making it through the music festival." It sounds pathetic. I instantly regret the words leaving my mouth that way. "Or wine mixer, I guess."

"I'm sorry. I wish he weren't here," she continues. "He's gonna be a jerk the whole time. I just feel it in my bones. He has bad energy, to say the least."

Smirking, I ask, "What's your sign?"

"Aquarius. Why?"

I bark out a laugh, and she clicks her tongue after realizing my question.

"Oh, okay," she drawls with sarcasm. "Yeah, yeah, hardy har."

"I'm not judging you," I explain. "Just makes sense you believe in feelings and energies."

"Don't you, Mr. Good for the Soul?"

I hum to myself. "Never really thought about it."

"Well, I'm rarely wrong about my gut feelings. As long as I listen."

"Do you get a gut feeling from me?" I ask.

It's quiet. Then, after a beat, I feel her shrug against my back.

"Only a good one," she answers.

Heat rises up my cheeks and to my ears. Even though she can't see me, I'd wager my face is burning red.

"Thanks," is all I can think to say.

We pass the clock tower on our right, traveling down most of Main, and distantly, I can see the road splitting, right where her dad's apartment sits at the edge of the docks.

I look both ways before crossing the street, reaching the bottom stairwell of Starkey's apartment. Marina twists to jump down, but I tighten my hold and stop her, striding up the stairwell quickly with her still bouncing on my back. Her arms tighten around my neck as she laughs with each step.

"Show-off."

"I need the workout," I explain. "I didn't get one in today."

We finally stand outside her dad's apartment. Tiny mosquitoes dart in and out of the warm flood light. I slide Marina off my back.

"Thanks for the ride," she says.

"Yeah. No problem. Get better shoes though."

She kicks out a toe. "They're new and trying their best."

Marina gives me that mischievous smile of hers, the kind with tan freckles scattered over her cute, scrunched nose. Her pink lips with that sheen that might be lip gloss or some other natural essence women have. I don't know what that essence is, but Marina definitely has it.

"Thanks for the company," I say.

"No, thank *you*."

"Anytime."

I'm talking in circles, but I don't want to leave her side. I've liked our night together, and especially when I consider just how much the townhome will echo when I walk in, it makes me want to not go home at all.

I do anyway, waving goodbye as Marina turns the handle. But I twist right back around when the air is ripped by the sound of multiple lawn mowers revving—inconsistent, jarring, and fumbling over each other.

I chuckle. "What the—"

I peer past Marina to see a large man lying on the carpet and snoring. William Jukes. His hand is splayed over his rising belly, rising and falling in loud fits and starts. In the bedroom beyond are two other lumps—likely Charles and Bobbi. It's a symphony of horrific snores.

Silently, Marina closes the door, staring at me and blinking to herself.

"I guess the crew is staying over," she whispers.

"Jukes saved you the sofa," I observe. "That's sweet."

She gives me a questioning look. "How often do they do this?"

I shrug. "They're always at The Hideaway. Didn't know they all bunked together after, like summer camp kids. That's sorta cute."

Her eyes swivel to the closed door, as if she could see through the wood. I can still hear the cacophony of sound buried behind it as worry etches in the lines of her forehead.

I hate seeing her apprehensive like this. She looks like she's stuck between a rock and a hard place. As it turns out, I enjoy being the rock that shatters to pebbles when people need me to. I'd shatter for her.

"Move in with me," I propose. I instantly laugh at how big her eyes get. "Move on in, honey. I've got room."

"No, that's your house."

I tilt my head side to side, as if thinking. "I mean, *technically*, it's still under the Starkey name."

Despite my joke, she shakes her head. "I can't just plop myself into your life one day and turn it upside down."

"What is right side up anyway?"

She squints at me. "Why? What's in it for you?"

"Feeling like you're not homeless," I say.

She snorts in response.

"It's only for the summer. I can handle a summer."

"I'd be a burden—"

"It's too quiet," I confess. "I just moved out from my parents' house, and … honestly, I'm kinda used to my little brothers and Bonnie. Or my dad cooking at all hours of the day or Ma's shows. I don't like the echo. I could use another voice around for a few weeks."

Marina blinks for a moment, looking at the door once more.

"I'm told I don't snore," I add.

Marina finally laughs, looking at me suspiciously. "By who? Because I heard those snores last night."

"As bad as all that in there?"

"Hmm … no."

"Come on," I say, tapping the toe of my sneaker to hers. "Give me some noise in my empty house."

"Seriously?"

I grin. "Seriously."

She bites her lip, maybe thinking some more. I wouldn't be surprised if she needed to think on it for a while. I'm a relative stranger. She barely knows me. It would be a pretty impulsive—

Marina shrugs. "All right. I could do that."

I bark out a laugh. "That was quick."

Her cheeks flash red, but she straightens her spine and jerks her palm out. I grin, clapping my hand to it in a full shake, like we're two companies striking a deal.

"Roomies," I agree.

"Good," she says.

"Good. Well, let's go."

She falters. "Wait, tonight?"

I nod toward the closed door. "Unless you wanna join their loud slumber party?"

She bites her bottom lip and shakes her head.

With the symphony of the three-person band left behind, Marina and I descend the stairs once more. And I try very, very hard not to watch my new roommate's ass bounce with each step.

- Chapter Nine -

SEE YOU IN HEAVEN, HONEY

Marina

I'm making yet another impulsive decision.

Cassidy turns the handle to the townhome and lowers me down from his arms. After I started limping again two blocks away, he decided to carry me the rest of the way. Back on the ground, I kick my shoes off as quick as I can. He laughs, but the least funny part is how much I liked his palms under my thighs.

"Well, here it is in all its glory."

He waves his palm out, and I realize just how little this place has changed since the last time I got a good look at it. The kitchen island is empty with two unstained wooden barstools tucked underneath. A wide threshold leads to the only sitting room. Built-in bookshelves stand along one wall, fairly empty, save for tabbed notebooks here and there. A rolling ladder leans against it with the bottom rung a different shade than the others. A single green sofa is plopped in the center of the room, facing a small media stand with a television precariously perched, as if Cassidy bought the biggest one he could manage with the table he had. A propped-open window spans the back wall, overlooking a tiny backyard.

Beyond the kitchen is a skinny hallway. No photos hang on the walls, but frames lean against, as if the intention to decorate was there. At the end, there are two doors for the bathroom and bedroom—only one of each in the whole house.

I'm not sure if moving in with someone I barely know is a good idea. Then again, I lived with a random girl from the internet. At least I knew Cassidy from high school. But who is he now, as a twenty-seven-year-old man?

It's only for the summer.

Only for the summer.

I exhale. "I'm gonna go wash my face, if that's cool."

"My *casa* is your *casa*," Cassidy answers.

I nod with a barely concealed grin, walking down the hall and shutting the bathroom door behind me.

I have no idea what I'm doing. Buyer's remorse is setting in quick.

I'm living with Cassidy Davies.

Strong, bulky Cassidy.

Hot Cassidy.

You know what? Maybe he's not that hot. Maybe I'm just in a dry spell, and he's incredibly nice.

He's sweet. Like a freshly planted gardenia.

A nice, nice man.

I splash water on my face, stare at the droplets running down my cheeks, then wipe them off with a towel. I exit, walking into the living room, and immediately halt in place.

Cassidy is squatting low, palms clutching the bottom of the sofa. A line curves down his shin as he flexes. His thighs stretch the boundaries of his gym shorts. Feet hip width apart, Cassidy lets out a slow, hissing breath, like a balloon letting out air, before quickly pushing up. The shapes of his body form a tantalizing landscape before me—biceps, triceps, even that little muscle over the forearm.

A couple seconds pass in strained silence as he scoots one half of the sofa across the floor. With a low, guttural grunt that has me crossing my legs in place, Cassidy lowers the sofa back down.

And when he stands up tall again, he flexes out his delicate wrist. His hand is wound with veins, and I could picture it dipping near so many inappropriate places.

"Am I interrupting something?"

"Oh." He laughs because that's what Cassidy seems to do. "Yeah, just moving the sofa a little farther from the window. There's a draft that annoys me sometimes."

"I don't think I've ever seen someone lift a sofa like that."

"That?" He throws a thumb over his shoulder. "That's nothing."

I bet. I wonder how roughly he could toss someone onto *that sofa.*

I shake the thought from my head.

There's an array of new blankets littering the cushions. A fitted sheet is tucked into them, still loose and bunched in areas, stretching over a surface it doesn't belong on.

"Thanks for setting this up for me," I say.

He leans back and laughs. "This is for me, not you."

I blink. "No, it's not."

"Yes," he says. "I'm taking the sofa."

"Don't be a macho man," I counter. "I'm not stealing your bed for the summer."

Then, his face falls, and I realize how serious he actually is.

"I'm sleeping on the sofa," he insists, the lips now in a line. "You're on the bed."

"I would rather die."

"Then, I'll see you in heaven, honey."

I cross my arms. "No."

He mirrors me, crossing his tree-trunk arms in mock defiance. "I'll carry you there if I have to."

"You wouldn't dare."

"I can, and I will." Cassidy says.

"Twenty bucks says you won't."

"Bet. Thirty."

"Fifty," I counter.

What the hell am I doing?

The word slips out like slithering snakes, hissing, *Yesss, you want him to throw you on that bed.*

"Fifty?" His eyebrows rise, and he smiles, the kind that sends part of his cheek deepening with that gorgeous dimple.

I smirk. "Well, I don't believe you would do it."

Yesss, you do.

He tilts his chin down and murmurs, "You'll eat those words."

It happens so fast. Cassidy bends at the waist. He buries his head under my arm. A rough palm slides over my thigh, and I'm lifted like a sack of potatoes over his shoulder. He pounds down the hallway, my ass bouncing beside his cheek, and I can feel my skirt starting to ride up with each step.

"Cassidy!"

Nerves erupt through me and only emerge as giggles.

"Hey, you made this bet!" he says.

Cassidy tips me forward, feet over head, depositing me onto the mattress. I land with a squeaking bounce that is like a Pavlovian shot straight to my pelvis.

He towers over me, one hand on his hip and the other pointing a finger in my direction.

"Now, stay," he demands.

And boy, do I.

Cassidy walks away, clicking off the light, and I scramble to the end of the bed.

"Hey, Cass? Thanks again. For everything."

He turns, eyes roaming over my position on the bed, crouched on all fours. I suddenly feel so ridiculous for crawling at all.

"I like walking," is all he says, as if that summarizes everything we decided tonight. "Night, Starkey."

"G'night, Davies."

He closes the door behind him. I move back to the headboard and dip my legs beneath the covers. As I pull the sheets up to my chin, I'm overwhelmed by the smell of this man and his fresh body wash.

I barely get a wink of sleep that night.

- *Chapter Ten* -

CASSIE AND DUSTY

Cassidy

Dustin paces across the lawn, tapping his fingers on his chin.

"How many booths can we fit in this park again?" he asks.

"About fifty," Laura answers.

I'm standing beside my limping boss, hand on her lower back, trying to make sure she's not two seconds away from collapsing. She's been hobbling on her crutch for a few more yards than she has the energy for, and we both know it.

The three of us walk through Never Harbor's park off Main. Colorful bunting hangs between lampposts, and though most of the grass is still lush, patches are stamped down here and there with dirt from past events. The clock tower has already signaled that it's twelve o'clock, so I know Laura must be hungry. Then again, our clock tower is never correct, no matter how many times they adjust it. Maybe I'm just ready to leave.

Dustin nods. "Good. We'll only need ten booths or so."

Ten?

What was once a music festival is now a certified wine mixer. A fancy event for our very unfancy town. I don't understand, but it's not my job to think. Though, if it were, this sounds like a shell of what was once a beloved event.

"And I think we can keep the jazz players," he continues.

"You just made my job super easy," I say. "Last thing I wanna do is tell Jukes he can't play."

"You're welcome, Cassie," Dustin says with a grin that might be genuine if my old nickname wasn't attached to it—a name only he ever used.

I'm not sure why Milo ever hung out with Dustin in the first place. Maybe it was their academic connection—Milo being valedictorian while Dustin was salutatorian—but my brother has never been condescending the way his friend was. What started as side-glances from Dustin became thinly veiled jokes at my intelligence. The comments always left me a little raw.

Can't say Dustin is entirely wrong, but he's also not right either. Maybe I can't give a book report on *Moby Dick*—probably because I laugh too much at the name—but I know all about optimal gym routines, how they affect different muscle groups, and the nutrition to pair with it.

I wish I weren't spending my morning with ol' Dusty. Instead, I would've preferred the company of a certain wavy-haired blonde, slender neck thrown back and laughing, but I wasn't so lucky.

I woke up before Marina this morning. My lumpy sofa was to blame. That antique had somehow survived decades in our family basement, and I know the spring stabbing my back all night was a result of my baseball-team number of siblings cushion-jumping on it for over thirty years. But as I lumbered to the kitchen to get ready, it wasn't the sofa I couldn't shake the feel of, but Marina's thighs when I'd carried her to the bedroom. I still can't forget it.

At least I'm distracted enough to not think about her all hours of the morning—just in small moments that make my fingers twitch at the memory.

I needed to get to the community center early to pick up Laura for our meeting with Dustin. We didn't know he'd want to walk the park though. And with both sides of Laura's body out of commission—the left leg, combined with the right arm in a sling—it's been nothing short of difficult.

"So, small plates here …" Dustin strolls a few paces over. "Servers here …"

"Servers?" Laura asks.

"The rest is just tiny, tiny details," Dustin says, waving off her concerned comment. I'm not sure he even notices her struggling. "I'll send a list."

"I just want to make sure I understand." Laura speaks as sweet as her tired voice will allow. She hops forward and exhales heavily when her crutch wobbles.

"Whoa there. You tired?" I murmur between us. "Want to get some rest?"

Laura shakes her head. I can see the deep purple exhaustion sinking under her eyes though.

"Only one jazz band?" she continues. "Lots of tall tables scattered around. And only ten booths with …"

"Wine distributors, suppliers—yeah, that sort of thing."

She slowly nods, and Dustin finally lets his eyes scan over her. He raises his eyebrows. If I didn't know better, I'd say he's worried, but I can't tell how genuine it truly is.

"You doing okay over there, Laura?" he asks.

"Yeah, I just need to sit down, I think."

"All right, break time," I insist.

Squatting low, I loop my arm under Laura's knees and another behind her back. I scoop her up, carrying her across the park to a lone bench near the street parking. Dustin follows with a *tsk*.

We have four weeks until the festival, and with this many changes and Laura mostly out of commission despite pending arrangements we need to make, I can't help but feel like this might be a lost cause. Or at least a certified disaster.

I set her down, and her eyes instantly close.

"I'll send you that list," Dustin says, gingerly stepping across the lawn so as not to dirty up his shoes.

Laura nods to herself. "Please."

Dustin glances at the clock tower, then at his wristwatch. He scowls under his breath. "Thirty years, and we can't get that clock tower fixed?" He rolls his eyes. "I've got a flight to catch. Keep in touch."

He extends his palm to shake Laura's hand, but seeing that her sling limits her movement, I hold out my hand instead. He reluctantly shakes it.

"Nice to see you again, Cassie."

Cassie.

"You too," I agree, and I'm not sure I've ever lied so blatantly in my life.

Once he strides to his car—some rental that is far beyond a price range I could ever afford—I turn back to Laura and sigh.

"Talk to me."

She returns my heavy exhale. "I feel worse."

"You look worse."

"Thanks," she says with a grunt.

"I'm serious. You need to go home and sleep it off."

"I could seriously use a chocolate bar or something."

"What kind?" I ask.

"I don't know … the one with little orange peels?"

"Noted," I say, also making a mental reminder to add it to my pocket notebook on the page titled *Laura*, which I know already contains her favorite chips and TV show.

She sighs. "We have way too much to do, Cass."

"He's emailing a list, right? I can tackle it."

She blinks at me. "The entire list?"

"Yes," I answer with a laugh. "The entire list."

"No," she says, shaking her head and sitting up, as if mentally vowing to do it all right now. She hisses in a breath. I place a hand on her shoulder, and she lowers to the bench again. "That's a lot of changes."

"And I've got tons of hours in the day."

"Do you?" she counters.

I open my mouth, then close it. "Of course."

"Cassidy, I adore you, but you're late to everything."

My face falls. But I can't exactly defend myself. I try to be punctual, but I can't leave people high and dry. If conversations linger, then it feels rude to break away. They're giving me their time; they deserve mine. Hell, even now, I should be heading out to meet Pete. But how else will Laura get home without me?

"It'll get done," I reassure her.

She shakes her head. "I can't ask that of you."

"You didn't. I offered."

"It's the *entire* festival, Cass."

That statement has my chest constricting, like maybe I truly don't know what I'm in for. But I want to help. It's like an itch that won't settle until I scratch it.

I can do it. I help all the time. This isn't any different.

I barrel forward with a confident, "I know."

I'm not confident though. Far from it. It suddenly feels like the entire event is resting on my shoulders, and I don't know how to feel about it. But I can't look at Laura's sling and crutch and do nothing.

I laugh. "You can barely stay awake. Let me help."

"I'll be fine in a few days."

"That's one week out of four," I insist. "And a very critical week, where we need to book people and get things reserved, and you know that."

She winces, and I can't blame her apprehension.

It's me.

Cassidy Davies.

So, I'm surprised when she slowly says, "You sure you're not stretching yourself too thin?"

"Absolutely not."

This is Never Harbor. If I can't pull off a wine mixer, then what can I do?

"I've got this, Laura," I say, attempting to convince myself more than her. "Promise."

My phone dings in my pocket. I pull it out and see a text from Peter.

Damn it.

Okay, so, sure, time management isn't my strength. But Laura deserves my time, just like Pete does and the person after that. How people can decide to simply *leave* while helping someone is baffling to me.

I text him that I'll be a few minutes late and grin to Laura. "Let's get you some orange chocolate, huh?"

"Yum."

"And some sour cream and onion chips. They'll make you feel better."

She smiles. "Those are my favorites."

"Are they? Huh. Had no clue."

She pushes my shoulder. "Cassidy, you are magic sometimes."

"I sure try."

Laura laughs, and I help her off the bench, escorting her to my car and wondering the whole way whether signing up for the entire festival was a good idea or not.

- *Chapter Eleven* -

SEXY GRIM REAPER

Marina

I open the door to the townhome with only my duffel bag and Fido in my arms.

"Hello?" I call.

My voice echoes back to me. Cassidy wasn't kidding. When you're alone in the townhome, it's way too quiet.

I walk over to the counter. There's a stack of brown packages—things I ordered before coming here, thinking I'd need to stock up this place again. Beside them lies Cassidy's note from this morning.

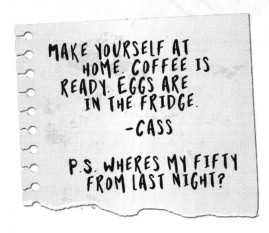

MAKE YOURSELF AT
HOME. COFFEE IS
READY. EGGS ARE
IN THE FRIDGE.
-CASS

P.S. WHERES MY FIFTY
FROM LAST NIGHT?

Placing Fido on the counter, I lower my bag off my shoulder. I stopped by my dad's house to pick up some things and forgot just how little I had. I've lived as an aimless borderline nomad for so long that my essentials come down to basic dresses and T-shirts, along with my little ficus. In lieu of forgetting my bathing suit, I bought some over-priced one marketed to tourists, getting stopped no less than five times to say hey to people I hadn't seen in forever, already asking about my job situation. I have no idea how people found out.

Never Harbor is nosy like that. I forget how small our town truly is. I already miss California.

Only for the summer.

I open the townhome window and find my old flower box outside, still nestled on the ledge. They're flourishing. I smile, seeing that some-one—maybe even Cassidy—has been tending to them. I place Fido next to the sink, letting him soak in the rays too.

"Oh my God, Marina?" a voice calls from outside.

I look up. Lulu is on the sidewalk across the street, grinning ear to ear and waving wildly.

Yeah, Never Harbor is definitely *too* small of a town if I'm seeing people outside the window.

I wave back, and without a second thought, Lulu crosses the street in a strut. Wearing funky-patterned shorts and a crop top with her long black hair plaited in two braids down her back, Lulu is a wonder to behold. The girl I once babysat always carried herself with pride, even at eleven years old. Now, as a twenty-one-year-old woman, she's confidence incarnate.

"You *dog*," she says, running through the yard and up to the win-dow. "Did you go home with Cass last night?"

My cheeks grow hot. "Oh, no, this is absolutely not what it looks like."

She rests her chin on the other side of the window. "Uh-huh. Tell me another lie. I love it when you talk dirty to me."

I laugh. "I'm serious. I only moved in with him. That's all."

She wiggles her shoulders. "Ooh, so we're skipping steps."

"Stop," I say, batting her tanned arm. "I couldn't live with my dad in good conscience. He's got a life and stuff now." Saying it aloud pains me more than thinking it. I wish I knew more about my dad's life. I wish I knew when he'd started dating Bobbi. "Cassidy offered."

"Because you're pretty," Lulu teases.

"Because I need a place to stay," I correct.

"And you're pretty."

I consider this for a moment—that maybe Cassidy only made the offer for all the same reasons Dustin had tried to make a move that day.

Don't think about that possibility.

Cassidy, sweet Cassidy, is nice and gentlemanly. If he wanted to make a move, he could have during our walk last night. Or he could have insisted we sleep in the same bed or something. As it is, he's only as flirty as he seems to naturally be, and I want to keep it that way.

Though that means I probably shouldn't get him to carry me to bed in those strong arms, but … well, moving forward, I'll be better.

"Oh, girl, I'm just kidding," Lulu says, placing a hand on my forearm. I must be wearing my expression on my face.

"No, I know," I say through a laugh. "I know."

She twists her lips to the side and clicks her tongue. "What are you doing today?"

I pause, looking around, eyeing Fido in the bare kitchen and the specks of dust floating in the living room. This townhome is depressingly empty. And I'm depressingly here, back in my hometown, with no prospects.

"Job-hunting later," I say with a shrug. "Maybe house-hunting."

"Perfect!" Lulu says on a relieved exhale. "Come with me."

"To where?"

"To be bored together."

"So, you just hang out here?" I ask.

"Forced to."

"It's beautiful."

Never Harbor's one and only flower shop, Florally Yours, is a greenhouse brought to life. Tables along the walls house glass arrangements. Shelves above those carry rolls of parchment paper and ribbon. The place is bursting with colorful buds and petals—from white to pink and violet and periwinkle blue. I reach out to trace my finger along a leaf, feeling the waxy surface weeping on my skin.

Okay, so maybe it's a fixer-upper greenhouse with wilting plants, but the life is still there. I'm listening to my gut for once, and the feeling is good.

"This place is barely holding on," Lulu says in passing, tossing her purse on the glass counter, where it slides precariously to the edge. "Pop bought it out of boredom last winter. You know it's their favorite thing to do."

"Spend money?" I ask with a grin.

"Of course." Lulu hops up to sit next to the cash register, her legs dangling over the edge with the heels of her red cowboy boots knocking against the empty display case. "New ventures or whatever."

Lulu's parents have always been that way. I was gainfully employed as her babysitter through most of high school while they went off to find new companies to acquire or investments that might or might not return.

"When Tina's husband kicked it last year—"

"Lu!"

"What? He did," she insists. "He passed, leaving her alone with this shop. And she's, like, eighty billion. She needs to live her best old-lady life with knitting and soap operas. So, Pop bought it from her and promised to keep it alive."

I smile, tracing fingers over the limp leaves. "That's really sweet."

"My parents loved this shop," Lulu says. "I think my dad bought flowers for Mom here for their first date or something. I don't know. Anyway, it's ours now. They couldn't let it die."

I run my finger over the flowers once more with a smile. "I love that. Except, well, it's only partially true. It's a little ... wilting."

Lulu laughs. "Well, that's the problem! They left me to run the dang thing this summer."

I slide my hand across more sad, drooping stems and leaves. "And what made them think you could do that?"

"Hey," she calls defensively.

I raise an eyebrow with a smile. "Well?"

"I mean, yeah, my first big project this summer was the high school prom." Her eyes widen as she blows out air. "Big failure."

"What happened?"

"Ugh. Organization. Delivery with a one-woman team. Bonnie and the Davies clan offered to help, but I told them I could handle it."

"Lord, why'd you think that?" I ask with a laugh.

She groans. "I don't know. I'm in 'business school,' " she says, assigning bunny ears to the two words. If phrases could feel emotions, those two words should feel offended with the sneer she attached.

"You don't like it?" I ask.

"I'm not a big flower person really."

"No, I mean, do you like business?"

Lulu hums, then laughs. "Nope, don't like a lot of that either."

I put a hand on my hip. "What *do* you like?"

She hops off the counter, smiling as she points an accusatory finger. "Okay, I invite you into my lovely flower shop that smells terrible, and you're attacking me? What's with the interrogation?"

"I have a spotlight, too, if you want me to grab that," I joke.

Lulu sticks out her tongue.

I tilt my head to the side, examining another plant.

My mom always wanted to open a shop of her own. She wasn't big on flowers or plants that much, but she loved books. She was the type of person who would forget about time when she disappeared into a story. As a kid, I'd toddle to the living room well past my bedtime to find my dad snoozing with his head in her lap, just waiting for her to finish the one last chapter that inevitably turned to three or four. He was always waiting on her.

I suck in a breath and let it out unsteadily. I wonder if she ever opened a shop after she moved. I jerk away from the plant's leaf.

"You okay?" Lulu asks.

I shift on the spot, the rubber soles of my sneakers squeaking on the tile floor.

"Yeah. Just thinking."

"Thinking about …"

"How this place smells," I joke.

"Farts," Lulu deadpans. "Smells like farts."

"It's because the plants are dying, Lu."

"Yeah. Makes sense."

"Certain plants need different types of water or sun," I explain. "That little guy in the window? Absolutely does not need to be there."

Lulu scrunches her nose. "Huh. So, is it dead?"

I shrug. "Yeah. The stems are already cut. No saving it. But that snake plant over there? It could be nursed back to health easily."

"And … what about that one?"

"Not totally lost either actually."

"And that?" She points to a withering brown plant that is one heavy breath away from disintegrating to dust.

"Oh, no, that one's definitely done."

Then, for a second, I think I hear a plant squeak. That doesn't seem right though. Only when my ankles feel suddenly warm do I look down and see a scraggly, lanky calico cat.

"And who is this?" I ask.

"Oh, that's Stinky," Lulu says. "He showed up at the door one day, so I let him in. I fed him once, and now, he doesn't leave."

"That's kinda what cats do if you feed them."

She grins. "I know. I wanted a little shop cat. Cute, right?"

I bend down, tracing two fingers over his bony back with a smile. He doesn't seem malnourished exactly—just that rough-and-tumble outdoorsy type with a rough coat and hoarse meow, like he's earned his way in the world.

"Why Stinky?" I ask her.

"He's the shop cat with these stinky plants. It was either that or Toot."

I scratch under Stinky's chin. His head tilts up, climbing on my foot and flexing his little paws on my toes.

"We should get him treats or something," I suggest.

"Girl, you understand this place already."

It's quiet for a moment as I admire him now winding through my legs.

Out of nowhere, Lulu gasps. Her eyes widen, and just like last night, it's like a light bulb exploded to life in her mind.

"Oh my *God*, wait, you should *work* here," she says.

"What?"

"Please. I know my parents would say yes." Lulu runs over to clutch my shoulders, rising to the top of her red cowboy boots and snapping back down to the heels. "Just fill out stupid paperwork and *please* work here."

"Oh, I—"

"You *just* said you were job-hunting."

"I'm not staying in town long."

"That's fine."

I want to fight against the idea. Somehow, a part-time flower-shop gig in my hometown feels too permanent. I plan on leaving, not settling.

But what else am I going to do?

I need money to pay Cassidy for rent. A sweep across the store has me worried about the future lives of these plants. One more moment in the sun, and that window plant will need a eulogy. Plus, Stinky Toot is ... well, stinky.

"Okay," I answer. "Yeah, I can help out for a bit."

Lulu squeals. "Perfect. We've got graduation coming up for the high school, and I have *no* idea what I'm gonna do, and if I screw up one more thing, I swear my parents will kill me. Marina, oh my God, we're gonna have so much fun, and—wait, is that the mayor's kid again? Dustin?"

His name has my blood pressure skyrocketing into my skull.

I dart my eyes toward the glass windows, and standing right outside is Dustin Barrie with his crooked smile and misplaced charm.

"He's just staring," Lulu says, scrunching her nose. "Is he the sexy Grim Reaper or something?"

"Maybe," I answer, almost tumbling my word over hers by how fast it comes out.

He tips his chin to me and gives a small wave. Only Lulu returns it.

"He probably wants to talk." I dust off the cat hair from my shorts. "I'll be back."

I walk out the door. The bell above the threshold chimes shrilly— we'll need to replace that—until the closed door muffles the sound.

"Hey," Dustin says first.

I hate the way he sounds so relaxed, squinting up at the sky like it's a beautiful day—which it is. I'm pretty sure I heard babies giggling by the clock tower. But the idyllic summer morning feels wrong with him here.

"Why are you here?" I ask.

"Looking around," he says. "Wanted to say bye before I left."

"Why?" The word is harsh, but I don't care. Okay, maybe a little. "And how'd you know I'd be here?"

"People talk in this town. I almost forgot how rampant gossip was." He says it with disdain. Suddenly, his disdain of the town makes me feel bad about my own. "I overheard some bike guy at Peg Leg Press who said he saw you with … her."

He pockets a hand, looking at the shop and giving another wave to Lulu, who is back on the counter, watching us like a television show on the opposite side of the glass screen. When we catch her, she digs in her purse to pull out a tattered paperback.

I don't like how he smiles at her one bit.

"Okay. You're saying bye. So, bye, Dustin."

"Harsh. I thought we were friends, kiddo."

I tilt my head to the side as if to say, *You're kidding*. "You fired me."

He shrugs. "Misunderstanding."

"Did you think I'd … come around?"

"Come back to work," is all he answers. "Christ, why do you think I'm doing this whole thing?" He waves to the buildings around us. "I'm trying to pick up the pieces and make the company look better."

I squint. "Is everything okay?"

"Apparently, you did a lot," he continues, ignoring my question. "I haven't stopped hearing the end of, 'Oh, our daily reports didn't come in.' " He flails his hands in the air, raising his tone in mockery, and I wonder if he knows how ridiculous he looks. "And you know we have that new label launch coming up. It was just a really bad time for you to leave."

"Maybe you should have thought about that before firing me."

"Maybe you shouldn't have sent mixed signals, and I wouldn't have had to."

My head juts back, and I tongue my cheek. I don't know how to argue with that.

"So, this is image control?" I ask. "And because you're the mayor's son, he just *gave* you this event?"

"I wouldn't say he *gave* it to me," he murmurs to himself.

I roll my eyes. "Grow up, Dustin."

His face falls, back into that ugly expression he gave before he fired me, and I can tell receiving a *no* from his former employee wasn't on his radar for today.

"*You* grow up, Marina," he hiss-whispers. "What, you're running a flower shop now?" His eyes dart to the fading sign overhead. "Some part-time gig for a college kid? I'm not even surprised."

"Bye, Dustin," I say, but it doesn't carry as much conviction as I'd like.

With a sigh, he bypasses my shoulder without even a spiteful bump—*the jerk*—and then his nice leather shoes clack on down the sidewalk to somewhere else. I don't know where. Toward the pits of hell or something?

I push the metal bar on the shop's door, the bell shrieking once more overhead. But this time, it feels more like a warning chime. Shame boils through me.

Lulu watches in silence, peering over her book. I cross back to the row of plants in front of the register.

"He's got that creepy, mysterious, attractive thing going on, doesn't he?" Lulu observes.

I feel my face contort at the same time my stomach churns.

"Don't waste your time," I answer.

Lulu watches the empty window, as if the shadow of him were still standing there. "Why?"

My whole body—from my whirring mind down to my tapping sneaker—wants to scream in protest. But I don't know how to explain what happened with Dustin. It's the same reason I haven't told Cassidy and why I won't tell my dad; the last thing I need is for word to get out in Never Harbor that I lost my job because I strung along my old boss.

"He's skeezy. Selfish. Thinks he can get whatever he wants," I say instead. "You don't want to get involved with a guy like that."

Lulu nods with a hum, watching the window. "Good to know."

Stinky winds through my legs again, low, purring rumbles echoing through the shop. I've always heard cat purrs are meant to calm your soul, but not even Mr. Stinky Toot can soothe away Dustin.

- *Chapter Twelve* -
TWO CAN PLAY AT THIS GAME

Cassidy

My feet are dragging by the end of the day. I worked three client appointments, hopped to The Hideaway to help Peter with inventory, rushed down Main to meet with some locals Laura had recommended for festival volunteering, then traveled to the docks to spend the afternoon with Wendy and Sam, as promised.

"Uncle Cass! Give me a math question!"

Now, I've got my seven-year-old nephew asking for multiplication problems, of all things.

"Isn't it the summer?" I ask. "Shouldn't you be burning your eyes out with television?"

He shrugs. "I wanna do math."

Behind him, Wendy smiles. "I don't question a kid who likes math."

During the summer, Wendy and Sam have their own adventures. Normally, it's playing pirates or watching cartoons. Occasionally, it's doing this—hanging out at the docks, waiting for Jasper to get off work. As port captain, Jasper stays busy, but I know he enjoys their company. Having me as a companionship buffer provides enough entertainment for them so he doesn't feel guilty about working.

It's like I'm the nanny for the nanny.

Though Wendy is much more than a nanny now. After last summer as Sam's actual babysitter, she and Jasper fell in love, and Sam is more her own son than simply a job now. I'm happy for them—both for my grumpy, eldest brother, who had trouble letting anyone in, and for Wendy, my oldest friend who deserves every bit of happiness after everything she's been through.

"Six times seven?" I propose to Sam, leaning against the thick wooden pole.

He throws his head back with an exaggerated groan. A very preteen gesture. I am definitely not prepared for that stage of his life. "Harder than that," he insists.

"A billion times three billion?"

"Wendy?" he asks her pointedly, as if done with my shenanigans.

She runs her fingers through his feathery blond locks. "Thirty-six times fifty-nine?"

"Got it!" Sam scampers off toward the break room, back to his abandoned pencils and papers scattered over metal tables and bench seats.

I swear I could blink and miss it. His little-kid limbs grow longer each day. He'll be taller than us by the time he's fourteen, I guarantee it.

"Since when does Sam like math?" I ask Wendy, smiling. "What happened to his dream of being a pirate?" I lean my forearms on the wooden railing, looking out at the bobbing boats.

Wendy gathers her chestnut hair up into a ponytail, securing it with a delicate blue ribbon. Wendy is a gentle, soft person—even with her playful jumpsuit. She makes dressing like a toddler look in style in the way only an elementary school teacher can pull off.

"Sam's got his mind set on being a marine biologist now," she answers, her curled ponytail bobbing behind her. "And I told him that required a lot of math, so here we are."

I can't help the immediate smile that bursts on my face. "Oh, don't break my heart like that. A marine biologist? Really?"

She grins. "Don't tell Jas I told you, but he definitely teared up when Sam told him."

"That old softy."

I can't blame my brother. Jasper took in Sam when he was only two years old, orphaned once Jasper's closest friends—two accomplished marine biologists—died at sea. Sam is so lucky to have my brother to lean on. It's weird to think I was Sam's current age when I found my home. And now, Sam wants to follow in his parents' footsteps? I'm surprised Jasper didn't break down right there.

"Math was never my forte," I say. "Or anything with numbers actually."

"Same," she agrees. "Though Bobbi said you're thinking about opening a business?"

My eyes widen. "She did?"

"Are you?"

I laugh. "No. Absolutely not. I don't know how she got that idea."

"She said you might do personal training outside the community center?"

I chuckle. "She suggested it. I said no."

God, this town's gossip train never stops. Not that I'm any better about it. I'm the one who spread the rumor about Jasper's eyes getting red when he's angry. It's a fact too.

"Why?"

"I don't know," I say, tilting my head side to side. "Maybe it'd be cool. But me? Open a business? Come on."

"And where was all this pessimism last summer with my drama?"

"I only have enough optimism for everyone but me."

She rolls her eyes, leaning her head on my shoulder. "Oh, Cass ..."

The dock planks beneath my feet creak, and down the narrow, open hallway, I see Starkey emerge from his office. I wave, and he curls a finger in his direction, gesturing me over to him.

Uh-oh.

"Speaking of," I murmur, "I think I'm in trouble."

"Is this about Marina?" she whispers to me.

"I don't even want to know how you know."

"Bonnie," she supplies.

"How does my sister already know?"

Wendy shrugs, then gives a kind wave to Starkey. He beams at her. Dang, I didn't get that type of reaction. Then again, everyone adores Wendy.

She prods my arm, coaxing me toward him. "Go walk the plank."

I trail down, my boots clunking on the wooden planks, past the rattling chains hanging from ceilings and whining rope.

"Starkey."

"Davies. I hear my daughter moved in with you?"

A laugh bubbles out of me. *Damn this town's gossip ...*

"You heard right, sir," I say. "She's probably settling in as we speak."

"That's nice of you to take her in. I hate that she doesn't feel like she can stay with me. I know Bobbi wouldn't mind, but ..."

"I get it," I say. "She's more than welcome in my house."

"Good. You should know she's a bit fragile right now. But she's a good kid."

I wouldn't call her a *kid*. We graduated in the same class, so I know she's likely twenty-seven. Regardless, her plump lips and slender legs are all woman. But I'm not gonna tell her dad that.

Starkey sighs, placing a meaty palm on my shoulder and giving a small squeeze.

"Davies, Davies, Davies …" he muses. "I'm watching you."

I stiffen at the sudden shift in the air. The threat said as if he were telling me the time or admiring the weather. It's paired with a wistful sigh as his palm tightens over me.

"No funny business, understand? I have eyes and ears everywhere."

With his reputation for knowing gossip, I wouldn't doubt it.

"Understood," I answer.

He claps me on the back, and it's hard enough to push my back forward.

"Good man."

I glance over at Wendy and Sam, who give a reassuring thumbs-up behind Starkey's back. I return a weak, uneasy smile.

I'm not scared of Charles Starkey, but that grimace under his wiry beard, combined with a heavily tattooed neck and gripping palm, isn't something to scoff at. He's like a biker version of my older brother, and I know Jasper wouldn't hesitate to murder anyone who messed with Sam or Wendy.

But more than pure intimidation, I respect the man. Charles Starkey was flexible with Jasper when he became Sam's guardian, he donates to the community center annually, and he volunteers at the music festival every single year.

If he thinks I'm a good man, then he's a great one.

So, it's settled. No more imagining Marina with her freckled nose and pink lips. Her long legs and firm thighs. Her gentle smile and melodic laugh. No more thoughts of how she's the most beautiful woman I've ever seen.

Should be easy.

Not a problem at all.

My nose is invaded by smells when I open the townhome door that evening. Vanilla, maybe lavender, is my first impression, but the overwhelming scent is sickly sweet. But that's nothing compared to how the townhome *looks*.

"Whoa ..."

The kitchen is overflowing with greenery, from top to bottom, side to side, counter and floor, cascading over the fridge, propped on the windowsill, and even spiraling out of empty cabinets. Flowers in an array of colors—from pink to white and yellow—are tucked into pots along the floor near the bay window.

It's a lush forest. And it's so *cool*.

Grinning, I walk toward the fridge to touch the bubble-looking plant relaxing over the side. Then, I notice, hidden somewhere beneath the variety of smells, is some type of spicy onion-garlic mixture floating from the active oven.

I place my own handful of grocery bags on the counter. I grabbed different vegetables, fruit, chips, and chocolate from Greta's Grocery. I don't know what Marina likes yet. Seems she had a similar idea.

I peek down the hall. Steam billows under the bathroom door. The shower is running. Muffed through the water, music plays. No, it's not music; it's Marina. She's singing.

I pause in place at the gentle tune, notes that rise like the tide, only to softly descend once more. It's deep and whole when her voice demands it and breathy as the notes fade away. I lean my head against the wall and listen as the music lulls me.

My day wasn't bad exactly.

"Days are only what you make of them," my dad always says.

But planning the entire music festival—*wine mixer*—was something I had to arrange in my mind and reorganize like jigsaw pieces to fit. Not to mention the borderline threat from Marina's dad. Yet somehow, the stress seems bearable with her hums floating down the hall.

The shower cuts off. A short minute later, she opens the bathroom door and steps one slender leg out the door. Then another.

If I was frozen before, I'm an iceberg now.

Marina Starkey emerges, wearing a loose T-shirt and shorts.

Tiny shorts.

My gym-rat brain is running on his wheel at top speed. Her posture tells me she's got a strong core. Her legs are lean, but her upper thighs look hard and toned. I wonder if she squats.

The only thing covering her soft skin are those teal shorts that are *short*, and I pray to God they aren't any shorter from behind, but, no, when she turns on the spot as if she forgot something, the bottom hem whooshes up. I spot the under curve of her ass, like a precious peach, glistening with shower droplets still clinging to her skin.

I want to look away. It's the nice thing to do. The appropriate thing. The thing Charles Starkey would approve of.

But I'm stunned in the same way I was when I discovered porn for the first time. Younger Cass didn't know bodies could look the way women's did, and Marina is his wet dream come to life.

She emerges from the bathroom once more with a bottle of lotion in hand, absentmindedly squeezing the tube while she hums the same melodic tune. Finally, she looks up and sees me. I expect her to scream, but instead, her lips tip into her cheeky, freckled smile.

"Oh, hey, Cass! How was your day?"

Cass. I like my nickname on her lips.

"I, uh …" I can't find any words. I blink repeatedly at the blank wall when she passes by me, the scent of lavender masking every other smell in the apartment. It's hypnotic; combined with her singing, she's like a siren song calling to me.

She plops the bottle of lotion on the kitchen island and hikes a bare leg onto the lowest rung of the barstool, running a hand down the length of her calf.

Oh. Good. God.

Charles Starkey is gonna murder me.

"Uh," I try again, and a laugh strangles its way out of me. "Good. Good day. How was yours?"

"Great! Oh, hey, good news! I got a job!"

"That's great."

"That's right," she singsongs. "Rent is on the way. I'm a certified roomie now."

Marina continues lathering her slender legs, stroking over her ridiculously perfect body as if it were nothing of consequence. When she goes to get another dollop, the bottle tips over and rattles to the ground.

"Whoops!"

She bends in half to pick it up, and I have to bite my lip to keep from groaning because, God, that ass is raised to the sky like a beacon. I look away, the lump caught in my throat.

Marina straightens up and recaps the lotion bottle with a small *snap*.

"So, you take baths at night," I observe. "Noted."

She dips a hand into her thick blonde waves, separating it into threes, and braids down from the nape of her neck.

"Are you a morning-shower person?" she asks.

"No, nighttime too."

She clicks her tongue and looks to the ceiling in thought. "I'll need to take one earlier."

"No, now is fine. I normally do it after dinner."

She gasps with a smile. "Oh, speaking of, I made a casserole. Wait, when do you normally have dinner?"

"Whenever. I'm flexible," I say on a chuckle. "I see what you're doing."

"You do?"

"Helping, accommodating, trying not to seem like a burden."

"I mean, I made enough food for both of us, so …" I must have an expression on my face—probably beaming like a goofball—because she laughs weakly. "Sorry. I'm trying not to invade your personal space more than I already am."

"Hey, make yourself at home. Though, I noticed we now have extra roommates too?"

I look around at the kitchen at the variety of greenery.

Her face flushes red. "Oh. Is that okay? I probably should have asked, but I assumed we had room?"

"I love them actually."

Her eyebrows rise.

"Really? I swear it's only temporary. The plants weren't thriving in the store, so I brought them here while I nurse them back to health. I didn't want the shop window displaying our wilted ones."

"That makes sense. Plus, it adds something this house needed. And it doesn't echo as much."

"I noticed that too. Think we could get some padding for the walls?"

"More plants maybe?"

She leans forward, biting her lower lip. "Don't tempt me with a good time."

I laugh but only to hopefully distract from the rising heat in my cheeks. "So, you're at the flower shop now, huh?"

"Yes!" Her eyes brighten. "Lulu brought me on."

"That's perfect for you."

"It is?" she asks.

I tip my chin to the only plant that existed before, still sitting on the counter in its terra-cotta pot. "I've noticed you're attached to that guy."

Her smile widens. "That's Fido. He's been with me forever. My mom actually named him. We couldn't have a dog when I was growing up. She was allergic," she explains. "I would change the name now, but … well … I mean, Fido didn't do anything wrong."

"Oh."

I feel ridiculous I could only come up with one word in response, but I don't know what to say to that.

I forget that Charles Starkey is a single dad. I've never pressed Jasper for details about his coworker's runaway wife, and my grumpy brother isn't the type to ask anyway. But here I am, staring in the face of the other side of the equation—the grown woman who lost her mother at too young of an age. I hate that I also understand abandoning parents all too well.

I must take too long to come up with something else because she laughs.

"It was a long time ago, Davies. I'm not gonna cry about it." Though the way she says it makes me wonder if that's only because she exhausted her tears already.

"If you did, I wouldn't judge you."

She gives me a sly smile. "I'll keep that in my back pocket."

"I just … I get it, y'know? With … me moving here at seven years old and all."

She slowly nods, and as if she realizes the full weight of what I said, her face falls. "Oh. Right. I guess you do get that better than most."

I give a crooked smile, and just as her expression dropped, it now slides back up into a pretty smile, like a mutual understanding settling between us. I try to hide my ever-growing grin.

"So, uh, you like plants, huh?"

"I actually majored in botany. Well, that and chemistry."

"No way." I lean back on the counter, tracing my fingers through that weird bubble plant again. "I didn't know that. That's so cool."

"Chemistry was just so I could go to pharmacy school. But I didn't. And, I mean, I'm not doing anything with that or botany, so …"

"You are now."

"I think I like your optimism, Cass."

I think about what Wendy said and comment, "I saved it all day just for you."

She continues to draw her fingers in and out of her braid, now halfway through, just beside her breasts. I see her nipples pebble against the fabric of her clothing, just as they did yesterday and the day before that. The fact that bras appear to be this woman's mortal enemy is more appealing than it should be.

I avert my gaze as she asks, "So, do you always get home this late?"

"No, not usually," I answer. "Well, maybe. I was helping around town."

"All day?"

"Here and there."

She nods to herself. "So, you're like … Mr. Never Harbor, huh?"

I laugh. "I don't know about that."

"It's not a bad thing."

Even though she says it isn't, her eyes float down to the counter. Is being active in the community something to be ashamed of?

She clears her throat. "So, how was work?"

"Oh. Work was … interesting."

Her fingers halt. "Why?"

"One guess as to why."

She gasps. "Dustin?"

"Yeah, ol' Dusty."

"He stopped by the flower shop too," she says. "What'd he say to you?"

I furrow my brow. "Wait, he stopped by the flower shop? Why?"

Her head dips, and she suddenly finds something on the counter interesting once more. She hesitates before answering, "Oh, he just asked me to work for him again or something."

I bark out a laugh. "You're kidding."

She peers up through hooded eyes. "That's what I said too."

"You said no, right?"

"Of course."

"Atta girl," I answer.

Her lips part. It takes me a whole five seconds to realize what the hell just came out of my mouth. The worst part is, I didn't mean it sexually. I'm just proud of her, is all.

"He's got a lot of demands for us," I say, barreling on like it didn't happen. "For the festival. Or, I guess, *wine mixer*."

"Wine mixer," she says on a snort.

"Yeah. It's a lot going on."

"Like what? I promise not to tell."

I chuckle. "Oh, yeah?"

"Pinkie promise."

"You're just as bad of a gossip as your dad and Bobbi."

"You're the one who started it."

I am, and I find her eager look only coaxes me on. I tell her what happened at the park today while she continues her braid. She's a good listener, the type of person who gasps at all the correct moments and tsks when it's obvious I'm irritated. I'm not sure I've ever had someone this invested in what I had to say.

It's nice. Really, really nice.

"Like, how am I supposed to make those changes to the festival—"

"Wine mixer," she corrects for me.

I slap my palm on the counter. "Exactly! It's barely a music festival anymore."

"What'd Laura say? I'm surprised she hasn't hit him with her crutch. The festival is basically her baby, isn't it?"

"Well … I'm actually running the whole thing now."

"What?! Cassidy! You didn't mention that!"

She drops the end of her braid and reaches up for a high five. I reluctantly meet her in the middle with a slap.

I'm not one to turn down a high five, but, "What was that for?"

"Because that's amazing!"

"It's … something, sure."

"No. It's *amazing*." She waves her index finger around. "I want none of that."

"None of what?"

"Your self-doubt," she says. "Not when I'm here. You're doing a cool thing, and you should be proud." I shake my head as she continues, "And! You've got a super-cool roommate who loves to help." She pulls a turquoise hair tie off her wrist and secures the end of her long braid, snapping it with a final *pop*. "And I'm free of charge."

"Well then, I made a good decision, didn't I?"

She tips up her chin. "I'd say so."

Marina's too cute for her own good. Hell, she's too attractive for this situation to be appropriate at all.

"Dinner?" she proposes.

I shake off my grin. "Sure. Dinner."

We eat the pre-prepped casserole. It's so different from my usual bachelor meals that I groan a little through the first bite. She laughs, and I toss my soft dinner roll at her. She tosses hers in retaliation.

"Not used to this?" she asks.

"I mean, I can make a mean PB&J, but this is on a different level."

Marina giggles. "Well, I'd love to try your PB&J."

Tonight is the first night I've felt good in this townhome. A warm meal. Good conversation. And just a bit of clutter. It feels like home.

I take both our plates to the sink. "All right, I'm gonna go hit the shower."

"Oh, I'll take the sofa tonight," she says.

I snort. "No, you won't."

"You're not gonna sleep on the sofa every night," she insists. "It's not fair. So, I figure we'll switch off."

"Cute, but no."

"Cass—"

"Nope."

Maybe she expected less of an argument, but my mom raised me better than that. Marina lets out a small *hmph*, and by the time I'm walking down the hall to the bathroom, she's shifted to humming once more, musical notes that ring all the way in the shower, where I stare down at my stiff erection with an irritated groan.

No. Not for her, buddy.

I turn the shower water to freezing and hurry out.

When I return to the living room, Marina is lying on my sofa, reading a book labeled *Kick Ass Your Way*, still humming to herself. Her legs are under the sheets, but I can still see their beautiful outline. She gives me a sly side-eye.

"Told you I'm getting the couch. G'night!"

I sigh, head to my bedroom, and instead return with a pillow, along with my thick comforter. I settle on the floor beside the sofa. When she blinks down at me with her lips parted in shock, I pump my eyebrows.

"Two can play at this game, honey."

"The floor? You can't be serious."

"I am."

"I don't believe you."

Maybe she thinks I'll eventually cave and head back to the bedroom. But I don't. A cold shower and a night on the floor might even be good for me.

I fall asleep easier than I thought I would. The smell of lavender is relaxing, but it's her small hums while she reads that finally lull me to sleep.

- *Chapter Thirteen* -
TWO PEAS IN A POD

Marina

I wake up with Cassidy lying on the floor next to the sofa. Never Harbor is still dark outside, but moonlight filters in through the large window, highlighting his form. I lean my cheek on my forearm and take him in.

He's handsome. There's no denying that. His brown curls fall away from his forehead, spiraling together and apart like loose springs. The layer of five-o'clock shadow masks most of his jawline, but it can't hide his lips, the color of a dusky rose, resting slightly parted. His dimple isn't there, but I can spot the beginning of it, like, even in sleep, he's on the cusp of a laugh.

And he snores.

I grin. He's like one of those curly-haired labradoodles that runs after rabbits in their sleep. When he twitches almost imperceptibly, I giggle.

I wonder if he's caught the rabbit yet.

Pulling back the thin guest sheets, I stand. But the moment I'm up, I almost fall back down. My lower back hurts. My hips feel out of alignment. Even my wrist is aching. I've aged ten years in one night.

It's the *sofa*. I can't believe Cassidy slept there.

I'll need a walk and fresh air to get this straightened out.

I change into my bathing suit, snatch a towel, and leave, gently closing the front door behind me.

I love Never Harbor first thing in the morning with its silence, aside from the lapping water and the rough shift of my sandals on the sidewalk. It's a peaceful quiet in the way the townhome's silence can't achieve—the kind of quiet nature accompanies.

I walk one block down toward the beach, then change my mind. I remember exactly where I can go to relax. It's a thirty-minute walk, but the trek to Mermaid Lagoon is worth it.

Mermaid Lagoon isn't an official Never Harbor tourist attraction, not like the shops on Main or even Skull Rock. It's concealed, tucked beyond The Hideaway and nestled into an alcove below a cliff.

I sneak down the secret trail behind the bed-and-breakfast's backyard and down to the rocky beach, and I skip over rock after rock, passing the signs of *DO NOT ENTER* until I reach it.

It's just as magical as I remember.

A cave, barely the size of a parlor, circles a large pool of water in the center. Craggy rocks emerge from the surface here and there, like seats you can perch on. The high ceiling is unreachable unless you pile three fully grown adults on each other's shoulders, circus-style, which I'm pretty sure the Davies crew did at a high school party one time.

It's a place of seclusion and privacy, respected by all, except for teenagers on Friday nights—guilty as charged.

I wade out. The cool water laps up to my waist, and my shoulders rise to my ears. Before I can rethink my decision, I plunge underwater. The world disappears below the surface, sounds muffled around me. I hold my breath as long as I can before emerging with a gasp, shaking off the fresh morning chill. Then, I lean onto my back and float.

I close my eyes and suddenly see Dustin Barrie tucking a loose piece of hair behind my ear. I shiver. The embarrassment of it all still bites at me, snapping like shackles around my wrists.

Filled to the brim with nerves, I switch to swimming strokes. I repeat until I'm panting and desperate to go home.

Home.

Back to the handsome, sleeping man who is the personification of Never Harbor. He's so entrenched in the lives of these locals. Why did he never leave after high school? Heck, why have most people stayed? It's just another small town. Doesn't anyone want to see the world? Have adventures?

My dad never left either. Only my mom. She understood the urge to travel. Then again, she's not exactly a shining example of stability.

Don't people feel stuck though? What's so special about Never Harbor?

Another small trek later, I open the townhome door, and our little kitchen forest is alive with sound. The fan hums over the stove, and angry bacon snaps on a skillet. Cassidy glances up from a book and greets me with a smile. A weird shift happens in my chest at the sight of that dimple, a giddiness.

"Morning, Starkey."

"Hi, Davies."

"Where'd you sneak off to?" he asks, setting down the notebook and tucking a pen in the crease.

"The ocean," I answer, wrapping my towel tighter around my chest. "The water is my happy place."

I practically skip to the barstool. He chuckles. I like the energy in this house with him.

"Any new gossip out on the town?" he teases.

"Why? Have you already heard something this morning?"

I start to braid my hair. His eyes linger on my working hands with a small smile.

"If I do, you'll be the first to know. Promise."

"Pinkie?"

"Swear."

He flips the bacon, glances at his watch, then turns on his heel toward the bedroom. I follow his lead, padding to the edge of the kitchen and leaning around the corner.

"Need me to watch the bacon?" I call to him.

"I'll be back in a sec. It won't burn," he responds down the hall.

I pace over to the stove again. He's right. The bacon looks almost perfect.

My eyes catch the small book set to the side. It's not a book though. It's a journal. Pint-sized and leather-bound with a ribbon and tabs trailing out the top. My finger twitches to grab it, eager for a peek into this man's deeper thoughts. But I don't. Instead, I walk away and into the living room.

Stacked on the sofa are the sleep pillows and folded sheets—even the fitted ones.

"You know how to fold a fitted sheet?" I call.

"You don't?"

I bark out a laugh in response, but I can't tell if he's joking or not. Maybe learning how to fold sheets is a rite of passage for adulthood I didn't get in my mess of nomad travel. Maybe that's something mothers teach you.

I walk to the bookshelves, noting a small stack of notebooks similar to the one on the kitchen counter. Different sizes, some spiraled, some not. All with little tabs.

Cassidy walks back to the kitchen, and I meet him there, plopping up on the kitchen island's wooden stool once more. He starts a new pan, cracking eggs one-handed and scooping the shell up just in time to grab the yolk. He tosses it in the trash, then does it again, moving swiftly and methodically, like it's a practiced routine.

I actually kinda hate how hot that is.

Cassidy's open laptop sits on the counter, clunky and thick and whirring with a spreadsheet pulled up. There's nothing fancy to it—a collection of information typed into blank columns that overlap without care. When I look up, Cassidy is staring at me, but his eyebrows are turned in.

"It's not good, is it?" he asks.

"The spreadsheet?"

He shakes his head. "Yeah, I tried to arrange it differently, but it's a mess."

"Want me to look at it?"

He scratches behind his head. "If you want, I guess. It's just … I don't know what I'm doing. Laura sent me the information she had, and I'm already lost."

"I'll help." I scan over the spreadsheet of musicians and laugh.

Cassidy cringes. "Oh God, what?"

"No, I just noticed Jukes has been working on a rendition of 'Yakety Sax.'"

Cassidy smiles weakly. "Don't know what that is, but I'm excited either way."

"Everyone in the English-speaking language has heard of 'Yakety Sax.'"

Cassidy shrugs, but something passes over his eyes. Shame? Embarrassment for not knowing?

"Cass, you don't know what 'Yakety Sax' is. I don't know how to fold a fitted sheet. Two peas in a pod."

Cassidy rocks back on his heels, a half smile forming again as he bites his lower lip. "Listen, I know I'm not the most knowledgeable so—"

"Okay, well, (a) you *are* bright, and (b) you'd totally know 'Yakety

Sax' if you heard it, and (c) spreadsheet knowledge is basically just being really good at searching the internet for solutions other people have already figured out."

Cassidy smiles and then laughs, running fingers through his curls and nodding. I like how they bounce back each time. I look away before I can admire it too long.

"Good to know," he says.

"I'm just earning my keep here," I say, then add, "I will have rent though. Promise."

Cassidy shrugs, turning back toward the stove and shifting the eggs with the spatula. "I know. And if not, I know where you sleep."

He gives me a sideways grin, and I have to shift in the chair to not think about how cute that dimple is.

"Sometimes."

"Sometimes," he agrees.

Cassidy twists off the stove and pulls down two plates, emptying half the eggs and a piece of bacon onto one and sliding it toward me.

I blink. "This is for me? You made me breakfast?"

"You made me dinner."

"Oh, a trade-off?"

His dimple deepens. "No. I would have made it for you either way. Hope I'm not making you late for work."

I shrug. "Lulu didn't give me a start time. But I figure getting there early can't hurt."

"Good. I need a walking buddy."

I laugh. "You're gonna walk me to work?"

He shrugs at my surprise. "I like walking."

I grin, then absentmindedly play with the eggs he prepared.

Cassidy Davies is a good guy. A really, really good guy with cute dimples and breakfast skills. But he's also my roommate, and more than that, he's a small-town guy with no intention of ever leaving. It would never work with someone like that.

In the silence, I joke, "By the way, that sofa sucks."

We both descend into laughter.

"Oh my God, hi, Mr. Starkey!"

I twist on my sneaker to see my dad's head poking through the threshold to Florally Yours. He waves.

Stinky darts from the back of the store, instantly stretching onto Dad's pant leg, his claws snagging on the denim.

"Mr. Toot!" Lulu calls, running over to un-cling him from the fabric. "Sorry. He's still learning manners."

"What are you doing here, Dad?"

My dad strokes the top of the cat's mangy head. "I'm here to bring you lunch," he says, wiry eyebrows rising up to his forehead as he lifts a fistful of two sagging brown bags.

I set my watering can aside as Lulu groans out, "Perfect! Get her out of here. She won't stop talking about plants and soil and—*ugh!* So useless with all that knowledge of hers. Can't stand it."

I give her a passing smile, and she scrunches her nose at me to show her obvious sarcasm.

"You're sure?" I ask.

"Take an hour," she says, walking behind the counter and whipping open her book on the glass counter. "Heck, take two."

I'm not even out the door before she's kicked back on the chair with her feet propped up.

"Huh," Dad says. "What's a girl like her doing, running a shop like that?"

I laugh. "She's not great with the plants, but she excels with customers, believe it or not."

It's true. And since rearranging the display windows—and removing the scorched plants—we've had a lot of familiar faces stop by.

"I didn't even know this place was still open after Tina sold it," Greta told us, which had Lulu cringing in embarrassment, but only until purchases started racking up.

Turns out, refreshing the display stock and propping open the door is the key to sales. Who knew?

It's been nice solving a puzzle for which plants match which occasions. Roses for bouquets are lovely, but I suggest pansies to Steve the paper delivery guy—as a quick "I'm thinking of you" for Laura. Tulips are timeless for the local book club. And when Mr. Davies comes for flowers, I suggest lilies, his wife's favorite according to Cassidy. Of course, he already knew, though.

I could get used to this. Maybe wherever I end up will have a flower shop.

Dad and I walk without discussing where we're headed. After years together, words can be translated from tiny gestures and small nods. I love that about us. We end up at a bench, right behind Main, over-looking the sea.

"So, how are you liking being home?" Dad asks, handing me a brown bag.

"I like it," I answer, rummaging through. "Tuna sandwiches? Classic."

"Reliable. So, it's been good?"

"Yeah, Lulu has been nothing but nice. I have a job. A place to live... ..." I shrug as my words fade off. "It's good."

"And how's that boy treating you?"

My lips part before I shut them again. Somehow, I'm at a loss for words when it comes to Cassidy. "Good. He's nice."

"Just nice?" Dad says through a bite of his sandwich, placing it back on the crinkling bag before clapping his hands together, as if washing away the crumbs.

"Yes, he's being an absolute gentleman. Don't kill him."

"You're being nice too?"

"Of course I am," I answer, straightening my spine. "You taught me better than that."

But the moment I say it, I think about Cassidy sleeping on the sofa and the floor. I can't in good conscience take his bed again. So, what are we supposed to do in this situation if he won't take it either? Share the sofa?

No. Not with those arms and hulking shoulders of his. And not because I worry both of us won't fit—although that's probably an issue too—but because I mentally can't sleep next to him. The proximity might kill me—or at least trigger a pregnancy when I accidentally brush against him in the middle of the night.

"How are you?" I ask quickly, changing the subject. "I feel like we haven't actually talked in forever."

Months, I want to correct myself, but I don't because it seems too real.

I haven't been present for a while now. After abandoning my life map post-college graduation, I didn't want to stay in Never Harbor. I fled to try other things. But now, it feels fruitless and cyclical. I somehow ended up back here.

"I'm good," he answers, clearing his throat again and knocking back part of his soda. "Practicing for the music festival a lot."

"Mixer," I correct.

"Mixer?"

"It's a long story. Sounds like you'll still be playing though."

Dad gives a small *hmph* and nods to himself. The sound alone expresses his disapproval.

I ask, "And how many neighbor complaints have you gotten about your trombone?"

This lightens his mood.

"I don't complain about Moira's mahogany candle whatzitcalled she's brewin', so she can't complain about my music."

"Can't or doesn't?"

He grunts, "She still does."

Though my dad has little to no fight here. Moira's candle shop is very successful even if she does practice in her apartment.

Dad sighs. "Your mom always got along better with her. Knew how to compliment her scents. I try, but I always get it wrong, and it only pisses off that woman more."

It goes silent between us. The tide rushes in, then back out. I try to think of something happier—something the opposite of my mom or Moira's whatzitcalled candle.

"How's Bobbi?" I ask.

Dad takes a bite of his sandwich at that exact moment.

I laugh. "Come on. You're living together. It's serious, isn't it?"

"Yes," he says through a muffled bite. "It's been nice. Fun."

I wave my hands. "Uh-uh! Don't say *fun*. If it's anything that implies you and sex, I don't want to know."

He drops his head with a laugh, and I join him. It feels comfortable for a moment until he sighs once more.

"Is that weird? I know she was like an aunt for you, growing up."

I pull in a breath that almost hurts my chest. "No. I mean, it's a little weird, but I like her. You know that."

After Mom left, I assumed he'd be a bachelor his whole life. Him dating someone is odd, but if it's gonna be anyone, I'm happy it's one of his oldest friends. But something about his scrunched expression is uneasy.

"Are *you* okay with it?" I ask.

"Yes. Of course. I just don't want this to be uncomfortable for you."

"It's not."

"And nobody can replace your mom—you know that."

I swallow and stiffly nod. "I know. But it's been a long time."

"I know," he echoes.

"Want to have a movie night?" I ask. "Get some over-buttered pop-corn that'll stop our hearts?"

Dad laughs but shifts to the side. "I … yes, let's do that, Guppy. I'd love to."

I squint. "You hesitated. If you have plans already …"

"No, I don't. It's fine," he says. "I want to spend time with you."

But just like how we can find a spot to eat without speaking, I can tell by his body language that he's lying to make me feel better.

"It's Bobbi, isn't it?" I say. "Go. Live your life!"

He sheepishly smiles. "I was gonna take her to Skull Rock tonight."

I gasp, covering my ears. "Oh, gross."

"Gross?"

"That's where teenagers go for their first time."

His face hardens. "Marina Starkey, how do you know—"

"I absolutely do not want to have this conversation. Got it. No movie night."

He snorts, but after a moment, his expression feels layered with pity. "I'm sorry," he says.

"Don't be."

"She's very special to me. But you'll always be my Guppy—you know that, right?"

I hate how guilty he looks. I'm the one in the wrong here. He's an empty nester, and I'm the baby bird that nudged my wing back through the sticks. My nose stings with tears, but I shove it down.

"Go," I insist. "Hang out with someone your own age. Not your weird daughter."

"I like my weird daughter."

I roll my eyes, but he leans in to rest his head on mine. His scraggly beard scratches my forehead.

"You're gonna hurt your back more, sitting like that," I observe.

He nods in sync to the tune of, "Yeah, yeah, yeah. You know what? You're right. You are the worst. Now, I definitely don't wanna be around ya."

"See? I'll go do my own thing. I'll make friends or something."

"Good. That's good for you."

I smile in agreement, but making friends feels entirely too daunting.

Chapter Fourteen

DOG OFF A LEASH

Cassidy

"They'd better be paying you buttloads of money to torture me like this," Bobbi grunts, huffing through her final box jump.

"One more."

"I swear, if you say that one more time—"

But she jumps, like I knew she could, and I throw my fists in the air and let out a loud, "*WOO!*" just to embarrass her properly. But when I do, my back cracks, and I instantly clutch it.

"You're not *that* old yet," Bobbi demands.

I laugh. "Just fell asleep in a weird position."

My pallet of blankets on the floor has had my back twinging all morning. Even the lumpy sofa would have been preferable, and that's saying something. But if Marina's gonna be stubborn, I will too.

"Steve said the same thing."

My eyes widen. "Steve? Paperboy Steve?"

Bobbi gives a mischievous smile. "I hear he's been visiting Laura every day since her fall."

I tongue my cheek. "Speaking of gossip, I have a bone to pick with you."

"Do you?"

"I hear you're spreading rumors that I'm gonna start a business."

"Ah, glad that made it to you," she says, not a bit ashamed of it.

"Have you thought about it?"

"Nah." I try to make the word casual as I shake my head. But I can feel the smile disappearing at the same rate my heart pumps faster. "I could never. You're confusing me with Peter."

"I am not," Bobbi counters. "Your brother is good at what he does, but so are you. I bet people would pay top dollar for more training sessions than the community center lets us schedule."

"I can't," I say on a laugh. "I can't keep a schedule."

"Well, that's the benefit of owning a business. Make your own schedule."

Bobbi Mullins always approaches things with a businesswoman's mindset. It's why Peg Leg Press is so successful. She makes the right moves, knows how to market, and—better yet—how to pivot. Her new licorice-flavored coffee might not be my thing, but it's exploding over town. I saw Moira carrying one just the other day.

"Think about it," Bobbi says, raising her eyebrows.

I nod but know I won't.

After she leaves, I wipe down the equipment and exit the building too, pulling out my phone from my hoodie pocket to call Milo.

"Cassidy Davies," is how he answers the phone, and I respond with an echoed, "Milo Davies."

It's our ritualistic greeting. Calling my older brother Milo after work just to talk is expected by now. And if he doesn't answer, I'll call my little sister, Bonnie, or even Jasper, who normally just hands the phone to Wendy. With six siblings and a future sister-in-law, I have enough family to make my walking commute pass by in a flash. Maybe we're that weird type of close family, but who cares? When you grow up in a chaotic house for the first quarter of your life, not keeping in touch feels weird. Not cherishing this family when I went seven years without is even more uncomfortable.

"How was work? Hear from Dustin again?" Milo asks.

"No. Not yet," I answer. "I knew he wouldn't stick around long."

"Good," my brother muses.

My brow furrows. "Thought you guys were pals?"

"High school friends," he clarifies. "Not so much now."

"What happened?"

"He's Dustin. What else is there to say?"

"Oh."

My brother will always be a small mystery to me—almost more so than our oldest brother, Jasper. Jasper might be quiet and solitary, but

Milo is … in his head a lot. His ideas are constantly shifting and calculating, and I can't keep track of which he's mulled over recently that might have changed an opinion or two.

"Well," I continue, "Marina seems to not like him either."

"She's got a good head on her shoulders then. How's that whole arrangement going?"

"Not too bad actually. Sleeping on the floor sucks, but—"

"Why are you on the floor?"

"She refuses to take the bed. And I won't either." I cross the street, holding up my palm to grin at Steve rolling his bike across the four-way. I wonder if he's headed to Laura's.

"That's incredibly stubborn, Cass," Milo says.

I laugh. "I don't have a lot of brain cells, but the ones left do what they can."

There's a moment of silence before Milo says, "Hey, you should invite Marina over for dinner tonight."

"Nah, she wouldn't want to go," I insist.

"How do you know that?"

I pause and then shrug. "I mean, I guess I don't. But she's probably with her dad or something."

"Well, Bonnie keeps calling me about it," Milo says. "Her obsession with your roommate is astounding to me."

"Why's she not calling me instead?" I ask.

"Probably still miffed you moved out. She thought you'd stay there forever."

"I had to grow up eventually."

I walk through the door. Marina is perched at the kitchen counter in a long, flowing dress, reading that same self-help book from last night. She waves eagerly, and I return it.

It's nice, coming home to someone. Not just someone, but this woman. Selfishly, I like how her ass plumps up when she perches on a stool. How her legs, long and elegant, fold over each other and how her posture is damn near perfect as she flips the page of her book.

I pull the phone from my ear and whisper to her, "Hey, you won't believe what I heard about Steve today."

She grins. "Spill."

"Later." I pull my phone back to my ear. "Sorry, just got home, Milo."

"Invite her," Milo repeats.

"Nah, it's not like *that*."

"That's vague," Milo says, and sometimes, I hate his perceptiveness. Too much time in the library. "Not like what?"

I don't know why I said it like *that*. I walk down the hall to the bathroom and shut the door behind me. I can't help but pace.

"We're just living together, you know," I say, running a palm through my hair, snagging my fingers on some of the curls. "Like a giant slumber party."

"Uh-huh."

I swallow. "What?"

He's silent, and I wonder how fast his mind is reeling. Milo's brain works like this, processing every option before speaking. Ultimately, he just says, "Invite her."

"You were quiet," I observe. "Why were you quiet?"

His laugh sputters out. "I was just thinking. Roommates. Close quarters …"

My body feels like it constricts all at once, folding in on itself until I'm an origami of nerves.

"What's that mean?" I ask.

"It means she's pretty, and you know it."

"That's … oh, come on now."

He sighs. "Don't say it's ridiculous because it's not."

"Okay." I lower my voice. "Yeah, she's gorgeous. So what? I'm not a dog off a leash though. I can control myself."

Milo laughs. "Invite her to dinner tonight. Before Bonnie leaves me another five-minute audio text about it."

I scratch the back of my head. "Yeah, yeah. I'll talk to her about it."

"Good."

"I'll see ya tonight."

I hang up but continue pacing the bathroom.

I pull my notebook out of my hoodie pocket, turning to a new page I started, titled *Marina*. It's already got a few lines of her favorites listed. *Veggie casserole. Lavender lotion. Swimming before sunrise.*

I have pages of notes for everyone in town, but why do these notes feel … different? More invasive?

Is it that obvious I find her attractive? Or is her beauty obvious to everyone, and Milo knows I'm simply a man with eyes?

I blow out a breath and pocket my notebook.

This is ridiculous. I can control myself. I can respect Starkey's wishes. I haven't masturbated in three days, and I shake off any thought of her breasts the moment they pop into my head. I call that an accomplishment.

I exit the bathroom and walk back down the hall. Marina's still there. Still pretty. Still poised with perfect posture and perky breasts poking beneath her dress.

Don't think about them. Don't think about how perfect they'd feel in your palms.

I clear my throat. "Hey, what are you doing tonight?" I ask with forced casualness.

"I was thinking we'd have some of your world-famous PB&Js."

"Well, apparently, you're invited to the world-famous Davies family Friday night dinners instead. If you want to come."

"Ooh, how formal."

"I mean, I don't know if you know this, but it's kind of a big deal."

"Hmm … can I see family photo albums?"

"Are you a mind reader?" I ask. "Because I was absolutely gonna force you to look at pictures of me as a kid."

"Perfect." Then, twisting her cute lips to the side, as if thinking, she nods. "Then, yes, I'll go."

"Great. Now"—I lean on my forearms on the counter—"let me tell you all about Steve and Laura."

She gasps. "I knew it. Let me tell you about his flowers."

"Flowers?"

"Oh, yes. A whole-ass *bouquet*, Davies."

She leans forward, too, so close that her lavender perfume seeps through me like a gentle lullaby.

And I hate that Milo might be right.

I need to watch myself around this gorgeous girl more than I already am.

- *Chapter Fifteen* -

CURLY

Cassidy

I haven't brought a woman home to a family dinner since high school. Every time I look over at Marina, my palms whine over the steering wheel. This isn't the same situation as arriving with a new girlfriend, but I somehow feel just as nervous.

My parents' house is only a twenty-minute walk from our townhome, but after a full day of work, we decide to drive. Five minutes later, I pull my truck into the driveway, rumbling off the concrete and into my usual spot in the yard. Other familiar cars are parked, and I can already hear the interior of our busy house.

My little brothers barreling up and down the stairs. The back door squeaking open without the return creak of it closing once more. Dad's music floating out from the open kitchen window. Our house is the poster child for potential defenestration.

I walk around the front of my truck.

"Welcome to chaos," I say, jerking open my truck door and walking backward to let her step down.

Marina giggles. "Why'd you open my door?"

I play it off with a shrug and a laugh.

Her lips curl up at the edges. I've never seen such a plush pink mouth. And when she smiles, it pronounces the apples of her cheeks, rising into perfect circles of blushed skin, like a filter over her smattering of freckles.

"Roommate of the year," she compliments, hopping down from the seat.

I nod more to myself than her, pulling my lips in and letting them out with a *pop* before shutting the car door behind her.

"Sure am." I play along. "Now, come on. I've got someone's night to ruin."

"Whose?"

"Yours."

We cross the threshold of the open door, and the cacophony of a busy house blasts around us.

My childhood home consists of three stories and next to no matching parts. Every piece of the house feels off-color from the one before, and the structure, while sound, has a lean to it, like maybe our stomping down the stairs permanently altered the architecture.

The interior is cluttered. Multiple jackets are hung on multiple coat racks. Shoes are in the hall and in only some of the cubbies, where they belong. Frames line the hallway, floral wallpaper barely visible behind the childhood photos and crayon drawings.

"Family pictures, as promised." I point to a photo of me in a little league jersey.

"Oh my God, that *hair*," Marina says, tracing her turquoise-painted nails over the glass frame.

"Pete called me Curly as a kid. It wasn't until he was in high school that he finally called me Cass."

She gasps. "Can I call you Curly?"

"Sure, let's bring back the childhood trauma of it all."

She giggles. Marina continues walking down the hall, glancing over pictures. She finally stops at our latest family photo, taken just a couple of weeks ago at a family dinner before I moved out.

"Sometimes, I forget how many of you there are," Marina observes.

"Yeah. My parents love on hard mode."

The Davies family is a big crew, and we're not getting any smaller either.

In the photo's far corner is my oldest brother, Jasper, with Wendy and Sam. Bracketing the opposite side is my brother Peter.

"Jasper and Peter were here before the rest of us," I tell her. "The family legend is that their excessive fighting forced Ma to need more kids."

"They had to even out the battlefield?"

"Exactly. You know, Jasper's eyes turn red when he's angry."

"I didn't know that."

"It's sorta true. I like to spread the rumor. Adds to his mystery."

Marina snorts and shakes her head. "Typical younger brother. So, when did you come along?"

"Well, it was a while after," I sigh. "They sorta struggled to have kids after Peter. Jasper was the only one old enough to remember, but apparently, it wrecked Ma. It worked out though. They had too much love to give to not figure something out. Milo was the first one adopted, same age as Peter. I was next. I've been told I arrived like a tornado."

"I bet."

Beside me in the photo is Bonnie, laughing at something I must have said.

"My parents adopted Bonnie as a baby," I explain. "She's a firecracker."

"Big, happy family," she says with a grin.

"Dream come true." I can't help but smile. "Feels like night and day from before."

Marina is quiet before murmuring, "Do you … do you remember much? Before here?"

I sigh. "A little. I'm the only one too. Milo and Bonnie were both adopted too young to remember life before living here. But honestly, to me, there was no time before them. Not really."

I look at Marina, who places a hand on my forearm. I smile. I remember how carefully she spoke about her mom the other night. I don't remember my birth mom, and sometimes, that's a gift. I can't imagine Marina's situation of knowing her mom for thirteen years before losing her.

Marina smiles at the photo again and laughs at Bonnie's curled fist, as if prepped for action. "You can tell Bonnie's got four older brothers. She's ready."

"Trust me," I say, "her attitude has nothing to do with us. Even when she was tiny, she had this thousand-yard stare that scared the hell outta me. Still does."

Marina laughs, and it only continues when she points out the last two Davies children. My two youngest brothers—now twelve years old—are at the end of our lineup, holding Nerf guns behind their backs. They were seconds away from attacking Dad once the picture snapped.

"Liam and Levi—or The Twins—were a happy surprise. Rainbow

babies, Ma says. Unexpected chaos demons who were born later than she'd have liked at her age."

"Whoa."

I shrug. "Can't deny a true miracle."

As if on cue, the stairwell shakes beside us, and The Twins shoot down the steps, each holding slingshots.

"Duck!" I command, wrapping an arm around Marina and pulling her to a squat.

Levi aims at Liam, shooting a marble from the slingshot's rubber band. The moment it *plunks* on the hardwood, near the open back door, Ma's sixth sense activates from the other room.

"That'd better not be marbles in my house, Twins!"

"Hey, don't hit me!" I blurt out randomly.

The Twins and Marina shoot me synchronized surprised glances. I cover my mouth with a laugh.

"Boys!" Ma yells again. "Are we shooting at family again?"

"You pot stirrer," Marina accuses.

"It was Liam!" Levi calls, but Liam instantly shoves him.

They dart out the back door with Levi cackling and Liam swearing his innocence.

Marina and I exchange a quick glance before sputtering into a fit of laughter. It's easy and nice. But after the laughter dies down, as I'm taking in her dotted freckles and smiling pink lips, I realize I'm still holding her. My palm presses against the dip in her back, supporting her from when we dodged the marble. I pull in a breath, and she takes one too.

We scramble to stand. I help her up, and once we're upright again, I tug my shirt down, and she's tucking a strand of her blonde waves behind one ear.

Ma comes around the corner, just barely missing our awkward interaction. Her face brightens. "Cass!"

She's still in her long white coat from the day, probably back from the office.

She instantly pulls me into her arms. Ma is shorter than me and plump but in a way that lends to only the best hugs. She's barely done tightening her grip on me before turning and doing the same to Marina.

"Hey again, dear."

"Oh!"

Marina's arms are stiff at first, but somewhere in that hug, Marina's eyes flutter closed. It suddenly dawns on me that maybe she hasn't been hugged by a mother figure in years. I remember that first Maggie Davies hug. I understand the moment where you allow yourself to sink into her arms. The comfort never really goes away, no matter how many hugs she gives.

"Hi, Mrs. Davies," Marina murmurs softly.

"Please, call me Maggie," Ma responds. She doesn't pull away until Marina does, and after, she cups her cheeks. "So nice to see you again. I know your father must be happy you're back."

Marina gives a smile that doesn't look as happy as it was seconds ago. "He is."

I tilt my head to the side but am brought back when my mom pokes me in the chest.

"And you," my mom says, "how are you? How's Laura doing?"

"She's healing. Trying to keep a low profile for now."

"Good. And Bobbi ..." She leans in conspiratorially. "Has she beaten my personal record yet?"

"You know I can't tell you that."

"She has, hasn't she?"

"Can't say," I say with a nonchalant shrug.

"Bah, you. How's the new house? When are you taking The Twins with you?"

My head rolls back. "Ma ..."

"I'm seriously gonna kill those kids," she says with wide eyes. "And watch out for him too," Ma warns Marina, poking me in the chest again. "He's no better than those two. He likes to eat all the food in the pantry."

"Ma!" I cry again.

"It's true." She taps Marina's shoulder. "He leaves no peanut butter for everyone else."

Marina laughs. "I'll keep that in mind."

My mom tosses me a wink, then looks over our shoulders, where Milo walks in behind us. "Lo!" Ma calls, and it's the same process all over again—a mother greeting her child like she didn't see all of us just one week ago.

"Wanna see the rest of the house?" I prompt.

Marina nods. "As long as I can get a slingshot for protection too."

"Definitely. It's standard issue in this house. The war room is our third stop on the tour."

"Perfect."

I hold a palm out to Marina, gesturing the way forward. She follows my lead through the doorway of the kitchen. My dad feverishly stirs a pot. Sitting on a stool nearby is my sister, Bonnie. Her eyes widen at the first sight of Marina.

I give my dad our typical three-pat hug—he's not nearly as touchy as Mom. Then, he does the same to Marina. Robotic but funny.

"Nice to see you, sweetheart."

"Oh," Marina says, almost stumbling backward. "Nice to see you too, Mr. Davies."

"I think all this affection is gonna kill you," I mutter to her.

Flushed, Marina shakes her head. "No. It's actually kinda nice."

Across the kitchen, Bonnie is still staring, blinking with ginger eyelashes. Her equally red hair is plopped haphazardly on the top of her head, like she took a small break from studying to come downstairs for this.

"Bon, you got something to say?" I ask.

Her face flushes.

"Oh, sorry, hi, Marina," Bonnie stumbles out. "You babysat my best friend as a kid."

Marina graciously laughs. "I remember you, Bon. No more braces though?"

Bonnie grins with all her teeth, flashing the lack of wires. "Got them off this year."

"Very cool."

"Nah. Not really." Bonnie's face flushes red.

"She thinks you're *super* cool," I say.

Bonnie's eyebrows rise. "Cass!"

"Oh," Marina says, jutting her head back with a smile. "I don't know about all that."

I see her faltering look, the way she gives a soft smile that feels like the same one she gave when my mom mentioned her dad.

"Let's go outside," I suggest. "It'll start to get hot in here with all the cooking." On instinct, I place my palm on her lower back again.

As we pass Bonnie, I whisper, "How's that teenage idolization going?"

Bonnie glares, hissing, "Ass."

"Bon," Dad warns.

Bonnie groans out a drawling, "Language. Got it," as she follows Marina and me out to the backyard.

The Twins and Sam run along the tree-house bridge. Bonnie joins them, serving as backup for Sam, who is currently fighting two-on-one. When she leaves, I lean in toward Marina.

"Sorry," I whisper.

Her demeanor shifts; she's confused at first, then sputtering out a laugh through a cheeky smile that seems too forced for her. "What do you mean?"

"I know my family can be weird sometimes. Bonnie thinks you're the coolest, and when my mom mentioned your dad—"

"Are you telling me I'm not cool?"

"Oh, no, you're cool, Starkey," I reassure with a grin. "Cooler than I'll ever be."

"Says who?"

"People."

"Oh, right, forgot about *people*," she says, grinning.

"But I get it if that was … a bit much."

"No, it's fine. It's just … I don't know exactly how *cool* I am."

She turns to walk away, but I take hold of her elbow.

"Marina, don't tell me you're not cool. Because then my standards will plummet down."

"What?"

"You're my baseline for cool, honey. And you set one hell of a bar for everyone else."

A slow smile rises on her face. It runs sparks down to my fingers still lingering on her arm. I don't know what to do, but I don't want to let go.

Thankfully, my indecision is solved by my brother's telltale crow of, "All right, the party has arrived! Don't worry!"

Peter strides outside on our open deck slab, announcing his presence like a king emerging to his throne room. He grins ear to ear, running a palm through his wild blond locks, like them being in control would be unsightly.

He bumps my fist as he walks by but saunters over to speak with Jasper and Wendy. The three of them are finally functioning well. But it's hard to miss how Pete's face falls when Wendy sidles closer to Jasper.

Marina leans toward me and whispers, "I must be super behind. What's all that about?"

"Them?" I suck in a breath. "It's a bit too much to explain in five seconds."

"Mind if I get the gossip?"

I chuckle. "Oh, I've got gossip. Pete and Wendy broke up a couple of years back."

We both watch Jasper's arm curl around Wendy's waist.

Marina gasps. "And are Jasper and Wendy ..."

"Uh-huh. Last summer. Wendy started nannying for Jasper. One thing led to another and ..."

"Drama," Marina responds with a smile.

"I like Wendy for Jasper," I admit. "Plus, I've known her since middle school. She should have been in our family years ago."

"Is Pete all right?"

"Of course. A cannonball couldn't take that guy down."

I admire my brother's inability to let bigger things bother him. Sure, he was pissed about it all. But anyone could see that Wendy's softness sands down Jasper's rough edges. Peter doesn't need that same tenderness for himself. It would be like putting out a fire with oil. He's only wilder when attempting to be tamed.

Bobbi thinks I can start a business, but I'm nothing like Pete—my brother who already has a successful business. I'm not as confident. Not as charismatic. Not as bulletproof.

I jump when soft fingers trail down to my wrist. A palm gently cups around mine. I follow the arm to Marina, who looks very grave.

"I didn't know roommates held hands," I joke.

"I don't know what's going on in that head of yours," she says seriously. "But I don't like the feeling coming off you right now."

"Bad energy?" I tease.

"You seem self-conscious," she corrects. Her eyes swivel to Peter, then back to me. "A cannonball could take *anyone* down. Not just him. Your brother's not invincible. Neither are you. And that's okay."

I run a thumb over the back of her palm, feeling just how smooth Marina's skin truly is. It's like silk under my gym-roughened calluses. My heart beats a little faster, and I pull away almost as soon as it starts.

"I'm all right," I say, forcing a grin. "Really. But I'll tell you what does hurt—the floor." I laugh, but she barely laughs with me. "Please sleep in the bed again tonight? I need that sofa."

I'm trying to play with her, but Marina weakly smiles back.

I knock my chin toward the rest of the crew hanging near the tree house. "Want to watch me annoy Jasper?"

She smiles and follows silently. "Sure."

But she's quieter now, and I can't help but wonder if it's because of me or something I said. Or worse, who I am in general.

- Chapter Sixteen -

ANOTHER STUBBORN GAME

Marina

The Davies family is a wild, cozy riot, if something like that could exist.

We spent all night at the long picnic table in their backyard, eating Mr. Davies's delicious pork chops, mashed potatoes, and greens. Cassidy went back for seconds and thirds of his meal, stepping over the bench seat with an overflowing plate and asking, "What? Ever seen a man eat?"

On one of those trips, after I told him I loved his dad's mac and cheese, he scooped some extra onto my plate. I'm not sure why that made me giddy, but it did. Cassidy is thoughtful, and I wish he recognized that as much as I'm starting to.

Maggie kept asking about everyone at the table. Even if they gave short answers, she demanded clarification with her and Mr. Davies leaning forward to listen with genuine interest, even when I talked about the flower shop. Bonnie rolled her eyes at her "embarrassing parents," but I loved every second, and judging by Cassidy's growing grin, I thought he might have too.

He loves his family so much—appreciates them, more like it. He bounced between conversations like a ping pong ball, making sure to give all his family equal time and attention. He even played with Nerf guns with The Twins at the end of the night when I was ready to fall asleep on the parlor sofa.

Cassidy gives a lot of himself, almost like he's in a happiness debt and he owes so much of it to them.

I wonder if he ever gets tired.

Something bothered him tonight that I couldn't put my finger on. I don't know him well enough to ask about it, but I also don't like this duality of Cassidy Davies. Outwardly, he's a puppy, but behind the curtain is someone different.

Not Mr. Never Harbor.

We walk through the townhome's door late. When I head to the bathroom for my shower, Cassidy settles on the sofa with his journal. Throughout my entire routine, I can't stop wondering what he's writing in there and whether there's more to his outgoing happy-go-lucky demeanor than he wants anyone else to see.

After I'm finished in the bathroom and Cassidy goes in to shower after, I eye the deposited journal on the kitchen counter. I keep looking at the hallway bathroom then back, and as the steam starts to billow from under the door, the temptation to read it snags at me. Eventually, the shower cuts off and I walk away.

I braid my hair, watching Cassidy, with his curls now deliciously damp, pile blankets and pillows on the sofa. He lays down and immediately winces. I know because it's the same face I made last night when I rolled over that spot.

I tsk. "Those springs are relentless, huh?"

"Nah," he says. "I'm comfortable here."

"Liar."

He snorts. "Hey, it's better than the floor."

I inhale, exhale, then click my tongue.

"Okay," I say slowly. "I have a crazy idea."

"Let me hear it."

"What if... we shared the bed?"

It's silent for a moment as his eyes flick over me. And then he throws his head back in laughter. "Starkey—"

"I'm serious! We're adults. You need something better than that stupid sofa."

"A sofa is fine."

"For how long?" I ask. "Weeks? Months? Whenever the flower shop pays me enough to afford my own place?"

"Maybe."

"No," I argue. "I can't stand to watch you suffer anymore. You've played your stubborn game. Let me play mine."

"You can't out-stubborn me," he challenges, and that has my eyebrows rising.

"Bet."

I cross to the kitchen, standing on my tiptoes to pull down a cup. I twist on the faucet.

"Wait, what are you doing?"

I don't respond.

"Starkey." It sounds like a warning.

I kind of like the tone. I shake my shoulders, letting the attraction slide out of my mind because I'm a woman on a mission.

The cup almost overflows with water before I stomp back into the living room and, staring him in the eye, unceremoniously dump it onto the sofa.

Cassidy shuffles to stand, ripping the blanket from the cushion. He blinks at the soaking wet sofa.

"You just did that."

"I sure did. Now, bed," I demand, following it with a small, "Please."

I honestly expect Cassidy to stay on the floor just to prove a point, but just like I've reached my breaking point, he must hit his. He snatches his pillow, thankfully untouched by water, and stalks over to me.

I'm tall, but Cassidy is taller, towering over me with his jaw winding back and forth as his eyes roam over my face. We're nearly toe to toe, which suddenly feels inappropriate. I should have thought about this more.

"You win," he finally announces, partially laughing but low and in a way that sends shivers down to my stomach.

"Great." I turn on my heel, shakily exhaling the heat from my body once more, and walk to the bedroom.

It should be illegal to be that unintentionally attractive. And I'm about to share a bed with this man?

Great job, Marina. Stellar problem solving.

When we reach the threshold, I pause.

"Should I change?" I ask.

"Why?"

"Because I've been sleeping in my tank top and shorts."

"Last I checked, I'm not a nun," he answers with a laugh. "And we're not gonna cuddle."

"We don't know that," I tease. "Maybe I like being the big spoon."

Cassidy runs a palm through his hair. "If you want to put on more clothes, go for it. But it gets hot in here, even with the window open."

"You sure?"

He leans toward me, inches from my nose. I can smell his minty toothpaste. "You won't be tempting me, you sinful woman."

The seductive hiss has my heart hammering in my chest. I choke out a playful laugh.

"I can't tell if that's an insult or not."

"Trust me, honey, there's no reality where you're not stunning. I'm just a gentleman. Or I try to be anyway."

And then the man winks.

I feel my cheeks flush. Heck, I almost collapse onto the bed.

"Go on," he coaxes.

I climb in bed, crawling across the sheets to the opposite side situated against the wall. I hope he can't see my ass pushed toward the ceiling as I move on my hands and knees, but when I turn around, looking over my shoulder, his face is stone.

Clearing his throat, Cassidy crawls in. Under the sheets, his warmth is a radiator next to me. Remembering his preference, I reach up to prop open the window.

With a laugh, he says, "Thanks."

We lie there in silence. His breathing is unchanged, but so is mine. I can't fall asleep. I'm too busy imagining his body, lying inches away. I hear him shift, and I wonder which parts of him flex under the movement. Is it the large muscle just under his arm and above his ribs? Or is it his forearm, twisting the roped veins with each motion?

Cassidy lets out an exhale, but instead of picturing his barrel chest—okay, so I might for a second—I instead notice how rough it sounds. Almost shaky. The other side of Cassidy Davies.

"Hey," I whisper in the dark.

"Hmm?" he answers.

"Can I ask what was wrong tonight, or is that too weird?"

I hear his lips part. "Uh …" He laughs quietly. "What do you mean?"

"Was everything okay? Or did I just imagine that you seemed sad? I'm normally pretty good at noticing these things, but I've been wrong before."

After a quiet moment, Cassidy rolls over to face me. I join him. Both of us prop our heads up in our palms. I feel thirteen again, at a sleepover with a friend.

"Do you always talk when going to sleep?" he asks.

"Maybe."

"Cute."

"So, was I wrong about tonight?"

It takes another beat or two, but he finally answers, "I get a little self-conscious sometimes."

"You? Mr. Muscles?"

"Yeah, me," he confirms, and I can hear the grin even if I can't fully see it in the dark.

"Why?"

"I just do. I don't know."

"Sounds like you *do* know."

He laughs again. "I just … I'm not my brothers, y'know?"

"No," I answer honestly.

"I'm … well, some piece is missing in me, I think. And that's fine. But"—he shrugs—"it is what it is."

"What …" I'm at a loss for words for a moment before asking, "What's that mean? '*It is what it is?*'"

"Well, my brothers have it together. I never really have."

"How long have you thought that?"

He chuckles. "Forever."

But this isn't so funny to me. "Why?"

"Eh, you go from family to family … why'd it take so long for me to find one that stuck? I'm just chaotic."

"I don't think that's true."

"No?"

"Absolutely not," I say, and my heart is breaking at even the thought. "So, because of that, you don't think you're like your brothers?"

"I try to be. I do."

"You are exactly as you should be. Good to your core. You know what your real problem is?" I tease.

He grins. "Do tell."

"You've got a wonky mindset."

"Wonky?" he says, his throaty laugh almost muffled in the sheets between us.

"Yeah. Okay, and I know it sounds ridiculous—"

"You don't sound ridiculous," he cuts in.

"And neither do you. You've basically got that cute little hamster running on a wheel in your head in a choke hold. He's self-conscious over nothing."

"Well, then how do I … let the hamster breathe, I guess?"

"I've got some things that help me. You gotta promise not to laugh though."

"I promise."

"Okay. Well, self-help books are great."

I hear the stifled laugh wanting to emerge as he asks, "Self-help books?"

"Hey, you promised not to laugh."

"I'm not making fun," he says. "They just seem too ... I don't know. Preachy? And don't they all basically say the same thing?"

"Sometimes, you just need things said in a certain way to let it sink in. At least, that's how I feel about it. They helped me a lot. Back then. When my mom left."

He hums for a moment, then says, "All right. From one lost kid to another, I'll give it a go."

I laugh at the dark humor. "Little Curly would be so proud."

He snorts. "Little Curly?"

"It's one big step forward for him."

"Little Curly," he echoes again. "Sorry, I can't let that go."

"Imagine if I reserved that nickname for something else."

"Marina ..."

"Kidding."

We lie there in silence again, and all I hear is the whistling breeze squeaking through the window on a gust of wind.

"Hey. Is everything okay with you and your dad?" he asks.

I hesitate before answering, "What?"

"Didn't seem that way when my mom brought it up."

"It's fine."

"Don't be shy. I just talked about my *missing pieces*."

I laugh. "It's fine. I ... really, it's fine. I just feel like I've missed a lot. I feel like I should have known he was dating Bobbi. I wonder if that makes me a terrible daughter."

"You're not. It's natural for people to fade apart."

"Not us. Feels wrong. It was just me and him against the world for so long, and now, he won't even tell me he and his best friend are boinking."

"Do you really *want* to know those details?"

"Sometimes ... I don't know ... I wonder if maybe I've failed him. That I left, just like Mom." I pick at a string sticking out from my pillow. "Maybe he resents me for it, y'know?"

I can feel the tears stinging behind my eyes at the admission, and I hate myself for it. Now is not the time.

"Hey. Marina. You're not her," he murmurs.

"You don't know that. Heck, I've never stuck with anything in my life."

"Are you seriously trying to convince me you're a bad person?" he asks with a quiet laugh.

"I am."

Suddenly, I feel his warm palm on my cheek. I'm startled by the motion as Cassidy runs a single knuckle down my jawline before taking my chin between his thumb and forefinger.

"Listen to me. You wanna talk about energy and all that stuff? Well, I only get the best feelings from you. Not a single sliver of bad, all right?"

I let out a shaky breath, feeling the warmth radiate off his hand before his rough fingers slowly slide away.

"Understand?" he whispers.

"Yeah."

"Good. Now, if I can't talk negatively about myself, you can't either. You've got me now, and I monitor that stuff. Deal?"

I smile. "Deal."

"Good. Now, let's get some sleep."

"Night, Davies."

"Night, Starkey."

I roll over to grab my Kindle, turning down the light and pulling the covers up to my chin while I read. But I can't concentrate, not with those words still barreling through me, right down to my stomach.

"You've got me now."

"Do you know you sing when you read?" Cassidy asks.

I lower my book. "What?"

"When you're concentrating, you sing."

I bite my lower lip. "I'm sorry. Does it bother you?"

"No," he murmurs. "No, keep going. It helps me fall asleep."

I start to smile. "Really?"

His pillow shifts as if he's settling in. "I don't hear that humming."

Grinning, I go back to reading, and as if I'm humming a lullaby, Cassidy's breathing gradually relaxes, and his low snores rumble out as he falls asleep next to me.

Chapter Seventeen

A BOY AND HIS WOMAN ON WINGS

Cassidy

I think I like self-help books.

I have a full week of juggling gym clients and planning the wine mixer. But in between, I flip through the book Marina let me borrow. Honestly, it isn't terrible. It makes me feel … seen?

Christ, that sounds so ridiculous; it almost makes me laugh. But some of the passages … well, let's just say, I understand the recommendation now.

My page flips echo through the main lobby of The Hideaway. Across the room, Peter paces from booth to booth in serious bar-owner mode. We had a meeting scheduled, but I got caught up helping Jukes carry bags to his car. When I texted Peter I'd be a few minutes behind, he took advantage of the extra time to knock out some small tasks. I feel bad, and I can't blame him for moving on. He's a busy guy.

"Just a couple more things, and then I'm all yours, Cass," he calls over.

"Not a couple more—a *few* more things," Izzy corrects him.

His bar manager, Isabel, flits behind him like a woman on wings. Despite how pint-sized she appears in comparison to Pete's towering height, we all know Izzy could suplex a grown man if she wanted to, and that man would likely be Peter.

I go back to my reading, then pull out my phone.

> ### Cassidy
> "The road map for your life is entirely up to you. It's all about mindset."

> ### Marina
> Ooh, yeah, that line changed my life.

> ### Cassidy
> I like it a lot.

> ### Marina
> I like that you like it. :)

Marina's reactions are my favorite part about this book. It's not that I'm reading the book for her—not entirely—but the encouragement, knowing that I'm not reading this alone, admittedly cements how often I turn the next page.

I like having someone to text who isn't my siblings. It's nice to know that when I have a thought, there's someone else who will acknowledge it.

But if I think about that too much, I feel guilty, like maybe I'm not appreciative of my family. I am, but not being known as the goofy younger brother for once is nice.

Izzy huffs from across the room. "Peter Davies, I need some focus here. After the stupid health inspector thing last week ..."

He places calming hands on either shoulder and bends down to look her in the eye. "You're stressed."

She scoffs, rolling her eyes. "Of course I'm stressed."

"Is the high school principal still giving you issues with graduation plans?"

"Yes. He won't return my calls. But after I saw him at dinner with Donna ..."

If I were a dog, my ears would have perked up. *Two school principals?*

Dang, Bobbi is right. I'm a sucker for gossip.

Peter barks out a laugh. "Dinner with Donna?"

Izzy snaps her fingers. "Focus, Pete."

His lips pull into a lazy grin. "Yes, ma'am."

"I'm serious," Izzy says. "Don't play with me today."

He leans in closer to her ear, murmuring, "But it's so fun, Bells."

If the room wasn't so empty, I might not have heard it. I wonder if

I was supposed to.

Izzy smirks up at him. She normally keeps him in line, but today, she's been more lenient. Izzy clicks her pen over the clipboard. She walks on. Though, for a small moment, I catch his eyes lingering on her ass when she does. I snort in amusement louder than I mean to, and both of them swivel to me. I jerk my head back down to my book.

I admire my brother's drive, but he'll need more than pure charisma if he's checking out his bar manager. Izzy likes things a certain way, and Peter is anything but *certain*.

And for some reason, I find myself pulling out my phone again.

> **Cassidy**
> I think my brother is playing with fire.

Marina
Can I guess which brother?

> **Cassidy**
> One guess.

Marina
Pete.

> **Cassidy**
> Ding, ding, ding.

Marina
Can't wait to hear about it at home.

I smile to myself, my heart beating that much quicker.
Home.
I like our routine.

I've never had a roommate who wasn't my family. I wonder if liking your roommate this much is normal. Roommates. Friends. That's all it is. Nothing serious.

Our slumber parties this past week have been fine. Normal. Not sexual at all. Except that the thought of touching her hasn't left my mind for one second, so, okay, maybe a little sexual.

In the middle of the night, if she rolls a little too close to me in bed, her curves press against my chest or leg or arm. And if I stretch out, forgetting she's there, then our hands bump, and I jerk back so fast that I'm surprised the sheets aren't on fire. But what's really heating up are the way my fingertips itch to reach out and trace along her soft skin once more.

Worse than that is her nightly routine—the long showers, the hot steam, the lavender scent, the ritualistic lotion application, and the way her elegant fingers slowly braid her long waves, past her perky breasts and down to her slender waist. I can't watch anymore if I want to uphold my integrity with Charles Starkey. But his daughter is driving me insane, and she doesn't even know it.

Peter and Izzy finally sit across from me, screeching up barstools to the high-top. Izzy eyes my book and smiles.

"Oh, hey, I've read that one too," she says. "I recommended it to Wendy."

Peter looks at her, then me. "Can I see it?"

I clear my throat, tuck my bookmark back in, and hand it to him.

"I didn't know you read self-help books," Peter says.

"It was just a recommendation from Marina."

"Why have you read this?" Peter asks Izzy.

She shrugs. "I read it back in business school." Izzy eyes me. "Do you want to start a business or something, Cass?"

I snort. "No." But then I think for a moment about my conversations with Bobbi and scoff. "Well, I don't know. If it were up to Bobbi Mullins, I would."

Izzy arches an eyebrow in question.

I stretch my arms up and over my head.

"She thinks I should … I don't know … start my own personal training business or something." I grin more, shaking my head at the ridiculousness of it all.

Peter nods. "Maybe you should."

I choke out a laugh mid-stretch. "What? Nah. I'm not a business guy like you, Pete."

"Me? I got this place on accident."

Izzy's eyes widen at the same time mine do.

Pete's been a little *off* since last summer—ever since Wendy started dating Jasper. Maybe the experience of losing his ex to his older brother was humbling. Maybe Wendy spit some hard truths at him. Whatever it was, sometimes, he now says one-liners like this that have everyone around him blinking a couple of times, like, *Where did our cocky Pete go?*

"Pardon me, Mr. Special-est Boy Ever?" Izzy asks, dripping with sarcasm.

Peter holds out his palm toward me. "What? I run a restaurant. It's not rocket surgery."

"Rocket science," Izzy corrects.

He looks at her with raised eyebrows, and she rolls her eyes. Something tells me that was the joke.

"Come on, Pete," I say, laughing it off.

Peter furrows his brow.

"Let's talk about what I came here for," I insist.

"The festival?"

"Mixer," I correct.

"Right."

Thankfully, Peter drops it once we discuss catering, but I'm still stuck on our conversation.

I appreciate the vote of confidence from my brother, but all this consistent talk of starting a business is edging too close to reality.

I know how I operate. I'm late to basically everything. I'm gonna miss dates, barrel past timelines, fumble a schedule … I can't let down Never Harbor like that. I can't disappoint the people I love like that.

Eventually, I check the time and realize I'm running behind if I want to catch Laura before she leaves for the day—because of course I am. I love giving Peter and Izzy my undivided attention, but Laura's still hobbling through the halls, and it makes me nervous.

"Hey, let's get some lunch soon," Peter says, catching me by the arm before I leave. "I really do believe you could do it."

"Do what?" I ask on a laugh, and his answer isn't what I want to hear.

"Start a business." The way he says it is so matter-of-fact that my instinct is to laugh again.

"We'll get lunch," I concede. "But not to discuss something ridiculous, okay?"

His eyes flick to Marina's book clutched in my palm, then back to me.

"*You're* ridiculous," he counters.

I shake my head and smile. "Later, Pete."

I descend the front porch stairs with a wave. But when I pull away in my car, he's still staring at me from the front door's threshold, arms crossed over his chest.

Start a business.

I couldn't. Without a shadow of a doubt, I know that. Plus, the idea of upcharging locals for training they already get relatively cheap through the community center makes my stomach feel raw.

When I get to the community center, an unfamiliar car is parked in my spot. Not that we have designated places, but in a small town, it's like classrooms in school. You choose your seat on day one, and everyone pretty much respects that decision. But seeing as I don't recognize the car, this visitor deserves a pass.

Instead, I pull one block down in front of Peg Leg Press, give Bobbi a wave through the window, and take the sidewalk to the community center.

I open the front door, and immediately, something feels off. No, I've just been reading that self-help book too much with all its talk of energies and vibes.

But then I spot a man down the hall, leaning forward and laughing with Laura. My breath catches in my throat at the sight of the fitted gray suit, the chin raised in the air like he owns the place, and the cocky grin that follows when his silver eyes catch mine.

And before anything else crosses my mind, my first thought is to tell Marina.

Dustin Barrie is back in town.

- Chapter Eighteen -

SOMETHING FISHY

Marina

Life has been good lately, and I'm not sure how I feel about it. Not that life *can't* be good, but the past few days have been oddly … enjoyable.

The flower shop is starting to be a reliable routine. I look forward to the sweet buds and lemon cleaner. We've slowly moved the rejuvenated plants back to the shop, so I bring Fido to work, too, clutching his pot in my arms as I walk the few blocks to work with Cassidy each morning.

"It's like Bring Your Kid to Work Day," I explain. "He can't be at the house alone. Obviously."

Cassidy gives that loud laugh of his and echoes, "*Obviously.*"

Day by day, the shop is getting more attention. The moment I flip the sign and prop open the door, people mosey in with their to-go coffees from Peg Leg Press. Tourists swing by for seaside dates, Mr. Davies grabs a couple of lilies for Mrs. Davies, and Steve, in his apparent pursuit of Laura, grabs a bouquet daily. Lulu and I look forward to ribbing him about his crush every morning. I personally look forward to my lunch breaks, sitting on a bench by the sea, letting the breeze whip past my hair, and listening to the distant ice cream truck rumbling by with its gentle melody.

Lulu and I have also been prepping for the high school's graduation, setting aside specific school colors for Never Harbor High in coolers when they arrive from our supplier greenhouses, arranging for bouquets and corsages to hand to the seniors as they cross the stage.

It's weird that I've nestled into a routine so quickly. I might have enjoyed Barrie Wine & Spirits, but I *love* Florally Yours. The chatty regulars, Lulu's eclectic energy, the sun beaming through the large front windows … I'm not sure how to reconcile this feeling with the fact that I'm also job-hunting before dinner every night. Everything I'm finding is in a fluorescent office space, sitting behind a computer and taking notes in meetings. I feel nauseous, just thinking about it.

Traipsing down an aisle, I check on our orchids, finally blossoming again.

I almost took them home, but when I ran it by Cassidy, he said, "We can't adopt them all. How will we afford their college tuition?"

He smiled, and I know he would have changed his mind if I'd asked a second time, but that knowledge alone made me not press further.

The flower shop is nice, but Cassidy is a ray of sunshine. We walk to work every morning, switch off making dinner, and gossip before bed. Sometimes my cheeks will hurt from smiling too much at night. And, okay, I maybe, possibly, definitely like sleeping in bed next to him.

I like the way his toothpaste smells when he lightly snores. I like the way his curls get messier throughout the night as he tosses and turns. I like it best when he bumps into me on accident. One night, he rolled over and brushed his palm over my back. I didn't move an inch.

For a split second the other day, as I was touching myself in the shower, his brown eyes passed through my mind. A flash of those hooded eyes sliding over my body, suffused with longing. I concentrated really hard on my usual celebrity crush after that, and thankfully, I imagined their rough hands over me. My orgasm was an unsatisfying whisper.

I'm starved for touch. That's all this is. I don't know how long it's been since I've had sex or even kissed someone. But I want to run my fingers through Cassidy's tight curls. I want to lick a line down to his dimpled cheek. I want to trace my nails down his abs. It's almost inhuman how beautiful he is and even more ridiculous how *so* out of bounds he is.

We *live* together. What if it ended poorly? What if I lost the one close friend I have in Never Harbor?

The devil on my shoulder likes to hiss in response, *But we're only here for the summer.*

Thankfully, I have an angel countering, *Exactly. We're* only *here for the summer.*

Why ruin our short time together? Why halt how wonderful things are?

I like what our friendship is turning into, and if something went south … I'm not sure I could handle losing this slice of peace I've gained.

I swallow, adjusting the leaves of the plant unnecessarily before walking away from both it and the thought of Cassidy in bed.

Except that deep, comforting tone finds me.

"Hey, Starkey."

I halt in my tracks as Cassidy himself crosses into our shop, his bulky shoulders barely fitting through the doorway. Without hesitation, a smile beams on my face. His expression mirrors mine instantly.

The devil whispers, *Yesss.*

Stinky winds through Cassidy's legs with loud meows.

"C'mere, mister," he says, scooping down and laying him over his chest.

Stinky purrs like an engine roaring to life whenever Cassidy cuddles him. It's like good can sense good. They nuzzle together like two lost souls, and I'm pretty sure my soul is oozing to soft goo at the sight.

"Wow, he's super nice today," Cassidy observes.

"Yeah, I had fish for lunch and gave him a tiny piece. I'm hoping it stops the *gifts* he brings us."

"Ah," Cassidy says, watching as Stinky buries his face in his hood as if digging for potential food there too. "You gonna bring Miss Marina another rat?" he coos. "Or a squirrel?"

Stinky purrs louder, as if confirming, *Yes, Mr. Cassidy. I will bring food for flower humans.*

I never know whether to be offended by cat behavior or not.

Cassidy looks around, tracing a thumb over Stinky's spine. "Where's Lu? No fish for her too?"

"Apparently, she doesn't like seafood, so she went to get ice cream with Bonnie."

"That's not a real meal."

I hold my hands up. "I don't question her decisions anymore."

"Gotcha. Oh, looks like Fido is sunbathing on the job." Cassidy nods to where the plant sits on the counter, attentive, leaves soaking in the sun. "How rude."

"We truly pay him too much." I play along.

"We'll ground him when he gets home," he says, pointing a finger in Fido's direction. "No special plant food for a week."

Stinky winds around Cassidy's shoulders, arching against his curls sprouting out from his headband. Cassidy lowers Stinky back to the ground, receiving a disdainful, offended meow.

"So, hey, I actually came here to tell ya something."

"Oh, wait, I have something to show you first."

I tuck my hand into his and tug him to the back of the flower shop. I love holding hands with Cassidy. His palms are rough to the touch, and veins wrap from his stiff forearms and wind down over his hands. It's hard not to imagine what those deft hands can do.

We squeak across the tiled floor, bypassing the rows of floral arrangements and the metal prep table. I open a fridge and wave my hand in front of the display. Cassidy blinks at the arrangement, then to me, and back to drooping white flowers.

"Well?" I ask.

"I ... they look fantastic, Marina."

"You don't know what they are."

"I don't."

I laugh. "They're lilies of the valley. They represent luck and joy. They're what I'll be putting in the centerpieces at the wine mixer. Plus, they're white, so they're automatically classy."

"*So* classy." A slow smile grows on his face, and eventually, the beautiful dimple pops. "That's really thoughtful, Marina."

I shrug. "My mom could never keep one alive. I'm just proud of that alone."

"Your mom wasn't good with plants?"

"Our living room was full of plants when I was growing up," I explain. "But they all died unless I watered them. Actually, they thrived a lot once she left."

I peer at the fridge again, both of our heads tilting to the side in contemplation.

"Was she good at growing anything?" he asks.

"Oh, she loved her ficus," I say through an exhale. "That's actually where Fido came from."

His eyes widen, and I love how his smile does too. "He was your mom's?"

"Yeah. Same one. I've propagated him over the years."

He squints. "Propo—"

"Planted and replanted," I define for him with a laugh. "Using seeds from the original. And he's still kickin' somehow."

"I like that." He tips his chin up. "And you know what? I think that gives off good energy."

"Okay, har har." I push a single finger against his hard chest. "I told you, you can ignore those parts of the book if you want."

But the smile on his face relaxes into something gentle. "I'm being serious."

I can't tell if it's the way he's looking at me or the cool air of the fridge spreading goose bumps over my skin, but a shiver rattles through me. He raises a single eyebrow at the movement. I shut the fridge door, but the chill doesn't go away.

Cassidy reaches out to run a rough palm over my bare shoulder, up, then down. He's trying to rub the chill away, but it only sends more skittering down my arm.

His hand gets slower. His touch lightens. I don't know how it happens, but gently, he runs his palm up my throat and to my jaw, where he lets his fingers rest.

I swallow. He traces a thumb over my cheek.

"Thanks," is all I can find to say.

As if he realizes what he's doing, Cassidy's face falls. He jerks his hand away.

"Um …"

"Sorry, you wanted to tell me something?" I ask.

"Oh, right." He cringes, rubbing a palm over the back of his neck— the one that was just touching me. "You're not gonna like it."

"Okay," I answer tentatively.

"Dustin's back in town," he explains.

"Oh," is all I get out because, suddenly, I am drowning.

"And he's staying."

I gasp for air. "Oh."

Never Harbor isn't big, so it's only a matter of time before I run into Dustin Barrie myself. It happens the very next day at Peg Leg Press.

"Do you think if I tell Bobbi I want jet engine fuel, she'll take me seriously?" Lulu asks, arms crossed as we stand in the afternoon coffee line.

It's been a busy day at Florally Yours. After I changed out the window arrangements, more people have been flocking in each hour. I could barely get through my leftovers from yesterday while working through customers. Some are here to ask if we have specific flowers, but some—like Steve and Mr. Davies—come in, grinning ear to ear, with their usual bouquet purchases.

"Surprise me with how many," Cassidy's dad said.

After he left with a bouquet of lilies in hand, Lulu sighed wistfully. "Those Davies men, huh?" She shook her head, turning the page of her book. "Mags is so lucky."

I glanced at the cover. "Is that the same one Milo was reading the other day?"

"Oh. Is it?" She flipped to the back. "Huh. I didn't notice."

I grinned and nodded with a humming, "Uh-huh."

At eleven years old, Lulu never stopped talking about her best friend's older brother. She and Milo are ten years apart, so I took it as a simple childhood infatuation. But the way Lulu darted her eyes to me after my innocuous acknowledgment makes me think that crush never disappeared.

"He just reads good books," she snapped. "I can't read the same ones?"

I popped my lips. "I said nothing, Lu."

"I was just saying the Davies men have a great dad."

"Mmhmm."

"That's all."

"Those Davies men."

She's not wrong about those Davies men. If I think about Cassidy, my day is a wistful dream. Fantasies piling one after the other—hand-holding, sleeping next to him, his arms wrapped around me, his thick thighs spread in front of me, him lowering his boxer briefs …

But then, inevitably, I remember that Dustin is back in town, and my body has the opposite reaction. I've been getting nauseous since I found out he came back yesterday, and after our morning rush, I'm downright exhausted.

We step forward in the coffee line, and I drag my feet behind me.

"Girl, you all right?" Lulu asks. "You look a little pale."

"I'm tired. Aren't you?"

"Oh, I wasn't kidding. I'm literally ordering jet fuel."

"If you want jet fuel, you get jet fuel, girl."

"How supportive," a voice croons from behind us.

A shudder racks down my spine. I know that voice all too well.

When I turn to see who it is, my whole world tilts. It's like when a wave unexpectedly crashes, flipping you over yourself, head over feet. Nausea again. I don't know which way is up or down, but I do know who's standing right there in a gray suit.

"Hi, kiddo," Dustin says.

"Hey," I reply with as much snap as I can muster.

Lulu's arms drop by her sides, but mine remain crossed over my chest, like a shield.

"Hi," Lulu says, shooting her hand out. "Lulu. Local nosy person."

"Dustin," he answers.

His eyes flick down to her lips and back up, and my back straightens instantly.

Sure don't like that.

"Marina worked for me out in California."

"Why are you doing introductions like you're a stranger? You're the mayor's son," Lulu points out through a scoffing laugh. "Who *doesn't* know you?"

He chuckles. "I suppose."

"Well, I'm her current boss," Lulu says, rising to the tips of her toes and back down, as if proud of it.

Dustin's eyes swivel to me with owl-like precision. "Friends with your bosses here too, huh?"

He's saying it like we ended on excellent terms, like I signed the termination paperwork with a smile on my face and a skip in my step. But it's not like I can call him out for the unspoken lie. Nothing I can say would make me not seem like the jerk here. Plus, I can't make a scene in Peg Leg Press in the middle of the day. Not in Bobbi's establishment.

"So, how've you been?" Dustin asks me, jutting out his elbow to nudge mine.

"Fantastic," I answer through gritted teeth.

"Fantastic? Wow. If Never Harbor's that great, I'm happy I came back." He eyes Lulu. "Place to be, right?"

"Why *are* you back?" I ask.

He pockets his hands, leaning back on his heels. "Wanted to make sure everything goes well."

Something feels off about that answer. Fishy.

"You should come to The Hideaway later," Lulu suggests. "That'll give you a real town welcome."

"Only if you promise to meet me there?" Dustin says.

Lulu's lips part then tilt up into a smile.

My stomach drops, and I feel sick again. I swallow.

I want to tell her exactly what happened. I'm usually good with words. But now, I feel so frozen, so helpless as we step forward in line again. I'm practically sweating when Bobbi sees me and smiles, and I'm even clammier after Dustin steps between us.

"I'll take a coffee," he interjects. "And I've got theirs too."

My head spins around.

"No," I demand.

"No?" Lulu asks, eyebrows cinched in.

"No?" Bobbi adds. She eyes Dustin suspiciously. "Well, if the lady says no …"

And thankfully, with a subtle wink, she takes my card instead before quickly looking away.

My stomach churns.

I haven't spent nearly enough time with Bobbi since I got back. I've never considered that maybe she feels uncomfortable about dating my dad—maybe as much as I do with interrupting their established routine.

Does she think I didn't live with them to avoid her?

The nausea builds.

Bobbi frowns. "You okay, Marina?"

"Yes, I'm fine." I blink repeatedly. *Is the world underwater?*

I watch as Dustin pulls out his wallet to pay for his own drink. I watch every single motion, how he strokes a thumb over the back of his leather wallet, how his eyes trace across my cheeks, and how he, not so subtly, steals a glance at Lulu.

I stand closer to Lulu like some bodyguard.

"Sure you're okay?" Lulu whispers to me, rubbing a hand over my arm. I didn't realize I had goose bumps.

"Yeah, I'm fine."

We get our drinks a couple of minutes later, and unfortunately, Dustin does as well.

"So, where are you headed?" he asks, falling in step beside us.

Ugh.

"Back to work," I answer dully.

"Ah, Florally Yours."

I narrow my eyes. How dare he know where I'm at nowadays.

He lazily brings his coffee up to his lips. "You look angry, Starkey."

I don't like when he calls me Starkey. It doesn't sound nearly as nice as when Cassidy does it.

"Why are you really in Never Harbor?" I snap.

I've never talked to Dustin like this. Then again, he was always my boss. But now, he's just a man. A snotty mayor's son outside a small-town coffee shop who thinks he can get whatever he wants.

I'm irritated and weirdly sweaty.

"The new wine label is important to me," he says. "The mixer is going to help promote that. And I mean, c'mon, kiddo ... don't you know that being in Never Harbor is important to *me* too?" he says, taken aback.

But he's faking it. He's such a fake, fake liar.

Lulu's hand lands on my shoulder again. "Hey ..."

My head feels like it's swimming. And when he gives me a nod and a subtle glance at Lulu, I realize I don't like how he stares at the girl I once babysat. I dislike even more how red her cheeks get afterward.

But what do I even say? How do I explain our history?

"Don't do that," I say to Dustin. "Don't—"

Lulu touches my arm again. "Okay ... Marina, you look terrible."

I *feel* terrible.

But I have to tell her exactly why he fired me. I don't care if I say it in front of him.

My words are jumbled. Caught in my throat.

I feel sick to my stomach.

Suddenly, I'm heaving forward.

Then, I puke all over Dustin Barrie's nice leather shoes.

Chapter Nineteen

THE EXORCISM OF MARINA STARKEY

Cassidy

After Lulu calls, it takes less than two minutes for me to leave work. I push through the community center's double doors with so much force that the wind tries to fight me back.

I kick open the townhome door when I arrive. Lulu is in the kitchen, picking up her keys.

"How is she?" I ask.

"Not too hot. I told her you're next on duty."

Marina's quivering voice floats from the bathroom. "Cass?"

"Marina?" I call out.

Lulu pats my back and heads out. I barely say goodbye before making a beeline down the hallway. Plastic bags crinkle in my fist from my quick pharmacy run. Ted, our pharmacist, looked scared at how quickly I threw items in my basket, and he rang me up in likely record time.

I hear a groan behind the bathroom door. It's cracked, so I gently push in. Marina is curled on the floor in just a tank top and panties, knees tucked around the toilet's base. Her wavy blonde hair pools on the tiles, held back in a loose ponytail with frizzy strands framing her ashen face. She blinks up at me, and it's so pathetically sweet.

"Hey, pretty girl," I coo. She groans in response, and I chuckle. "I brought some things that will hopefully help—"

Suddenly, Marina grabs the edge of the toilet and hoists herself up.

I dump the bags to the floor, land on my knees, and grab a fistful of her hair right before she begins sacrificing everything she's eaten in the past three months to the porcelain gods.

"There we go. Let it out." I stroke her back.

"I'm so sorry," she whines into the toilet.

"Don't be."

She sniffs and chokes on a sob. "I'm disgusting."

"Impossible. You're a knockout."

"I smell like fish."

I tilt my head side to side. "If anyone can pull off fishy perfume, it's you."

"I think it was the leftovers."

I can't help but laugh. She groans then pukes again. I continue to stroke my hand across her back over the next minute or two as a borderline exorcism is performed in our bathroom.

I sit down on the tiles behind her, spreading out my thighs on either side of her waist to cage her in near the toilet. I remove her turquoise hair tie, separate her long waves into three strands, and start to braid down her back.

"What are you doing?" she mumbles.

"Getting your hair out of your face."

"You know how to braid?"

"Your hair is thicker and longer than Bonnie's, but yeah. I've had practice with a little sister."

"Oh," she mutters. "Thank you."

We sit in comfortable silence, her head hanging limp in the toilet as my fingers thread through her wavy strands. I've always wondered what her hair would feel like, and I'm not surprised it's angelically soft.

Occasionally, Marina heaves. I hold her hair and rub circles over her spine, repeating the motion again and again.

"Let it all out."

"I don't wanna," she moans.

"I know."

"I puked on Dustin Barrie's shoes."

"Good aim."

Once the demon expulsion sounds subside, I tear off some toilet paper and hand it to her. She wipes her mouth. I tie off the braid and lay it across her back.

"Would you like saltines or toast?" I ask.

"Neither."

"I'm gonna ask you to at least try something. I also bought ginger ale," I say, leaning back to dig through the plastic bags. "It doesn't actually make you feel any better, but Ma always got it for us."

She whispers, "Mine did too."

"See? There you go. The placebo effect will work on you then. How are you feeling?"

"Empty."

"Good enough to maybe abandon the porcelain throne for a while?"

After a moment, she silently nods in agreement.

"All right, then hang tight. I'll be gentle, okay?"

I stand, lower down to a squat, and hook my arm under her knees and another behind her back to carry her in my arms to the living room. My sofa isn't great for overnight sleep, but boy, does it feel good when you're sick in front of the television.

I set her down on the cushions. Marina instantly curls into a tight ball. But that's when I notice a sick stain on her shirt.

I cringe. "We should get you out of this tank top."

"I already took my pants off."

Chuckling, I respond, "I know. And you did great, honey. But let's get you a new shirt too, okay?"

I barely hear a, "Mmkay."

I walk back to the bedroom and rummage through my closet to pull out an old 2016 Never Harbor Music Festival tee. It's hard not to reminisce on better days, to think about Dustin's changes to the mixer and how many other things seem to be changing as well. But when I get back to the living room and see Marina's knees pulled up to her chest, I don't want to linger on Dustin or so-called better days.

She sees me approaching and slowly sits up.

"All right, hands up."

"I'm not wearing a bra."

"I know," I admit. "I'll close my eyes, okay?"

She weakly nods. I reach down to grab the hem of her shirt. I forgot how smooth her skin is—how it feels like silk against my calluses. Swallowing, I start to edge it up, and just as I see the start of her breasts—the beautiful curve of the underside—I do as I promised. I shut my eyes.

I pull the shirt over her head and throw it to the side. Blindly, I locate the new tee on the arm of the sofa and shake it out to find the hem. I scrunch it so the arm holes are easily navigable, then hold it out.

"I'm gonna try to find your hands now, all right?"

I think I hear her swallow. "You can look if it's easier," she sheepishly whispers. "I don't care."

I freeze in place. I've thought about her body a lot, not just the breasts, but also the long torso, the line that must dip between her ribs, and the flat surface just above her belly button. The thought of seeing her, of viewing what must be perky pink nipples, is all too tempting. But despite my desperation and with all my willpower, I don't look.

"I promised I wouldn't."

My hands bump against her raised ones as I poise the shirt over her head. I slide it over her fingers, guiding them through the arm holes and tugging the hem down. My knuckles nudge the soft curve of her breasts, and it almost kills me to think about it, but I continue the rest of the way without stopping.

When I open my eyes, she's blinking up at me.

I give her a smile, which she slowly returns.

"Thanks," she murmurs.

"Anytime."

She lowers back down to the cushions, pulling her knees up to her chest once more.

"Be right back, okay?"

She nods in the pillow, and I leave, grabbing the trash can from the bathroom to place in front of the sofa. I drag the comforter and a few pillows from the bedroom and tuck them around her. In the kitchen, I prep toast with a thin layer of peanut butter and crack open a can of ginger ale. I place it on the side table next to her, then grab the remote.

She tentatively takes a bite. "Aw, I made you butcher your PB&J, Curly."

"Nah, a good chef knows how to alter his recipes. Now, let's see …" I browse through various streaming services before navigating to the show at the top of my mind.

For the first time in ten minutes, Marina tips her pretty lips into a smile.

"How'd you remember I like *Survivor*?"

I shrug. "I remember stuff. Now, if you need anything, let me know."

She sits up. "Wait, where are you going?"

I halt in the doorway. "I was gonna hang out in the bedroom. Give you some space."

Marina slowly shakes her head, then lifts up the opposite side of the comforter, murmuring weakly, "I don't want space. Stay with me?"

She looks so delicate like this. Dark, sunken circles creep beneath her eyes. Color is only just returning to her cheeks. But she looks at me like I'm holding the stars and she wants to borrow a bit of their sparkle.

"As long as you promise to eat," I say, smiling as I take the offered comforter.

I slide under it until I bump against her body. Her feet touch my thighs, and I immediately pull in a hiss.

"God, your toes are cold." Lifting up my thigh, I drag both her feet beneath me and sit back down. "I'll be your heater. No worries."

The smile she returns is worth every inch of frostbite I'll get.

"Thanks," she says.

"Always," I tell her because saying *anytime* now feels so insignificant. I'd do this with Marina whenever she asked.

We sit there for the rest of the afternoon—Marina occasionally sipping ginger ale and me stroking her back, hands, and feet. Even though we chose a random season of *Survivor*, she still knows everyone, spilling facts like an encyclopedia of reality television.

When a contestant says, "I'm not here to make friends," she mouths it along with them.

By the evening, we've fallen asleep on our lumpy, uncomfortable sofa together.

- *Chapter Twenty* -
SECRETS

Marina

Forty-eight hours later, I'm finally shuffling my way back to Floral-ly Yours, just in time for Never Harbor High's graduation to creep up in a few days. Lulu and I are running a little behind, to say the least.

She's been operating the shop on her own. When I get back, the storage is a little messy, and paperwork has piled up, but overall, the plants are fine. Everything is just how I left it. Something that is undeniably new though is Lulu's attachment to her phone.

I peer over her shoulder, but she jerks it away from my eyesight.

"Who's the boy?" I joke with a grin.

She bites her lip.

"Oh, wait, I'm right? It's a guy?"

"He's nobody. We're just talking," she says.

"Ooh, is nobody cute?"

"I'm just thanking him."

"For a lovely night?" I tease.

She pushes my arm, and I laugh. "No, he helped me while you were gone, is all."

I halt mid-watering-can pour. "Wait, someone came here to help?"

"Yeah, but he was just being nice."

"Uh-huh. The mystery man. In our shop."

"Don't be weird about it."

I snort. "We have a cash register, Lu. I have to be a little weird about it."

I'm not upset, but I feel a bit protective of this place now. Having a stranger in here feels … *wrong.* But aren't I a stranger for the summer?

"It was only a couple of hours." She places her phone to the side with a smirk. "Just trust me, okay? Now, are we planning graduation or not?"

Another conversation for another time, it seems.

I laugh. "So testy."

Lulu rolls her eyes, and we continue prepping graduation arrangements between the influx of customers. After closing the shop late afternoon, I join Cassidy down Main to spread flyers. Pinning the paper brings me eye to eye with the headline—*Never Harbor's First Annual Wine Mixer.*

"Blegh," I sneer.

Cassidy laughs, but the boyishness fades off. "Yeahhh."

"Has he come to a meeting yet?"

"Nah."

Dustin Barrie apparently stalks everywhere in Never Harbor, except for where he should be—in mixer planning meetings. The past two nights have been consumed by small venting sessions as we lay in bed, Cassidy clenching his fists in irritation. Seeing my goldendoodle Cass mimic a rottweiler is both saddening and weirdly thrilling.

"I keep sending him emails with items for approval," he explains. "But I get nothing."

"Why's he even here then?" I ask, stapling a flyer to a telephone pole.

Cassidy digs through the box in his arms and hands me another flyer. "Laura says he's maintaining a *presence.*"

"To destroy the peace of Never Harbor?"

Cassidy laughs again. "Okay, he's annoying, not evil."

My eyes widen, as if to imply, *Maybe!*

He shakes his head with a smile, pointing to the bulletin board on the other side of the street. We cross, Cassidy hands me a pushpin, and I spear the paper into the cork with a decisive *schwick.*

"Watch it there, killer."

I twist on the heel of my sneaker. "You really don't think he's that bad?"

"I mean, he's a little full of himself. But we're getting things done even if he isn't involved. I can't be too upset." His face falls. "Plus, I don't have to talk to him."

I squint. "What happened between you two?"

Cassidy looks away, mouth open, on the verge of a laugh he can't seem to force out.

"He's never been too nice to me," he explains.

"Pardon?" I swear heat rises in my chest like fuel to my existing flame.

"It's fine. We've never understood each other, is what it is."

"Has he talked down to you?"

"It's whatever."

I shake my head. "No, it's not."

"You get so riled up, talking about him," Cassidy teases, handing me another flyer. "Sometimes, I feel like there's something *you're* not telling me."

That clams me up real quick. "It's nothing."

I haven't told Cassidy—or anyone—why I got fired. The last thing I want is people thinking differently of me. That I smiled too much or was too nice. I want to remain the carefree girl Cassidy, Lulu, and even Bonnie admires. That girl wouldn't have gotten fired.

"Sure it's nothing?" Cassidy asks.

I stab another flyer into the cork. "Absolutely nothing."

"That cork might disagree."

He places a palm on my shoulder, and his hand skims down my spine to rest at my lower back. I turn away to hide my giddy smile.

And it's so freaking giddy.

Ever since I was sick, Cassidy and I have been more casual with our touches. When I was sick, it was gentle. Caring. But now ... well, it's something different, but I don't dare address it.

If I talk about it, it might go away.

Cassidy and I deposit more promotional flyers around Main, dropping in shops along the way. We sample some ice cream; visit Moira's chandlery, where Cassidy helps her put a large box in storage; and finally say hi to Jukes at Jukes's Jambalaya. He insists we stay for dinner and that our bill is on the house.

"Your dad would kill me if I let you pay," he tells me, pinching my shoulder affectionately, like he's done since I was a kid.

My dad.

I haven't seen him in a couple of days. He dropped by the house when small-town gossip informed him I was sick, bringing heaps of ginger ale and crackers. But nothing since. I know he's busy with work, and I've been distracted too, haven't I?

Cassidy and I journey into another shop. He chats with the owner like they're best friends, but even during the conversation, he discreetly reaches out to tug on my skirt when I walk too far away. Cassidy is so entrenched in this community, and yet I'm the one person Mr. Never Harbor can't keep his hands away from.

I remind myself to stop smiling so freaking big.

We end our route at Rafe's screen print shop, right on the edge of Main. He's standing outside, one boot kicked against the brick wall and a limp cigarette between his fingers. He gestures to the bulletin board with a nod of his chin, as if anticipating our arrival.

"How's it going, Rafe?" Cassidy asks.

"Fine," is all he answers.

Cassidy waggles his finger. "One day, you'll say more than a single word to me."

"One day," he murmurs.

"Hey, that's two already."

Rafe smirks, bringing his cigarette to his lips. While Cassidy is large and rough, Rafe is lean and ethereally beautiful. His high cheekbones and heavily lidded eyes make him look tired, but in a lazy way an ancient god might appear bored. The black ink illustrated on his arms and neck harshly contrasts his beige skin. The blatant display of art makes me trust him more, probably a result of growing up with my dad's plethora of tattoos.

I pin a flyer to the bulletin board and peer in his shop to look at the colorful screen prints. They're the same posters I saw hanging in Maggie's clinic.

"These are beautiful."

He grabs a to-go cup of coffee from the ledge and tips it to me. "Take a look around."

"Four words," Cassidy adds, then sniffs. "Wait, is that licorice coffee? God, that got around fast."

"He wasn't talking to you," I say, sticking out my tongue.

Cassidy reaches out as if to grab my tongue, but I pull it back in. I poke it out again, he whips out his hand, and then we repeat the game. Both of us descend into laughter.

I pinch Cassidy's side. He pinches back. And then, suddenly, he picks me up, hoisting me over his shoulder with a laugh. The flyers in my hand flutter down to the open cardboard box. He dips down to pick it up with one hand, carrying both me and the box down the sidewalk.

"Wait, Cass, no!" I say through giggles. "We have to put the flyers up!"

"Nah, we got 'em all."

He thuds down the wooden ramp toward the rocky shore. "Cass!"

I can't stop laughing as he deposits the box on the rocky beach, then slowly wades us into the ocean with our clothes still on.

My dress billows in the breeze until it catches the surface of the water. The hem darkens, the stain of soaked water spreading up the back like inky blotches until I'm up to my shoulders. Then, he throws me under.

It's quiet under the water. Peaceful. Cool. But where Cassidy's hands still grip my waist are full of heat. Protective. Exciting.

I swim back to the surface. Cassidy is mid-laugh, head thrown back and boisterous. I crawl up his chest like he's a jungle gym, pushing his shoulders with my palms, dunking him underwater.

He resurfaces, shaking out his curls. They slap his forehead and send sprays of water onto my cheeks. His shirt sticks to his hard chest, the white of his tee now see-through, highlighting each ridge of his abs and curve of his collarbone. I'm ashamed by how long my gaze lingers.

I distract myself by leaning back and floating on the surface, eyes turned toward the cloudy sky instead. Cassidy joins me.

I can feel my nipples pebbling against the thin fabric as wind gusts over us. My dress gathers in a mess at the area between my thighs. Suddenly, I wonder how appropriate this is, given our situation. I glance over to find Cassidy staring at me.

"Cass?"

He snaps his eyes up to mine.

So, I'm not the only one sneaking glances.

I notice he's floating away, so I reach out, cupping his palm in mine. Water laps between our arms when I tug him closer. I realize I don't want him to leave my side. Or maybe I'm scared that he will.

"We'll be like otters," I say by way of an excuse. "They hold hands, so they don't get lost from their friend."

He smiles. "I'd love to be an otter with you, Starkey."

"Perfect." The word leaves me on a breath, and I close my eyes to the echoes it leaves in my mind.

Perfect.

I start to hum to myself, an absentminded ballad. It leads us into amiable silence. After a few minutes—could be five or twenty, I don't know—Cassidy finally speaks.

"So, tell me your game plan for the graduation."

"I'm still waiting on the all clear from the principal."

"I bet I know why he's taking his time."

I look over, and Cassidy flashes me that dimpled smile.

"Do you have secrets, Davies?"

"You know I do. Want to hear?"

"Of course."

My heart beats faster, nerves sparking through my body enough that I give Cassidy's palm a gentle squeeze. Because even though there's plenty to worry about—the flower shop, Dustin Barrie, or even where the end of this summer might take me—my mind is focused on something else entirely.

All the frustration, all the worries of the day, float out with the tide as I lie in the sun and gossip, and the undeniable sensation I've been denying washes over me.

Want.

I want Cassidy Davies.

- *Chapter Twenty-One* -
SHOWER THOUGHTS

Cassidy

The night before my sister's graduation, I attend our usual Friday night family dinner. Marina doesn't come; she and Lulu are too busy finalizing arrangements at Florally Yours. But my mind drifts in her absence.

The wisps of hair separating over her face in the breeze. Her freckled cheeks. Her plump lips, sometimes parted, as if anticipating something from me—a laugh or a look—maybe just the way my eyes roam over her, which I cannot stop doing for the life of me.

I think about the way her hand slips so easily into mine.

How maybe we could slip just as easily together.

"Where's Marina tonight?" Wendy asks.

I swallow, coming back to reality with my siblings mulling around in the front yard. It's the twenty-minute goodbye ritual, having started in the kitchen after dinner and traveling to our cars. Jasper was two seconds away from closing his car door, but Ma barely mentioned dessert to Sam, and he went running back in the house. Jasper's head fell back on the seat with a groan. Now, another ten minutes later, Wendy is sitting next to me on the porch with Jasper lurking like a gargoyle beside her.

"Huh?" I ask.

"Marina?" Jasper reminds me, leaning against the porch railing with his arms crossed.

"Oh." I blink. "Working."

I smile to myself. I love seeing her among the plants. I have an Eve-like fantasy of her with just a single plant covering her, and if I just push it aside—

Wendy grins. "Did we interrupt your daydreams?"

I scoff. "I'm not daydreaming."

She holds her hands up. "Sorry, *fantasizing*."

"That's not—" I look at Jasper for reassurance, but all he does is shrug. I sputter out a laugh. "I'm not fantasizing about anything."

"Right. Your face definitely doesn't transform when we talk about your roomie."

I link my fingers together and shake my head. I try to make my laugh casual. "Yeah, she's gorgeous. I'm not blind. But nothing is happening."

Except for my massive crush.

Except that I think about her constantly.

Except that I keep imagining her soaking wet dress draped over her perfect figure.

"I don't believe you," Wendy says. "You can't wait to get home to her. Come on. Details, please."

Jasper nudges Wendy with the toe of his boot. "Cass doesn't have to talk about it."

She pinches the knee of his jeans, tugging on the fabric. "Not everyone keeps everything inside, like you," she teases.

He scrunches his nose with a playful smile. Wendy's elementary school teacher demeanor is exactly what he needed in his life.

But Wendy is right.

I cannot wait to get home to my girl.

No, my friend. My roommate. Not *my* girl. That's ridiculous.

But that thought follows me as I take the footpaths home—dirt trails with backyards on one side and tall grass overlooking the sea on the other. It's silent, as Never Harbor always is. But my mind is loud as hell.

I walk through the townhome front door, scuffing my shoes on the mat Marina recently purchased saying *hello!* while *goodbye!* is upside down on the opposite side. She knows how to make this place a home, and I've never enjoyed coming back to it as much as I have lately.

I silently shut the door behind me. Shower water is running. She must have just gotten home. I'm surprised to not hear her singing, like she normally does. I miss the hums.

I toe off my shoes and walk down the hall. I raise my fist to knock on the bathroom door, but a low sound halts me before my knuckles hit the wood.

Wait——

Then hear it again.

It's a breathy, whining moan.

All the blood in my body rushes up my neck and to my head. I feel lightheaded.

Marina hisses in a gasp. The thump of water on the shower floor gets rhythmic.

For a moment I consider whether someone else is in there with her, but I only hear Marina's sounds.

Is she touching herself? How long has she been doing this?

I swallow, taking a step back from the door.

She thinks she's home alone. I can't listen to this. This is such an invasion of her privacy. My eavesdropping is breaking too many unspoken agreements between us. We're roommates. We're friends. She's my landlord's only daughter.

"Yes," she moans. "Please."

You've got to be kidding me.

I can't handle this.

I walk backward in the bedroom across the hall, slowly pulling the door shut but leaving a small crack so the snick doesn't echo through the house.

But why? She should know I'm here. I should be making *more* noise. Instead, I'm frozen like a statue, staring at the blank wall with my hands flexing out, then back.

The thumping shower water picks up speed. And suddenly—

"Yes, I'm all yours, Cassidy."

Holy. Fucking. Shit.

I don't know what happens next. Not really. I'm a man driven by lust and want and everything in between. I'm a caveman, blinded by my name leaving her beautiful lips.

I tuck a thumb in the waist of my gym shorts and pull them down just enough so my cock bobs out into my palm. I'm hard as a rock, thick veins bulging down my pelvis and pulsing around the length of me. The tip is already beet red, twitching to burst.

It's embarrassing. Torturous.

No.

I can't. I can't do it.

"Yes," she hisses. "Yes, Cass."

I don't know what fantasy Cassidy is coaxing out of her, but real-life Cassidy is at his wits' end.

So, well … fuck it, I guess.

I clutch my cock and pump.

The thrill is instantaneous. My stomach leaps to my chest, and the groan I can't hold back rumbles low in my throat. I grip myself harder, to the point where it's nearly painful but the tightness is just right—exactly how I imagine her to feel.

I close my eyes. I can see her almost clear as day. On all fours on the bed. I'm standing behind her, my palm stroking over the round globes of her ass. I reach back and slap it.

As if on cue, real-life Marina moans from the shower.

Fuck me.

I run my cock along the outside of her, the wetness coating me. She *would* be wet, wouldn't she? Dripping even.

"That's right. So ready for me." I imagine the words leaving my mouth.

I lick my dry lips, letting out a small pant as she responds, *"Always."*

Always.

I lower down onto my knees behind her and bury my face between her thighs. I consume her. Allow her to wet my face. I can't imagine how she'd taste, but it must be sweet.

I imagine her pushing back against my face, bucking, and I go until she seems on the edge. I rise back up, settling my palm in the dip of her waist, my fingers pressing into the top of her thighs.

"Lean back, pretty girl."

I guide her hips back and imagine as, slowly, inch by inch, I disappear inside her. Tight. Wet. Warm.

I thrust my hips forward into my palm and groan.

It's almost too real. Or maybe I've just been depriving myself for too long. I haven't come since Marina moved in—not when my thoughts kept drifting to her each time I tried to touch myself. Her flawless body, now owned by me in my fantasy. Her pink cheeks, now flushed as she looks over her shoulder at me. Her soft exhale as I sink deeper.

I'm pumping wildly now. My other palm is keeping me upright against the wall as I lean forward. My knees are weak. My legs shake.

"I'm close," Marina whines from the bathroom.

Damn.

I look around. I don't have a trash can in here. I don't have condoms either. So, instead, with a cringe, I choose the last resort. Old faithful. I snatch a sock from my dresser drawer and slide it halfway up my cock.

Not my proudest moment.

But the moment I'm thrusting again, I don't care that much. I think I black out, honestly. My back is turned to the door as my palm races over my cock. My breathing is heavy and labored. My teeth gritted as each movement is hell on earth. Rough and wonderful and so overdue.

In my mind, we're moving the bed. The springs whine. The bedpost creaks. My mind is so loud that it almost feels real, like the sound is in the room with me. I'm drowning in my fantasy.

Then, it rushes out. I barely have time to process it. With a whine of my own, I empty into the godforsaken sock for what feels like forever, left flushed and weak.

When I come to, when my ears stop ringing and the fantasy fades, that's when I realize the shower water is off.

My stomach drops.

No.

I rip the sock off, throw it in the clothes hamper, and try to steady my breathing.

How long has she been out?

I peek through the cracked door. The bathroom door is still closed. She's humming to herself.

She seems relaxed.

Please, God, tell me she has no idea.

"Hey, uh, Marina?" I say, clearing the roughness from my throat. "I'm home."

"Oh! Hi, Cass!" Her response is instant. Almost shaky. Embarrassed.

No. There's no way she heard me. She's just flustered because of her own session. Not me.

Please not because of me.

"How, uh, how was your graduation prep?"

"Good!" The word is almost a squeak.

"Good. Hey, you wanna maybe watch *Survivor*?" I ask.

I'm babbling. I don't know what else to say. I'm panicking.

"Yeah," she answers. "Mmhmm. Sounds great, Cass. Whatever you want."

"Whatever you want."

Because, apparently in her fantasies, she's mine, isn't she?

I bite my fist to hold in my groan.

She's making it hard to keep my promise to her dad. And I don't know how much resolve I have left in me.

Chapter Twenty-Two

WHAT AM I GONNA DO WITH YOU?

Marina

I saw him.

I saw Cassidy Davies masturbating.

And I'm pretty sure no other man, or any version of the filthiest porn I could search for, will ever live up to that sight.

It was perfection.

At least until I realized he must have heard me too.

Oh God, the mortification. The guilt. The *shame*. Just thinking about it gives me full-body shivers.

I was home alone. I assumed he'd be gone for hours, and I was taking advantage of my time alone. Don't ask me why, but something about moaning out loud while masturbating makes the whole experience ten times more enjoyable. I don't know the science behind it or if it's just me who loves it, but if I can moan, I'm gonna moan.

I came hard too. I came to the thought of Cassidy Davies. I lived out the fantasy that'd been bouncing in my head for so long now—a demanding other side to that golden retriever of a man. I bet he's a giver. But I'd love him to be a taker as well.

I got out of the shower, fully satisfied and ready to conquer a few more weeks of living with Mr. Muscles, when I heard a noise.

I froze.

Sometimes, I hear things in the house. A creak, a door shutting from the breeze … it's the natural settling of a house near the shore, affected by waves and sand and whatever else over time. But I was raised by my dad, who taught me nobody is to be trusted, including houses. Being the independent woman that I am, I snatched the toilet bowl brush and snuck out of the bathroom, still naked and prepared to knock anyone over the head if necessary.

But then a small moan came from the bedroom. I tiptoed closer. The door was cracked enough for me to peer in.

I wasn't prepared.

I saw Cassidy, facing away from the door, head thrown back in ecstasy, exhaling rhythmic sighs as his large arm pumped back and forth. It took me a second to register what was happening, but once I did, I couldn't look away.

My pulse skyrocketed. Goose bumps skittered over every inch of my naked body. My heartbeat traveled immediately between my thighs.

I watched as Cassidy's massive biceps flexed and strained against his T-shirt; his forearm, roped with veins, jerked back and forth; and his large thighs quivered as he thrust into what I had to imagine was his palm.

I'll be honest; I shuffled to a different vantage point to try and catch a glimpse of something more, but I wasn't so lucky. I was, however, lucky enough to be granted a small, whining groan again.

Gorgeous.

He moved faster. Pumped harder. Shivers visibly rolled down his spine.

A large exhale.

I bolted back to the bathroom. I tried to act natural. I tried humming—I know I do that too often—but I couldn't recover from the whole thing.

It didn't register with me, until I was humming to myself, that Cassidy must have heard *me* too.

Oh God, no.

Cassidy had heard me. My moans. His *name*. Oh God, I'd said his *name.*

Wait . . .

Did he touch himself because he'd heard me?

He must have.

Cassidy Davies couldn't help himself. Because of *me.*

We were both quiet all night. I kept stealing a glance at him on the couch.

I know he knows. Does he know I know? Or does he know I know he knows?

We went to sleep side by side in deathly silence.

And now, I'm supposed to work? Like nothing happened?

It's Never Harbor High's graduation ceremony, and I'm struggling to pay attention to anything but the memories of last night.

Lulu and I arrived early while they loaded folding chairs onto the football field. We placed flower arrangements down the aisles and on stage—wreaths and garlands with accents of baby's breath and hydrangeas. Throughout the ceremony, we stood on the side, handing small corsages to the graduating class of around fifty people. Our whole contribution was likely excessive, but I wanted to blow my first big event out of the water. I was proud to see my alma mater in such lush foliage and vibrant petals.

The only thing that crushed the energy was Dustin's speech. He was the guest speaker—because *of course he was*. Rumor is, his dad had pushed him to do it since he was conveniently in town. I wonder what other things he and his dad are talking about behind closed doors and if that's why he's still here. After a few handshakes and glances toward the audience, he left as quick as he came. But not before slinking by to wave at Lulu.

Ass.

Nothing—not even Dustin—could steal the ceremony's magic though. When Bonnie crossed the stage, the Davies clan erupted in cheers. Mr. and Mrs. Davies were leading the charge with a drumstick clanging a cowbell; Peter gave a loud crow; Jasper, Wendy, and Sam shook homemade maracas; Milo and Cassidy whistled through their fingers; and The Twins shot firecrackers in the air, and their mother promptly snatched the rest away.

Her, "*Where did you get those?!*" echoed over the football field.

After the closing remarks and caps are thrown, I look around.

I know who I'm searching for.

And he finds me.

Cassidy crosses the football field with a grin plastered on his face.

I stiffen at the memory of his flexing arms. The moans.

Maybe it's the nerves from last night or the excitement from a successful day, but I run over and hug him. Those same beautifully filthy arms wrap around me. He picks me up, twirling me on the spot, sending my dress flying in the wind around me. By the time my sneakers hit the ground, I can barely breathe.

He came straight to me. I don't know if anyone has ever chosen me first.

"You did fantastic," he says, gripping my waist in his palms, sending butterflies fluttering up my throat.

I laugh, gesturing to the open field, laden with crushed flowers and plant leaves. "I mean, I think it went well, right?"

"It was *amazing*," he says.

I shove his shoulder. He grunts, and the heady moans from last night replay again.

I've got to pull it together.

"Ugh, get a room," Lulu says beside us with a wink. I forgot she was standing there. "By the way, my parents texted and said they wanna hop on a call with us tomorrow. Touch base on this whole thing."

I beam. "Really?"

Cassidy strokes a single finger up the back of my arm, and I shiver. "Hey, that sounds fun."

He can't do stuff like that anymore. He can't.

Lulu rolls her eyes. "Sounds *boring*. It'll probably be typical shop stuff."

"It'll be fine," I say. "We can handle it."

"Hey, come take pictures with me, loser!" Bonnie calls over to Lulu.

Lulu looks at me pleadingly.

I shoo her off. "Go. I'll clean up."

"I promise I'll be back in time to load the van."

"I'm not worried. Go be with your best friend."

Cassidy eyes me as I start to stack vases in my arms. "Need help packing up?"

"Oh. No, you don't have to. You're here with family."

The wind blows, and strands from my braid frame my face in an erratic, wispy mess. I sputter to blow them away, but then it happens.

It.

In what feels like slow motion, Cassidy reaches out with a steady hand and tucks a strand of my hair behind my ear. It's like déjà vu. Except this touch isn't greedy like Dustin's attempt, but instead gentle. Caring. Adjusting hair that needs to be moved rather than using it as an excuse to get closer. Cassidy doesn't clumsily flirt. It's all with good intention.

I blink up at him, still feeling the warmth of his palm near my face. I inhale and let it out shakily. But I want him to do it again. All of it.

Near the chain-link fence separating the field from the bleachers,

Wendy glances over at us. I give a small wave; she returns it. When Cassidy shoots a look at her, she immediately looks away.

Bonnie jumps on Milo's back, holding her diploma above her head. Lulu snaps a photo of them, making some joke about jumping on Milo's back too. All three of them laugh.

"Best friends connected at the hip," Cassidy observes with a crooked smile.

"I never had that," I say. "I mean, my dad was my best friend. Does that count?"

"Of course it does."

"A real best friend might have been nice too, I guess. Less … old and hairy."

He laughs. "You've got a roommate who likes you. Is that good enough?"

Gently, just like before, Cassidy slides his palm into mine, first from my wrist down to cup my hand.

"Yeah, my roommate is better than good enough," I answer.

He gives a squeeze before disconnecting our palms. I instantly miss his touch the moment it's gone.

Suddenly, I'm thinking less about last night and more about *him*.

His softness. His kindness. His support.

I'm not just attracted to Cassidy; I like him.

A lot.

We gather up arrangements from the stage, including discarded bouquets on the ground and various petals I can repurpose into potpourri.

"Let me take that," Cassidy says every time I hold more than one vase at a time. He's to the point of balancing eight, so I twirl away.

I giggle. "We'll drop off what we have."

"Want me to get Lu?"

I look around for my helper, who is still at the fence, taking pictures with her best friend. "No. I'll let them enjoy today."

"Celebrate before the real world hits, huh?"

I laugh. "I don't know. The real world hasn't been so bad lately."

His eyes relax. I've never met a man who can truly smile through only his eyes. "It hasn't, has it?"

We walk across the field, where we'll likely be photo-bombing about fifty family memories. We pass discussions about college or summer jobs or vacations, all greeted with unrivaled optimism that only comes from recent high school graduates.

"I remember when the world seemed so much bigger than it is now," I admit.

Cassidy adjusts the vases in his arms. "Oh, yeah?"

"Everything felt possible after high school. I could've been easily convinced I'd end up at NASA and go to the moon."

"Did you want to be an astronaut?"

I laugh. "No."

Cassidy attempts to nudge open the gate, but his arms overflow with vases. I roll my eyes with a laugh, opening it for him instead.

"Try a little less to be helpful for once," I joke.

"Never," he argues.

He gives me space to slide through, then follows behind. We stroll around the bleachers, passing Bonnie, who's now taking pictures with her mom, who mirrors her daughter's pose of a peace sign held in the air. I wish I'd had that on my graduation day. Sometimes, I wonder how I'll be as a mom one day. I want to be so much more than what I had. The Davies kids got lucky.

"Cass!" Bonnie calls to us. "Come here! It's your picture time!"

"I'll be back!" Cassidy yells over to her. "Let me drop these off!"

"Hurry!" she yells back.

I pick up my pace, but Cassidy shakes his head.

"Don't bother. Bonnie thinks everything is an emergency. Gets it from Dad. I swear she could drive an ambulance and be happy."

"Maybe she should. Or a rocket."

"Ah, so the astronaut dream is alive."

"The world is her oyster."

"She wants to go to art school," he says. "If it were up to her, she would have graduated yesterday. She's always in a hurry to grow up."

"Who isn't at that age?"

He shrugs. "I sure wasn't. What did you want to do after graduation?"

I pull in a large inhale. "Well, I majored in botany and chemistry in undergrad."

"Oh, that's right."

"And pharmacy school was the end goal. But honestly, I just wanted to play in the dirt."

He chuckles. "You and your plants."

"Pharmacy seemed so boring in comparison."

We journey under the bleachers, shadowed from the metal seats above. Without the sun beating down, it's a little cooler and breezier, like a small wind tunnel gusting past my ankles, trailing to my abandoned worktable. The setup is exactly as I left it—messy with unused packing materials, scissors, and spare plants with bits of leaves discarded to the ground.

"What did you want to do when you graduated high school, Davies?" I ask.

"I wanted to play professional football."

"And now?"

"Not that," Cassidy deadpans with a barking laugh. "Definitely not that."

I set down my load, and one by one, I remove the bundles of clattering vases from Cassidy's arms.

"So, what is your dream now?" I ask.

"I don't have one."

"Lies," I whisper.

He glances down at me with a crooked grin.

"Come on. What is it? Think big."

It takes him a second, huffing out a strangled exhale before hemming and hawing.

"Curly ..."

"Fine, yeah, okay, maybe having my own personal training business would be cool." He says it reluctantly. "Just a recent thought."

"Oh, wow. You could absolutely do that."

He runs a rough palm through his hair. "Nah, I couldn't. I'm not good at this kind of stuff."

"What kind of stuff?"

"This," he says, gesturing to the table. "The stuff you're doing. Running a business and being the boss."

"Aren't you planning an entire festival?" I ask.

"With Laura's help."

"She's barely involved. You don't give yourself enough credit."

"I'm giving myself the right amount of credit," he says, emptying the rest of his armful onto the table. I watch his forearms flex with the motion. "I'm just hoping some of your hard work rubs off on me."

I click my tongue. "You want me rubbing off on you?" It slips out before I can stop it.

It's his biceps. The veins. The way his dimple appears after I say it. *Oh boy.*

Instead of laughing, like I expect him to, he lets out a very low, very heavy exhale.

Bad idea. Got it.

I quickly pace away from him, depositing the remainder of the vases on the table. I need to control myself. This is a tenuous tightrope we're balancing on, and I'm tempting fate. I'll fall if I'm not careful.

"You know, I used to sneak under here during football games," I say, changing the subject.

"That seems like a recipe for disaster."

I snort. "I was a cheerleader. I wanted to get away from the crowds for a second."

"I remember."

"Remember what?"

"The uniform." He smiles. "Like I could forget those short skirts."

I freeze. He's pushing the limits now too.

Playfully, I shove him, forcing out a laugh. "Pig."

Cassidy reaches up to cover the back of my hand, holding me there. His eyes soften, and it's like something in him—something delicate— turns. Clicks into place. Like a key unlocking a part of him I'm scared to face.

Cassidy Davies looks at me like he wants me.

I try to play it off with a laugh. "I never thought I was cool enough to be a cheerleader. Like it was an accident I got on the team."

"I don't like how you talk about yourself sometimes, Starkey."

I smile, but he doesn't. His eyes are hooded over.

"If I could be half the person your sister or Lulu thinks I am, I'd be golden," I continue to joke.

But he's not budging. Not looking away in shame like I want to. My heart is racing.

"You are," he says.

"I'm not—"

"What? Motivated?" he says. "Effortless? And gorgeous to boot?"

Underneath my palm, I can feel his heart beating in sync with my pulse.

"You think I'm gorgeous?" I ask.

He looks away, tonguing his cheek before swiveling his eyes back to me. "Come on. You know you're a total knockout, Starkey."

"Every night in bed with me, and you've never mentioned this," I joke. At least, it's supposed to be a tease, but the words barely make it past a whisper.

His eyebrows furrow inward. "Should I be mentioning it?"

And here we are.

The line neither of us wants to cross is abandoned.

We're hopping right over.

"Maybe," I exhale.

"I've tried not to," he admits.

"Why?" The word leaves before I can stop it, the devil on my shoulder driving me forward, just as his does the same. I don't want to tell that horny demon no. I want this.

Cassidy slowly, deliberately, rotates his palm in mine, adjusting our hands from cupping like shy teenagers to slowly fitting into the grooves, entwining our fingers together. It's more intimate, something I didn't know hand-holding could be until now.

"Why?" he echoes. "Because I won't be able to stop once I start."

He walks forward as I take a step back. My head bumps against the metal bleacher behind me. Cassidy's hand rises to cup behind my neck.

"Ouch," he says on a gentle laugh. "Did that hurt?"

I shake my head side to side. The only thing hurting is the tension in my bones, the way my skin feels like it'll burst from how my nerves are thrumming at a frequency that seems one beat away from a heart attack.

Cassidy's palm lowers from the back of my head to around my neck before rising to meet my cheek. His rough thumb traces over my jawline and down to my lips. I tilt my chin up, letting his thumb drag my bottom lip down along the way. It pops back up, and Cassidy pulls in a hissing breath.

Our hands remain linked, the only thing keeping my chest from hitting his with every deep inhalation. He leans closer. I can feel his lips hovering over mine, smelling like spearmint. I want to taste the toothpaste that's been teasing me every night. I want to feel how soft his lips actually are, then revel when his rough stubble cuts my chin.

I tilt my mouth higher, feeling his palm dip around my head, fingers coursing through locks of my hair tangled at the nape of my neck.

"Marina," he whispers, and the word zips down to my stomach, leaping between my thighs. It's a shot of adrenaline, a spark of a flame that's been unlit for far too long.

"Cass," I practically whine back, and he responds with a low grunt. But then another voice calls his name too.

"Cass!" Mrs. Davies calls from the fence. "Cass? Where'd you go?"

His mom's voice is like being slapped in the face with another eviction notice.

Cassidy rests his forehead against mine, hissing out the most pained, "Fuuuck," I've ever heard in my life.

I can't help but laugh as he nods against me.

"Right," he says on a low breath. "Family pictures."

"I should keep packing anyway."

He nods again, and I laugh at how his forehead rubs against mine. "Of course."

"Cass?" Maggie Davies yells again. "Are you back there?"

Cassidy groans and calls, "Yeah, Ma! Coming!"

I curl in my bottom lip and whisper, "Are you, Cass?"

"What?"

"Coming?" I finish.

His brown eyes shadow over, roaming down to my mouth and back up. The look could raze me to the ground. The corners of his mouth slowly perk up, indenting the familiar dimple.

"Would you like me to?" he murmurs.

"Only if I can watch."

A low groan rumbles in his throat. "Want me to come apart in front of you?"

I don't know what bold streak takes over, but I lean in. I let go.

"No," I amend. "I want you to come apart inside me."

Cassidy pushes against the metal seats behind my head and paces away. He runs a hand through his curly locks, choking out laughter. He points his index finger in my direction, shaking it as if thinking of what to say. I giggle at his frustration.

"What am I gonna do with you?" he asks. All I can do is shrug in response. He tongues the inside of his cheek, then gives the most boyish grin imaginable. Dimples and all. "Don't be cute."

"I'm not doing anything," I say innocently.

"No, you are," he says, stalking back to me. "You're doing so many things to me. Do you have any idea how often I think about that? About simply kissing you? Or, God, getting on my knees for you?"

"Like last night?"

His eyes widen before steadying once more. "Yes. Just like last night."

"You heard me," I say, but it isn't a question.

"Yes," he confirms. "I did. I heard ..." And he hesitates before taking a step closer, making us chest to chest. His mouth close to mine. "I heard *my* girl coming, is what I heard."

My body lights on fire, my heart shooting up to my brain, my knees weak.

"Cass—"

"Oh, I'm not finished."

That, combined with how his eyes take me in with possessive greed, has my mouth slamming shut. His palm buries in my hair. He sucks in a breath and slowly lets it out.

"God, I want to bury my head between those thighs of yours. I'd eat you so good, honey."

Cassidy leans closer. My heart ratchets into my throat as his lips nearly brush against mine.

"I'd eat you so good; you'd never want another man's tongue down there again."

When he pulls back, I realize just how heavily I'm breathing. His eyes scan me head to toe, to the way I'm practically in shock.

"You all right?" he asks.

"No."

"No?"

"Recovering," I confess with a grin. "Y'know, I like this demanding type of Cass."

He smirks. "I know."

I choke out a laugh. *Of course he does now.*

"Are you going to The Hideaway tonight? For the graduation party?"

"I might."

And Cassidy, in only the way he can, gives a command with a smile. "You'd better, Starkey."

- *Chapter Twenty-Three* -
THE INTENDED AUDIENCE

Cassidy

I'm a goner, and against my better judgment, I can't turn back now. It's too late.

Her siren song has captured me too well, and it's maddening to wait for her melodic voice to lull me over once more.

The Hideaway is humming with high energy. Graduates flood the top floor that Peter usually reserves for either family or over twenty-one visitors only. Tonight though, it's for Never Harbor High.

I wouldn't say it's the most exciting party. They're only serving non-alcoholic drinks, and it's a lot of awkward, hormone-charged interactions I wish I weren't witnessing.

I'm happy for my sister. Hell, she's happy enough for all of us combined, throwing her arms up on the dance floor to party songs and waving her drink around. But it's just not as fun without a certain someone.

All evening, I give obligatory laughs, make a toast when asked, and sip my drink. But I'm just biding my time, nodding and smiling, like maybe getting through yet another conversation will get me one step closer to Marina. I'm thankful I don't run into her dad. I have no idea how to explain this. I can barely explain it to myself.

Eventually, I'm leaning my forearms on the railing overlooking Crocodile Cove. I have my glass clutched in my fist, practically shaking in my grasp as I look down at my watch that can't seem to move past a snail's pace.

"You're acting different tonight," a voice observes.

I'm not surprised when my older brother Milo sidles up next to me with a pop in hand.

I force out a laugh. "No, I'm not."

He squints. "You're checking your watch. What are you waiting on?"

I give a little *psht*. "Nothing. I'm celebrating our sister."

"Our sister who doesn't care if anyone lives or dies here, except her best friend?"

We both laugh, watching Bonnie and Lulu dance together with their hands raised in the air around a circle of other locals. Bonnie's laughing with Lulu, only occasionally looking elsewhere. Though, when she does, her eyes snag the same area—the far corner of the porch where a plume of smoke billows in the air, arrowing down to the end of a cigarette held by Rafe, who stares back at my sister.

I glance at Milo the same time he looks at me.

"You saw that," he says quickly. It's not a question.

I clear my throat. "I don't like it—I'll say that."

"He's not a bad guy though."

"No," I agree. "Absolutely not."

Milo tilts his head to the side. "Little edgy."

"Sure."

"Older," he observes.

"*Much* older." I sniff. "I could beat him up if I wanted to."

"Yeah," Milo says, sipping his drink. "You could take him."

The dancing crowd grows larger as more graduates arrive with their parents. In the center, Lulu tosses her long inky-black hair over her shoulder. The motion reminds me so much of Marina that it's unbearable.

It's clawing at me. Frustrating. All-consuming.

And, as if I wished her into existence, she ascends the stairwell.

Her hair is a sea of blonde, braided back in an attempt to tame the heavy waves. She's changed into a shorter dress, the type that hugs her ribs, then flows down to kiss just above her knees. It's weird how one part of me wants to hold her hand and make jokes like we usually do, but the opposite side of that coin wants to hike up that dress and take, take, take.

Marina stops to say hi to Tina, previous owner of Florally Yours, sitting at the bar. I don't think God was playing fair when he made Marina both sweet and a bombshell. But here she is, and I'm barely keeping it together.

Searching around, she finally catches my eyes. She gives a small wave. I return it, and I can already feel my cheeks heating at the simple exchange.

"Oh," Milo says.

"What?"

"I see."

I laugh, but it's only to break the tension, to maybe keep up the obvious facade that, with each step Marina takes toward us, I'm not floating toward her like a sailor drawn to a mermaid at sea.

"Hey, guys." Her tone is casual as she looks more at Milo than me, as if avoiding my eye contact.

I find I can't stop looking out at Crocodile Cove, almost too excited to meet her eyes. We're so close yet so far. I know if I steal one glance at her, it will all be over for me.

"Hey, Marina," Milo answers for the both of us. From my peripheral vision, I see his eyes flick to me, then back to her. "Congratulations on today, by the way. The flowers looked great."

"Thanks," she replies on a breathy exhale. "Felt good. To accomplish something, y'know?"

I want to laugh at the small talk, and I can hear the smile in her voice too. I imagine her beautiful smile. The barely there freckles dotting the apples of her cheeks, the subtle curve of her crinkled nose, and her plump pink lips. I need to see it.

"I guess I should go congratulate the graduate," Marina says.

Bonnie is by the bar now, heaving out breaths after leaving the dance floor. Lulu is beside her, their arms looped together. Inseparable, as always. Once they finish chugging water, they run back out.

Marina throws a thumb over her shoulder. "I'll be back."

"Have fun," Milo says.

I don't respond, but I do finally turn around to see her. I wish I hadn't because what ensues is pure agony.

Slowly, she edges her way to the dance floor. She begins moving with the crowd. Her hips shift side to side. Her back arches. Her breasts push against the fabric of her dress. Each step flows together in a slow, graceful motion. It's like she's swimming through air.

I swallow, watching Marina dance her way through to Bonnie and Lulu. I can't hear their words, but I see Marina talking, the way her lips part and close. Her smile, straight and white and perfect. Then, the three of them start dancing together.

My sister is terrible at it, jerky and barely holding it together. But beside her, Lulu is feeling the music as much as Marina. The Hideaway's music thrums through the speakers fencing in the makeshift dance floor, and I can feel it in my chest, pounding to the beat of my heart.

Marina won't meet my gaze, but Lulu consistently glances in our direction, only to look away again.

Milo tenses beside me. "I'm gonna get another drink. Want one?"

"No," I answer, but my voice sounds like it's coming from someone else, distant and breathy.

He claps me on the shoulder, then walks off without another word. Lulu's eyes follow him, and furrowing her eyebrows, she leaves the dance floor.

It's one of those weird moments that domino-effects the rest of the circle. Bonnie sees her best friend leave and frowns. Marina whispers to Bonnie. They exchange a hug as Bonnie leaves. Marina, alone, shifts through the crowd and walks straight toward me.

I don't know what I'll do when it's just us again. It feels almost irresponsible, being alone with her. But when Marina's eyes finally meet mine, low and hooded, blinking like the curtains are parting on the stage around me, irresponsibility is suddenly my only option.

She's barely by my side before my palm finds its way to her lower back.

"Hey," I murmur.

"Hi."

"Having fun?"

She peers up at me, giving an innocent smile. "Sure."

"Sure?" I echo.

"Yeah," She bites the corner of her bottom lip. "Sure."

"How'd cleanup go?" I ask.

"Are we really gonna talk about flowers right now?"

I grip her waist tighter, the fabric of her dress fumbling through my fingers. "What do you want to talk about?" I murmur.

"Something else."

"I'll say anything you like."

She leans into my touch, huffing out a laugh. "I just assumed I had an audience while dancing."

"Oh, you did."

Marina's lips pull into a sly smile. "Then … what's going on here, Cass?"

Our eyes dance between each other's. I've never noticed just how green her eyes are, the type of bubbling sea-foam that sucks you in and holds you under. I'd happily let her drown me, and I'd give thanks the whole way down.

I nod. "Let's get out of here."

My sentence is barely out before she says, "Please."

Chapter Twenty-Four

A BETTER IDEA

Marina

Have you ever looked at a man and known exactly what he was thinking? Cassidy's eyes roam over my body like he needs it. Tense jaw. Flexed shoulders. God help me, my mind is already there too.

I don't care that I just walked through the door. I would have left the moment my feet hit the front step if he'd been there waiting. Now, as he spreads his hand over my back and guides me toward the stairwell, I wish he had been.

We don't say goodbyes to anyone else. We only sneak peeks at each other. I catch his eyes darting to my lips at the same time I'm taking in his jawline. We both laugh.

Cassidy and I descend the stairs quickly, down one floor, then another, before crossing through the propped-open front doors. I link my hand in his, but before we can walk farther, I yank him to the opposite side of the porch, around the corner of the wrapped railing to the side with no windows. Our hiding spot is shrouded from the dim warmth of the string lights looping between tree branches, and suddenly, we're alone.

Cassidy's palms bracket my hips, gripping with intention to own, walking me backward to the wooden frame of The Hideaway. The floor creaks under our hurried feet, punctuated by my heavy breaths. My back hits the wall with a small *thump*, and I gasp at the sudden closeness of him.

We're positioned just like we were this afternoon. The energy around us is charged, like electricity is crackling between clouds before a storm. Everything moves in slow motion—the way Cassidy's hand cups around the nape of my neck, how my own hands rise to tangle in his curls, and the gentle pull toward each other as our lips ghost mere inches apart.

I catalog all of his features. The thick eyelashes that feel too beautiful for a man, the way his eyes shadow over, swiveling down to trail over my mouth. I revel in how he tugs his lips to one side, indenting the dimple into his cheek, amused by my arousal.

He dips down, and slowly, gently, agonizingly—like savoring every second—Cassidy presses his lips against mine.

It's hard to describe how wild my heart beats in that moment, how my whole body arches into him, as if my soul were trying to escape my chest. He hisses in a breath, cupping my head to bring me closer. I nearly stumble, rocking back on my heels as I grip his hair to keep me upright, chasing his kiss with my own.

Our lips grow feverish, exhalations shared as his fingers trace down my neck, curling around to tip my head back so he can taste more of me. His opposite hand grips my hip tighter, tugging forward in an attempt to step closer, as if that were possible.

I could make out with Cassidy forever. I love the way his stubble scrapes against my cheeks. I love how he lets out a small groan when my hands curve over his jawline, how he nips at my bottom lip, and most of all, how his dimple doesn't disappear because he keeps smiling.

"Did you …" I ask against his lips, but we keep kissing, each one silencing future words. "Did—" I try again, but he deepens the kiss, and so do I; I can't stop.

His thumb runs circles over my ribs, tracing underneath the curve of my breast, as if he wants so badly to touch, but won't allow himself the freedom. I bend my knee to meet his waist, and his palm darts to clutch my thigh, curling his fingers around it and squeezing. The rough fabric of his jeans greets the juncture of my thighs. He lets out a strangled groan.

Cassidy rips his lips away, leaning his forehead on mine, both of our chests heaving up and down. I continue grinding my hips over him. His erection pressing beneath my hiked-up skirt is a sensation I'm already addicted to.

"I'm sorry," he asks between breaths. "You were asking something?"

"Did you drive?"

"No, carpooled," he responds. "You?"

"Walked."

He swallows. "So, we have to walk back to the house?"

"We can."

It's honestly our only option unless we ask for a ride. Rideshare apps don't extend to Never Harbor.

He leans back, glancing to the right, then left of us.

"Yeah, screw that." Cassidy plants his large hands on my hips and, in one swoop, tosses me over his shoulder.

"Cass!" I squeal on a laugh, but he's already turning us around.

He walks me down a narrow driveway, past a fence separating the outdoor patio from the sea. I watch from over his back as The Hideaway gradually bounces away.

A gate creaks open, and we journey down a wooden ramp to the rocky shore of Crocodile Cove.

"Are you trespassing?" I ask playfully after we clear a sign hanging on the fence, reading, *EMPLOYEES ONLY.*

"Like I care right now," Cassidy answers, and his boyish tone, now layered with haughty sarcasm, shoots right down between my thighs.

Cassidy is a man on a mission. His shoes crunch over pebbled sand, shifting and crackling with each purposeful step. My skirt rises further up my thighs as we walk. The night air sighs on the back of my legs and eventually on the curve under my ass.

The beach grows darker, the farther we move from the bar's lit windows and hanging lights. I wonder how far he's traversing. Before I know it, we're alone with only the moon as our guide. Cassidy places me down in a small alcove, cornered on two sides by craggy, rocky walls.

We move quick. Our hands explore blindly. His palm snakes up my waist, splaying out over my ribs and stomach. I grasp the fabric of his shirt in mine.

"Been thinking about me all day?" I ask cheekily.

"I'm never *not* thinking of you," he murmurs, bending down to place a single kiss on my neck as shivers explode over my skin. "Of your lips. Your legs. These ..." Cassidy's thumb slides up to my puckered nipple, showing through my thin dress fabric. He swipes over the peak, striking nerves through me. "I'm ready to think of only you for a while, if you're all right with that."

"Please," I breathe.

He groans in relief. "Fantastic."

Cassidy's hands dive into my hair at the same time my hands lace behind his head. Our mouths crash together. Pushing, pulling, stumbling, he grabs under both my knees. I leap. I land in his arms and hook my ankles behind his back. His palm skates up my spine, rough but easily supporting me at the same time. The only struggle seems to be in his resolve.

I can feel his erection straining against his jeans, thick and insistent against me as he thrusts between kisses, bunching my skirt around my waist. I ground down, the rough denim shifting against the outside of my thin fabric. I haven't felt this excitement in so long—the desperate wanting and newness of feverish touches, blocked by layers of constraints.

Screw constraints.

I reach between us, thumbing his pants button through the loop and jerking the zipper down with a hiss. I dip my palm down the waistband of his boxers. I can't see the cock I grip in my hand, but I already like it. Thick with veins cording around every inch I touch and long enough that I can't feel the end yet.

Cassidy's head falls back with a choked groan.

I move my hand up, then back down his cock. His palms grip my thighs tight. Pressing his forehead against mine, he looks down between us. He watches as I stroke him.

"God," he groans. "That's hot, Marina. You're such a fucking knockout."

I stroke faster, and he pulls back.

"Too hard?" I ask.

"No, I just have better ideas."

He bands an arm around my back to hold me in place as he lifts me higher.

And higher.

"Cass—"

Suddenly, my legs aren't wrapped around his waist. They're on either side of his head. I have no idea how he's holding me up. It's gotta be all those hours in the gym. I've never dated a fit guy before, but I could definitely get used to this.

He walks forward until my back lands against the wall. I lean against it, thighs still hiked on either of his shoulders. He swats away my skirt with his nose and buries his head beneath it.

Oh.

I feel his warm tongue slide along my inner thigh. My legs shake terribly.

Don't stop. Don't stop.

I'm already shivering at his touch when he reaches the pinnacle of my thighs and licks a slow, sensual line over the fabric.

I gasp, closing my eyes, tightening my thighs around his ears. He hooks his teeth in the hem of my underwear, nudges it aside, and slowly slips his tongue over me.

I'm breathless, barely holding it together as Cassidy tastes me again. I swallow with each subsequent lick until he's lapping like a man desperate for more. He has a rhythm, starting slow, only to pick up pace exactly where I need him to, then stopping to tease me once more.

I've never—*never*—had a man understand this dynamic so quickly. The combination of both needs required to get me off. Honestly, that knowledge alone gets me closer than I should be by now.

I'm sure we should be concerned about being caught. But I'm too busy enjoying our symphony of huffs and groans, the slick slide of his tongue, the embarrassing whines leaving my throat. It's desperate, messy, but *so* good.

"God, I could taste you all night," Cassidy moans under my skirt. "Being between your thighs is my new favorite thing, honey."

"Me too."

This has him laughing. I can feel his warm breath against me. Then, he navigates exactly where he knows he should, where I've squirmed the most, made the most noises. Teasing, teasing, teasing …

My eyebrows cinch in as pleasure crests like a wave through me. Building and curling and then crashing.

"Cass—" I barely say his name before I tumble over the edge, shaking in his touch, my thighs tight around his head.

My orgasm courses through me like a hurricane, barreling over every sense of rationality I had.

It was perfect. *This* is perfect.

Out of breath himself, Cassidy removes his head from under my skirt and begins lowering me back down. My body skims between the wall and his chest, inch by inch, zipping sparks over every touch. When I land on the rocks below, he adjusts my skirt back down, patting my ass outside the fabric once it's in place.

I reach toward him, but Cassidy halts my wrist. "Next time." He tucks himself back in his pants and zips back up. "I'm honestly a little worried your moans might have woken all of Never Harbor."

I grin. "But that's your fault."

"And I'd do it again too. But we have a party to get back to, don't we?"

I wish we didn't, but I'm too exhilarated by him to say no. And ultimately, he's Cassidy. I can't change him. He's a people person, and he has all of Never Harbor waiting for him back at The Hideaway.

I'm swooped into his arms again, laughing as my hot roommate carries me across the pebbled beach and back toward The Hideaway. I have to curl my lips in to stop from smiling too much. Cassidy doesn't need to know that my tiny, innocent crush on him just grew to something far bigger.

- *Chapter Twenty-Five* -
BETS, BOUQUETS, & BUSINESS

Marina

I wake up the next morning, splayed out in bed.

Our bed.

Cassidy's limbs are tangled with mine, his bulky arm lying under my head as my leg drapes over his waist.

I run a palm over his stubbled jawline and into the base of his curly hair. I twist it around my finger, letting it snap back in place. I already miss his gorgeous grin. I like being around him. And now, curled together under the sheets like some blanket burrito, I don't want to go anywhere.

Memories of last night rush in. His palm stroking over my stomach. His tongue whipping over me. It stopped there; we went back to The Hideaway and drank two more shots than needed. We were too tired when we got home. I was almost asleep when Bonnie and Lulu dropped us off at our front stoop.

I wonder what Dad will think about us. Here I am, in town temporarily, and I impulsively jump into bed with my roommate. But, God, my roommate happens to be a big man with an even bigger heart. I was a goner from the first time I crawled under these sheets with him on day one.

Cassidy feels familiar. A bright spot in the world, like my parents used to describe each other. It hurts to imagine that now—that my dad could be so obsessed with a woman who ultimately might not have felt the same way. But I wonder if I've found my own bright spot.

I kiss Cassidy's stubbled jaw and lay my head back on his arm. He shifts beside me, waking up with a low murmur. Then, he sees me, and that dimpled grin returns like my own personal sunbeam.

"Well, good morning, you," he says, kissing the top of my head. There's no hesitation at all, like kissing me has been normal for years now.

"Good morning, Curly," I answer, gripping his hair and pulling him down to meet my lips.

Our kisses are lazy, slow, but wanting. We stroke through each other's hair or trace along lines of our faces. Just as we're settling into something nice and consistent, with his lips growing more insistent and awake, Cassidy's alarm blares from the side table. He groans, pressing a final kiss to the tip of my nose before rolling over to turn it off.

"What day is it?" he asks.

"Sunday."

"Sunday … Sunday …" he mumbles to himself, closing his eyes in thought.

I stroke down his neck and to his shoulder. "You've got Bobbi scheduled again."

Cassidy's eyes pop open, darting between mine, crinkles forming beside his eyes as he slowly grins.

"I think you're right," he answers. "How'd you know that?"

"I listen."

"Oh, Marina," he rasps. "You do, don't you?" There's another kiss, on my cheek, my chin, and neck. He grasps my waist in his palms and noses down between my breasts. "I want to listen to you too."

I'm peppered with kisses until I'm laughing my way out of bed.

"Where're you going?" he asks.

"I've got to get moving so we can unload the van from yesterday," I say. "And we're talking with Lulu's parents today too."

Cassidy props his cheek onto his palm. "Big meeting?"

"I don't think so," I say, grabbing my dress off the floor. "Just kinda reviewing graduation and how it went, I guess."

I slip the dress over my head, and Cassidy's face falls when I'm clothed.

He knocks his chin toward my breasts. "Bring them back now."

"Later."

"Promise?" he says, leaning up to kiss me when I pass by.

I meet him in the middle for a peck before pulling away to braid my hair. He sighs, and I'll admit, it's too much fun, toying with him.

"Down, boy," I command.

He gives another sigh, more frustrated this time.

"Well," he starts, standing up and crossing the floor, "I have no doubt you'll rock it."

As he pulls gym shorts from his closet, I stare at his back and shoulders, trailing all the way down to his toned ass. He tugs his shorts on, grabbing the tiny, tabbed notebook off the floor and pocketing it.

The ever-mysterious notebook.

"I feel cheated," I voice out loud.

He twists around. "Oh, yeah? More tongue?" He winks. "Put me back in, Coach. I can do better."

I choke out a shocked laugh. "No ..." I say slowly.

He grins playfully.

"I just haven't had the chance to touch you yet. Or see you. All of you."

"Don't worry about that," he says, taking tentative steps closer, bracketing my hips with his large hands. "I'll come home tonight, and you can have your way with me. I bet I'll even make you come three more times. At least."

"How much?"

"Twenty dollars."

"Ten," I counter.

He laughs. "Why go lower?"

"Because I know you can do it."

His brown eyes scan me for the second time this morning with something in them I can't decipher.

"What?" I ask.

"I like you, Marina Starkey," he says with a gentle smile. "That's all."

When Cassidy's brown eyes scan over me, I don't feel them on my skin, but deeper in my core. I can't resist my subsequent smile, how it almost hurts my cheeks because I'm never *not* smiling with him.

"I like you too, Curly."

I leave earlier than I should and stop by Mermaid Lagoon again. I haven't been since my second day here, but it feels different now. Even though I'm alone, it feels less secluded than before.

It feels nice.

I'm already dressed for work, so I don't swim. Instead, I dip my feet in the water, letting my toes rummage through the sandy depths.

I used to come here a lot after Mom left. Even more when she passed. It was solace. Peace in this cave was exactly what I needed.

But I don't know what I need anymore. After last night, being alone feels like the worst reality—a future my hurt teenage self wanted instead of the current Marina.

I don't want to be alone. I want to spend more time with Cassidy and less time thinking.

I regret not walking to work with Cassidy this morning. Seeing the familiar faces on the sidewalk, waving to shop owners as we pass by, watching that muscled goofball attempt to make conversation with quiet Rafe.

I like our routine.

And that fact is enough to make me hop off the rock and continue with my day instead of continuing to mull.

Never Harbor is becoming a comfortable routine, and I might like it.

Maybe.

Possibly.

Lulu practically stumbled into the flower shop this morning, bleary-eyed and clutching a to-go coffee. I was almost done opening the computer for the store when she plopped down on her usual chair behind the counter, leaned her head back, and let out a dramatic whine.

"Did you just remember we're talking to your parents today?" I asked.

"Yes," she groaned out on a lower tone, dragging the word like it offended her before tipping back her coffee cup and chugging.

"Wish you hadn't partied so hard?"

"Yes, and no. Yes because ..." She waved her hand across the shop, as if it symbolized her parents' arrival. "But also *no* … because …" Lulu then smiled in a way I'd never seen from her before. But I saw a similar dazed expression in the mirror this morning too. "Because there might be a *boy*."

"Lulu," I accused on a low gasp. "Did you go home with someone last night?"

But before I could ask who the lucky guy was, Steve walked in to buy his usual bouquet, followed by a consistent line of customers until we temporarily closed two hours later. Conversation forgotten.

Now, Lulu is back on the less-than-thrilled side of the spectrum, sipping yet another coffee.

We're sitting under the white gazebo across the street from the beach, shimmers of sun pouring through the slats of the roof, casting rays along the wooden planks and over my knees.

"Did they say whether they're running late?" I ask.

Lulu sighs. "They just show up when they want. Give them another five."

The shop's tablet is balanced on the railing as we wait in a virtual meeting room. Lulu insisted on getting out of the shop for a while and that the Wi-Fi near the beach was better. But judging how she's lying on the long bench in the direct sun, I think she just wanted an excuse to tan.

Lulu sighs, sitting up. "I swear if they're more than ten minutes— Mama! Pop! Hi!" Her voice changes on a dime as another video pops up.

Her parents sit side by side in what looks like an airport terminal. It's been a while since I've seen Lulu's parents, but there's no denying the relation to their daughter. Lulu has her father's long nose, cheeky smile, and thick eyelashes. Her inky-black hair and rustic, sun-kissed skin comes from her mother.

"You look tired, Tallulah," her mom observes.

"That's because I am tired," Lulu responds.

"Don't be sarcastic," her dad rebukes.

"Wouldn't dream of it."

"Oh, Marina! My love!" Though harsh on Lulu, her mom is quick to wiggle an index finger at me in greeting.

"Hi. It's nice to see you two."

"Marina," her dad says. "Pleasure." Much more formal.

He's the type of man with a permanent line between his brow that maybe disappears if his soccer team wins the cup.

"Let's keep this quick," he says, flicking his eyes to something off-screen. Maybe they're boarding soon. "We've been looking at the numbers, Marina. It seems like you're really turning this place around. Meeting deadlines at least," he adds, pointedly looking at his daughter, who shakes her head with a small *ugh*.

"I'm really enjoying it," I respond. "It's a great challenge, and I get to use my degree. I can't thank you enough for the opportunity."

"You seem happy," Lulu's mom says.

"I am."

I love Florally Yours. I love the smells, the squeak of my shoes on the tiles first thing in the morning, the familiar faces, and the daily conversations. But most of all, I love the freedom. There's no sitting behind a desk or counting the fluorescent lights. It feels … right.

I haven't felt *right* in so long.

And now, sitting here with Lulu's parents, it feels more formal. More official.

Happy, I think. *You're happy.*

"I have a degree in botany," I say. "Happy to put it to good use."

"Ah, you can see the passion," Lulu's mom says with a nod. "Tallulah, why didn't you tell us she had a degree?"

"You never asked. Want me to switch majors?"

I can feel her sarcasm, and maybe they can too.

"You need to stay in business," her dad quickly commands, like this is a conversation they've had too many times.

"So, Marina"—Lulu's dad claps his hands together—"we're looking to the future. The music festival—"

"Wine mixer," Lulu corrects under her breath.

"The festival has our contract."

"Yes, and I've already got ideas," I say.

He exchanges a look with Lulu's mom. "That's what we like to hear. If it goes well, we'd like to keep you on past the summer."

"Oh." I can't stop myself from blinking in disbelief. "Oh, wow, well, I'm not sure I—"

"She'll think about it," Lulu interjects.

I'm thankful she does, but I don't know how to react.

I'm not sure who said that terrible things come in threes, but I worry that, instead, it's good things that come in threes. First Cassidy. Now the flower shop …

I'm scared of what else the universe will throw my way.

I'm happy. I shouldn't be happy in the town where I graduated high school, right? Aren't you supposed to leave?

Lulu's tablet buzzes, but she quickly swipes the notification away. I smirk at her. I wonder if it's the guy from last night. With how embarrassed she looks, something tells me it is. Given this small town, there's really only a few options.

It's funny, thinking of her with anyone but Milo. She's only ever had eyes for him. But Milo is far too old for Lulu—ten years older. Plus, he's practical. And Lulu's ... well, Lulu.

Lulu pulls out her phone, likely responding to the text.

Her mom tsks. "Texting at a business meeting, Tallulah?"

"She's learning nothing at college," her dad says, irritation in his tone.

"Lulu's actually been an amazing help at the shop," I chime in. "She's there every single day, even after we close. She helps with arrangements and keeping things up-to-date. I really couldn't do this without her."

They eye her, and for a moment, I spot pride in the way her dad's chin tips to the sky. He even straightens his posture more, if that were possible.

Lulu tosses me a smile, and I return it with a wink.

But then the tablet buzzes again.

And this time, I see who it is.

"Dustin?" I ask.

Her mom squints. "What did you say, Marina?"

But I'm already frozen to the spot, feeling needles prickling down my spine and realization setting in.

Why is Dustin texting Lulu?

Did Lulu go home with him last night?

I didn't even see Dustin there. For the first time, he wasn't even remotely on my radar. All I saw was Cassidy.

"Marina?" her father asks.

"Sorry. Just remembered something from yesterday." I shake my head. "The speaker at the graduation."

"Barrie's boy, right?"

"Mmhmm."

"Bet he did a fine job."

I cringe, but Lulu sits up a little straighter, as if proud of her new man.

I'm gonna be sick.

"We need to wrap it up," Lulu's mom whispers.

Being the businessman that he is, Lulu's dad does exactly that in less than three sentences. We're off the phone in fewer minutes.

The moment the call ends and the meeting room disappears, I look to Lulu.

"Are you talking with Dustin Barrie?" I ask.

"Sort of. Not really. It's complicated."

My mouth feels dry. "I mean, isn't he too old for you?"

"Only by ten years," she counters. "Wendy and Jasper are seven years apart."

"Yeah, but she was twenty-six when they got together. You're only twenty-one."

"Okay, *Mom*."

My head jerks back. That hits harder than it should. My nose stings, but I shake it off. Now is *not* the time for tears.

"I don't trust him," I confess. "I told you he was a walking red flag."

"He's been nice to me," she counters. "He gives me flowers."

"We have flowers at our store."

"He walked me to my car after we left The Hideaway. He texted me good morning. He's texting me good afternoon. He asks about me and what I like and—"

"Yeah, those are basic things any guy should be doing." This is too much. She has to know. "Lu, I should tell you …"

"It's nice to have someone want me, Marina," she snaps. "Okay?"

All the blood drains from my face.

She deflates. "I'm sorry. I just …" She sighs. "Dustin is nice. Is he pretentious? Sure. But he likes me. Which is more than I can say for … other people."

I swallow. I don't know what to say.

I need to tell her everything—how terrible Dustin is. I need to tell her the truth.

Lulu sees the world in me, and it'll hurt to see what she thinks of me after. And yet I was naive enough to lead on my boss to the point where he thought he could hit on me. What kind of role model does that? Dustin was only acting in a way he thought was appropriate because I'd made him feel that way. He tucked that hair behind my ear because it made sense. Because I'd inadvertently told him it was okay.

No. He crossed a boundary. And she needs to know.

She winces. "Are you mad?"

"No," I say quickly. "No, of course not. I just … I should tell you something."

"Does he eat his boogers?" she jokes.

"No, Lulu … he … he's just not a good guy." I'm so embarrassed by the truth. So ashamed. But this is *Lulu*. "I told you I got fired from my job, right?"

"Yeah …"

"He fired me. He …" I sigh, and her eyebrows furrow. Like she is confused. Heck, I'm confused. I haven't told anyone this yet, and saying it out loud might feel too real. But I have to. I close my eyes and spill. "He came on to me. He hit on me and then fired me when I didn't feel the same way."

Silence. Pure silence, aside from the waves lapping the rocks across the street.

Lulu blinks. "He *what*?!"

Her incredulous response has my head jutting back.

"I'm so sorry—"

"Don't be sorry," she snaps. She leans in and jerks me toward her into a tight hug.

And suddenly, I feel much younger than her. For once, she's taking care of me. I can feel my nose stinging.

No. Don't cry. You're being silly.

But Lulu isn't being silly at all. She's being nice.

I don't know what I expected. If she'd insist I was wrong or blame me. I don't know.

But this is so different.

So kind.

"I'm done with him," she announces.

"What? I … you believe me?"

She leans back, her dark eyebrows raised to almost her hairline. "You're kidding. Of course I do. Come on. You take me for a woman who puts up with that bullshit?"

I laugh. "No. I guess not."

"Good. Don't make that assumption again, girl." She pulls me back in, tucking me under her arm. "He's done. Gone."

I smile and curl closer.

Good things do come in threes, and here is the third. I'm still a woman floundering in the past. I'm not sure what to expect anymore, but here, under a gazebo beside the shore, I feel welcome for the first time in a while.

It's hard to reconcile how kind everyone is with how I imagined Never Harbor to be.

- *Chapter Twenty-Six* -
SPELL ENTREPRENEURIAL

Cassidy

Water laps against the side of the boat as my and three of my brothers' folding chairs line the railing. It's mid-afternoon, and Milo, Peter, and I dragged Jasper and his boat out to sea near Skull Rock.

"Hey, you got something," Milo says, pointing to the taut line in the water.

I reel and pull, but the line goes slack again.

"One of these days," I say, rotating the crank on my pole before flinging the line in the water once more.

I love these slow afternoons with my siblings, floating on the gentle waves under the summer sun. We've asked Bonnie to join, but she wants nothing to do with fishing. One day, we'll invite The Twins—when they're older and not at risk of sinking the boat.

"I bet the fish love when you're around," Peter says with a laugh.

"Yeah, yeah, hilarious."

It's normally pretty quiet out here. Jasper insists fishing is meant to be experienced in dead silence. With Peter, there are still some jokes exchanged, but for the most part, Jasper has the right idea. It gives me time to think. Maybe that's why I suck so bad at it. Thinking isn't my strong suit.

My mind is overwhelmed by the last twenty-four hours. The Hideaway. The beach, dimly lit and echoed by Marina's hurried breaths.

How her thighs tightened around my ears.

Last night was the hottest sex I'd ever had, and we didn't even have it. That's got to say something, right? Though *what* it exactly says, I don't know. Maybe that when you're doing it with the right person, the pieces fall together. That it's just *good* without even trying.

I'd be rushing home to touch her more if I knew I could, but Marina has a late day at the shop, recouping from graduation. I'd spend every moment with her if she let me—working in the shop alongside Stinky, moving boxes wherever she needed. But I'm not going to tag along like a puppy while she's making waves.

Peter looks down at his watch and sighs. "Oh boy. Let's pack it up. Izzy's gonna kill me."

"We lose track of time again?" I ask, breaking from my thoughts.

Milo sighs. "I asked if I should set an alarm, guys."

"It's fine," Peter says, muttering, "Damn, I promised not to piss her off again."

"Ever?" Jasper grunts.

Peter smirks. "Maybe not *ever*. That's an awfully long time. But maybe in the immediate future. So, she won't hate me any more than she already does."

"Hate," Milo muses. "Sure."

"She does," Peter insists. "She threw a Styrofoam cup at me yesterday. I swear that woman's only got room for one emotion at a time. The one she's mentally assigned to me is disdain."

"Or something like that," I add with a chuckle.

Peter scoffs, reeling in his line and tucking the pole back in the boat. "I'm not even gonna ask what that means."

"You and Izzy?" I ask. "Come on, Pete."

He laughs. "What?"

I glance at Milo, but he's already looking at me. And when we turn to Jasper, a single eyebrow is arched.

"You don't think she hates me," Peter states, hands on hips.

"Oh, no, I think she does," Milo corrects.

I shrug. "We just think she's, like, *into* that, right, guys?"

"Absolutely," Milo says at the same time Jasper grunts in assent.

Peter throws his head back and laughs. "Screw you guys. She's my bar manager."

"And?" I ask. "Wait." I lean forward on a whisper. "Is it because you're into it too?"

"Get out of here," Peter scoffs. "She'd choke me if she could."

"I bet," Jasper says.

Peter shakes his head. "*Et tu, Brute?*"

"She's the only person who keeps you in line," Milo comments. "I don't think that's a bad thing."

I shrug. "She's also been your friend since high school. You're really gonna say you haven't thought about it?"

"Wendy was your friend forever," Peter observes. "You never considered it."

I snort. "Nah, but she was always one of the boys. Or maybe like the mom of the group. Well"—I look between Peter and Jasper—"to some of us."

"Watch it," Jasper warns.

I hold up my hands, feigning innocence. "Just saying that I wouldn't sleep with Ma."

We all laugh, but Peter's fades off quickly. Jasper's laugh is nonexistent. They exchange a quick look before Peter turns away.

"It's in the past," Peter says. "I'm not worried about it. But let's go before Izzy does choke me out. And not in a fun way."

Milo grins. "Is that an admission of guilt?"

I dig into my hoodie pocket and pull out my notebook where I log everyone's favorite things, saying out loud, "Peter loves choking."

"Don't write that down!" Peter says, knocking the book out of my hands. I laugh and pick it back up. "It isn't easy, running that place. I need her by my side."

"Running a business," I muse, shaking my head. "I wouldn't know where to start."

"You're learning though, right?" Peter asks. "How's that whole self-help thing coming along?"

Jasper quirks up a single eyebrow. "Self-help?"

"Oh …" I laugh sheepishly. "Yeah, just … Marina let me borrow a book. That's all."

"Are you okay?" Jasper asks with a squint.

"Yes," I say with another laugh. "Yes, I'm fine, everyone. No issues here. Just trying to better myself. That's all."

Milo shrugs. "I respect that."

"Yeah, but you said you were thinking about starting a business?" Peter asks.

"No," I say. "I don't know why everyone is insisting I did."

Jasper exchanges a look with my brothers, and I hate when I'm left out of the unspoken conversation. "Well," he says, "tell us about it."

"Nothing to tell."

"Well then, if it's nothing …" Milo coaxes.

I sigh. "I mean, sure, personal training would be fun, I guess. But, guys—"

"Personal training?" Jasper asks. "That sounds up your alley."

"Nah," I say. "I'm just a meathead with silly ideas."

"Yeah, but you're our meathead," Milo says.

"Our little ground beef," Peter adds with a grin.

Jasper nods. "Well, go on, Cass. Tell us more."

"It's just an idea, guys."

Peter says, "So?"

"Well, I just … couldn't," I explain through another laugh, but they're not laughing with me anymore. "Come on," I counter with a grin to Milo. "We all know I'm not management material, like Jas, or bookish, like you, or, heck, entrepreneurial, like Pete."

"You know the word *entrepreneurial*, and honestly, that's the hardest step," Peter says. "Took me forever to spell it."

"Didn't say I could spell it."

"That's beside the point," he says, waving me off. "I don't know what you're worried about. You'd kill the business."

"In a good way," Jasper adds.

"That's what I meant," Peter says with a laugh.

"Hey, I'm happy, all right? I'm just taking life day by day and hoping for the best," I say.

"Exactly," Jasper grunts. "We all are."

He knows that better than anyone. My nephew was thrust on him at two years old, and Jasper had to learn how to be a parent out of nowhere. I could have never managed that, but Jasper can. That's where we differ. I'd forget to pick up the kid at school or something.

I must remain silent for too long because Peter stops smiling.

I sigh. "Guys, we heading back or—"

"You're actually serious right now, aren't you?" Peter interrupts, and the disbelief in his voice echoes over the water.

"I …"

My older brothers stare at me with various expressions I don't like. Peter with an uncharacteristic line between his brow, Milo with his glasses tipped to the end of his nose, and Jasper with a scowl—but I guess that one's pretty normal.

"Guys"—I laugh—"we're having fun! Don't be weird about it."

"We're being logical," Milo counters.

"It requires a lot of organization and—"

Milo nods. "You said it yourself. Pete runs a business, and Jas is a manager. I've got the entire library at my disposal. Let us help you."

I open my mouth, then shut it. "I don't ..."

But I can't find the words.

I'm not the youngest in our family—The Twins take that title. But I was the little brother with these three, always chasing behind their footsteps with play swords and jokes I hoped made them laugh. It didn't matter if they did though—not if they helped or gave me any additional effort. The Davies family had unconditionally gifted me so much by then.

I'm the helper in this family.

"No," I insist.

"No?" Peter says on a laugh.

"No," I repeat. "I can't do it. So, I won't."

"Why?" Milo asks.

"Because I'm just me. Heck, even your pal Dustin knew it." I toss a palm to Milo.

At that, Milo goes very quiet, almost eerily so. "Knew what?"

"That I'm just ... here. I'm an average guy."

"He said *what?*"

"It was just side comments and stuff. It wasn't a big deal. But come on—"

Milo, very steadily, very precise, like the tip of a knife, says, "Dustin can eat shit, Cass. He doesn't know what he's talking about."

The boat jerks forward, and with one hand on the wheel, Jasper announces in irritation, "Don't listen to what the snot-nosed mayor's son thinks. Cass, you take on more every day than any two regular people, and you do it smiling. So, cut this shit out."

Peter shrugs. "Yeah, sucks to suck, but you're in it now, Curly. You're doing this."

Milo shakes his head. "We're just doing this for your own good. Sorry."

"My own good?"

"Yes, because clearly, you've been living with some lie. Some kid told you that you weren't smart, and you believed them," Milo says, but I don't miss how his face contorts in disgust. I can't decide if it's for me or Dustin. "In fact, a lot of people might have let you down," he finishes. And I realize it might not be for Dustin at all. But for pre-seven-year-old Cassidy. Pre-Davies Cassidy. "So, we're helping you. And that's final."

Peter lets out a low whistle. "Man, how embarrassing for you. Brothers who care. Disgusting."

I shake my head, but the collective laughter—humor that is *with* me and not *at* me—has my clenched fists relaxing. My heart rate, once raised, is descending, slower and slower.

For once, I wonder if there's something I'm missing here, and maybe it's a part of me I left behind in high school. Or even younger. Maybe it's the part Dustin Barrie, or anyone else, couldn't reach—shards still left in the shattered parts of my brain. Or maybe my brain isn't as shattered as I thought.

My brothers believe in me.

My *family* believes in me.

Even Marina believes in me. I imagine her smile if I told her I was doing it—really doing it—and, God, I'd do anything for that freckled smile.

We ride in the boat in relative silence, except for the occasional observation and pacing from Peter, who can't stop moving to save his life. But when we dock again, I finally talk.

"Hey, uh, Milo, how long are you gonna be at the library tonight?" I ask.

"I'm closing up, so at least ten. Why?"

"Mind if I steal a desk after my last client?"

All three of them pause, slowly grinning, like they got me hook, line, and sinker.

"You gonna do some research?" Peter asks.

"Maybe." I shrug. "I don't know. I might."

Milo nods. "I'll pick out some books for you."

"I'll lend a hand," Jasper says.

"I've got my laptop," Peter adds. "I can pull up my old business plan and walk you through it."

"All of you are coming?" I ask. "But why?"

"Because we believe in you," Jasper says. "Don't you?"

Don't I?

I don't know yet, but I think I'd like to find out.

I laugh. "Wait, don't you have to work, Pete?"

"Eh, I like Izzy being mad at me," Peter says with a shrug. "What can I say?"

"Knew it," Jasper grunts.

"Well, if you're all coming, then you're helping stock shelves too,"

Milo says.

I grin, grabbing my bag and pole from the seat.
"Deal."

- *Chapter Twenty-Seven* -

DON'T BE GENTLE

Cassidy

The house is quiet when I get home. I didn't realize how late it'd gotten at the library, and I'm mentally kicking myself at being late to something—*again*—as I trail across the creaking hardwood, feeling around in the dark to place my keys on the hook beside the door.

Not a single lamp is lit. Even the window is closed.

I exhale, silently walking down the hallway and pushing open the bedroom door. The streetlights shine in through the window, illuminating a sleeping Marina. She's in her usual position, facing the window, with both knees curled to her chest, cheek resting on her arm.

I can't stop the chuckle escaping my throat.

I might be too late to touch her, but I don't mind. Just seeing her here, giving light, breathy exhales just one octave short of a snore, makes me happy.

I move around as silently as I can, toeing off my sneakers, unbuckling my belt, and shucking my pants down to the floor with a silent rattle. I pull my shirt over my head, toss it in the laundry basket, then crawl into bed. The mattress sinks under my weight as I curl around Marina.

"Cass?" she whispers.

"Hey," I murmur back. "How was your day?"

"It was … good."

Something shimmers beneath the surface in her voice. It's almost reluctant.

"Everything okay?"

"Yeah, I'm just … it was a long day."

"How did unloading the van go?"

"Good."

"Was the meeting with Lulu's parents okay?"

"Yeah … can we just …"

Marina scoots back, pushing her round, perfectly peach-shaped cheeks against me and rubbing a long, tantalizing line over the length of my half-hard cock. I let out a low groan I wish I didn't, but am met by a soft exhale in response.

I still a palm on her stomach.

"Hey, wait." I choke out a laugh. "As much as I'd love to do this, I want to make sure you're fine."

"Cass, not every day is perfect."

"But I want all of your days to be perfect."

"Then, make it better for me. Please?"

I tuck my knees behind hers and pull her back against my chest.

"How so?" I murmur.

My palms slowly trail down her shoulder and forearm, tracing along her skin until I reach her hips. It's almost maddening how well my palm curls around her waist, gripping her side as she pushes back into me again.

I press my lips to her ear, nipping the lobe between my teeth. Shivers break out over her skin.

"That," she whispers. "By doing that."

I flex my palm against her hip, pulling her back against me at the same time she pushes herself against my groin once more. It would be so easy to slide inside were there not two layers of fabric between her and my greedy cock, now almost at full mast.

"I'll make it better," I rasp against her ear, dipping my hand past her hip, palming across her stomach and trailing lower to the hem of her underwear. I nudge my middle finger past the fabric.

I slide my hand down until I reach the softest part of her, silky and wet beneath my fingertips. I dip my middle finger down, stroking a small circle over her before burying it inside. She lets out a small gasp.

"Is that it?" I ask. "That where you need me?"

Marina nods as I push one of my knees between her legs, spreading them wider. I add a second finger, finding that same spot from before, teasing it until her gasp transforms into a whine.

She reaches behind her back, between our bodies, taking a handful of me outside my boxers. It only makes me dig my fingers deeper into her, pulsing in and out.

She rubs her palm over me, finally shoving her way past my waistband until I'm in her hand, stroking up and down.

I press my forehead against her neck, kissing against her shoulder while she grips me tighter, rougher, harder. I thrust into her fist at the same rhythm I bury my fingers inside.

"Don't be gentle, honey," I demand.

She jerks my cock faster, the sound of her hand bumping my abs echoing through the room. I press my palm against the outside of her, feeling the small bump of her clit tease against my rough hand.

"Right there," she whispers, the words barely there.

It's intoxicating, hearing her respond like this. Hearing how she can't even form sentences as I have her in my palm.

I feel my own body tighten, the influx of tension in my stomach.

It's the crude sounds of our bodies shifting in the sheets; my fingers thrusting inside her; her fist pumping my cock … all of it is too much and not enough.

"Give me some noise in this empty house," I demand.

Marina does, letting out a breathy moan and sharp inhale.

I close my eyes, letting the zips of pleasure course through my body, from my stomach out to my fingertips, as I drag in and out of her fist on repeated moans. My orgasm makes me feel like I'm blacking out. Spots explode behind my eyes.

Marina follows quickly, squeezing around my fingers, moaning my name on an exhale. "Cassidy."

I rest my forehead against her back, planting kiss after kiss down her spine and back up until my chin nestles between her shoulder blades. I entwine my hand with hers, bringing it up to kiss her fingertips.

I don't know how to describe the feelings pounding through me like a heartbeat. Instead, I murmur against her ear a small, "That's my girl," and maybe it'll give her an ounce of how I feel.

Maybe she'll sense that this new sensation is possession.

I want Marina to be mine.

Chapter Twenty-Eight

ALMOST SWEET

Marina

"Lulu, can you grab more roses from the back?"
She's in a daze as she continues to text.
"Lu?"
"Sorry," she answers.
Stinky hops on the counter, and Lulu lowers him down with one hand. He repeats the jump, now batting at Fido's leaves.
"Lu, control him, please?"
"Sorry, sorry," she says, finally placing her phone down and hugging Stinky in her arms. "Come on, Toot. Down you go."
I peer at her phone when it buzzes again. She's been texting Bonnie all morning. I wonder if it's about Dustin—if what I told her crushed her world.
I know I did the right thing, but her words still linger. *It's nice to have someone want me.*
I get it. It's nice to have someone *kind* want me for once. It's only mid-morning, and I miss Cassidy.
I attempt to shove the thought away and refocus on Steve, grinning as he purchases his daily bouquet. His bicycle leans on the glass window outside, the basket normally filled with mail now empty and reserved for the incoming arrangement.
"Do you like Laura, Steve?" Lulu blurts out.

He opens his mouth, then closes it, sheepishly scratching his neck.

I pat his arm. "You don't have to tell us."

"But we'd love to know," Lulu insists.

"She's injured, and I thought that it'd …" Steve starts, the words petering off. "I would like flowers if I were her, on crutches and stuff. It's no big deal."

I smile. "Well, I'll go get the no-big-deal, get-well-soon bouquet prepped."

Lulu hops on the counter, arms wrapped around a discontent Stinky, who's scrambling to get down. "So, is it her smile or her ass, Steve? Or do you just like that air of older woman confidence?"

"That's not—"

"It's okay. I like older men," she whispers conspiratorially. "You can like older women."

I barely hear his flustered stammering before walking to the back of the shop. Lulu could kill a man with her blunt words. I pity the one who vows to endure them forever.

I gather roses from our back stock, laying stems down on the steel table to cut and arrange.

My phone vibrates in my pocket, and I pull it out to see yet another text from Peter and the other Davies brothers. They reached out this morning, asking for help with Cassidy's business. I respond, then set it aside, turning to the flowers on the table, splayed out in a beautiful array of petals.

This is what I always wanted—to play in beautiful nature every day. To be with people. To have someone like Cassidy. Sweet, giving Cassidy, who encouraged me from the beginning and still does.

I should be thinking about how thankful I am for my wonderful new life.

Instead, I'm stuck on what this all means and what I will do when summer ends. What happens when I find a job—which, admittedly, I haven't applied to or searched for in a week?

What happens when I get the itch to leave, like my mom?

What happens to the life I'm creating here? I always knew it would be temporary. I can't get lost in the possibility that it isn't.

I mix and match the flowers before rolling them with parchment paper and walking back to the front.

I only catch the tail end of Lulu saying, "… because flowers won't heal a broken heart."

"Very insightful, Lu." I hand over the bouquet to a very anxious

Steve. "Tell Laura we said hi."

"I'll do that," he answers, quickly exiting through the door with a borderline fretful *ding*, running his bicycle down the street and away from our shop.

"You didn't scare him away just now, did you?" I ask Lulu.

She shrugs. "We're his only supplier in town. He can't get flowers without us."

I laugh. Why am I worried about her anyway? It'd take a lot to topple this girl. Maybe she sees something I don't. Maybe—

Then, like summoning the devil himself, Dustin Barrie crosses in front of our shop window. He's wearing that same tailored gray suit. I bet his closet is full of them, or maybe—I can hope—he simply wears the same outfit every day. We could call *him* Stinky.

Lulu's face hardens. She tips her chin up defiantly, crossing her legs, one over the other, with intention and elegance.

I take a purposeful step forward—I don't know why—but Stinky jumps on the counter.

"Hey, off the counter, Stinks," I say.

But that colorful fuzz ball glares at me dead in the face and yowls.

I wonder if he's telling me to back off. That Lulu can handle this situation. Or maybe I'm just trying to find meaning in a mangy cat's demand for food.

Lulu gives Dustin a sickly-sweet smile and gently waves her hand, saying, "Run along."

Dustin must be able to read her lips because he grimaces, flashing me a quick glare before walking away.

The hair on the back of my neck stands on end.

Why do I feel like I'm in trouble?

Lulu exhales a few seconds after he's gone, crossing over to the counter. The book—Milo's book—remains in her purse, untouched. I watch her sit there on her phone, but after a few moments, she swivels her eyes up.

"I'm fine."

"I know," I say.

"Good. He's just … pushy." She shakes her head. "That's all."

"I know."

"And he holds grudges."

I nod. "I know that too."

She sighs. "Why is our taste in men so different?"

I blink. "Wait, what?"

"You have Cassidy," she says matter-of-factly. "He's nice. A soft kinda guy. Unpretentious. Not like Dust-bag."

I choke on nothing. "Who said I'm with Cass?"

"Oh, *please*. You've been holding hands like teenagers for weeks."

"We're friends."

Lulu responds with her head tilted to the side, raised eyebrows, and a sly smile—a *that's a cute lie* kind of smile.

Thing is, I don't know how to label Cassidy and me. But the idea that we're associated together—that I'm *with* him as a couple—is exciting. She's right.

"See?" she says. "I like men who value fancy shoes and nerdy glasses. You like gym shorts and hoodies."

"Hey now," I say with a laugh. "Cassidy is more than gym shorts."

"Aha. You're defensive. Only girlfriends get that defensive."

"I'm not—whatever."

Lulu smiles as if she's won. I want to argue more, but our conversation is interrupted when Jasper rushes in with heavy breaths, palms splayed on the counter instantly.

I freeze. He's just that type of man to stop you in your tracks. If it's not the stern way his lips flatten beneath his thick beard, then it's his piercing periwinkle eyes. I remember Cassidy's rumor about Jasper's eyes turning red when he's angry. I don't know how cheery Wendy tamed this beast, but props to her accomplishment.

My head juts back. "Whoa, what's the emergency?"

"I pissed her off," he answers.

I laugh. "Who?"

"Wendy?" Lulu fills in the blank.

He clenches his jaw. "I need the biggest bouquet you have."

"I mean … would she even like that?" I ask.

Jasper runs a rough hand over his bearded cheek. I've never seen this man so stressed. Then again, I don't see much of Jasper anyway. Maybe he's stressed a lot, and I just don't see it. I reach out to touch his forearm for comfort, and then I remember it's Jasper and think he might gut me like a fish for doing so. I instead play with the edge of the counter.

"I just … I can't have her mad at me. I don't want to lose her," he says. "I refuse."

Refuse.

Lulu and I exchange a glance, likely both hanging on that word.

"Well, let's get her something that matters," I suggest. "What's her favorite color?"

"Yellow," he answers.

Lulu barks out a laugh, hopping off the counter. "God, you are *far* from in the doghouse."

He furrows his eyebrows in question.

Lulu sighs. "Because you know her favorite color."

Jaspers squints.

"It means a lot to know those things," I clarify.

"Why wouldn't I know that?" he deadpans.

Lulu slouches, letting out a small whine.

He grimaces. "Listen, I'm good at certain things. Repairing ladders. Binding books …"

Lulu bemoans, "You bound her a book? Are you kidding me?"

He blinks. "Is that bad?"

She tosses her hand in the air, as if signaling to God. "It's unfair, is what it is."

Jasper swivels his gaze to me. "I'm not good at flowers. When can it be ready?"

"I'd need maybe thirty minutes."

"My lunch break is almost over." He looks at his hands, as if considering. "I can come back at—"

I twist my lips to the side. "How about this: is she at home?"

"Yes."

"Well, how about I deliver it to her personally? And then you get one more bouquet after work too. On the house. It'll be double the surprise—like you couldn't stop thinking about her all day."

His lips pull up into a secret smile, barely visible beneath his thick beard. "I never stop thinking about her."

Lulu groans, "God, stop. Please. I've never felt more single in my life."

I smile at him. "Of course you don't stop thinking about her. You're a Davies man."

Jasper and Wendy's cottage is a dream. Down a little ways from the main sidewalk, their tiny blue house sits on flat seaside property, separated by only a white picket fence. According to Lulu, they live closer to Never Harbor than they did last summer. She says they renovated this house over the winter. You can tell.

The wraparound porch railings look newly painted white, the navy-blue siding isn't windblown by the salty sea breeze yet, and the gravel looks freshly laid down. The tinkling of wind chimes greets me when I reach the end of their driveway.

There's only one other neighbor on their left, in a house looking a little less new, save for a porch that is under construction. A trampoline sits between both houses. Two abandoned child-sized bikes lie in the front yards.

I walk up Jasper and Wendy's porch steps with my hand clutched around a small collection of yellow daylilies. I knock on the door. After a minute, it creaks open. But it's not Wendy I see. Instead, it's Izzy.

Isabel, the bar manager for The Hideaway, has her blonde hair pulled into a frizzy bun. She arches a single eyebrow. Her green summer shorts expose curved legs. Her hips tilt to the side—attitude apparent in such a simple gesture.

I haven't seen her in a long time, and I could have sworn she and Wendy weren't exactly speaking anymore. But things tend to change around here, I suppose.

"What are those for?" she asks.

I swallow. "Do I have the right house?"

From behind her, Wendy appears, brown hair tied back in a delicate ribbon and barefoot under her sundress.

"These are for you," I announce, reaching over Izzy's head to hand them over. Even with the high bun, she's short enough that it isn't difficult.

Wendy takes the bouquet. "From who?"

Izzy twists her lips to the side. "Who else?"

"Jasper," I answer.

A smile twitches at the side of Wendy's mouth as she leans in to smell them.

In the house, shoes squeak over hardwood, and two faces appear behind Wendy's legs. I recognize one—Sam with his feathery blond hair and toothy grin. The other is a freckled girl with short, curly brown hair. I could mistake her for Shirley Temple if I didn't get a better glance.

She gasps. "Ooh, flowers!"

Wendy twists around and hands them to Sam. "Mind putting these in a vase for me, bud?"

"You got it!"

He holds them delicately, as if worried they'll break. The other girl runs through the kitchen.

"Sam, we have to cut the stems first!" she commands.

I snort, and Wendy laughs to herself. "That's the girl from next door. I watch her when her parents are at work. She's—"

"Awesome," Izzy finishes for her.

Wendy nods, wincing at me. "A little bossy. I worry Sam gets pushed around too much."

I peer past them and watch as Sam cradles the bouquet into the vase she holds out for him. She stumbles a little, knocking a lemon off the kitchen island. But once they're securely inside, she holds up her hand, and he high-fives it. Then, hand in hand, she drags him through the back door and back down to the rocky shore.

"Want to come inside?" Wendy asks. "We're making lemonade."

"Oh, sure," I say, following in with Izzy behind me shutting the door.

I take a seat at the kitchen island barstool. Wendy gets down glasses while Izzy pushes a precut lemon through a squeezer.

Wendy slides a glass my way. "Thank you again."

"For delivering flowers?" I shrug. "It's my job."

"Yeah, but you didn't have to come all this way. And you walked, right?"

"I like walking."

She laughs, like maybe she can hear the excuse in my words. "I really appreciate it. I'm sure Jasper does too."

"It's a decent apology," Izzy says, tossing a leftover lemon in the trash and grabbing another.

I run a finger over the rim of the glass. "If you don't mind me asking … what happened?"

Wendy looks at Izzy, and both of them smile—Wendy's gentler and Izzy's with a playful eye roll.

"He made plans for Saturday," Wendy explains. "But we already had plans. It was simple miscommunication."

"I planned a whole celebration for her," Izzy adds. "She finished another book. She deserves it."

"Oh no, what'd he plan instead?" I ask.

Izzy grumbles, "A surprise book release party too."

"And you got mad?" I ask Wendy.

Wendy laughs. "Well, sorta. It was a surprise, so he wouldn't tell me what it was for. I thought he'd forgotten about my book."

Izzy squeezes another lemon with a bit more force than needed. "I might have gotten pissed on her behalf and said he was being a bad boyfriend."

Wendy traces a finger over the flowers, wistfully musing, "He could never be."

Izzy sighs. "I should probably be the one sending flowers to him."

"Want me to?" I tease.

With a half smirk, Izzy surprisingly nods. "Do it. Confuse the hell out of him."

All three of us laugh, and Wendy shakes her head. "He's just so stubborn sometimes."

"They're all stubborn," Izzy adds.

"Who?" But I think I know.

"Those darn Davies men," Wendy says through bubbled laughter. It's light, airy. Pretty and elegant, just like her ribbon and flowy sundress.

Izzy smiles at Wendy, and suddenly, I don't blame the woman who seems to be pessimism incarnate being protective of her friend. She probably likes Wendy's sunshine.

Wendy hands another lemon to Izzy. "How's Cass?"

I swallow and almost choke, giving my own—less cute—laughter. "Good," I answer.

"Really good?" Izzy asks, snickering.

"Yes," I say slowly.

Wendy bites her bottom lip. "Can I ask something else?"

"Sure."

"Is something … going on? Between you two?"

How does word keep spreading so fast in Never Harbor? Everyone seems to know things before even I've had time to process, as if the town itself has decided we're a couple and that's that.

A blush creeps up my neck, and I shrug.

Izzy smirks. "Say less."

"He likes you, you know," Wendy says.

"How long are you planning on staying in town?" Izzy asks.

My balloon pops.

"Oh." I tap on the side of my glass. "Yeah, I don't know actually. Just the summer?"

Izzy's eyebrows furrow, like she's almost offended on the town's behalf. She might be one of the most abrasive people I've ever met. I can't tell if I like it or not.

"What's stopping you from staying past that?" she asks.

I grew up here, I want to say.

"I don't know," I answer.

"Are you worried about someone judging you for staying?" Wendy asks, like she's reading my mind. But instead of being offended, the words are accompanied by another light laugh. "Why?"

"I'm not sure," I admit. *I'm not. Not anymore.* "Why do you two love it here?"

Izzy shrugs. "I ask myself that every day."

"Hush," Wendy says, nudging her. "You're not helping."

Izzy smirks. "In all seriousness? It's home. I like my job. I like the regulars at The Hideaway, even when they get drunk." She huffs a laugh. "Maybe *especially* when they get drunk. And I like … other people too." Her words fade off. She looks at Wendy, who stifles a laugh for some reason I can't interpret. "I guess. Reluctantly."

"What about you?" I ask Wendy.

"I can't leave Never Harbor," she answers simply. "The kids I teach are so special. The events we have are perfect. I love it all. You can't beat being so close to the sea either. I did try moving away once. For a bit. It didn't work out."

"Why?"

As if on cue, Sam and the neighbor girl with the wild hair barrel back into the house with the back door still wrenched open. "Wendy, can we buy some kazoos?"

She blinks at the two children beaming up at her. "I'm afraid to ask why."

"Thanks!"

Sam accepts Wendy's concern as affirmation with a tight hug, and the two run off again.

I smile, but it instantly falls.

This life feels idyllic. Why did my mom want to leave something like this—me? What am I missing—on either side? Did she know something about this town everyone else didn't, or am I trying to find truth in a selfish woman's pursuit of happiness?

"This place is home," Wendy says. "It's the kind of town where you don't have to grow up. You can just *exist*."

Izzy gives a half smile. "Agree."

I nod to myself, silent for a moment, before Wendy holds up the full pitcher. "Lemonade?"

As she fills my glass, I look around at Wendy's little slice of paradise, and I wonder if I've found mine as well.

- *Chapter Twenty-Nine* -

"I'M NOT HERE TO MAKE FRIENDS."

Cassidy

We're one week out from the festival—no, mixer—and I'm surprised by how it's all coming together. The light-blue linens are ordered, the Chiavari chairs we're renting should arrive soon, and Ma even threw in a red carpet to lead musicians toward the stage. I swear, she thrifts everything.

I'm running from one moment to the next. For once, I can't afford to be late. I'm setting alarms and trying to leave quicker than the usual, lingering goodbyes that are normal to Never Harbor.

It's different … odd. Responsible, sure, but uncomfortable. I'm not sure how I feel about it.

Our music-festival-turned-wine-mixer schmoozefest is not what I wanted it to be at the beginning of summer. The end result will honestly look nothing like a Never Harbor event, but for what it is, I'm satisfied with Dustin's vision.

Though, honestly, I have no idea if this is what he wants.

Ol' Dust-bin won't show for any meetings, and it's increasingly frustrating as the days pass. We have no final approval on items; we're still operating off the vague notes he sent through bullet points in an email. But what we have planned isn't too shabby.

Laura, now off her crutch, takes one look at my laptop with organized spreadsheets and PowerPoints—thanks to Marina—and grins.

"Well, looks like you've got this, Cass. Proud of you."

Proud.

It's such a funny feeling to receive.

Peter
Cass! Shooting over a link on LLCs. Ma sent some info too.

Jasper
Spoke with Rafe. He'll design a logo.

Bonnie
I want to help! What can I do?

Milo
Cass, I looked over the certifications you might need. You already have one, but I think the second one on nutrition is required, and I don't believe you have that. Correct me if I'm wrong.

The texts from my siblings keep coming in throughout the day. They're filled with bite-sized advice or reassurance, and even Jasper's curt texts feel welcoming.

I push out the community center's double doors that afternoon, feeling energized. That maybe I can do this. If the wine mixer is coming together without a hitch, maybe I'm on the right path.

"Hey, Curly." Down the sidewalk saunters a familiar, sunny blonde with a potted plant curled in her arms.

I'm definitely on the right path if the sidewalk ends with her.

"Well, hey there, honey."

Marina smiles with those gorgeous pink lips, and my heart fills to the brim. Like a balloon that's so big that it's set to pop at any second.

I descend the stairs and take Fido from her, cradling the pot in my arms.

"You don't have to do that," she says.

"Can't I carry the kid home?" I joke. "How was work?"

"Oh. It was fine," she answers.

The sentence is short and a little worrisome. I raise my eyebrows, waiting for more, but it never comes.

"Alllll right," I say, dragging out the word. "Well, that's good."

Marina hasn't been the same since our night at The Hideaway. Quiet, distant, and vague. If no clothes are involved, we're fine. She's sexy, demanding, and clearly into me. But outside of that, it's almost awkward. If I consider why for too long, it twists my stomach in ways I don't like.

"How's business prep coming along?" she asks me.

I shush her playfully. "Haven't told Laura I'm doing that yet."

"But she'll be so happy for you! Did you look at that certification I sent you?"

I chuckle. "Milo sent me the same one."

"Perfect. I also have timelines and study guides pulled down too."

I pull her hand to mine as we cross the sidewalk, kissing the back of her knuckles.

"Sometimes, I underestimate how great all of you are," I admit.

"I think you underestimate *yourself*," she corrects me. "Including how many people care about you."

"Maybe."

But that's not the case. It's not me. It's her. Her reassurance. Her happiness. Her light.

Marina rises to her toes and kisses my stubbled cheek. "Definitely."

I feel my cheeks flush. She kissed me in public. In front of all of Never Harbor.

Receiving my family's help is one thing, but Marina's assistance is all-consuming. I live for the way she runs a thumb over the back of my palm or how her freckled cheeks flush red whenever I look at her … it's overwhelming that anyone could support me that much.

Except there's the problem of how her expression fades when she thinks I'm not looking.

Marina's nose loses its cute scrunch, and while her skin isn't as pale as it was when the fish leftovers betrayed her, it's ashen in a different way.

We walk hand in hand down the sidewalk, cutting through a grassy park area between two rows of houses—a shortcut to our townhome. I open the white fence for her, and she slips through. Her long dress whips near me, and I reach out for it, letting the fabric flow through my fingers. Airy. Weightless. Unlike this new version of her.

I squeeze her palm, halting her in place. "Hey, is everything all right, Starkey?"

She blinks, like resurfacing from deep thoughts.

"Yeah," she answers, but her words are a ghostly whisper.

"Okay, spill the hot goss."

She smirks. "Hot goss?"

"That's what cool kids say, right? For gossip?"

She clicks her tongue, looking over my shoulder and into the distance, but I reach up to redirect her chin so she's looking at me once more.

"Hey. What's going on?"

Her green eyes dart between mine for a moment, and I'm almost relieved to hear, "It's complicated."

I'd rather have the truth than tiptoe around a lie.

"Try me."

"It's just … well, I'm only here for the summer, right?"

"Yeah, and …"

"I just worry … what we'll be like after that."

"Uh-huh. Well, that kinda sounds like a problem for us in a few weeks, don't you think?" I step forward. "Not now." I lean down and nip at her ear. "When I could have my girl's thighs around my head."

She lets out a shaky breath. "You are"—she laughs and pushes my chest—"too hot for your own good."

"I'll be good to *you* if you let me."

She gives me a side-eye, then sighs.

"Is that all?" I ask. "Worrying about the future?"

She tongues her cheek. "How's the wine mixer going?"

"We're gonna talk about work?"

"Of course."

I sigh. "Well, Dustin still won't respond to our meeting invites—"

"Dustin." She stops me suddenly. "Do you talk to him much?"

I try to shake out the sudden twinge in my chest, the way my heart beats a little faster at the idea that what might be wrong with her actually includes another man.

That man in particular.

"Nah, not often," I admit. "Why?"

She twists her lips to the side. "I don't know …"

Marina was on top of the world a week ago, and now, she can't get out of her head. I shift Fido to one arm and reach out to grab her dress in my other. I tug her into my arms. She smiles, but it looks forced.

"Hey, are you still thinking about your job there? Do you want to go back?"

"God, no."

But that's all she says before silence creeps between us. Water trickles in the park's koi pond. The community garden plants sway on either side of us. I inhale the scent of Marina. I could easily drown in her.

I squeeze her waist. "How about we have a *Survivor* night, huh? Binge a whole season? It'll be good times."

She smiles weakly. "I like your good times."

"I know you do."

"But, um," she says, "can I rain-check until tomorrow?" Marina slowly disentangles herself from me. "I want to see my dad tonight, if that's all right. I haven't talked to him in a while."

"Oh." I try not to show how quickly I deflate. "Yeah, for sure. But tomorrow ..."

She grins. "Yeah, tomorrow is for us." She winks.

My heart sinks at the idea that she only seems happy when it might involve sex. I've had my fair share of friends with benefits, but Marina is different. At least, I thought she was. Maybe she doesn't feel the same way. Maybe this is just her summer fling.

If all she wants is something physical, then I can fulfill that need for her.

But I hope that's not the case.

I kiss her goodbye, and she takes Fido from me. We slowly walk backward, hand in hand, in opposite directions until we finally disconnect.

But something isn't right.

"Hey," I call before she closes the fence. "Is there something you aren't telling me? Honestly."

Marina swallows. "Honestly? Yes."

My stomach twists.

"Okay," I say slowly. "Is it bad?"

She's quiet for a moment before asking, "Can you trust me?"

"Of course."

"Then, I need to keep this bit of gossip just for me. For now at least."

And because I'm a man of my word, I nod.

"Okay. I trust you."

And I do. Maybe it's not smart, but I never said I was that smart of a guy anyway.

- *Chapter Thirty* -

UNTETHERED

Marina

The nerves in my chest feel like an itch I can't scratch, so I go to the one place that solves all issues—my dad's fishy-scented place of employment, the Never Harbor docks.

By the time I arrive, creaking over wooden planks and past rattling chains and hooks, the fresh air has made me feel slightly better. Or maybe it was Cassidy's unconditional acceptance—that he was able to basically say, point blank, *I trust you to keep something from me.*

I take a deep inhale and blow it out before knocking on my dad's office door.

"Dad?"

Inside, my dad sits at the desk. Standing beside it, with arms crossed over his chest, is Jasper.

"Am I interrupting business stuff?" I ask with a grin.

Jasper shakes his head. "It's fine. We'll circle back tomorrow."

"Oh, no, don't let me—"

"If Sam dropped by, I'd drop everything too," Jasper explains, raising a single eyebrow. "Tomorrow, Starkey."

"Aye, aye, Cap'n," my dad says with a salute.

I step aside, giving Jasper enough berth to quietly pass by.

"Oh, Lulu is holding your flowers at the shop," I add. "Grab them anytime."

He towers over me, smiling—another secret one beneath the beard. "Thanks."

Only the sound of his work boots echoing down the hall alert me of his absence.

"Boy, he's intimidating," I finally breathe.

My dad smiles, rapping his knuckles on the desk. "What's up, Guppy? Want coffee?"

"No, I'm all set." I walk in, choosing my usual seat in the creaking wooden chair next to the window, setting down Fido, and pulling my knees up to my chin. "Just feeling a little out of sorts, I guess."

"Cass treatin' you right?"

I laugh. "Right off the bat, huh?"

"Well, you're living with a man. I have to ask."

I'm close with my dad, but I can never tell him just *exactly* how well my roommate is treating me. Even if I kept the details vague, I wouldn't know where to start. Where Cassidy and I started is unclear, even to me.

All I know is I like it.

I like him.

A lot.

And the last thing I want is to ruin a good thing by sharing it with the man who might kill Cassidy if he knew.

"He's good," I answer.

My dad squints. "Y'know … there's been word something is going on at the house. Between you two."

I stiffen but try to play it off by scratching some of the old paint from the wooden table.

"Small-town rumors aren't always true, Dad. You know that."

He snorts. "No, what I do know is, there's usually a kernel of truth."

I don't want to lie, but I also don't want him thinking I just moved in with someone and instantly started sleeping with them. I mean, I did. That's pretty much exactly what happened. But it's different with Cass.

"Nothing's going on," I answer.

My dad slowly nods. "All right …" He says it slow enough that I can tell he doesn't believe me, but I can't worry about that right now. "What's got you feeling out of sorts then?"

I sigh. "Everything?"

"Go on," he grunts.

"I should job-hunt," I say. "I haven't done it lately."

"Why do you need to job-hunt?"

"Well, I have to get a job somewhere."

"You have a job," he counters.

"Yeah. Here. Not ... somewhere else."

He narrows his eyes. "Why not stay here? What's so wrong about it?"

I can't answer that. I don't know how. Not with how much I might be falling for Never Harbor. Wendy and Izzy were right—something about here feels like home.

I adjust in my seat. "How are you and Bobbi?"

"Changing the subject?"

"Please."

"We're good. Is that what's bothering you? Me and Bobbi?"

"No!" I shake my head. "No. I mean, how is she?"

"Fine," he says, then tilts his head to the side. "Well, a little irritated, but fine." Dad leans back in his chair, the leather whining with the motion. "Turns out, the mayor's boy is a bit of a nuisance to her."

It always comes back to Dustin Barrie, doesn't it?

"What?" I ask.

Dad shrugs. "He's making a lot of demands."

"Wait, what?" *Does Cassidy know this?*

"Yeah, he comes into her coffee shop every day with some off-the-wall order, and if he's not served immediately, he gets snippy."

"Someone gets *snippy* with Bobbi? Isn't that illegal?"

My dad chortles out a laugh. "Seems like it should be, huh? It also sounds like he's getting difficult with the music festival."

"Wine mixer," I correct.

Dad throws his hands in the air. "Whatever it is. Did you know he's adding tablecloth linens? Jukes might riot if he finds out we have to use different forks for salad and steak. It's a music festival—"

"Wine mixer."

"Christ's sake, Marina!"

I cover my mouth with my palm to hide my laugh, instead muttering, "Tablecloths. The audacity."

He leers at me.

"Well, how do you even know all this?"

"People say things at The Hideaway." He jabs a meaty finger at me. "*Some* gossip is true."

"Some."

He chuckles. "Hmm. Y'know, your mom always thought it was a

talent of mine to simply … *know* things. Back then, I told her every-thing."

My stomach drops at the mention of her. It's funny how my dad keeps wearing these rose-colored glasses when it comes to the version of her before she left us. I think about my parents' relationship, and it's hard not to compare it to mine now.

Would Cassidy ever leave me like she did?

I shift uncomfortably in my chair. "Well, you tell *me* everything now, right?"

"And Bobbi."

I smile, but I know it looks weak. I'm happy for him. But I hate that he seems unsure about it every time Bobbi is brought up.

He squints. "Are you all right with that?"

"Of course I am." I blow out a breath. "I'm honestly offended you'd even ask."

Dad gives a crooked smile. "Will you stay here? In Never Harbor?"

I shrug. "I … I'm not sure anymore. This place does feel … differ-ent."

It's a good different, and I don't know what to think about it. Home is good because of Cassidy. Florally Yours. Lulu and the Davies crew.

I swallow and look away. "So, tablecloths, huh?" I tease.

Dad shakes his head. "Fuckin' tablecloths."

Chapter Thirty-One

NEVER TRUST A SUMMER SUIT

Marina

"Eggs, bacon, and …" Cassidy kisses me on the lips hard with the full weight of his lazy morning demeanor. "Me."

"Breakfast of champions," I say with a smile.

"I thought so too."

I'm in better spirits this morning. Maybe it was visiting my dad, or maybe it's because Cassidy is happy too. At least partially.

I watch from the corner of my eye as he lets out a large yawn. He has slight purple circles under his eyes. He told me he fit in another client last night when I visited Dad, then helped Peter at The Hideaway. He didn't get home until two in the morning. Now, it's seven o'clock, and he's trying to make breakfast as if he had more than five hours of sleep.

Cassidy crawled out of bed before me—giving my ass a squeeze he probably thought I wouldn't notice—then hunkered down at the kitchen table with his laptop to work on mixer and business tasks before making breakfast.

I'm proud of him, but he's working himself too hard. I don't think he notices just how hard. In fact, he's zoned out over the stove, absent-mindedly pushing eggs here and there.

I kiss him on the cheek, bringing him back to the present.

"Are you excited?" I ask.

He blinks. "About what?"

I shake his forearm with a grin. "All the changes! The business."

"Oh. Yeah. Hey, we're hanging out tonight, right?"

"Only if you make sure you're home by four. No late appointments. No nothing, okay?"

"Twist my arm."

"And I'm also joining you to go to Rafe's this morning."

His brow furrows, which is the exact reaction I wanted. "We're going to Rafe's?"

"He told me to drop by the store before he opens," I explain, biting my bottom lip. "He has mock-ups for your business logo."

He laughs, reaching out to stroke my hair. I revel in the motion.

"And how do you know that?"

"We've got an email chain going on," I say. "Me and the rest of the Davies crew."

"Emails?"

I shrug innocuously. "And maybe a couple of shared folders too."

He pulls me closer, kissing my forehead. He continues for more time than usual, and the longer it lasts, the more I giggle until we both descend into laughter—the type that bubbles over and is unstoppable once you start.

That's Cassidy though. Unstoppable. Here. Present.

Rafe spins the paper around and raps his knuckles on the counter.

Cassidy's jaw drops. "Whoa."

"That looks stunning, Rafe," I breathe.

He shrugs, keeping that usual lazy look about him. But nobody can deny Rafe's talent. Cassidy's new logo is perfect.

A dumbbell sits front and center, overlaid with a sketch of a bear, stylized in browns, reds, and blacks. Cassidy's name is scrawled in cursive over the top. Beneath, in small block letters, are the words *personal trainer*.

"It's so great," Cassidy says through an ever-growing grin.

I nudge him with my elbow. "It looks *amazing*."

"Yes, sorry, I'm just …" He can't stop smiling. It's so cute. "Rafe, thank you."

Rafe nods. "No problem. Don't just thank me though. Bonnie actually came up with the concept."

Cassidy's brow furrows. "That's … uh …" He shakes whatever thought he was having and nods. "I can't believe it's really happening."

"Soon," I say, rubbing up and down his forearm. "Just gotta get through this mixer."

Rafe gives a scoffing half laugh.

Cassidy darts his eyes to him. "That's a reaction if I've ever seen one."

"It's gonna be a mess," he answers.

"Whoa, what?" Cassidy asks, and my blood pressure rises faster than it should.

"Pardon?" I snap. "Cass has put a lot of work into that."

Cassidy places a hand on my waist. "Easy there, killer."

"No," Rafe says, rolling his eyes. "Not because of you. You're doing good, man."

Cassidy straightens up. I wonder if it's rare to get a compliment from this guy, clad in leather and ink.

"It's the mayor's kid who's giving everyone problems."

My head swims. "What's going on with Dustin?"

"What *isn't*? Let's just say, we've got a history now. I'm done with him," Rafe says with a casual shrug.

"Why?" Cassidy asks.

Rafe's eyes hood over more. I didn't know he could look more bored than he already did.

"I don't like when someone fucks over my friends."

"I didn't know you had fr—"

I whip my hand out to hit Cassidy's stomach. "Cass."

Rafe smirks. "I get it. Guy owns a little shop on Main. Sleeps in the apartment above. Doesn't talk to anyone. Must be lonely."

"Well, yeah," Cassidy replies on a laugh, but the moment it comes out, Rafe rolls his eyes, and it dawns on me that maybe nobody really knows Rafe that well at all.

Rafe sighs. "First night he was here, after he *didn't* help you guys take Laura to the clinic, he got a little rowdy at the bar. Tried to hit on Izzy, and she wasn't having any of it. She kicked him out. He wouldn't leave, so I had to drag the guy out by his suit jacket. Izzy came back the next morning to a health inspection with no notice. She *always* receives notice from another restaurant nearby."

"That's just a coincidence though, right?" I ask.

"Is it? Guy in a liquor supply business? A company whose whole business model includes having connections with anyone and everyone in the restaurant industry?"

I twist my lips to the side. "Did she fail it?"

"They're all right," Rafe answers. "But I'll be damned if I support something of his after."

"Dad actually mentioned something similar with Bobbi."

Cassidy whips his head to me. "What?"

"Yeah." I wince. "Seems like Dustin's kinda difficult with everyone."

Rafe raises his eyebrows. "See? He's just here to boost his ego. I'm not getting near anything of his."

"Wait, but"—Cassidy closes his eyes and shakes his head—"I thought you had a booth at the festival."

"The festival, sure," Rafe confirms. "But not the *mixer*. My art isn't made for their crowd anyway. It's nothing personal, yeah?"

Cassidy looks shocked. I wonder if he's thinking the same thing I am—that maybe Dustin scared off other vendors too.

I glance at the logo again, tracing my hand over the ink. "Well, thanks for this."

"Good luck," Rafe says to Cassidy. "I like it when people go the small business route."

"Can I expect to see you at the gym?"

He smirks. "Maybe so, Cass."

The three of us empty onto the sidewalk with Rafe trailing behind us, lighter poised near the end of his cigarette.

"I never trust a man who wears a suit in the middle of summer for no good reason," Rafe drawls.

He lifts his eyebrows, and both of us nod in response. Because it resonates far more than it should with us. And probably for different ways.

We wave goodbye, and he gives his signature chin tilt before billowing smoke rises above his head.

Cassidy looks like his brain is already turning. "I should go talk to Laura. Maybe she—"

"I thought you had a meeting with Bobbi?"

He shakes his head, touching his thumb and forefinger to his temple. "Right. Yeah. No, you're right."

I reach for his hand, giving it a squeeze. "You okay?"

"Yeah, I just have to … there's a lot of …"

The dark circles under his eyes are deeper than I noticed. "Whoa, big guy. Let me ask again. You *okay?*"

He nods, but his smile is forced. "Yeah, just let me send some texts."

"To who?"

"Laura … she's gotta know—"

"No," I blurt out.

"What?"

"No. You're worrying about something you can't change. You've stretched yourself too thin. You're done."

He pulls in a disbelieving breath. "I'm *done?*"

"Give me your phone," I demand.

Staring at me for a second, Cassidy surprisingly ends up handing it to me.

Does he truly trust me that much?

"I'm canceling everything for you today," I say.

"Everything?"

I stare at him pointedly. "Everything. You need a break. And I'm making you take one."

"What about—"

"Nope. No *what abouts* or *what ifs* or *can I please stay out late and lift more weights.*"

He smirks. "You read my mind."

"It's just you and a comfy bed all day, okay? And stay there."

"Can I watch television?"

"If you're good."

"Oh, I can be your good boy."

I roll my eyes even if goose bumps spread over my arms.

"People always say you should celebrate the small milestones," I say. "And you've had a lot lately, so it deserves a celebration."

"Right, those darn *people*," he says. "Giving great advice."

I reach up to trace my thumb over the sunken purple circles under his eyes.

I sigh. "Get rest, okay, honey?"

"Don't *honey* me," he says. "You're honey. I'm … meathead."

I snort. "Then, get rest, meathead."

"Yes, ma'am."

I like him. I like him *so* much.

And I don't think that feeling is going anywhere.

I don't know if I am either.

Chapter Thirty-Two

MERMAID LAGOON

Cassidy

I spend all day in bed, as Marina instructed.

It doesn't feel good to stay at home all day, but it doesn't feel bad either. I don't like holing up all day like a hermit, missing friendly faces, and not answering texts. It guts me to miss appointments, like I'm letting people down even though they were all notified well beforehand. But I do like the freedom of an empty day, roaming from one room to the next with coffee in hand. I even peer out the parlor window for a time, the large one Wendy always kept cracked. I've never spent time sitting on the bench, just listening to the sounds of kids playing at the beach one block over or hearing the ice cream truck rolling by. I hear the thump of a rolled-up newspaper hitting my stoop. I wonder if I should say hi to Steve, but then remember I don't have to.

The house is quiet, but it's not as daunting as it was a few weeks ago. Because I know who will be back home later. She always comes back.

Marina gets home in the early afternoon, finding me splayed on the couch, watching *Survivor*.

"Are you watching without me?" she asks.

I smile. "It's an older season. I'd never continue ours without you."

The flush of pink across her cheeks is all the affirmation I need.

"Sit down," I say, patting the seat next to me.

But all she does is look at me—really look—as if taking me in, eyeing my lips, down to my chest, and back up. She winds her hands together.

"Actually," she says, "I'd like to take you somewhere."

"Oh, yeah?"

Slowly, her lips tip up, and she nods. "Yeah. Somewhere special to me."

"Well, let me grab our treat first …"

"Treat?"

I put on my shoes, walk into the kitchen, and hold up two sandwich bags.

She gasps. "Your world-famous PB&J?"

"The very one. Had a feeling we'd go for a picnic."

"Always reading my mind."

I laugh. "Or I was planning on it either way."

"I'll pretend you read my mind anyway."

"I could only be so lucky."

We leave the house and start our trek on the sidewalk with Marina leading the way. A couple blocks down, we open our sandwich bags, knocking our PB&Js together in a *cheers!* motion before digging in.

"This is good," she says through a mouthful.

I chuckle at her enthusiasm, wiping peanut butter from the corner of her lips and licking it off my thumb.

"You're ridiculous," I say because I can't tell her what I really want to, which is, *I adore you. I can't stop thinking about you. You make my days incredible.*

I don't know where she's taking me, but as long as I'm there with her, I don't mind.

Eventually, we pass The Hideaway, down the road to the bed-and-breakfast. She shamelessly cuts through their yard, and I realize where we're headed.

"Mermaid Lagoon?" I ask. "I haven't been here since high school."

"It's my favorite place in Never Harbor," she says. "I've never taken anyone with me."

My eyes widen, and I can't stop looking at her. We hop rock to rock across the beach, her dress billowing out in the sea breeze. I place a hand on her waist to steady her once she endures a slick surface, but it's also just to feel her.

She's taking me to *her* place. Her secret spot.

We finally turn a corner into the small alcove, and I'm amazed at how unchanged it feels from ten years ago.

Large. Cavernous. A pool of water takes up most of the area, craggy rocks shooting out here and there. Water drips from the ceiling, plunking in random intervals as a distant echo. I watch Marina eye the high ceiling. I remember all the parties Peter hosted here before he owned The Hideaway. I wonder if teens still come here.

"Did you know I touched the ceiling once?" I ask. "Somehow, Milo propped me on his shoulders, and I got it barely with the tips of my fingers."

She grins. "I was just thinking about that."

I bark out a laugh that echoes through the cavern. "Were you really thinking that?"

"Yeah."

"Then, maybe I can read your mind," I say with a wink.

Her cheeks flush pink again. I like that even after a few times, I can still make her blush.

"Try to read mine now," she says.

She pulls down the straps of her dress, letting it fall in a pool around her ankles. Goose bumps instantly scatter across her skin, and I can't look away.

My lips part at the vision of her perky breasts, the hardened nipples, the smooth plane of her stomach, down to turquoise panties. My mouth runs dry.

"You know, getting naked isn't exactly what I expected on our picnic," I joke.

"I know," she confesses. "You're not that conniving."

I choke out a laugh. "I'm really not."

"That's what I like about you."

"Well, I like that you don't wear a bra, honey."

She shrugs innocuously, and my eyes follow the bounce of her breasts as her shoulders rise and fall. "Bras are too uncomfortable."

"Too inconvenient," I correct.

She pulls in the corner of her bottom lip. "Well, are you going to join me?"

"You didn't even have to ask."

I grab the corner of my T-shirt, ripping it over my head. She shamelessly stares at my bare chest, and I toss her a wink while shucking my gym shorts to the floor and stepping out in only boxer briefs.

"We're swimming like this?" I ask playfully. I look at the cool water. "It might be cold."

But when I glance back at her, she's still staring at me—though now at the bulge in my boxers.

She hooks her thumbs into her panties and tugs them down, stepping one leg out, then the other until she's wearing nothing at all. Chills break out over my skin, but something about her being naked in public is exhilarating.

"No," she says, tilting her head. "I'm thinking we swim *this* way."

I don't take my eyes off her once as she slowly enters the water, the dimples in her lower back disappearing under the surface. And even though she hisses at how cold it must be and her shoulders hike up to her ears, she laughs out of sheer excitement.

Wading to a smooth rock in the center, she climbs on top, and I admire the sight—her naked body with water sluicing over her breasts and thighs, feet playing in the water, sending ripples over to me. She runs fingers through her long blonde locks, taking a small section and beginning to braid. Marina is a vision.

She smirks at me. "Well?"

I chuckle. "You want to play that game?"

"I want to play that game."

"Just know you started it." I grip my boxers by the waist and wind them down my body.

Every time we've touched each other, it's been in the dark. She's never gotten a full look at my cock, but the moment it pops out from my boxers, bobbing over the waistband and hanging between my thick legs, her tongue darts out to lick dry lips. It's hard to contain my massive grin.

I step out of my underwear, then take steps toward the water.

"God, yep, okay, stings a bit," I say once the cold waves lap over my waist.

She dips back in the pool, sloshing over to me, water spraying over her smooth stomach.

I take her hand and pull her closer. "Come here, otter friend. Make me warm."

Her breasts hit my chest, the radiating warmth between us like an instant furnace. We exchange laughs, simultaneously dipping lower until the water reaches our shoulders.

She rests her head under my chin. I wrap my arms around her waist, stroking my palms up and down her spine.

I love it.

I love … us.

No. It's more than that.

Suddenly, my stomach drops in fear, like there's nobody spotting me at the bench in the gym.

I love her.

Every morning, I watch the sun beam in through the window, splaying over Marina's pink cheeks and halo of blonde hair. Specks of dust glimmer around her, like the shimmers of magic. And every morning, I want to sit there and watch her for longer.

But she's leaving. I've dealt with people leaving before. Too many times. I can't do it again. So, I hold her and try not to fantasize about how it would sound to say *I love you* even though it feels perfect in my head.

"This is nice," she says, breaking the silence with a sigh.

"You seem happier," I observe.

"Happier?"

I nod against her. "You've just seemed off for a couple of days now."

She clears her throat. "You don't miss a thing, do you?"

"It's the gut feeling, y'know? Your energy is off."

Marina snorts. "Are you teasing me?"

"Maybe."

My arms pull her tighter to me, sloshing the water against our backs and necks. We both gasp at the new place of contact with the cool water, and both of us laugh.

"You also seem better after today," she says.

"I didn't like taking a day off," I admit. "But you were right."

"I'm always right."

"I'll take your word for it."

"Everyone understood, didn't they?"

I slowly nod. "My family ... this town ... they've never let me down. Not once."

"Which is why you can't let them down either?"

"Yeah. I think so. But I should have known they wouldn't be upset."

She opens her mouth, then closes it, and as if knowing I saw, she shakes her head.

"What's up, honey?"

"You were right," she admits. "I have felt off. Ugh, that sounds so weak."

"You're far from weak."

"It's all a front, I swear."

"I think we all have a front."

She leans back to look me in the eyes. I wonder if she expected me to disagree with her, to tell her, *No, you couldn't possibly have a front.* But I know Marina. I know she doesn't think that way. Her small smile in response confirms this.

I stroke a wet hand over her head. "I'm trying my best with this mixer, but do I think it'll be a raving success?" The nerves in me shift as I realize the truth of what I'm about to confess. "No. No, I don't."

"Why?"

"Because it's me," I say with a laugh. "That's why. My confidence to everyone else is a front."

"But you're knocking it out of the park."

"We'll see, won't we?"

She taps my chest. "No. No negative thoughts, okay?"

"Okay," I say with a smile. "And, hey, for the record, you're rocking it, too, at that flower shop."

"Lies."

"No, as your man—"

"Wait, you're my man?" Marina's head juts back as she smiles. "Am I your woman?"

"Of course."

That quiet satisfaction crosses over her face again. "I'm honored."

"Anyway, as *your* man, I can honestly say that I think you are doing great. I wouldn't lie to you. Seriously."

She nods against me and pulls in a breath. "Then, can I confess something to you?"

"Always."

She bites her bottom lip. "I'm scared. I don't know what to do now."

My chest twinges. "What do you mean?"

"I wanted to leave. I planned to be here for just the summer, but now ..."

"Has that changed?"

"I don't know. I just don't."

"Is it the flower shop?" I ask the question, knowing full well I long for another answer. I want her to say it's *me.* But I can't be selfish like that.

"A little," she says. "But maybe ... I don't know."

I reach my forefinger under her chin, so she looks at me. "Maybe?"

She shrugs. "Maybe ... there's more I'm unsure about."

I swallow. "Can I tell you something?"

"Sure."

"I …" *I love you.* "I think you can do whatever you set your mind to. If there's more here, then follow that feeling." I hope it's me. But I won't be the person who keeps her here. I won't hold her back. "But if it's elsewhere … I get that too."

Like a flash of lightning, Marina kisses me.

Thoughts silence. My heart pummels into my throat. She slings her arms from the water, splashing and dripping onto my chest as she clasps her hands behind my neck.

Our kiss is needy, mouths opening and closing. I groan when she nips my bottom lip. My tongue slips past her mouth to taste. More of her, all of her, every piece I can get.

She hikes her leg to my waist. My cock—now hard, even in the cool water—glides between her legs. We're stumbling in the water together, feverish touches, combined with rough tugs of my hair and scratches across my back. She grinds against the length of me. So needy. Wanting.

"You're so perfect, Marina," I whisper against her mouth.

I glide my palms down from her hair to her jaw, gripping, pulling. She pushes against my lips, and I chase it. We have no room for words, just the sensation of each other. I stroke a thumb over her cheek, my other hand roaming over her neck, to her collar, then down to her soft breast. I clutch a handful, whipping my thumb over the peak.

More sparks, more energy, more desperation.

Then, I break our kiss. I lower into the water, letting it lap over my shoulders and neck. I clutch under her thighs and lift her in my arms. She reaches between us, grasping my cock in her fist. We're thinking in tandem—or maybe not thinking at all. But when I line my tip at her entrance, she lowers down, sinking slowly onto my cock.

I swear I black out in the second it takes for us to realize how far we've gone. But we're exactly that—too far gone. No discussions, no questions … just us. Moving, thrusting and pushing.

Marina grips my shoulder.

"God, you're big," she moans, and, well, if that doesn't just make my entire fucking day.

Her body squeezes around me, and with every thrust I make, I'm panting. She's so tight. I edge my way in, out, then further. Each inch touches more of her—running over nerves that send sensations up to my stomach and out to my fingertips.

"Cass," is the only word she can manage when, on another push, I bury myself fully.

Water splashes around us, waves hitting my chest and spraying my neck.

"Perfect," I breathe. "So, so perfect for me."

I thrust against the water's resistance, grinding fingertips into her thighs. It's wild and loud and … not nearly enough of what I want from her.

I rise from the pool with Marina in my arms. She wraps her legs around my waist, hooking them at the ankles. We're out of the water, droplets sluicing down from our bodies, scattering on the surface as I carry her to the shore. I walk us to a mossy wall, pushing her back against it. With one arm around her waist and the other palm pressed beside her head, I thrust into her again.

Less encumbered by the pool, we're both greedy. Rough. Our bodies echo through the cave, slick from the water as we collide together, each push more intoxicating than the last.

"My legs are shaking, Cass," leaves her mouth before I realize just how true it is.

"Too much?"

"Harder," she moans.

I do as she asked, sending her head whipping back. She runs her hands over my back. I lick a line over her neck.

She exhales against my ear. "You're perfect for me too, Cass."

I swallow, almost tensing up at the words. But I keep thrusting.

Don't think about it.

Don't say it.

I love you.

"God, I need you," I growl.

That is safer. Safe and true.

"Need?" she asks on a breathy exhale.

"*Need*," I insist.

"Oh, I need you too," she whines.

That alone—the possession I crave so badly—gets me there. I quickly jerk into her, pounding against the place that feels like heaven, sending sparks down my spine.

She tightens around my cock, the sensation shooting down to my shuddering thighs.

I know most sex doesn't end in well-timed orgasms—not outside of porn or movies. So, now, when Marina and I orgasm together, I can't help but think that it's fate.

I let out unsteady breaths.

She's here—right here with me—gripping and shaking in my arms.

Maybe she said it in the moment, or maybe it came from the depths of her soul—I don't know. But even if Marina Starkey doesn't actually need me, I can live with thinking maybe she did, even if only a moment.

Chapter Thirty-Three

THE NEVER HARBOR MOB

Marina

I love watching Cassidy in his element. It's a balancing act, entertaining existing vendors while greeting new people. And he's a people person through and through.

It's the final mixer meeting. All vendors were invited to the community center to get a run-down of Saturday's schedule and ask any questions before the big event. A doughnut box is propped open in the corner, remnants of halves taken or pieces left behind. The coffee is already almost gone. But the conversation is just getting started.

"Jukes! My man!" Cassidy reaches out the same time my dad's drinking buddy does, and they clap each other's palm at the same time.

William Jukes's opposite hand pats the back of Cassidy's. "Excited to blast the pants off these wine people."

"You didn't bring your sax?" Cassidy asks. "Darn! I wanted you to open the meeting with a little number."

"Bah, I'm so unprepared!" Jukes waves his hands in the air, playing along with the bit.

Cassidy barks out a laugh. "Next time, buddy."

He catches me watching once Jukes walks away and winks—a gesture that sends shivers down my spine. He rounds to the other side of the table to talk to Laura about something, but I'm still distracted by the smiles he keeps flashing my way.

Last night was perfect. Mermaid Lagoon felt complete with him there, and by the end, as he confessed that he needed me—whether in the throes of passion or not—I realized just how much I might need him.

I think I might stay in Never Harbor. Sure, for the flower shop I love and the people I've grown to admire, but mostly for him. My man.

Because I think I might be falling for the first time in my life, and it's somehow not as scary as I thought love might be. I imagine my dad's love for my mom—unconditional yet painful—or my mom's love, which was selfish and limited. This isn't like that at all. Cassidy isn't conditional with his affection.

"Leave it to Cass to make this feel like a night at The Hideaway," my dad says from beside me.

"He's so good at this," Lulu observes from my other side right as Laura breaks into a smile.

I nod with an unrestrained grin. "Yeah. He really knows how to read people."

Dad rubs a rough palm over my back, narrowing his eyes at Cassidy. "Sure nothin's going on there?" he asks.

My face feels hot, and discreetly, Lulu elbows me and clears her throat.

"Dad," I mutter.

My dad stares at me in the only way Charles Starkey can—steady eyes and a small vein popping in his tattooed neck. I can't tell if he'd approve or not, and I don't ask because the conference room door whips open again.

Dustin Barrie strides in, unbuttoning his gray suit jacket like he means business.

Conversation still hums throughout the room, the coffee carafe rattling, loud laughter from Peter and Milo in the corner, and a small, "Hi, guys," murmured from Bobbi as she takes the seat opposite my dad.

He kisses her temple, and she gives a sheepish wave to me.

We still haven't talked. We need to. And if I stay, if I actually commit to this, I need to let Bobbi know this is okay. That she will always be my auntie Bobbi, regardless of whether she's with my dad.

I open my mouth to talk, but Dustin clears his throat.

"Ahem."

The room continues to overflow with chatter. Lulu snorts at his attempt. Cassidy crosses the room to Dustin, shaking his hand and exchanging greetings I can't hear. Dustin attempts to straighten his posture, as if he can simply command the room to quiet down by his sheer presence.

It's Cassidy that commands it instead.

"Hey," Cassidy shouts. "Hey, guys. Come on. Settle down." He gestures his palms in the air. "Gossip later. And, Charles, yes, I'm looking at you." He points a playful finger at my dad, who holds up a guilty hand while the room laughs.

The power Cassidy holds over these people and the fact that Dustin can't control the wild Never Harbor crowd—it has me grinning ear to ear. Dustin, on the other hand, is grinding his jaw like there's taffy stuck between his teeth.

Cassidy claps his palms together, rubbing, and exhales.

"Thanks, everyone, for coming today," he announces. "Big moment! The wine mixer is in four days. I want to touch base with everyone, go through the day's events, and answer any last-minute questions. Sound good, team?"

Cassidy swivels his eyes to me. I quickly toss him a wink, just like he does for me. With a grin, Cassidy grabs the presentation clicker and rotates toward the projector screen.

"Pete, can you—" The overhead lights click off, making the image clearer. "Thanks. All right. First, we've got the linens coming in on Thursday evening. I know Steve offered to house those for a day— thanks, man—but I'm gonna need a few helping hands to spread them out Friday morning, so—"

"Are those blue tablecloths?"

I, and everyone else in the room, turns toward the drawling voice in the corner. Dustin Barrie leans back in his chair, one ankle crossed over the opposite knee. His fingers steeple together.

"What?" Cassidy asks.

"Are those blue?"

"Yes. Well, powder blue, technically."

"This is a *white* tablecloth event." Dustin's tone drips with obviousness. Like the words *of course* should be implied.

Cassidy slowly nods. "Right."

"We've got some pretty important people attending," Dustin says with a condescending laugh. "We're not gonna have the tablecloths be white?"

"Sure, we can. Easy fix," Cassidy answers. But I don't miss the way his smile goes from confident to forced in one fell swoop. "Does anyone have—yeah, thanks, Laura."

Cassidy slides over the pen and sticky note pad from Laura, jotting down a quick reminder. He pops back up, and the smile is back. Somehow, someway. Because Cassidy is Cassidy.

"All right, so the *white* linens will arrive on Thursday evening," he says. "That's also when Jasper and his crew are assembling the stage. Yes?"

"We'll actually be there earlier in the day," Jasper announces.

"Aye, aye, Captain," Jukes, Bobbi, and my dad chime at the same time.

Despite himself, Jasper smirks.

"Don't expect much movement at the docks that day," Jasper explains to everyone. "It'll just be Noodler manning the office."

A low hum carries through the room with mutters of, "We'll avoid it," but peppered with, "Good kid though."

Cassidy clicks to the next slide, displaying a 3D mock-up of the stage. "All right. So, for the stage, this is what we're looking at. A little smaller from years before since we don't need to worry about a lot of bands, but there's an added—"

"It is quite small," Dustin interjects.

Everyone turns their head once more, and this time, you can hear the shifting shirt collars or swish of summer jackets.

Cassidy's face falls. "Is it? We confirmed this a few weeks ago before Jas started work on it."

"I wasn't here for that."

"Well, we can … Jas, you want to chat after?"

Jasper nods stiffly while Cassidy scribbles yet another reminder on the sticky note. Jasper doesn't move his sharp stare from Dustin though. And though it might be a rumor, I swear there's a hint of red anger in them.

"All right," Cassidy continues. "So, Friday, we'll mostly be setting up booths and tables." He clicks to a map of the clock tower park, rows of rectangles with numbers assigned and vendors displayed in columns beside it.

"This is where everyone will be," Cassidy says. "Any questions?"

While nobody asks a question, there's rustling as a whole room of eyes peers over at Dustin. A weird unheard relief washes over the room when he's too busy tapping on his phone screen to object.

"Okay, moving on to Saturday morning."

Grins flash across the room. Low murmurs are exchanged between neighbors.

"First thing in the morning," Cassidy says proudly, "right at the crack of dawn, we've got our very own Florally Yours team—Marina Starkey and Lulu Kitt—delivering flowers."

I refocus right as Cassidy holds out his palm toward us. Lulu gives a dramatic hand wave. Claps erupt through the room. My dad slings his other arm over my shoulders, giving it a tight squeeze.

The excitement is palpable.

And I get it.

I truly get it.

This is why people stay in Never Harbor.

This is the feeling of what it's like to belong. How could anyone leave a place that shows this much excitement over a festival that they don't even want? This might not be their classic music festival, but it's something they're doing together.

How could my mom ever leave this town?

I glance over, watching my dad squeeze Bobbi's shoulder, and I smile.

How could my mom leave that man?

How could I leave *my* man? Cassidy.

"Ahem." Dustin Barrie's voice echoes through the room.

Everyone whips their head to him. He casually pockets his phone, leaning forward.

"Everything okay?" Cassidy asks gently, as if Dustin were a child who just fell and scraped his knee.

Dustin gives a huff of a laugh. "Well, no, not really. I'm sorry, are our flowers really going to be catered by Marina Starkey?"

My heart sinks, plummeting to the depths of me like an anchor. I feel stuck in place.

"What?" Cassidy asks, blinking with a smile, as if he simply misheard.

Heads swivel again—from him back to Dustin.

"Well, just"—Dustin laughs again, like he's embarrassed he even has to explain himself—"she's only been working there as an employee for a few weeks now, hasn't she? What kind of experience does she have?"

"*She* is right there," Lulu chimes in, knocking her chin in my direction.

"*And* she was just a receptionist earlier this summer," he counters harshly.

Lulu's head jerks back. I guess any affection he had toward her is long gone, or maybe she's finally seeing the type of man he truly is.

I watch nervously as the rest of the town's faces fall into variations of anger. A line cuts between Milo's brows as he looks between Dustin and Lulu; Jukes's face is near purple now; Laura's fist clenches around her pen; and Peter, standing in the corner, overlooking the situation, has his arms crossed. It's the same gesture he gets when someone is being unruly at The Hideaway. He's ready to kindly—or not so kind-ly—escort Dustin out.

But most intimidating of all is Cassidy, standing at the front of the room, gritting his teeth, clenching his fists, rippling the muscles along his forearms and up to his shoulders.

"What the hell's that supposed to mean?" he asks.

Dustin stands, brushing off his tailored slacks. "Listen, you've clearly not put enough thought into this. We're four days away, and it's barely presentable. We'll need to scrap a lot of this. It'll be hard work, but"—he smirks—"I believe in you."

Then, he turns to leave. The whole room starts to murmur.

It's quickly silenced when Cassidy calls after Dustin, "Where are you going?"

He turns on the squeaky heel of his overly polished shoe. "Well, I'm not needed here, am I? You have a lot of work to do. And I know it takes you some time to get through things, Cassie."

My stomach drops, and suddenly, my whole body feels hot. You can hear a pin drop in the room. Not a breath or a mutter or even a shift of clothing indicates the room is alive.

Dustin exits the room.

Cassidy looks around and holds up a single finger. "Be right back, gang."

He leaves. The door clicks behind him. A second passes. Maybe two.

Then, Peter's face contorts, and he calls out a, "What the f—"

All hell breaks loose.

There's a mad rush to the door. Chairs screeching back, clipboards and notebooks thrown aside ... the conference room transforms into an erratic school of fish as people bump into the conference room table and each other. I faintly see Lulu grab a hard ruler from the chalkboard, wielding it like a weapon. Milo jerks it away and tosses it to the side.

Everyone crowds out of the conference room. Cassidy is halfway down the hall, following after Dustin, who exits through the double doors. I run faster, catching up behind Cassidy, who pushes the doors before they can snick shut again.

"Dustin!" he calls.

Dustin turns around with a smirk. If he were a smart man, he'd be intimidated by this jacked guy barreling toward him. And if not that, then maybe the mob of Never Harbor townsfolk pacing behind us.

"Yes?" Dustin responds haughtily.

"You can't walk in here after weeks of missing planning meetings and demand we change everything."

Instinctually, I want to reach out for Cass's hand, but he's in fight-or-flight mode, and I think fight is winning.

Dustin furrows his brows. "Uh"—he laughs, shaking his head, and he speaks slower, like Cassidy has a hard time understanding—"yes, I can. Because it's my event."

The community center doors rip open, and everyone files out in a cacophony of shoes and angry murmurs. They all stop at the top stair, looking down at me, Cassidy, and Dustin, frozen on the sidewalk. Lulu descends the stairs to loop arms with me.

"Your event?" Cassidy shakes his head. "You haven't done a thing, Dustin."

Dustin holds out his palms. "I made this festival—"

"Mixer," the crowd chimes in unison.

Dustin closes his eyes in frustration. "I made this mixer what it is."

Cassidy barks out a laugh. "Yeah, you gave us white tablecloths. Great job. You think this town can handle the color *white*?"

There's a low murmur behind us, including Jukes muttering more to himself than anyone else, "I'm a messy eater; so what?"

"You don't know this town," Cassidy continues. "Or these people. And how *dare* you say anything at all about Marina! You don't know her work ethic. How hard she's been busting her ass every day to turn that flower shop around."

I glance at Lulu, who gives a nonchalant shrug and admits, "I'll be honest; it sucked before."

Dustin laughs. "Don't know her work ethic?" He takes a step forward. "All she's good for is a pretty face."

A collective gasp captures the crowd.

Cassidy's teeth clench together. "Watch it—"

"Do you know how she got fired? What happened between us?"

Then, the world goes dead silent. I almost wish another comedic, synchronous gasp filled the air, but instead, I'm left with the daunting pain that follows something as terrible as the truth.

On the stairs, held back by Jasper's banded arm, my dad stares at me with his eyebrows slammed together.

But it's the look Cassidy gives me that breaks my heart to pieces.

His lips part on a breath. A line deepens between his eyebrows.

Cassidy averts his gaze from me and takes one threatening step closer to Dustin.

"What the hell are you talking about?" he sneers.

His bulky frame towers over Dustin. He's radiating with unbridled rage. He's not the happy Cassidy who laughs at every joke or the generous man who carries me on his back when my feet hurt. Any trace of his gentle murmurs calling me *honey* is gone.

Dustin walks forward. "Marina is a tease. She spent her entire time at my company flirting with me. Day in and day out. Stayed late whenever she could. And then she came into my office one evening and ..." The words fade off, but the implication is there. "Well, I had to fire her. I had no choice."

I'm falling, aren't I? That's the only way to describe this world-tilting feeling in my stomach. I must be close to hitting the sidewalk pavement, and the fact that I don't means I'm still here. Still living in this moment. And it isn't a dream.

"That's not true," I whisper, but I'm not sure who hears me.

"She's not catering our flowers," Dustin demands, then composes himself again. He sighs. "But I'm not surprised that someone like you couldn't see past her pretty face."

"Excuse you?!" The words leave my mouth before I can stop them.

The sidewalk erupts into movement. Stomps of shoes down the front steps of the community center, calls of curse words I didn't know Laura or Steve were capable of, and then there's me—barreling forward at the same time Cassidy does.

Rough hands grab my elbows. Two sets of arms wrap around Cassidy's middle.

I struggle harder against whoever is holding me, my sneakers scraping on the sidewalk, my shirt tugging back from the strain of the fingers digging into my forearms.

"Easy, Guppy," my dad growls behind me. It's his rough hands on me.

My heart is racing. I look at Cassidy, and he's already staring back at me. Peter and Jasper grip his torso, like they're attempting to control a bear.

Dustin stumbles back, glancing at Lulu. I wonder if he wants her as an ally again.

She scrunches her nose with a girlishly disgusted, "Ew."

Dustin's nostrils flare. "Brat."

Milo races over to Lulu, stepping in front of both of us like a guardian. He presses a single finger into Dustin. "You've said enough."

"Milo, please, like you haven't thought the same thing about Cassie."

Cassidy jerks his head to Milo, who shakes his head immediately.

"That's not true," Milo argues.

"No? How many times did you apologize for your meathead little brother?"

Milo opens his mouth and closes it. Finally, he says, "We were joking. You know that."

"You said that?" Cassidy asks.

Milo shakes his head. "I had no idea Dustin was serious."

Dustin huffs a laugh, sticking his nose in the air, hands held high in defeat. "Do whatever you like, everyone. Throw this whole thing to the wolves. See if I care. I'm just trying to get tourists here for you. Isn't that the goal? But no, feel free to ruin it all for yourselves. You already look like you're trying too hard. Can't wait to see the rest of it burn."

With most of us held back by someone or another, Dustin walks backward, turning to glare at Lulu and Milo, who now look aimed to kill, before striding down the sidewalk and turning the corner toward the mayor's house.

Tension is high for a few moments that follow. Heavy breaths and disbelief seeping through us, and we absorb them like a sponge.

Gently, my dad's fingers lighten and release my arms. Peter and Jasper release Cassidy. Other movements indicate wild locals getting released as well—Steve, the skinny paper guy, being one of them.

In the midst of confusion, it's finally Bobbi who says, "Well, shit, now what?"

All of us turn to Cassidy, but he's not looking at Milo, like I expect. His eyes are stuck on me.

Emotions cross his face I wish I could decipher. I thought I'd gotten good at reading him like a book over the past few weeks. But this type of hurt feels indescribable.

"Marina ..."

He takes a step closer, but I take one back. He must be disappointed in me, but he doesn't need to be. I'm already too disappointed in myself.

I avert my gaze. I can feel the tears bubbling up, and I can't hold them back this time.

My dad's tattooed arm swings over my shoulders. "I got you, Guppy."

I follow wherever my dad leads, leaving every ounce of energy, motivation, and care I had behind me.

Cassidy Davies owns those parts of me now, and I don't want them back.

Chapter Thirty-Four

MEATHEADS ALL THE WAY DOWN

Cassidy

Even though he's Marina's dad, it feels wrong for her to leave with Charles Starkey and not me.

She needs me.

I take a step forward, like my soul is losing its other half, but Jasper puts out an arm to shield me.

He claps a palm on my shoulder. "Easy, brother. Let's calm down for a second, okay?"

Peter places his hands on his hips. "Let's get out of here. I'll tell Izzy we're coming."

I watch Marina turn the corner, deflating. I want to follow, but I have no strength to argue. With the rest of my brothers and Lulu, we drive our cars to The Hideaway.

Izzy is poised behind the bar with a clipboard, one ankle casually crossed over the other. But when we bustle in, her expression falls. Nobody got bruised, but my curls feel astray, and I wouldn't be surprised if our clothes were rumpled from the chaos.

Peter throws her a wry smile. "The meeting didn't go well."

"You don't say," she breathes.

We navigate to a table, most of us taking an overturned chair from the top and placing it down. Milo takes two, one for him and one for Lulu. Peter continues to stand, pacing.

"So …" Izzy starts, walking over to Peter. Her hand rests on his shoulder. "Who got punched this time?"

He and Jasper exchange a knowing glance, and surprisingly, Jasper is smiling with him.

Peter shakes his head with a laugh. "No black eye for me."

"Turns out, Cassidy is more civilized than those two," Milo says.

"So, what happened?" Izzy asks.

"Dustin Barrie is a cock," Jasper grunts.

Lulu threads her fingers through her long black locks, flowing through like an inky mess. "God, I liked that guy. I feel so ridiculous."

Milo squeezes her shoulder. She jumps. "You didn't do anything wrong."

"He was right about one thing though," Peter says. "This mixer isn't fit for Never Harbor. We do seem like we're trying too hard."

We all deflate at once.

"*Blue* linens," I say with a rush of air. "What was I thinking?"

"You were thinking it was a good idea," Milo explains. "And it was."

"No, it wasn't. I should have followed up with him more. Forced him to come to the meetings or something."

"He wouldn't have," Lulu says. "Dustin does what Dustin wants."

We all glance at her, but she doesn't elaborate further. Milo gives a half smile, and when she notices, her eyes don't move from his for even a second.

"No," Jasper says. "Dustin is the problem, not you or anyone else."

"So, what?" I say, tossing my hands up. "We just … go ahead with some idea that might not even go over well?"

"This is your shindig," Peter says. "You lead the way. We'll follow."

"Me?"

"Yes," Milo says. "You."

"Haven't I messed this up enough?"

Jasper shakes his head. "It's not your fault he didn't help."

I blink to my brothers, opening my mouth and closing. I've never been the leader with them. They're my older brothers, and for once, they're looking to me. They're asking *me* what's best. Even Milo.

"What was that all about?" I ask Milo. "The meathead thing."

"Listen … it wasn't supposed to be anything—"

"Everyone called you a meathead," Jasper interrupts. "Hell, I called Milo a meathead."

"He's definitely called me one," Peter interjects. "You're our little brother. It's our job to rag on you."

Milo nods. "I had no idea he meant it, Cass. You're smart. Not even for a second have I thought differently. But I'm sorry. So, tell us what to do here. I trust you."

"We do," Peter adds.

"Really? But … I'm … well, what makes you think I can do this?"

"Because you already have," Lulu says.

Milo nods. "You show up every single time. Nobody's doubted that."

I smile. They believe in me, which is crazy because what I want to do is littered with a vengefulness I can't shake. What Dustin said about Marina … I don't know which parts of that were true. But just like my family believes in me, I believe in Marina.

Maybe she did have a fling with him. And maybe he was lying. But even if he was, Marina can do whatever she likes. I'm not here to live in the past, and she shouldn't be forced to either.

Past Cassidy would let this roll off his back. But I'm about ready to throw down instead.

I won't forgive what he said about my roommate. My best friend. No, my *woman.*

"Honestly?" I say on a sigh. "I wanna fuck his whole day up."

Peter gives a crooked grin. Jasper arches a single eyebrow. Even Milo curls his lips into a smile.

Lulu, beaming ear to ear, says, "Oh, I am one petty bitch; let's do this."

"I love to mess up people's lives," Izzy adds.

Peter grins, snaking his arm around Izzy's waist. I expect her to pull away, but she instead settles into it, a sly smile growing on her pink cheeks.

"Any ideas?" Milo asks me.

"I don't know yet," I say. "But I'm angry."

"Cool, let's run with that emotion," Lulu says.

"Why was he the end-all decision-maker for things anyway?" Izzy asks.

"Because he's the mayor's son," Jasper grumbles.

"He doesn't even know what this town is like anymore," Lulu adds on a scoff. "He called Live, Laugh, Taffy too sugary."

I throw my arms in the air. "That's the whole point!"

"Exactly," she adds with an eye roll. "Who doesn't get that?"

"Cass gets it," Jasper says.

"Of course he does," Peter adds. "Cass knows this town better than anyone."

"No, I don't."

"You do," he insists. "I run the bar, sure. I know things. But you know the *people*. You understand what makes each individual person and place tick."

"Pete just knows how to entertain the masses," Izzy says, tilting her head up to him. "Like a clown or something."

"Hey!" His head jerks back, but his smile never falters.

She grins. "We need to find little bells to put on your shoes."

"I second that," Milo says with a grin.

"Fine." Peter scoffs. "I'm a jester. Sure. Whatever."

I point at him. "Do you need cute green tights too or—"

He shoots me a look, tonguing the inside of his cheek and nodding. "Uh-huh. Very funny." He eyes Izzy for a moment or two before turning back to me seriously. "So, what are we doing, Cass?"

"Not having wine," I say with a chuckle.

Peter winces. "Well, there *is* a question of contracts and money here," he says. "Has Dustin paid deposits or anything?"

Izzy nods. "That could make things messy."

But that only makes me laugh. A lot.

She and Peter exchange some co-business-owner-y look.

Izzy blows a sharp breath of air through her nose. "I'm not kidding, Cass."

I pull out my phone, angling it toward them. On the screen are the repeated reminders I sent to Dustin about e-signing paperwork. Paperwork he never signed.

Realization pops in my head like a light bulb.

Bobbi and her licorice coffee.

The pirate trio and their jazz band.

Jukes's clear mistreatment of white linens.

And Marina.

Marina, always at the forefront of my mind, laughing with that scrunched nose, the sound like music on her sweet lips.

They're right. I know this town. And I know what it wants.

"All right," I announce, "I've got a plan. Think we can get everyone to meet tonight?"

"Everyone?" Peter asks, eyes widening.

"Everyone."

Peter glances down at Izzy, who nods determinedly.

She makes her way behind the bar, grabbing her clipboard. "Where?"

"Somewhere secret."

"Mermaid Lagoon?" Lulu suggests.

My heart stops. It feels like forever ago when Marina and I were there. I wish I could go back to last night, us swimming hand in hand, just the sound of water lapping against the edges of the pool.

Everyone looks at me. I shake my head.

We can't. That's her sacred place. Our special place.

"Anywhere else?"

"We could go to my old cottage," Jasper offers. "That's out of town."

"I like that," I agree.

"All right then." Peter claps his hands together. "Bells?"

Izzy nods. "On it." She grabs the corded bar phone off the wall and begins dialing.

"Looks like we've got a speakeasy party," Peter announces with a grin.

I watch as Izzy murmurs into the phone.

"God, is *that* how news travels so fast?" I ask.

Peter shrugs. "The worst gossip comes from Never Harbor business owners."

I grin, but it only lasts for a moment before my mind is elsewhere. I have other things to do.

"I'll meet you guys there," I say.

Milo frowns. "Where are you going?"

"To find my girl."

I exit through the front door, down the steps, and away from the increased chatter of my brothers. Maybe it's more gossip. Maybe Izzy will spread the word.

I don't care. I need to find Marina. I need to talk to her, to tell her that, regardless of what happened between her and Dustin, it doesn't matter. Nothing in our pasts should affect our present. Not words from bullies, misconceptions of our capabilities, or old relationships. All we have is right now, and my world is filled with my family, this town, and her.

Most of all, *her*.

- *Chapter Thirty-Five* -
RECKLESS

Marina

My dad's apartment is a blur through my tears. I think I hear him make coffee, but I'm not sure until a warm cup is in my hand.

"Hey." My dad's voice is gentle beneath that scraggly beard and tattoos. "Guppy, look at me."

I blink through my mess of tears and sniffles and everything else that lets loose more than I wish it had.

"I'm sorry," I blurt out.

His eyebrows cinch in as he stares, his eyes like blades that can cut through me. "For what?"

"For … being impulsive and reckless and … everything else you don't need me to be."

"Me? What are you talking about?"

"I'm just like her," I say. "Like Mom."

"Hey. No." He grabs my shoulders. "You are who you are, Marina. You're a little reckless, but the good kind."

"I don't know," I murmur.

"Guppy …"

"I don't want to talk about it."

My dad sucks on his teeth before shaking his head. I wonder if he's disappointed and if he'll be the one to abandon me after all this. Because looking at the old potted plants around the apartment, I know what life still lingers here. The good memories of mom. My dad still lives in those moments. The fact that I only took her impulsive traits, like moving every couple of years, never using my degree, inadvertently flirting with my boss, and never growing past being impulsive … it can't be easy on him.

I swallow, sipping the coffee already spiked with my three sugar packets.

"Dad, I …"

"Hush," he snaps, returning with a blanket in his arms.

He spreads it over me, throwing another on top as well. Bending down, he roughly shoves his palms beneath my body, tucking the blanket in as tight as it can go. I know my goofy, burly dad is trying to make me laugh by burrito'ing me, just like he did when I was a kid. He grins, but I can't find the heart to join him.

His cell phone buzzes on the counter, but he waves it away.

"Later," he says to my unspoken question.

Then, falling down next to me on the sofa with the remote, he clicks on the TV and props his feet on the coffee table.

"Let's see …" he says, flicking through the channels. "Ah. There we are. *M*A*S*H* marathon."

He looks at me, maybe wondering if I'll protest. I don't. He wraps his arm around my shoulders and pulls me closer. Somewhere during the third commercial break, I fall asleep.

I wake up on the sofa sometime later, dreary-eyed and blinking through blurriness again. I don't know how much time has passed, but I'm warm from the setting sun beaming through the window and highlighting the sofa. The two blankets feel claustrophobic, too fluffy and heavy. I shimmy them off.

Looking around the small apartment, I don't spot Dad anywhere. Suddenly, the room feels cold again. Has word already spread throughout the town? What must everyone think of me now? Does Cassidy believe Dustin?

My heart sinks.

The look on Cassidy's face is a memory I can't shake.

He's going to leave me for this.

In one simple morning, this place feels less like home and more like a prison. I know the small-town gossip is spreading, swift and true like a shot to the heart.

My body settles into the sofa.

I'm not sure I've ever truly understood my mom the way I do now.

Was this why she left?

It's weird; for once, I truly felt like I found a home. I love the people. I love the flower shop. I have purpose. Laughing with Lulu over who orders which bouquets and for whom. Picking up Stinky with his protesting yowls.

Most of all, I love waking up next to Cassidy. I love running my fingers through his curls. I love his boisterous laughter, his dimpled smiles, his affinity for gossip, and how he makes me feel like I'm the only person in the room, even among a slew of locals. Even when everyone else wants his attention, he gives it all to me.

But what is left?

What motive does he have to stay with me now?

Cassidy is the soil foundation of this small town, and I'm the girl who tried to break ground and tangle myself in existing roots.

I'm trying to make something work that simply won't.

It's time for me to face reality.

It's time for me to leave the magic of Never Harbor. It doesn't belong to me anyway.

- *Chapter Thirty-Six* -
FLYING AWAY

Cassidy

I knock on Charles Starkey's door. I don't know if she's here, but it's where my gut told me to go first when Marina wouldn't answer my texts.

I knock again, and on the second one, the door rips open.

I don't like how quickly Starkey's thick eyebrows furrow inward.

"Cass? What are you doing here?"

Immediately, he steps aside to let me in, but I'm not sure why. I accept the invite anyway and bypass him into the apartment.

"I'm looking for Marina," I explain.

Starkey shuts the door with a snick and crosses his burly arms over his chest. "She's not with you?"

Something inside me twists, a weird sense of dread I can't pinpoint.

The apartment seems mostly untouched or maybe recently cleaned. Two blankets lie folded on the sofa, one on top of the other. Marina's bright turquoise hair tie lies on the coffee table.

"She was here, wasn't she?" I ask.

He nods.

"Yeah, I went out to get food while she was asleep. I came back, and she was gone. I assumed she had gone back home."

On the kitchen counter is an unopened six-pack of ginger ale and prepackaged tuna sandwiches.

Something is wrong.

She wouldn't leave her dad like that. Not after a day like today. Being alone at the house isn't how Marina functions best. She needs to be around people she loves.

I swallow. "She hasn't answered my texts in a couple of hours."

Starkey notices my face contorting in thought. His lips part.

"Shit," he breathes.

"What?"

"She's running."

My stomach drops to the ground, and the dread seeps into my bones like poison.

He shakes his head, slamming his fist on the kitchen counter. "Her mom did this too."

"She's not her mom though," I interject. "We both know that."

His head jerks to me like a whip. "I know that. She's much better than her mother ever was or could be. But if she thinks she has no other options? That changes the game a little, don't you think?"

"But she has options," I explain. "This town is her option. The flower shop is her option. *I'm* her option."

Starkey looks me over from head to toe, taking in my wild curls and unshaved stubble that won't disappear no matter how much I try.

"There is something going on with you two, isn't there?" he asks.

Something tells me this isn't the first time he's asked this question, and now knowing Marina's shame with Dustin, I understand why he wasn't given a straight answer.

"I care for your daughter very much," I answer. "And I respect you, so I'm comfortable telling you that, yes, we're a little more than room-mates at this point. And while I wish I could also say that, yes, I'm dating your daughter, that's up to her to decide. If we can find her."

Slowly, he nods. "Then, we'd better find her."

"I'll try the townhome first," I say. "See if maybe we're just overre-acting."

"Let's hope that's the case. I'll also call around to ask if anyone's seen her."

I cross the room toward the door and twist the handle. But Star-key's palm whips out to hit the wood, slamming it shut once more. He stares me down, and I tense on the spot.

"Listen to me, Cassidy Davies. If I find out you're the reason she left, that somehow you took advantage of my daughter while living under *my* roof, I will strangle you until I watch the life leave your little turd-colored eyes. Do you understand me, kid?"

I'm not gonna lie and say that doesn't scare the wits out of me.

I swallow. "Don't worry. I'll hate myself enough to go around."

"Attaboy. Glad we have an understanding."

He claps my back, and I descend the stairwell, trying not to feel his eyes burning through the back of my head as I walk quickly down the sidewalk.

Eventually, a walk turns into a jog.

A jog turns into a run.

It feels like Marina is slipping through my fingers if I can't get to her fast enough.

I sprint past familiar faces on the sidewalk, bypassing little conspiratorial whispers of, "See you at the cottage tonight, Cass!" and, "Eight o'clock, right?"

But I don't care. The last thing I care about is this stupid wine mixer or whatever plan we can construct to fix it.

I love Never Harbor, but I love Marina Starkey more. The woman who's changed my life in only a short summer. The woman who believes in me.

I take the stoop steps two at a time and burst through the townhome door. The *hello!/goodbye!* rug Marina bought feels like it's taunting me.

The house looks relatively the same. Same counter with same barstools, bookshelves, and lumpy sofa. But I spot the crucial missing piece—Fido is no longer here.

I'd wager that it's denial making me rush down the hallway to our bedroom. I cross to the dresser, ripping open her middle drawer. My whole world turns on its head when I'm greeted with the bare wooden base. Only pieces of lint and another turquoise hair tie remain.

"Shit," I breathe.

I close my eyes, trying to inhale or recall any notes in all her self-help books that might apply to this moment. But most books don't discuss how to react in the moment someone leaves you; it's just how to rearrange your newly missing pieces.

I slam the drawer shut. A splinter rebounds off the floor. I'm not proud of it, but all the stress from this summer compounds in me. The mixer that's spiraled, the business I've taken on, and the love I've now lost.

I look at my phone with the two outgoing, unanswered calls to Marina, and it starts buzzing in my palm. I bring the phone to my ear.

"Hey, Starkey, she's not—"

"Greta just saw her walking past the fire station," he interrupts. "She's headed to the commuter train."

"On my way."

- Chapter Thirty-Seven -

AN AWFULLY BIG ADVENTURE

Marina

My arms circle around Fido's pot, holding him close to my chest while my duffel bag slumps on the concrete below.

I'm sitting on a metal bench under the train station awning, swiping through my phone to purchase a ticket. The online schedule says it's only one stop away, five minutes out. I got here just in time.

I don't know where I'm headed next. Maybe somewhere in Boston or to some other suburb on the opposite side of Massachusetts. Maybe I'll go down South, to Nashville or Atlanta. Bonnie always talks about some theme park in North Georgia. Maybe they're hiring.

With my ticket purchased, I slide to my texts. I've gotten two from my dad.

Dad
Where are you?

Dad
Don't make me ground you.

I smile, but it fades when I see the tiny red bubble, indicating five missed calls. I already know who they're from.

I pocket my phone again, holding Fido closer.

"Just you and me again," I whisper, leaning my chin on the flimsy leaves and sighing.

"Got room for an extra friend?" a voice asks.

I jerk my head around.

My heart plummets.

Cassidy steps onto the platform, sheepishly waving. I want to smile; it's hard not to around him, especially when his eyebrows tilt inward. He's cute, and I wish he weren't.

I look away, trying to control my heavy breathing. "Sure."

"Mind if I sit next to you?"

"If you want."

"I want very much," he answers.

From the corner of my eye, I see him grin. That damn dimple taunting me.

I clear my throat as he sits on the opposite side of the bench, leaving a respectful two feet between us.

He winds his palms together, running thumb over thumb. His thighs spread, almost overwhelming the bench with his bulk. It looks so similar to how Dustin sat on the coffee table almost one month ago. Casual, legs spread, slight smile to his features. But Dustin pales in comparison to Cass. He doesn't have the same approachability, the same gentle eyes, or his casual shrug, as if sitting at a train station with your runaway roommate is no big deal.

"How ya feeling?" Cassidy asks, and just the question alone has my mind spinning.

"Fine."

"Good, good."

I clear my throat. There's a squeak as Cassidy scoots one foot closer on the bench.

"I want you to know," he says, "that I don't care what happened. I don't care if you liked Dustin or not. People go for their bosses all the time."

I feel my nose sting. I blink to stifle the emotion rising up.

"I didn't sleep with him."

"Okay," he says slowly.

"I didn't even like him."

"Okay."

I slowly shake my head side to side. "Don't be mad."

"I could never."

Never. He could never.

"I ... on my last day of work, he tried to make a move. He said I'd been putting out the signs for months. I flirted or touched his arm or … whatever it is I guess I do. But, Cass, I didn't like him," I insist. "He was just my boss. That was it."

When he doesn't talk again, I look over. His jaw is clenched. The veins in his forearm shift as he taps thumb to thumb.

"So … he came on to you. Without you wanting it."

"All he did was touch my hair—"

"Don't lessen your feelings," he snaps. "Don't think you're in the wrong for this, okay?"

His hand reaches out, cupping my face, his thumb stroking over my cheek. I lean into it.

"So, what, he hit on you, then fired you when you didn't wanna be with him?"

I swallow and nod.

"Son of a …" Cassidy bites his bottom lip, shaking his head. "I wish you'd told me sooner."

Suddenly, I wish I had too. "I know."

"Is this the secret you kept to yourself?"

I nod, and he mirrors it.

I sigh. "Listen, this has happened a lot. Maybe I—"

"No," Cassidy says, his glare returning. "You're kind. Generous. Beautiful. It's a combination that's appealing, sure, but just because a man sees what he wants to see doesn't make it your problem."

My eyes burn. My body feels tight, and suddenly, I can't hold it in anymore.

I let out half a sob before Cassidy erases the distance between us on the bench and gathers me into his arms. I place Fido down beside me and bury my face in Cassidy's chest.

I can't stop the tears. They run down my face, smearing over Cassidy's hoodie. I can't catch my breath. I can barely think. The fact that I'm letting all this out in front of Cassidy, the strongest guy I know, is embarrassing.

I'm humiliated.

Cassidy rubs a palm over my back. "It's all right. Let it out," he says.

He squeezes me tight, and I scoot closer, clutching his hoodie tighter until he finally pulls me onto his lap. I let his body engulf me like we're back in bed. He strokes his thumb over my cheek again, wiping away the tears.

"Why are you running?" he whispers. "This isn't you."

"It is me."

"It's not. I know you."

"Do you?" I ask.

"Oh, Marina ..."

He digs into his pocket, pulling out the small, tabbed notebook I've been tempted to read from day one. Is he going to read it to me now?

He flips to a random page, then clears his throat. "*Marina Starkey. Loves plants and the beach. Enjoys ginger ale. Favorite show is* Survivor. *Likes showers at night. Three sugar packets in her coffee. Does not like when I tickle below her knee. But loves when I hold her hand.*"

I choke out a tear-soaked laugh. "What?"

"*Likes the left pillow, not the right. Doesn't care for the cool side. Doesn't like doughnuts, but loves ruffled chips. But not the super-salty kind—*"

"Wait, Cass ... what is that?"

"A notebook I keep of things people like." He turns the pages. One, two, then three. "You've got the most pages out of anyone so far. I can't stop thinking of things that will make you happy, so I write it all down, just in case. So, see, this isn't you. Because I think I know you."

In the distance, the commuter train turns the corner. The train tracks rattle under its approach. It gradually slows down, stopping just in front of our bench.

I lean back, looking into Cassidy's beautiful brown eyes. I love how they trace over me, crinkling at the edges with his smile.

"I adore you, Marina," he says. "You know that?"

"I think so."

And yet, at the tip of my tongue, I want to say something else entirely.

I love you, Cassidy Davies.

I've never felt this type of need before. This overwhelming possession to keep this man and for him to keep me.

I love you.

Cassidy looks up at the stopped train and heaves a sigh. "So, where are we headed?"

I blink. "What?"

"Got a place in mind?"

He's here.

He's not going anywhere.

I weakly admit, "I don't know."

"Perfect," he says with a grin. "This sounds like an awfully big adventure then."

I start to laugh, nearly sobbing again in the process, but Cassidy stops it by clutching my jaw and kissing me. It's light, soft, and beneath it all, understanding. It's Cassidy through and through.

"If you want to board that train and go, that's fine. I'll be your roommate anywhere else too." He threads his fingers through mine. "You're my otter. I'm not gonna let you drift away."

I look at the train and back at him. He gives a boyish shrug.

"I don't want to leave," I confess on a whisper. "I like it here."

"I like you here too."

So, ultimately, I don't stand up from the bench. And after another minute, the train starts moving away from Never Harbor once more.

"Hi, roomie," I whisper.

"Hey, honey," he responds with a quirk of a smile.

Suddenly, footsteps pound on the train station stairs. At the other end, my dad stands with a duffel bag in his palm, staring at us with raised eyebrows.

"You're still here," Dad says.

I nod. "I'm staying in Never Harbor."

It's something special to see a grown man's shoulders collapse in place. An exhale ruffles his wiry beard.

I eye the dropped bag. "Were you planning to come with me?"

"I wasn't letting my girl leave without me," he says. "Not this time."

"What about Bobbi?"

He smiles. "She knows I'm a little bit reckless. You get that from me, not your mom."

I stand from Cassidy's lap and run until I hit my dad's chest.

He grunts when we collide. "Love you, Guppy."

"Love you, Dad."

He pulls back, running the back of his inked wrist over his nose, and coughs. "All right, well, to the cottage then?"

"What cottage?"

"Jasper's," Cassidy answers.

"Why?"

"Because Dustin Barrie sucks," is all Dad answers.

"And I think we should kick his teeth in," Cassidy says. "So to speak."

"Nah, I say we literally kick his teeth in," my dad adds.

"Dad!"

"I'm only sorta joking."

Cassidy laughs.

"Wait, I'm so confused. Why are we really going?" I ask.

"Impromptu town hall," Dad grunts, knocking his chin to Cassidy. "Led by your knight in shining armor here."

Cassidy pumps his eyebrows at me, and if I could fall in love all over again, I might.

"We're fixing this mixer. We're taking down Dustin Barrie."

- *Chapter Thirty-Eight* -
A SPEAKEASY PARTY

Cassidy

Jasper's old cottage, with its empty, echoing walls and minimal square footage, does not feel like a place where one hundred locals should congregate. But desperate times call for desperate measures.

When we arrive, familiar faces are moving down to the rocky shore, bodies shoved shoulder to shoulder like sardines, forming a crowd at the bottom of the wooden ramp. Sleepy people cling on to different mugs of to-go coffee from Peg Leg Press. The place smells overwhelmingly like licorice.

I bump my way through the crowd, hand in hand with Marina, dragging her behind me.

Peter and Milo secured a craggy, raised rock in the corner as a makeshift stage. Izzy stands nearby with both Rafe and Wendy. She waves happily while Rafe just knocks his chin in my direction.

I shake hands with Peter. "Hey, man. So, when I said everyone, you guys took it seriously, huh?"

Peter puffs out his chest. "Yes, sir, we did. Right, Bells?"

Izzy gives a lazy, eye-rolling salute just above her smirk.

I look out at the slew of locals who have known me since I was a kid—the same faces that greeted me at the library or gave me free cookies at the grocery store or who scared me on Halloween.

And they're here to listen to me—the middle kid in that overcrowded house down the lane.

My gut wants to insist, *God, why in the world would they do that? You're* you. *Just Cass,* but I can't think that anymore.

The whole town is here because they believe in me. Because they trust me.

God, they *trust* me.

Suddenly, I can't find the words I need to say. I had a planned speech an hour ago, but now, it feels lost in time. A distant memory. But just as I start to breathe heavier, a beautiful hand slides into mine from one step below. Marina, blinking up at me like I was born from the stars, gives a small squeeze.

"Don't drift away, otter friend," she says.

I smile, rubbing a thumb over the back of her hand. "I'll try not to."

Milo nudges me with his elbow. "Hey. You're gonna do great, all right?"

I exhale. "How'd you do your valedictorian speech?"

"Oh, I vomited immediately after," he confesses, clapping me on the back. "Best vomit of my life though."

I bark out a laugh. "I always thought speeches were nothing for you."

"We're all imperfect in our own ways, Cass," he says. "Confidence is just an illusion. Ready?"

"Yeah, I'm ready." I grin, then cup my palms around my hands and yell, "Hey!"

It booms far louder than I expected, echoing out to the ocean. Any semblance of conversation is finished.

"Hey," I repeat at a lower volume. A few people laugh. "All right, so we all know why we're here."

"To kill Dustin Barrie!" Jukes yells from the back.

There's a collective gasp, and I quickly shake my head.

"No! No, not that. What in the world, Jukes?"

Peter waves his palm to the crowd. "Did nobody fill him in?"

Bobbi strokes Jukes's back, mouthing to me, *It's fine.*

A woman in the middle of the crowd I recognize as the elementary school principal steadily raises a thin hand.

I point to her. "Yeah, Donna?"

"Um, so we actually *don't* know why we're here," she admits, twisting her lips to the side.

Many people nod in agreement, shrugging and murmuring together.

"Yeah," Steve agrees in the back. "We were pretty much just told we're scheming against the mayor's kid."

"But we *love* scheming!" Lulu calls with two thumbs-up.

More of the crowd nods together.

I cringe and lean over to Milo. "Oh. Right, I didn't actually say anything, did I?"

Milo clears his throat. "Nope."

I straighten back up. "Okay, so, we're all wondering why we're here then …" I run a palm through my curls, letting them bounce back. "So," I start, "obviously, the festival—"

"Mixer," the crowd choruses.

"Right. The mixer …" I laugh. But that word settles in my chest uncomfortably, so I tongue my cheek and shake my head. "No. No, we're not calling it that. I don't want it to be a mixer."

"So, what are we gonna call it now?" Donna asks.

"Yeah, we've already made flyers," Bonnie adds.

Izzy groans. "The flyers are irrelevant at this point, guys. Those who want to know, know. We're four days out."

Marina cups her hands over her mouth and says, "So, what's it called?"

I laugh at her attempt to focus the crowd again.

"It's the Never Harbor Music Festival," I announce. "Guys, it's always been our music festival."

"What about all the wine we ordered?" Laura asks. "And the table-cloths?"

Peter shrugs. "I don't think extra wine will be any issue with this crowd."

Jukes, Bobbi, and Starkey give a collective, "Yarr!"

"What about the music acts?" Laura asks. "The booths? The food? All of it is for a mixer."

"That's true," I admit. "But who cares?"

"Who cares?!"

Mumbles erupt into a hum of chatter and then exhaustive concern.

"We've lost 'em," Izzy mutters. "Great."

"Wait!" a voice yells from the back. "Now, hold on, everyone!"

We turn to see Mayor Barrie emerging from the crowd, mustache twitching, hands on hips. He's older, walking with a small hunch in his back and a limp in his step. It's been so long since I've seen him away from his garden. He doesn't need to be present. We practically run ourselves.

"Mayor Barrie," Peter says, stepping down from the rocky platform as the mayor makes his way through the crowd toward us.

I follow Peter's lead, letting the mayor use my shoulder as an assist onto the makeshift stage.

He licks his lips, tucks his hands behind his back, and nods. "I'm sorry. I'm sorry I didn't notice everything going on before. This mixer? It's stupid. We can all agree?"

There are nods, but mostly everyone is quiet, cautious not to insult his son.

"I'm not proud of how my son handled this. I'm less proud of how uninvolved I've been."

"How'd he even find out about this meeting?" Marina whispers to me.

"He's probably got eyes and ears everywhere," I murmur back.

"But my son means well," Barrie continues. "I hope. He just doesn't know this town anymore. We can't fault him for that. We're welcoming, aren't we? So, let's think, everyone." He points a finger at his temple. "We can use the food. We can find bands. This is the damn music festival. Are we Never Harborians or not?"

They start to talk again, and Izzy groans from behind me.

I step onto the stage. "All right, listen up," I say, holding my palms out to quiet down the chatter. "Mayor Barrie is right. We have traditions here, guys. And traditions … well, sometimes, they're things passed down that aren't that fun. Like having to be nice to someone who sucks. Or having to stand there while people sing you 'Happy Birthday.' Or making New Year's resolutions you know you won't keep. Or when your brother puts stupid coal in your stocking—"

"Classic prank," Peter muses.

Izzy elbows him.

"And sometimes," I continue, "*sometimes*, traditions are great. Like a parent always having ginger ale ready to go when you're sick. Or going to The Hideaway for some random party even though we all know Pete probably just made up some holiday."

Low chuckling follows Peter's puffed-out chest.

"Or it's going to our festivals every year.

"I love our traditions. I love this town. It's my home. I was seven when I moved here. And I was seven when Tina called me 'just another one of those crazy Davies boys' right outside her flower shop. And she was right. I am a crazy Davies boy. Proud of it. And I'm also proud to call Never Harbor my home. Music festival and all. So, let's do what we do best. Let's put on a great music festival. Let's figure it out."

"Hell yeah!" Jukes yells, and everyone follows suit.

"Dustin Barrie thinks his mixer is getting ruined?" I ask before leaning in. "Then, let's prove him dead wrong."

Chapter Thirty-Nine

THE FIRST ANNUAL NEVER HARBOR WINE MIXER

Marina

The wine mixer is a massive failure.

The Never Harbor Music Festival, however, is a smashing success.

Our harsh pivot was blasted two days prior on any website we had control over. Employees at city hall adjusted the home page, and business owners shouted it on social media. However, the biggest influence of all was Noodler, who accidentally beached his boat, making Boston area news.

His comment? "Come see the music festival at Never Harbor this Saturday."

The call to action did its job.

On Saturday, the park off of Main was crowded with tourists from dawn until dusk. Tents with colorful bunting strung between posts were scattered over the lawn. Guests strolled booth to booth, departing with brown bags stuffed with Moira's candles or Rafe's screen prints. Hands were full of free ice cream from one of our four shops in town, and we tried to set up photo opportunities throughout the park, utilizing most of the back stock from Florally Yours to arrange flowers on picnic tables and as summer wreaths along the stage. Cassidy even got his petting zoo. Though how I'm still not sure.

We scrounged together last-minute home-cooked meals when the catering company said they couldn't pivot from oyster and hors d'oeuvres on such a tight turnaround. Our own Jukes's Jambalaya prepped two days before with the help of Mr. Davies and Peter, working late nights and early mornings. Tourists feasted on shrimp gumbo, fish fillet po'boys, and lobster rolls at picnic tables, covered with red-and-white checkered tablecloths. Given the messiness of the meal, Jukes rightly assumed white tablecloths would have been useless.

Musicians came from everywhere. Most were called in through favors from Peter and Izzy, whose connections are well known in the night-life industry. But all of us were shocked when some punk band showed up, saying they owed Rafe a favor. Apparently, both Lulu and Bonnie were big fans, along with half of the younger crowd, who screamed and rushed the stage.

And when they broke out into a polka rendition of "Yakety Sax," I looked at Cassidy, whose eyes grew as he yelled, "Wait, is *this* 'Yakety Sax'?"

Dustin arrived mid-morning, stumbling through the crowds, tapping shoulders of the nicer-dressed people he'd likely invited. But they were too interested in the festival—too distracted by what made Never Harbor special rather than what we weren't. I don't think they missed the wine at all.

Once the sun faded beyond the horizon, warm string lights wound through the tents and trees, illuminating the smattering of outdoor sofas and chairs set up to listen to calmer musical acts. Dad, Bobbi, and Jukes finished the night with smooth jazz. It was Steve who established the dance floor with Laura by his side. She covered her red face the whole way.

Tourists filter out, and mostly familiar faces remain. Jukes's soft saxophone solo has been going on for at least three minutes. I tug Cassidy to the slow dance floor. His large hands hold my waist as we sway. I lean my head on his chest.

"This was perfect, Cass," I say.

"You think so?"

"I know so." I look around. "Have you talked to Dustin?"

He inhales and shakes his head on the breath out. "No. He left pretty quick. His dad looks like he's having a good time though."

Both of us laugh at the memory of Mayor Barrie at the opening ceremonies. With a lobster roll halfway to his mouth at eight in the morning, Mayor Barrie laughed through most of his speech. It was still tailored for the white-tablecloth mixer rather than today's festivities with messy food and loud music. Most of the town mocked his overly formal speech as much as he did.

Cassidy holds out his hand to twirl me out and bring me back in.

"Ooh, fancy," I say.

He smooths back my hair, kissing my forehead. "I feel like I need to prove I'm better than a mayor's son."

"No competition," I say. "Fun fact: did you know he told me my shoes were too tempting for him?"

Cassidy leans back, staring down at my boots. I went to Boston yesterday for some last-minute festival items. While at the outdoor mall, I bought this short brown pair. They're similar to my old ones, but just different enough to feel like a fresh start.

"Those *are* some sexy shoes," Cassidy says.

"Are they?" I ask, leaning in.

"Absolutely," he murmurs, quietly connecting his mouth to mine.

Kissing Cassidy is like being swept off my feet every time. And sometimes, he actually does.

But given that we haven't exactly told everyone we're together, or whatever it is that we are—even though the whole town likely sees us in the center of the dance floor—we pull away, grinning smiles that neither of us can seem to leave behind.

I laugh, and he joins me, and if I could tuck this moment away—all of our moments where we're just enjoying life together—I would. And I'd open that drawer again and again.

There's a tap on my shoulder, and Bobbi appears next to us. She smiles, the little wrinkles beside her eyes like happy check marks.

"Mind if I cut in?" she asks.

I step back. "Of course. He's all yours."

She snorts. "I don't wanna dance with Cass."

"Hey," Cassidy says in mock offense.

She nudges him. "Maybe next time, big guy. I wanna talk with you, Marina, if that's all right."

My mouth opens and closes. "Oh. Sure."

I follow behind her, turning around to see Cassidy mouth, *Spill later!*

That alone makes everything so much easier. Outside of my dad, I've never had someone I can look to in these moments, someone who will know exactly what I'm thinking. Seeing this festival, I realize I've never had a place to feel like *this* either. Never Harbor is a community, highlighted in shimmering string lights with the symphony of laughter, jazz, and a gentle lapping sea. It's home. Cassidy is home.

Bobbi takes tentative steps past the silent auction table, adorned with too many bottles of Dustin Barrie's wine. She picks one up and gives me a sideways glance. The two of us burst into laughter.

It's always easy with Bobbi.

She sighs. "We haven't had time to talk much this summer, have we?"

I shake my head. "It's been a wild few weeks. I understand."

"No, this is on me. I felt guilty, and … I'm sorry your dad and I didn't tell you things had changed between us. We were still figuring it out ourselves."

"You don't need to apologize."

"I love the guy. You know that."

I grin. "Yeah, who wouldn't?"

She looks to the ground, winding her palms together. Bobbi Mullins is nervous. I'm not sure I've ever seen her bashful in my life. She's been my dad's best friend forever. If he was going to open his heart to anyone, of course it would be her. I wouldn't want it to be anyone *but* her.

She sighs. "I know it's probably weird. I'm not gonna ask to be your stepmom. I'll always be Auntie Bobbi, who will feed you way too much hot chocolate, even when your dad tells me not to. And if you still want to call me Auntie, you can. Hell, you're an adult; I can be whoever you want. Trash Bag Bobbi is fine too."

I laugh, and she takes my hand.

"But just know, I do love him. And I love you. And I'm not here to be a tornado in your relationship, okay?"

"I know. I'm happy for you. I hope you know that, Bobbi."

"Trash Bag Bobbi, if you please."

I laugh. "It's different. But different doesn't seem so bad lately. I'm happy he's happy. I'm happy *you're* happy."

"Thanks."

I lean on her shoulder, watching the tide wash in and sigh. "You're welcome, Auntie Trash Bag."

She yowls with laughter.

I can't wait to hear that sound more often.

- *Chapter Forty* -

PEOPLE

Cassidy

"How much can I pay for Tuesday nights? Are any slots open?"

I run a hand through my hair, puffing out a breath through a smile. "Donna, I don't exactly have a calendar just—"

"Yes, he does!" Marina leans her forearms on the bar top, whipping out her phone. "What date do you have in mind specifically?"

I roll my head back, laughing. This is the third person who's approached me about personal training while having casual drinks at The Hideaway. This is also the third time Marina has taken over for me, making a reservation in some new app Milo set up for scheduling.

It's been two days since the music festival. Watching as an event came together due to my organization triggered a leadership itch in me that I can't scratch fast enough. I spoke to Laura this morning about potentially transitioning out of the community center to start my own personal training business. I'd expected her to be upset, but by lunch, Laura had posted my new logo all over social media.

"We've got you down for the sixth." Marina tilts the phone to me. "Does that work, Cass?"

I chuckle. "If it says I'm free, I'm free. But, hey, Donna, just know I might be late, okay? It won't ever be *too* late, and I'll always stay late for you—"

"He'll make it," Marina says. "He's got a thirty-minute buffer between clients. So he can give you all the extra attention."

I blink at her. "I do?"

"You do," she confirms with a knowing grin.

"Even if you didn't, I trust you," Donna says simply with a shrug. "You're Cassidy Davies."

Marina sticks out her palm, heartily shaking Donna's hand. "Pleasure doing business with you, principal. You can expect a welcome package in the next day or so."

"A welcome package?" I mutter, pinching her side once Donna is out of earshot.

"I've got ideas," Marina says back, kissing my cheek. "Ten bucks you get a fourth customer in the next hour."

"Twenty it doesn't happen."

"Bet."

The requests have been arriving through texts and emails. Though I shouldn't be surprised it followed me here, too, considering how busy tonight is.

After everyone banded together to clean up the mess from the festival, Peter announced that Monday would be the official post-festival celebration. The Hideaway was transformed overnight. Old wine mixer flyers plaster the walls, corks litter down from the ceiling on fishing wire, and the red carpet directs the way to the third floor.

"The place looks like an art piece, Bon," Milo observes when she takes a seat next to us.

Two tables are pushed together to house as much of our family and friends as possible. Milo sits across from me, Wendy beside him with her pink drink, Jasper sits at the head of the table with Lulu on the opposite end, Bonnie scooted a chair next to her, and beside me is my woman.

"It looks really cool," Wendy says.

"It's my first installation," Bonnie explains, puffing out her chest. "I think that's what it's called? I'm sure I'll learn all about it soon."

"I don't know what they're gonna teach you in art school, but it already scares me," I say with a snort.

"If it's half as great as this one, you're gonna knock their socks off," Marina says.

Bonnie beams at the compliment. I'm not sure she'll ever see Marina as anything less than her best friend's cool babysitter. One look at Lulu, resting her chin in her hands, makes me wonder if the same is true for her.

"Hey," Lulu whispers to Marina. She leans over. "My parents are gonna be back at the end of this week. To talk about the flower shop."

Marina's eyes grow wide. "Really? Like, *here*, here?"

"Yeah, here in town," she says with a grin.

"Why?"

"I guess they kinda heard about the festival," Lulu says. "Friend of a friend of a friend."

"Typical Never Harbor gossip," I butt in with a laugh.

"Right? Oh! Psst." Lulu suddenly juts out her elbow to nudge Bonnie. "Ten o'clock."

I'm not sure I was supposed to hear the exchange or not. Marina meets my eye, and we nod in unspoken agreement, following the girls' eyeline to the corner of The Hideaway to consume the secret gossip.

Rafe stands near the stairwell with one hand in his leather jacket pocket, the other putting out his cigarette in an ashtray, looking over at our table. At my little sister.

His eyes find me, and he lazily nods his chin. I nod back. I like the guy. He really pulled through for the festival. But I don't like how unbothered he is. The girl he's staring at is surrounded by her four older brothers. Shouldn't he be shaking in his motorcycle boots? Maybe he's not acting like it's a big deal because it simply isn't. It's probably just some one-sided teenage crush.

When Bonnie and Lulu get up to refill their drinks—and I ensure they go specifically to the bar and only to the bar—I lean across the table to Milo.

"So, I think we need to discuss Bonnie," I murmur.

"Discuss what?" Wendy butts in.

I glance at Marina, and she shakes her head.

"No, Cass. C'mon. She graduated. She's an adult."

"Discuss what?" Milo repeats for Wendy.

I lift my eyebrows. "I think she's got a thing for Rafe."

Our eyes swivel over to Lulu and Bonnie at the bar.

"I mean, she *is* an adult," Wendy says.

Lulu turns around, sees us watching, then quickly looks away.

Milo sighs, shrugging. "Wendy's right. She's an adult."

Wendy nods. "I agree. Let her exist and figure out her own mistakes. I'm sure there are tons left to make."

I narrow my eyes. "I hate how logical you all are."

Milo tips his drink to me. "Blessing and a curse."

Peter plops down at our table, adorned in varying bead necklaces and leis.

"Speaking of adults with mistakes left to make, where did you get those?" Wendy asks.

"I don't know," Peter answers honestly, shrugging. "People."

"It's always *people*," Marina mutters under her breath.

I run my palm over her knee with a grin and squeeze.

"More wine, everyone?" Peter asks, swinging up a bottle by its neck.

"Why does this feel illegal?" Marina asks, holding up her wineglass anyway.

He scoffs. "Excuse you, this wine was bought and paid for in the auction by yours truly. Well, technically The Hideaway's money, but that's beside the point."

"It's actually really good wine," Izzy says, coming up behind Peter, draping a palm over his shoulder.

It's almost funny how all of us avert our eyes at the same time, all except Wendy, who curls her lips in to hide a growing smile.

It's not that we're not nosy about our brother's romance life. It's that Izzy might punch us if we asked in front of her.

"So, has anyone talked to Dustin yet?" Marina asks.

"I actually hear the mayor might be keeping a closer eye on his company," Milo says.

Peter scoffs. "Oh no, is Daddy mad?"

"Why?" Wendy asks.

"He almost ruined the music festival," Jasper grunts. "Right?"

"Yes," Milo agrees. "But also"—all of us lean forward at once—"rumor is, Dustin's profits haven't been great for a while now. He's been covering up a lot of stuff along the way. That's why he was in town. Trying to schmooze Mayor Barrie for more investment money."

I bark out a laugh. "No kidding? How do you know that?"

He shrugs. "I know things."

I look toward Marina to share in the gossip, but her eyebrows tilt inward at the stairwell.

Taking the last step in the bar is Dustin, clad in his gray suit—a little more unkempt than usual. His slicked-back hair is out of place, strands loose here and there. His glasses look smudged, even from here.

He saunters to the bar, tossing a finger up to get the attention of an employee. The barkeep swivels his head to Peter, as if requesting approval to serve him. Peter nods with permission.

"That was really nice, Pete," Wendy observes.

"We're Never Harbor locals," he answers with a shrug. "We're the kind of people to ruin a guy's wine mixer by making it better; we're not the kind of people to kick him out of the local bar."

Dustin spots Lulu, and she turns away. I see Marina tense, so I grip her thigh once more in solidarity.

Dustin runs a hand through his hair, peering around the top floor, watching as everyone else averts from his gaze. He looks uneasy, but he stiffens fully when Charles Starkey rises from his table with his arms crossed, looking between Bobbi in the booth behind him and over at Marina with us.

Nobody messes with Starkey's women.

Peter sighs. "Well, I guess I can't control if locals make him feel unwanted though."

Suddenly, Dustin's silver-gray eyes land on me. I hold his gaze. I want him to know I'm aware of his character, the type of man he thinks he is and that I know the true man that lies beneath.

He empties his drink and pays with cash.

For a split second, he looks like he might walk over. Like maybe he'll congratulate us on the festival or he'll apologize to Marina. Maybe, in some warped reality, I want him to apologize to me—for the years of making me feel like a lesser man than I am.

Instead, Dustin Barrie throws our entire group the middle finger and leaves the way he came.

I swallow, letting the tension sweep over my shoulders and down to the planked floor. Marina rubs my knee under the table, and I place my palm over her hand.

I can grow from my past, and I love that my girl can too. But some people never can.

"Hey, Cass?"

I'm brought back to see Steve winding his hands at our table.

"I heard you're picking up clients. Could I talk to you about Wednesdays?"

Marina grins at me.

"Absolutely," I answer. "Let's see what openings I've got."

- *Chapter Forty-One* -
DAVIES & STARKEY

Marina

Stinky paces over my feet, winding through my legs and eyeing Lulu's parents with suspicion. Though maybe that's just because Stinky is a cat and cats look that way. Similarly, so do Lulu's parents.

They're kind people, beaming whenever they talk to me, especially when I pulled out the business plan for the next six months. But with Lulu, the room grows a bit chillier.

"I never would've considered setting up a newsletter for a floral shop," her dad says, peering over the statistics I printed, displaying the usefulness of email communication for small businesses. "But whatever you've got in mind, I trust you. And we'll make sure you're getting quality candidates for help here."

"Thanks. I mean, Lu here has been an excellent help this summer," I say. "Any more like her, and we'll be golden."

His eyes flash to her. "We'll be discussing how she gets to spend her summers, moving forward. That is, if she wants college paid for."

"I graduate after this year anyway," she murmurs.

"We'll write up a new contract for you, Marina," Lulu's dad says, and the irritation in his tone says we're likely done with this conversation. "Glad to hear you're staying."

We all say goodbyes, shaking hands and side hugs with an extra hug each from Lulu's mom, who doesn't seem nearly as livid as her dad.

Lulu and I wave when they announce they have dinner in Boston. And the moment they're out of sight, Lulu's posture drops, and she groans.

"They're never gonna see me as an adult, are they? I didn't even do anything wrong."

I wince, running a palm over her shoulder. "Tough luck, girl."

"Makes me wanna do something that'll really piss them off."

"Gonna go buy a motorcycle?"

She scrunches her nose. "More Bonnie's style, not mine. Maybe I'll go be a stripper or something." I snort, and she grins. "I wanna do whatever I like with my business degree when I finish."

"Start your own strip club, if you want," I suggest.

She raises her eyebrows. "Now, there's a thought."

She looks more relaxed than she's been in days. Her parents' return has been doing a number on her. I've found two broken acrylic nails on the counter this week. But now that they're gone, she's slouching into the chair behind the counter and whipping out an old, tattered book, like usual.

"Hey, Lu, can I ask you something?"

Stinky hops in her lap, stepping over the book to demand attention.

Lulu snorts. "Yeah, sure."

"Why him?" I ask. "Why Dustin?"

She sighs, placing her book to the side. "He was nice. And here. And he paid attention to me."

I nod, looking from the book, then back to her.

"One more question?" I ask.

She smiles. "So curious today."

"Do you still have a thing for Milo? Even now?"

Her back goes ramrod straight. She closes the book and shakes her head, sputtering out, "No. Why would I?"

"Just curious. They're kinda similar in a way. Dustin is pretty much second-rate Milo."

"Salutatorian Milo," she agrees.

The bell above the door dings, and Cassidy pokes his head in. He's already grinning, clutching a handful of flowers.

"How'd it go?" he asks.

I laugh. "Where'd you get flowers? We're the only shop in town."

"Picked them from our yard," he answers with a shrug.

I love when he says things like *our* yard.

"Had to surprise you somehow," Cassidy says. "And how do you surprise a woman with flowers when she runs the flower shop?" He waggles his eyebrows. "You ... *do* manage this place now, right?"

I grin and eagerly nod. "You're looking at the new manager."

"Hell yeah!"

Cassidy runs in, picking me up and spinning me around, the bouquet crinkling between us as he peppers me with kiss after kiss.

"I knew it," he says, setting me down. "I did."

I believe him. Cassidy's just that type of guy—the guy who sees the best in everyone. And not once has he not seen the best in me too.

"Ugh, go," Lulu says. "Stop being so happy around here; it's depressing me. I'll run the shop for the afternoon. You guys go celebrate or whatever it is happy couples do."

Couple.

It's so funny how I've never even considered Cassidy my boyfriend or partner or anything in between.

He's my roommate. My best friend. My Cassidy. The guy I hold hands with and tell everything to and the first person I want to see every morning.

Couple? Suddenly, that doesn't feel like enough.

"Oh, I couldn't possibly—"

"Up we go," Cassidy says, throwing me over his shoulder.

"Wait, Cass!"

"See ya," Lulu lazily says, flashing a peace sign as I flop out the door on Cassidy's shoulder.

I laugh and yell, "Cass!" even though I know he won't drop me.

We quickly end up at the rocky shore, him walking us into the water with our clothes still on, soaking us through.

We're careless, but careless together in all the best ways.

I dunk him first. He resurfaces, shaking his curls with a barreling laugh.

Cassidy Davies is so happy, so filled with overwhelming joy; it's hard not to laugh with him.

He gets his revenge by dipping underwater, rising with me on his shoulders, then falling backward so that we both go under at the same time. Once we're underwater, I grab his cheek and pull him closer, entwining our limbs together to kiss under the sea with just the low hum of water in our ears—in a muffled world, just our own.

It doesn't take long for us to swim farther out, peeking around for any onlookers and laughing to ourselves as we find an alcove hidden from the shore.

"Hop on up for me," he teases with a grin.

I wrap my legs around his waist, my dress billowing on the water's surface.

"Now, stay quiet, all right?"

I bite my bottom lip, nodding eagerly as he reaches underwater to tug down his gym shorts. He moves my thong to the side, then thrusts into me.

His palm supports my neck as I lean backward, breathing out sighs of pleasure. Each thrust is slow. Each movement restrained by the water as it laps around our waists.

But I love it.

I like the slower life. The calm, coastal life.

A life where I'm unconditionally loved by this man.

"Nice and easy, honey," he whispers in my ear, goose bumps trailing over me.

I don't know how long we're hidden, slowly kissing and thrusting. At one point, I moan a little too loud, and his palm whips up to cover my mouth.

He chuckles out a, "Shh."

The secrecy takes me over the edge. It's not the type of orgasm that comes in sparks and lightning. It's slow and overwhelming, building on steady thrusts and pressured circles of his thumb rubbing over me. It's like a cresting wave curling over my stomach and washing down my trembling limbs.

We would have kept going if he hadn't heard footsteps. We escape right before Officer John's shoes plunk down the docks.

We spend the rest of the afternoon floating on the ocean surface together, telling stories we've heard around town, talking about his business and my plans for the flower shop, about this and that and everything in between.

He reaches out for my hand at the same time I reach for his.

"Don't float away," I say with a smile.

"You neither."

But for the first time in my life, I know that I'm here to stay.

Chapter Forty-Two

SMALL FRY

Marina

Four Months Later

Bobbi Mullins looks amazing in white. She looks even better as Bobbi Starkey.

The townhome's small backyard is packed with Never Harbor locals, sitting in white folding chairs, faces beaming up at two of my favorite people exchanging vows. I stand behind my dad in a long teal dress, holding a bouquet of flowers as his best woman. Across from me, holding a bouquet as well, is Jukes, Bobbi's man of honor.

Dad and Bobbi didn't want a big production at the chapel or even city hall. They knew we'd get too wily for that, and they were right. The moment Jasper pronounces them man and wife under the large floral arch, the backyard erupts into cheers, whistles, cowbells, and kazoos.

With wide eyes, I glance at Cassidy.

He's already nodding at me with his bottom lip poked out, as if to say, *Yep, not surprised they're loud either.*

Drinks are instantly abound, held in the air like beacons, liquid sloshing over the lips of glasses like my dad and his friends are pirates celebrating a pillage instead of a wedding. In their defense, it's the only way to stave off the cold.

I told Bobbi an outdoor November wedding was a silly idea. But she said she couldn't wait anymore. She'd waited for my dad long enough. I couldn't say no to that.

I hand Bobbi her bouquet, and she throws it at the crowd. I laugh when everyone leaps at it. Noodler emerges victorious, flowers smashed and held high.

With the ceremony over, everyone mingles, re-pouring pints upon pints. I'm not sure how long they'll last in the frigid weather. Peter's already on standby at The Hideaway, heater turned on and more drinks ready.

I hurry across the yard, back to the warm indoors. Unlike others, I can't depend on alcohol to keep me warm. Halfway to the back door, Maggie and Bobbi catch up to me, rubbing my arms and escorting me in.

"Guys, I'm fine," I groan through laughs.

"Not out here you're not," Bobbi says.

"Yes, you are in *no* state," Maggie insists.

Cassidy appears behind me, placing a hand on the small of my back.

"Listen, I know I can be a little reckless," I joke with a grin, running a palm over my poked-out belly, "but c'mon, guys. The cold is fine."

Life is a wild ride, and my impulsivity landed me exactly where I am today. It was impulsive that I moved back to Never Harbor. It was careless that I moved in with a man I barely knew. And we were the most reckless when we had sex without protection in Mermaid Lagoon four months ago.

It's funny; the moment I saw those two pink lines, I wasn't scared. I just imagined all the ways I'd love this kid that my mom couldn't. How they'd have a big, loving family through the Davies crew and an even bigger, supportive town to show them adventure. This was our new start, building a future just for us. I felt stability. I felt purpose.

Cassidy and I laughed together at those two lines, and I didn't need to ask to know he felt just as happy as I did.

The first two months were hell; Cassidy braided my hair back nearly every night because we knew I'd inevitably wake up sick the next morning. But even so, I'd lie there with my head in Cassidy's lap as sunbeams scattered across our bathroom floor, rubbing my curved stomach and smiling at the man above me.

He tells me every morning how strong I am. But that doesn't stop the two mothers from acting like I'm made of glass.

Bobbi and Maggie escort me through the back door.

"She runs a shop," Cassidy says, batting their hands away. "She put together the whole flower arch for this wedding. Trust me, she's fine."

What he doesn't say is that he was just as fretful when I stood on the ladder, placing the finishing touches this morning. I had to insist I had a pregnancy craving for PB&J just to get him distracted elsewhere in the kitchen.

"Hey, don't carry that," Maggie says, reaching for the two growlers of beer held in each of my hands.

"Yeah, I've got it," Bobbi adds.

"I can lift more than you, Bob!"

"Not anymore you can't, Mags!"

I groan, elbowing past both of them and refusing to relinquish the jugs. According to Cass, I actually lift more than either of them now.

"It's my house; let me through," I insist. "I can still do things."

Cassidy sweeps in and takes the two growlers in his tree-trunk arms anyway, tossing me a wink.

"Rude." I pout.

"Just protectin' my girls."

I'm capable of carrying two jugs, but still, watching him lug the growlers out and play host is comforting.

Ten minutes later, jazz music starts in the corner of the yard as my dad, his bride, and Jukes break out their instruments.

"I didn't even know they'd brought them," I tell Cassidy.

"I think they had Steve deliver them."

We simultaneously lean back to see Steve and Laura now swing dancing to the jazz. Since the music festival, they've gotten pretty good.

We sway to the music as well. Cassidy places a palm on my stomach. He loves to do that, leaning his chin on my head and giving a big sigh.

"Glad you moved in with me," he muses.

"See, I thought you'd moved in with *me*," I counter. "Considering, y'know, it's my family's house."

"Who says it's your house?"

"People," I answer.

"Gah, those darn *people*," he says, kissing my forehead and sighing. "Hey, you think you'll move in permanently?"

"Permanently? That's a big step, Davies."

He strokes my stomach. "Figured I had a good chance of you saying yes."

"Maybe. If you play your cards right."

"Bet," he says.

"What are you thinking? Twenty bucks you propose to me by New Year?"

"Make it ten."

"Lower?" I ask.

"Losing bet," he says, smiling down at me. "You know I'll do it."

I kiss him, and I probably clutch his face to mine for longer than is appropriate. But Cassidy sinks into it, embracing me as tight as he can too.

I love it. I love him. And he understands I need this. Only Cassidy understands the comfort in having someone who will never let you go.

- *Epilogue* -

Cassidy

Seven Months Later

"All right, rep number three. Here we go."

I squat down, supporting one hand behind my daughter's head as I pick up the plank of wood with another.

"And we hand it to Mommy." I hold out the wood, and Marina meets me in the middle with a kiss. "Okay, now, rep number four. We gotta push real hard this time."

I let out a faux grunt, cupping her head closer. Melody's head isn't going anywhere; she's tightly wrapped to my chest, barely moving with each motion. Doesn't mean I'm not gonna triple-check she's good though. I grab the last plank, then hand it to Marina.

"She's gonna be outlifting both her grandmas in no time," Marina says with a smile.

"Oof, don't tell that to them," I say before cooing down to Melody, "But you absolutely will be."

The two grandparents are the least of my worries. A couple of weeks after my business took off, I found out most of the older women in Never Harbor started a group text for weight-lifting personal bests. Then, Peter, being Peter, found out and added a living scoreboard behind the bar at The Hideaway. Laura is five pounds behind Bobbi's personal best. I don't want to be in the same room when she beats her.

I tuck a flower into the wrap beside Melody. A meow at my feet tells me maybe I handed it to the wrong child.

"Sorry, Mr. Toot." I pluck another flower from the old flower disposal and tie the stem to his collar.

Head raised high, he stalks off.

Melody squirms against my chest. I rub her back and kiss her forehead. It settles her down almost as easily as it settles Marina. But I can already tell my little girl will be just as restless and adventurous, just like her mom and her grandmother. I hear that's not a terrible trait to pass on though. Nine weeks after giving birth, Marina was back on her feet and renovating the flower shop. She couldn't help herself.

I join Marina at the front of the store again. She's wrapping up the new window display. It reads, *Free plant starters.*

It's nice weather, so the door is propped open, letting in the distant rush of the ocean and shimmering sun. Just outside the door, Fido sits in the dirt, soaking up the rays.

Marina finally let him place roots somewhere permanently. It took some time for her to give him a home, just like it took time to allow herself one as well.

I tuck Melody closer to my chest, then pull Marina in as well.

Never Harbor is my home. The Davies family took me in and I've never looked back. It was only a matter of time before I did the same for someone else. Except, funnily enough, I think Marina was part of our family the whole time; I was maybe just waiting for her to join us.

I hear otters mate for life. Maybe it's the engagement ring burning a hole in my pocket, but I think I've found my otter for good. And I have a good feeling my otter will hold my hand like always and say, yes, she's found me too.

The End

Never Harbor will continue in book 3

On Midnight Shores

- Also by Julie Olivia -

NEVER HARBOR SERIES
Off the Hook (Jasper & Wendy)
Out with the Tide (Cassidy & Marina)
—

HONEYWOOD FUN PARK SERIES
All Downhill With You (Emory & Lorelei)
The Fiction Between Us (Landon & Quinn)
Our Ride to Forever (Orson & Theo)
Their Freefall At Last (Bennett & Ruby)
—

INTO YOU SERIES
In Too Deep (Cameron & Grace)
In His Eyes (Ian & Nia)
In The Wild (Harry & Saria)
—

FOXE HILL SERIES
Match Cut (Keaton & Violet)
Present Perfect (Asher & Delaney)
—

STANDALONES
Fake Santa Apology Tour (Nicholas & Birdie Mae)
Across the Night (Aiden & Sadie)
Thick As Thieves (Owen & Fran)

- *Thanks, Etc.* -

I never thought anyone would be interested in a *Peter Pan*-inspired cozy small town. I'm grateful every day that I've found people who are. So, thank you. Thank you so much for picking up my magical seaside town (and if you're returning, hello again!)

This book wouldn't be what it is without a slew of wonderful souls I'm proud to call friends. I'm not sure what I did to deserve these amazing people, and I could thank them until the end of time, but we'll settle on book acknowledgements for now!

Thank you to my best friend, Jenny Bailey. Words can't describe the wonderful impact you've had on my life. I'm so proud of you for taking the leap and pursuing your dreams. I'm ready for PenPal PR to take over the world!

My editor, Jovana. Book six, baby! Thanks for putting up with my terrible grammar.

My cover artist, Alison Cote. You knocked it out of the park with this one. This is my best cover yet! I'm so proud to have your art on my shelves once more.

Dad. No amount of thanks will be enough for being the best dad ever. You're the reason I can write fantastic role models like Charles Starkey and Mr. Davies.

Rusty. For being the cooler sibling always.

Allie G. My other half. The Jenna to my Angela. I cannot wait to hug you again real soon.

Jillian Liota. I don't believe in fate or anything, but if I did, I'd say it was fate that you moved to Georgia. I want to be you when I grow up.

Caroline Laine. Our husbands were right. If we just got coffee together once, we'd definitely be close friends. I'll see you next week for our weekly coffee, my cozy fantasy romance queen.

Jere Anthony. You keep me sane. And, week after week, you push me one step closer to being an astrology believer.

Becca. I'm pretty sure you're an actual genius. I would follow you into the depths of Mordor.

My beta team!! Thank you to Jenny, Allie, Angie, Carrie, Emily, Elizabeth, Erin, Rebeca, and Kolin. This book gets its sparkle from your feedback.

To my reader group, all the lovely romance readers I've met through Instagram, TikTok, and other parts of the internet… thank you for your endless support and love for reading.

And finally, to my husband. My favorite person in the world. The funniest person I've ever met. The inspiration for every wonderful hero I've ever created. But, even though I try to write the swooniest men I can, my wildest imagination could never rival the real thing. I love you.

- *About the Author* -

Julie Olivia writes cozy love stories filled with humor, saucy bedroom scenes, and close friend groups that feel like a warm hug in book form.

She lives in Atlanta, Georgia with her husband who has a swoon-worthy low voice and their cat, Tina, whose meows are not swoony one bit.

Sign-up for the newsletter for book updates, special offers, and VIP exclusives!: julieoliviaauthor.com/ newsletter

Made in the USA
Monee, IL
09 March 2025